LITTLE GIRL TAKEN

BOOKS BY WENDY DRANFIELD

Shadow Falls
Cry for Help

LITTLE GIRL TAKEN

WENDY DRANFIELD

bookouture

Published by Bookouture in 2021

An imprint of Storyfire Ltd.
Carmelite House
50 Victoria Embankment
London EC4Y 0DZ

www.bookouture.com

ISBN: 978-1-80019-842-5
eBook ISBN: 978-1-80019-841-8

This book is dedicated to my readers.

PROLOGUE

Seven years ago

Kelly feels weighed down. Not just by the rocks in her pockets, but by the enormity of how her ordinary life, and that of her best friend, has been thrown so horrifically off course. She looks across at Janie, with her frizzy red hair, struggling to pull her heaving backpack over both shoulders. It's turquoise, with mermaids swimming across it, and her name is stitched in pink cotton across the front compartment. Janie, who always used to have a smile on her face, looks pale and scared but determined as she climbs the railings.

With butterflies in her stomach, Kelly glances over her shoulder, checking the road in both directions. There are no passing cars. Janie takes a sharp breath beside her as she realizes how high up they are. The river far below them sparkles with dancing sunlight, and in the shallow parts, Kelly can make out the pretty oval pebbles through the clear water. The water runs steadily away from them, carrying dead logs and debris to their final resting place. The birdsong coming from the trees is comforting as a breeze blows through her hair, making her tilt her face to the rising sun. On a normal day she'd be starting breakfast right about now before getting her books together for another day at school.

She hears rocks hitting the ground. They've escaped from Janie's cardigan, and Kelly watches as she climbs down to retrieve them. It's a chance for her friend to change her mind, to go home and try to rebuild her shattered confidence. To pretend none of it ever happened. She isn't surprised when Janie re-pockets the rocks and immediately climbs back up onto the railing. This was an easy decision for Janie. But a little harder for Kelly. Her own doubt was amplified when she saw Janie write the note that's sitting in a waterproof snack bag in the front compartment of her backpack.

Sorry, Mommy and Daddy. I love you.

It made Kelly consider how their parents will react, which is something she has tried hard not to do. She knows they'll be devastated, but she can't put their needs first. They've tried hard to help, of course, but neither she nor Janie has been able to open up to them about what happened. There are certain words you should never have to speak aloud in front of your parents. The police suspect it was bad, but they don't know the intimate details. Would they have thought she was overreacting? Would they have taken sides? Perhaps if the detectives had been women, she might have found the strength. She'll never know.

She feels hot tears sting her eyes, but she can't let them fall. She can't back out. She has to do this, for Janie more than for herself. If it were just her, she might be able to cope. To find a way to forget or pretend it never happened. But Janie won't be able to move on. She's not like everyone else. She needs to be able to grow up unharmed. But she *was* harmed. They both were.

"Ready?"

Janie smiles at her, and it's clear she's relieved to be here at last. It's clear they're doing the right thing for her. "You've always been my best friend," she says.

Kelly swallows the lump in her throat. *Focus.* "We need to sit on top of the railing now. Think you can manage it?"

"It's like PE at school."

Except at school there's a padded gym mat to catch them when they fall. Kelly's heart beats hard against her chest as she positions herself on top of the railing. The metal is cold underneath her, despite the warm start to the day. Next to her, Janie moves with ease. She's small for a twelve-year-old. Delicate. But she doesn't let the rocks tip her too soon.

Kelly resists the urge to look back over her shoulder one final time. Instead, she slowly leans forward. Her fear stops her hands from releasing the rail. She looks at her best friend and returns her smile. Then they clasp hands, her left with Janie's right. And as they slide off the bridge, they let go of the pain.

CHAPTER ONE

Detective Madison Harper is already running late for her first day working at Lost Creek Police Department in southern Colorado. Her first day in seven years, anyway. She took an unexpected career break when she spent six years in prison for a crime she didn't commit, and today finally signals the end of that whole inexplicable nightmare.

The rain is pelting so hard against her windshield that she's forced to drive slowly to avoid hitting anyone. The road that winds through the White Woods is challenging at the best of times, but more so today. The beautiful aspen trees with their haunting white trunks stand strong against a backdrop of evergreen pines dancing in the blustery wind. With one eye on the road, she leans forward to turn up the heating in the car. Thanks to the rain, it's not as cold as last week, but there's still a chill in the air at 6.30 on this October morning. The early mist is slow to clear, and it's still dark, making visibility poor, but she's pretty much the only car out here on the road right now.

Shivering, she breathes into her balled-up right hand, trying to warm it. As she rounds a bend in the road, her headlights illuminate the roof of a red car at the bottom of the embankment in the woods to her right.

She slows down as she approaches. "Oh my God."

It's definitely a car, and there's obviously been some kind of accident for it to end up down there. Damaged trees and broken branches give away the vehicle's route off the road, and it's clear it was headed out of town. She pulls over and switches her hazard lights on just as her cell phone rings. It's Owen, her seventeen-year-old son.

"Mom? Where are you?" He sounds harassed.

"I'm on my way to work," she says. "I can't talk right now. I did try waking you before I left, but you wouldn't even open your eyes."

He sighs down the line. "I was asleep, Mom. I'm a teenager; it takes me forever to wake up in the morning. Any normal mother would know that."

She bristles at the insult. He knows it's not her fault they spent seven years apart, but he's good at blaming her when he's lashing out. She can't get into an argument with him. Not again. Not now. Since their reunion four months ago, she's found herself biting her tongue more than she normally would. She has to be patient. Owen was only ten when she was taken from him, after her conviction for killing another cop. Child services whisked him away and never told her what happened to him. They're still adjusting to living together again after all this time, but it's not been easy. She had been hoping to pick up where they left off and make up for lost time, but it's like Owen's still holding on to resentment for what happened. It doesn't help that he experienced seven years of his father's influence.

She sees his father in his face and gestures sometimes, and it scares her. Because he wasn't a good man and she doesn't want Owen to turn out anything like him. Not that he could ever be capable of the things his father did. Images from the night Owen was conceived flash before her, briefly forcing her to close her eyes. The woods, the shotgun to the back of her head, the overwhelming feeling of helplessness. It all comes flooding back. She forces herself to focus on the here and now. "I've just come across a road traffic accident, so I have to go. What do you need, Owen?"

"I can't find my chemistry books. Did you move them?"

It's her turn to sigh. He knows it's her first day back at work; does he really need to bother her about stuff like this today of all days? "They're in the kitchen, on the dining table, possibly under a pile of laundry. I'm sorry, but I've really got to go. I need to check no one is hurt."

She doesn't think Owen's going to reply, but eventually he does. "Sure. Sorry, Mom. I hope today goes well."

Her heart aches. He's a good kid, but they're struggling to communicate and she knows it's going to take time.

She opens her door, shivering at the thought of getting out of the warm car into the rain. She considers using her umbrella, but it would be useless on a day like today, so she pulls her hood up instead and walks to the side of the road, peering through the trees. From up here, she can tell the fender on the driver's side is damaged, but there's no one to be seen. "Hello?" she yells. "Is anyone down there?"

A baby cries.

She listens hard. Did she really just hear a baby, or was it an animal? She hears a car slowing as it sloshes through the puddles behind her, but it doesn't stop, and by the time she turns around, it's gone. She listens again, but the heavy beat of the rain pelting down on both vehicles, combined with the persistent whistling of the wind, makes it difficult to distinguish any other sounds. Pulling her coat tighter around her, she slides down the slope into the dense undergrowth. Her leather boots are instantly covered in mud.

Moving toward the car, she peers through the rear window. She can't see in; it's all steamed up with condensation, which would suggest there's someone inside. She goes to the driver's side, and hesitates as she reaches for the door handle. She hasn't picked up any latex gloves from the station yet, so her prints will contaminate any others present. But someone's life could be at risk. Knowing she has to get to them, she struggles to pull the door open. The steel is misshapen from the crash. When it finally comes free, she's faced with blood spatter covering the deployed airbags and the windshield on the driver's side.

But there's no driver.

After a moment's hesitation, she leans her head in, careful not to touch anything. As she turns to look beyond the front seats, two eyes stare back at her from the dark. A baby girl is lying across the back seat, wrapped up warm in a pink snow suit and a blanket, with nothing securing her in place. Her eyes widen, registering surprise at seeing Madison, but tears quickly materialize. She clearly needs comforting after being left all alone out here in the dark.

Her mother is nowhere to be found.

CHAPTER TWO

Within an hour, the accident scene is a hive of activity, and Madison is bouncing the abandoned baby gently in her arms. She looks to be around twelve months old and healthy, but Madison has no way of knowing how long she's been here and when she was last fed. She remembers cradling Owen at this age. He was a quiet, smiley baby, but this beautiful girl is angry, with tears streaming down her warm pink cheeks. Madison softly sings a lullaby into her ear as they wait, which helps her settle a little.

Officer Gloria Williams joins her at the bottom of the embankment. She's wearing full rain protection and taking a lashing from the wind, but she still manages to have a smile on her face as if it's the height of summer. Madison hasn't worked with her before, but Gloria knows her. Everyone in Lost Creek knows her thanks to her highly publicized trial, conviction and eventual exoneration.

"Morning, Detective," says the officer. She smiles at the baby, reaching for her cheek, but the baby recoils and starts sobbing again. Gloria has to raise her voice to be heard. "I've closed the road. This weather's making people's driving even worse than usual, and I don't want anyone making the same mistake as this guy." She nods to the car.

"Great, thanks."

Gloria's cell phone rings, so she steps aside to answer it.

Madison turns back to the car, where the beams of two flashlights are dancing inside. She pulls her blue raincoat around the baby and wipes raindrops from her face. Her own hood gets swept off her blonde hair, making it wet within seconds. The wind adds its own flourish, and she just knows she's going to look like a hot mess by the time she gets to the station later, which is not how she wanted to turn up for her first day back at work.

An approaching ambulance siren wails behind her as Officer Shelley Vickers, someone Madison does know well, reverses out from the car and stands up straight.

"What a way to mark your return," she says with a smile. "Glad to be back?"

Madison smiles. "Let's see how today goes."

Shelley nods to the baby. "She can't have been out here all night, surely?" She instinctively reaches for the girl's chubby hand. "Hey, sweetie. Don't cry."

Madison swaps arms. "I don't think so, but it's hard to say. She's wrapped up well at least." Still, the car would have quickly lost its heat the minute the engine was switched off. Maybe the accident happened just a few hours ago.

"And you found her?" asks Shelley.

"Right. There's blood over the front interior of the car, but no sign of her parents." Madison strokes the baby's head. "You were just lying across the back seat waiting for me, weren't you? There's no child seat in the car."

An EMT slides down the embankment next to them and looks at the baby with concern. "Any obvious injuries?" he asks.

Madison shakes her head. "None at all. I checked under her clothes, but apart from a wet diaper, she appears to be unharmed. And as you can hear, she has a fine set of lungs on her."

He smiles. "That's what I like to hear. Does anyone else need assistance?"

Shelley says, "We've not found anyone else yet. The driver appears to have left the scene."

He nods and carefully takes the baby from Madison. "Hey, sweetheart. Want to come for a ride in my ambulance?" The baby finally stops crying as she reaches for his crackling radio. Looking at Madison, he says, "Jake Rubio. Pleasure to meet you."

"Detective Madison Harper." She gets a thrill out of using her job title for the first time in so long.

"You're the new detective I keep hearing about. I'm sure I'll be seeing you around, but hopefully not too much." He has a glint in his eye as he smiles.

"Let's hope so. No offense."

Jake laughs. "Is anyone accompanying this little one to the hospital?"

Shelley quickly answers. "I'll go with you."

Gloria has joined them and starts walking toward the ambulance. "I'll go. I'm near the end of my shift anyway, and I need to check in on my mom. She's in the hospital with pneumonia. Shelley, it's your turn to keep an eye on traffic."

Jake follows her, the baby safely tucked in his arms.

Moving to the driver's door, Madison says, "The blood's only located in the front of the vehicle, indicating the driver was injured in the crash. The windshield is shattered but intact, so we can rule out the driver being thrown clear with the impact. They must have walked away."

"Who has the car keys?" asks Shelley.

"Good question." Madison leans in to see if they're in the ignition. "They're not here. The car wasn't locked when I found it. I've called Alex, by the way."

Alex is Lost Creek PD's forensic technician. Madison met him briefly over the summer, but she's looking forward to working with him. They didn't have a forensic tech when she worked here before. With Lost Creek being a small town, the police department has never been huge, as it only has jurisdiction here and in Gold Rock, an even smaller town nearby. They're surrounded by mountains and woods, with the nearest large town—Prospect Springs—a two-hour drive away.

She sighs. "We need to search the wider area for the driver. It could be that they made it out of the car okay but now they're concussed or lying injured somewhere. Also, run a license plate check so we can see who the car is registered to." She leans in for a closer look. "That's a lot of blood for a walking wounded."

"It must've been a head wound. They bleed a lot. Officer Goodwin has been searching the immediate vicinity but not found anything yet. We'll expand the search area." Shelley looks at the damage to the outside of the vehicle. "The weather must've made them lose control. It's amazing the baby wasn't hurt with no child seat to protect her."

Madison agrees. But *why* was there no child seat? And why did the driver leave their baby alone down here? Maybe they set off to get help and realized the baby was too heavy to carry far, especially if they had a broken arm or rib. They must have thought she was safer in the car. Or it could suggest they weren't capable of thinking straight due to their injuries. She looks again at the amount of blood present. Could this have been the result of foul play?

She hopes not. That little girl needs her mother.

CHAPTER THREE

Nate Monroe leans back against the leather booth as he enjoys breakfast in Ruby's Diner. A flashing ambulance sped by a few minutes ago and he wonders what's going on. He knows today is Madison's first day back in law enforcement, and he has everything crossed that it goes well for her.

He glances around at the other customers. It's starting to get busy with breakfast orders, and the place smells strongly of bacon. In honor of it being Halloween week, there are pumpkins hollowed out with candles burning inside, and the special for this afternoon's dessert is pumpkin pie served with pumpkin spice latte. He smiles as he wonders whether the owner has ordered too many pumpkins.

"Care for a refill?" asks a waitress. Her badge says her name is Carla.

He thinks about it. He has no place to be today, so he nods. "Why not?"

She pours with a smile. "I hope you're going to be a new regular in here. I'm getting a little sick of the locals." She nods behind her, where several old-timers are sitting at the counter animatedly discussing what's playing out in the news on the small TV above them.

"I'm not sure how long I'll be in town, truth be told."

"Shame. It's about time we had some eye candy." She winks before walking away.

Nate laughs. He's almost forty, so he's not exactly eye candy, but he is significantly younger than the guys sitting at the counter.

Having driven through the night, he's just arrived back in town after spending two months in San Diego visiting his close friend Rex Hartley. He'd gone there to catch up, as it had been almost six months since they last saw each other in person. Other than having lost some weight, Rex was the same as always, witty and hospitable, and he'd been delighted to have company. He had been crucial in helping Nate and Madison with their last couple of investigations, even though he did so from afar, so Nate wanted to thank him in person. Working as an unlicensed private investigator requires reliable sources in various establishments, and Rex is irreplaceable in that regard.

He had also gone there to see whether Rex would home Brody, the dog Nate had inadvertently rescued from a summer camp that had to shut down after the disappearance of one of its kids. Rex lives on a large ranch filled with rescue animals that no one else wants, and Nate knew it would be the perfect home for Brody. He didn't think keeping the dog himself was a good idea, as he doesn't have anywhere to call home. He's always on the road to the next job, the next victim. But when it came time for him to leave San Diego and travel back to Colorado, Brody wouldn't be left behind. He jumped into the passenger seat of Nate's Jeep Grand Cherokee, and when Nate tried to coax him out, Brody growled at him in that way only large dogs can: deep and menacing. He's a former police K9—a German shepherd–husky mix—and he'd never hurt anyone who didn't deserve it. That doesn't mean he's not intimidating, though.

So Nate climbed in beside him, to the delight of an excited Brody, and the dog kept him company on the fifteen-hour drive back to Lost Creek, Colorado, the location of his last investigation.

Right now, Brody's sitting outside in the rain, as dogs aren't allowed in Ruby's Diner. But he prefers the outdoors, and loves people-watching. It's like he's trying to figure out which passers-by could be potential criminals.

Nate thinks about Rex's reaction to him leaving. His friend was reluctant to say goodbye. It felt like he was holding something back, that there were words left unspoken. It left him with a heavy heart, as he wasn't even sure why he was returning to Lost Creek. This is Madison's home town, not his.

"She's obviously going to be late again. Maybe the baby's sick."

He glances behind him and sees Carla whispering with a younger waitress.

"If she's not careful, Vince will fire her," says the other woman.

"No, he'd never do that. He loves Kacie. He may come across as gruff, but he's a sweetie under all that pseudo hostility."

"Well, she better get here before he comes down from upstairs." The woman sighs. "I'll try calling her again."

They walk away and Nate's attention turns to the TV. It's switched to a news channel. A notorious sex offender from Denver was sensationally released early from his life sentence last month. The bloodthirsty media can't get enough of the case, and they're still covering it four weeks on. Cody Stevens was twenty-seven at the time of his crimes, and recently, aged thirty-four, he was granted a retrial after it was found that a witness for the prosecution perjured himself during the original trial, throwing doubt on whether Stevens was in fact guilty. To make the negative press go away, the state offered him a plea deal, which he decided to accept instead of risking a retrial. He was allowed to enter an Alford plea—accepting guilt whilst denying it, essentially—in order to be released with immediate effect. Since then he's maintained a low profile and stayed out of the media, presumably in the hope of living as ordinary a life as he can.

Nate watched a documentary about him before all this happened. Unfortunately, because of his own experience with law enforcement, he has a vested interest in cases like Cody Stevens's.

"I can't believe they let him out," says one of the old guys at the counter. "Just look at his mean eyes! He's a rapist alright and you'll never convince me otherwise."

"You bet your ass he is," says his friend, a middle-aged man in dirty jeans. "The only reason that asshole got to walk free is because one of the witnesses lied."

Their friends agree, but the waitresses are more impartial. "They wouldn't have let him out with no reason, Barry," says Carla. "If he was guilty, the prosecution wouldn't have encouraged the witness to lie about him under oath. The evidence would have spoken for itself. You need to be more open-minded."

Barry's not convinced. "You don't know all the facts like I do."

"Oh, is that right?" She puts her hands on her hips. "Why? Because I'm a woman, or because I'm a waitress?"

He rolls his eyes. "Don't pull the feminist card on me, Carla. I meant because I've been following the case closely."

"Oh, and I haven't? You guys make me watch this stuff all day, every day!"

Nate turns away. He hears more sirens outside and feels his stomach flip with excited nerves. Something's happening. Something he might be able to help with. Then he remembers Madison's probably got it covered and won't be needing his help anymore. Not now she's got her son and her job back. It makes him question again why he even came back to Colorado. Perhaps he should have stayed in San Diego with Rex.

Wiping away some of the steam from the window, he watches as a cruiser speeds by. He has to resist the urge to jump in his car and go after it.

CHAPTER FOUR

Arriving at the police station, Madison hesitates to approach the front desk. She hasn't yet received keys to the building or her detective badge and service weapon. As she walks in, a shudder runs through her. Last time she was this side of the desk, she was fighting with the detectives in charge and trying to stop them from arresting her son for murder.

"Morning, Detective," says the male officer. He nods to the inner security door. "Go right on through."

She smiles. "Thanks."

Nerves flutter in her stomach as she walks through to the offices out back. She'd give anything for a cigarette right now, but she's a month clean of them. Owen insisted she stop smoking because he hated the smell on her, and so far, she's complied. In front of him at least.

The phones are ringing non-stop and the familiar smell of stale coffee reminds her of the good old days, pre-conviction. She looks around to see who's in. The two female dispatchers are in their shared cubicle, and Sergeant Steve Tanner is talking on the phone. Two officers are on their way out, pulling on waterproof jackets. They nod at her as they pass. She had a brief introductory meeting with everyone once her new job was negotiated, but the team is mostly made up of people who didn't work here during her time. There are only three remaining staff members from back then: Stella Myers from dispatch, Officer Shelley Vickers, and Detective Don Douglas. But Douglas works fewer hours since being injured on duty back in July, and now that Madison has been appointed, he'll be working later in the day whenever he can get away with it.

Once Madison was cleared of the manslaughter of her co-worker, she was asked by the chief of Lost Creek PD whether she wanted to apply for compensation for her wrongful incarceration, and whether she would be suing the department seeing as it was their flawed investigation that had led to her conviction. At the time of her arrest, she had worked for the department for five years as a police officer, a job she loved. She'd battled hard for a promotion, and almost as soon as she started her new role as detective, Officer Ryan Levy was killed and she was framed for his murder. That was seven years ago, and it's been a long, painful journey to clear her name. So when newly appointed police chief Carmen Mendes asked what would settle the whole sorry affair for her, Madison didn't hesitate. All she wanted was her name legally cleared and her old job back. She didn't need to sue anyone, and the people involved in framing her were now either dead or locked up awaiting trial.

Chief Mendes worked with the state governor to overturn the conviction, but she was apprehensive about having Madison return to the department. She thought it would be difficult for her to regain the trust of the community after everything that had been said about her at her trial, and after serving time in prison. But Madison was adamant she wanted the chance to prove herself. She had to wait a long time for Mendes's decision, but finally it had been agreed.

Now, Chief Mendes emerges from her office to greet her. "Morning, Detective. Welcome back to the team."

Madison smiles, whilst inwardly cringing. She hasn't had time to fix her hair yet, and windswept doesn't quite cover it. Chief Mendes, on the other hand, who at forty-five is eight years older than her, always looks pristine in her crisp pant suits and heels. Her shiny black hair is swept back in a stylish ponytail and her makeup is perfect. Every time Madison sees her, she remembers how striking and self-assured the woman is, probably because Mendes used to work for the Colorado Bureau of Investigation and has a hell of a lot of experience in law enforcement.

"Thanks. It's good to be back."

"Let me show you to your desk. I have some paperwork for you to sign."

Madison follows her and self-consciously smiles at people as they pass, because they all glance up at her with interest. Her new desk is by a window overlooking the parking lot. She also has a good internal view of most of the office from here. She pulls her wet raincoat off and tries her best to look confident.

"Detective Douglas sits opposite you—he'll be in this afternoon—and that's Stella behind. You know each other, I take it?"

Madison turns to smile at Stella Myers. "Everyone knows Stella."

LCPD's longest serving dispatcher stands up and comes in for a big hug. "That's a polite way of saying I'm old. Welcome back to the madhouse." She winks.

Madison would guess Stella is nearing sixty now, as she's worked the graveyard shift since forever, but her short grey hair—a wig—has bright blue dyed tips, and both her reading glasses and her fingernails match the vivid color. Her desk is covered with an array of scrap paper with all kinds of messages scrawled across, plus a couple of small house plants and a stack of romance novels. It looks messy to Madison, but she knows from experience it's how Stella likes to work.

She turns back to Chief Mendes, who unlocks a drawer in the desk. "Here's a set of keys for the station. You can sign for those while I grab your service weapon and badge."

With shaky hands, Madison signs all the various documents put in front of her. She slips her service weapon—a Glock pistol—into the holster on her waistband, and when Mendes hands over her detective badge, she has to resist the urge to stare at the gold shield in awe. It's the same one they took off her all those years ago.

"Just remember what I told you," says Mendes. "You need to be prepared for backlash from the community, and the media will be watching you closely, waiting for you to screw up. You need to rebuild trust and pay your dues."

Madison raises an eyebrow. "I didn't already pay them in prison?"

Chief Mendes smiles wryly. "Thinking like that won't help you with the whackos who will be clinging to the false belief that you had something to do with Officer Levy's murder, despite the public apology I put out from our department."

Madison tries hard not to scoff. The apology was about as wishy-washy as you'd expect from a law enforcement agency that doesn't want to admit it's capable of making mistakes. At the time she let it go, because she was just grateful to get her job back, but it doesn't mean it didn't annoy her.

"And they won't care that your conviction has been overturned," continues Mendes. "They saw you serve time. You have to prove yourself all over again."

Madison feels shame burning her face. She'll never be free of what happened.

Mendes crosses her arms. "Now, you assured me you could handle the scrutiny, so don't let me down, okay?"

"I'll do my best."

"Good. So what happened out in the woods this morning? I heard you found a baby in an abandoned car, is that right?"

Standing straight and focusing on the present, Madison says, "Right. We haven't managed to find the driver yet, but the baby's unharmed."

Mendes nods. "Do you think the driver may be disorientated, or left to fetch help?"

"Possibly. There was blood in the car, so we need to find them asap. And I need a team of uniforms to help search the area, because the weather is making it difficult."

"Take whoever you need. Find the driver by the end of the day. I want an update before you clock off." She walks back to her office.

Madison is a little taken aback by the defined time limit. She sighs and heads to the kitchen to grab a coffee. The room is unloved, with dirty mugs in the sink and the smell of stale food coming from the microwave. That's the problem with shared spaces like this: no one wants to take responsibility and clean them. As she pours coffee into her new, specially bought stainless-steel travel mug, her cell phone rings, and when she sees who's calling, her face lights up. Speaking to Nate will help settle her nerves.

"Hey, stranger. How are you?" She hears him laugh and instantly feels better.

"I'm good. I'm back in town, actually."

She raises her eyebrows. "You didn't say you were coming back today."

"Thought I'd surprise you. How's your first day going?"

"Well, I've already got an RTA to deal with, and the weather couldn't be nicer for it."

He laughs. "Let me know if you need any help. In the meantime, can I stay with you tonight? I still have the spare key."

She doesn't hesitate. "Sure." She knows Owen won't mind; he thinks the sun shines out of Nate's ass, and he's right. Despite being dubbed the "killer priest" by the media and serving seventeen years on death row for a murder he didn't commit, somehow Nate still manages to be a kind and compassionate individual. Their shared experience of being wrongfully convicted meant he took a risk on her when no one else would. "Did Rex agree to take Brody in?"

"Actually, Brody came back with me."

"Really? How come?"

"Let's just say he wouldn't take no for an answer."

She laughs. "I look forward to receiving my hundred bucks." Before he'd left town, she'd bet Nate he wouldn't be able to leave the dog behind in San Diego. Not after what the three of them had been through together. She suddenly realizes Brody could help with the search. "I don't suppose you fancy joining me out in the rain? I'm looking for the driver of the crashed vehicle. They could be bleeding to death, so I could really do with Brody's help."

"Sure. I bet he'd love that."

There's excitement in Nate's voice, and it's clear he'd love it too. She tells him where to meet her and ends the call, feeling better now that he's back. He's only been gone two months, but she missed him. He helped her get where she is today, and for that she'll always be grateful.

"Detective?"

She spins around to see Steve standing in the doorway of the tiny kitchen. "Yes?"

"Stella's just taken a call from one of the officers out in the White Woods. He's found a woman's sneaker and it appears to be stained with blood."

Her heart skips a beat. "On my way."

CHAPTER FIVE

Before Nate can leave Ruby's Diner to join Madison in the rain, a middle-aged guy with graying brown hair cut military-style comes over, and he doesn't look friendly.

"Mind if I have a quick word?" he asks.

"Sure," says Nate, taking a final sip of coffee. "But I have to be somewhere."

"This won't take long." The man holds his hand out. "Vince Rader. I own this place."

Nate shakes it but doesn't give his own name yet. He rarely offers his name to strangers, in the hope he can remain anonymous for as long as possible. He hates being spotted by people who watched his story play out on the news.

Vince nods. "Nate Monroe, right?"

Taken aback, Nate doesn't reply as Vince sits down. Being a tall guy means his legs don't fit under the table.

"Don't look so worried," says Vince. "I've been keeping tabs on Madison Harper since her return to town in the summer, which means I learned who you are."

Nate's instinct tells him to leave. This guy could be an undercover cop. At least that's where his mind goes when someone takes an interest in him. "Why would you do that?"

Vince leans back and crosses his arms, careful to think before he speaks. "Not for the reason you're probably thinking. I run a true-crime podcast from my apartment upstairs. It's called *Crime and Dine* and you can listen to it online or in here every Friday between two and three p.m. 'Get your crime while you dine.'" He smiles, but it's awkward, almost like he doesn't do it much. "It might sound cheesy to you, but there are a lot of folks interested in that kind of thing. The people who pay attention are painfully aware it can happen to them. Crime rates in this country are through the roof, and I help raise awareness of how to increase your chances of surviving the crazies out there."

"Forewarned is forearmed," says Nate, humoring him, but he doesn't smile. He feels on the back foot. This guy has obviously researched him, and now thinks he knows everything there is to know.

"Precisely. I'd love to interview you. And Madison Harper about her case too."

He relaxes slightly. He's been approached more than once to give interviews about his exoneration. "Thanks, but I try to fly under the radar. I don't need a constant reminder of what happened. I'm sure you can appreciate that."

"Oh, sure. What you went through…" Vince shakes his head. "Man, I don't know how you survived seventeen years on death row in Texas. And that's why you'd make a fascinating guest. I have a lot of listeners who requested you. And you never know, it could lead to some agent somewhere hearing your story and offering you a book or movie deal."

Nate laughs good-naturedly, because he doesn't want to offend the guy. "To be honest, Vince, that sounds like my worst nightmare."

Vince leans forward. "But why? Why not tell the world what really happened and expose how corrupt our criminal justice system can be? You can tell the listeners all about how you made it out unscathed."

Nate is starting to feel uncomfortable. For him, the whole situation isn't resolved yet, and he's not exactly unscathed. Sure, he's out of prison and he's been cleared of his fiancée's murder. But until he tracks down Father Jack Connor—the person he has no doubt killed Stacey—he can't even begin to think of his ordeal as over. Besides, this guy doesn't know about the random cocaine habit that gets him through the bad days. "That's not a good idea."

Vince sighs and crosses his arms. "I just thought we could dissect the ins and outs of Father Connor and perhaps think of a way to track him down and hand him to the feds. I thought you'd want revenge for your fiancée's murder."

Nate grits his teeth. He doesn't need this guy's help to track down Connor. And he doesn't need witnesses around when he eventually finds him. Besides, it's none of Vince's goddam business.

Vince at least notices his discomfort. He stands up. "It's up to you, but think about it. And mention it to your friend for me, would you? She never comes in here, for some reason."

Nate nods, but he thinks he'll follow Madison's lead and stay away from this place now he's met the owner. As soon as Vince is gone, he pulls out his wallet and leaves a tip for the waitresses before heading to his car.

Brody's sitting by the driver's side, but he's soaking wet. "Great." Nate retrieves a towel from the trunk and dries him roughly, something the dog always enjoys. It doesn't matter how dry Nate gets him, though, Brody always shakes off again once he's in the car. It means he's spending more money on air fresheners than coffee these days.

"Come on, boy. Your nose has been requested."

CHAPTER SIX

Madison is soaking wet and chilled to the bone as she stands in the blustery woods. She's holding a woman's bloody shoe in her gloved hand. It's a white Converse sneaker with red laces, US size 7. It certainly looks like it hasn't been out here longer than overnight; there's no mold growing on it and the bloodstain has turned a light shade of pink from all the rain.

"What do you think?" someone asks over her shoulder.

She turns around to come face to face with Detective Don Douglas. Three months ago, that would have sent shivers down her spine, but she's had time to adjust to the idea that she'll be working with the cop who arrested her for murder. Well, she's working on it at least. "I thought you weren't due in until this afternoon?"

"I heard the sirens pass my house earlier and resisted for as long as I could." He shrugs.

She understands. It's difficult for cops to ignore sirens when they're off duty. She looks at the sneaker. "Could be the driver's."

"Has anyone called into the station to report a missing person yet today?"

She shakes her head. "Not yet. Hopefully it's just a matter of time before someone realizes their loved one is missing. I'm waiting for Alex to tell me whether the car was deliberately run off the road, or whether it was an accident." She looks over at Alex Parker, who has erected a large plastic awning over the car to stop potential evidence being washed away. Despite the feet being held down with pegs, the wind keeps threatening to tear it away.

"Is it true a baby was found in the car?" asks Douglas.

"Yes, a girl about a year old, give or take. She's a real cutie and thankfully she was unharmed."

Douglas looks away, his jaw tense. He lost his six-year-old daughter as part of a revenge killing several years ago.

"She's at the hospital with Gloria. I need to go there and make sure someone from child services turns up." Madison doesn't have the best experience with child services since they took her son off her, so she wants to make sure the baby's welfare is prioritized.

He holds his hand up. "I'll go. I can relieve Officer Williams and get a social worker assigned to the baby."

"Thanks. Stick with her until a doctor gives her the all-clear. For all we know, a family member could turn up at the hospital looking for her, or maybe someone else…" Her thoughts trail off.

He tilts his head. "What do you mean?"

She nods to the damaged fender. "Looks like it was run off the road, if you ask me. Although I'm waiting for Alex's opinion, because there's a possibility it could have been damaged by trees rather than another car."

"And you think that maybe whoever did it might come back to finish the job?"

"It's possible."

"That would mean it was deliberate and the driver could have been abducted."

"Exactly." Until she finds the driver, they have to consider all possibilities. "A license plate check has revealed the car's a rental, which would make sense, because Alex found a large number of prints inside. I guess the rental company didn't do an interior valet between customers." She sighs. "He said it'll take some time to go through all the prints, and even then they might not tell us who was actually driving the car when it crashed."

Douglas nods. "Which company is it registered to?"

She checks her notebook. "Voyager Rent-A-Car. They have offices across the country, but the nearest to us is in Utah. Would you give them a call and see if we can get the name of the person who last hired it?"

He nods. "I'll try. Companies don't like giving out people's personal details these days, though." He clears his throat and suddenly looks a little uncomfortable. He fixes his brown eyes on her. "Look, Madison, I know we don't have a great history, but I just want you to know that I'm hoping to start afresh with you. And I'm sorry for what you went through. For what *I* put you through. I want you to know it weighs heavy on me that I was responsible for putting a fellow cop in prison unnecessarily."

She's surprised. She wasn't expecting that. So far, she's only seen his tough, arrogant side, but he appears to be sincere. "Thanks, I appreciate it. And I agree, we do need to start afresh. Because somehow we have to work together." She takes a deep breath and smiles. "Just do me a favor, would you? Don't ever arrest me again, no matter how damning the evidence."

He doesn't smile at her attempt to lighten the mood, which doesn't surprise her, as he's a serious guy. She'd love to be able to break through his wall and earn his trust.

"Just keep me in the loop while I'm working reduced hours," he says. "I don't want to be caught out by the media, you know what I'm saying?"

She nods. "Sure. How's your shoulder healing?" He took a bullet in July, but she heard the wound got infected and has been slow to heal.

"It's a pain in the ass. Did Chief Mendes warn you that you'd have to take the lead for a while? Just until I'm back to full strength."

She nods. It's a little unsettling to know she's already the lead detective on her first week in the job, and that she won't have a full-time partner for support. She thinks of Nate. Maybe she can utilize his PI skills if necessary. "You're going to physio and the gun range regularly, I heard? To improve your reaction times and range of movement."

"Right. But it's a slower process than I'd like. For now, that means you get to be the hotshot and I'll take the routine stuff." He sighs. "It's going to drive me crazy."

"It's probably for the best."

He looks at her questioningly.

"Well, I wouldn't want to embarrass you." She smiles. "At least this way you have an excuse to be slower than me."

Unexpectedly, he laughs. She can't remember ever seeing him do that before. When Douglas lost his daughter, he also lost his detective partner. They were both killed by an ex-con. After his loss, then a divorce, he transferred down here to LCPD as a stranger. He kept his background secret from everyone in the department, and remained at arm's length, acting cold so no one would ever get close. He never socialized and just came off as an arrogant asshole. So seeing him finally laugh at something she said makes Madison feel like they've had a tiny but significant breakthrough.

"That's funny," he says with a sarcastic smile. "I'll remember that one." His face is brighter as he heads back toward the road. He stops and shouts over his shoulder, "I'll call you when I know what's happening with the baby."

As she watches him drive away, another car appears. Nate has arrived.

CHAPTER SEVEN

Madison smiles as Nate parks on the road above. Brody jumps out of the car ahead of him and wanders down into the woods. He must pick up her scent, because he stops, sniffs the air, then turns to her and zooms over so fast she braces for impact. He jumps up with his front paws resting on her chest and his tongue trying to find her face. She can feel his tail going crazy. He was so reserved when she and Nate first came across him in Shadow Falls, but once he makes a connection with someone, he's their best friend.

She laughs as she strokes his soft brown ears. "Hey, Brody. I've missed you."

Nate makes his way down to them. He's wearing two-day-old stubble but somehow manages to look refreshed. The constant frown lines on his forehead are gone and he's sporting a golden tan. The break from investigating must have done him some good. Or maybe Rex managed to get him to relax for the first time since his release from prison.

When Brody has said his hello, he relieves himself against a tree and then immediately starts sniffing the ground. Madison walks over to Nate. "I've missed you too." She hugs him and says into his warm neck, "How are you?"

"We're both good. Rex sends his regards." He pulls back. "How's Owen? He handling high school okay?"

She takes a deep breath. "He's doing surprisingly well considering he was home-schooled for so long. He has a new set of friends and is enjoying the structure of classes. But I'm not going to lie, he and

I are struggling to adapt to living together. He's certainly not the little boy I used to know."

"I know it's tough, but you just need to give it time. His whole world has changed since you came back into his life."

She knows he's right, but she expected their connection to be immediate, so it feels like a personal failure that it's not. Changing the subject, she says, "You look good. Did you manage to catch up on some sleep while you were gone?"

"Yeah, Rex likes late nights and lazy mornings, so I had plenty of downtime, but it felt like the right time to leave. I was getting restless. I drove through the night to get back here. I've been at Ruby's Diner for breakfast and countless coffee refills, so I'll probably crash and burn in an hour or two."

She considers asking whether he's heard from Father Connor recently, but decides she doesn't want to spoil his good mood.

Glancing over her shoulder into the open door of the abandoned car, his eyes widen with interest. "That's a lot of blood. Any sign of the driver yet?"

She shows him the sneaker. "Just this." Brody jumps up to sniff it. "Can you find the other one, boy?" After inhaling the scent, he runs off with his nose down and his tail high.

"I better follow him," says Nate. "Do the officers know I'm allowed to be here? I don't want to get arrested again." He smiles playfully. One of them always seems to be getting themselves arrested for something or other.

"Yeah, I let them know we had an ex-K9 and his handler coming."

He winces. "Is that what I've been reduced to? A dog handler?"

"Afraid so!"

He laughs.

Alex Parker approaches them carefully, trying not to get his feet tangled in the fallen branches. "Perfect weather for this, wouldn't you say? It's almost like being back home." His British accent is strong, suggesting he hasn't lived in the US for long. Madison guesses he's around thirty, the same age as Shelley. He nods to Nate. The pair have met briefly once before.

Madison asks, "Have you found anything to indicate why the car came off the road and how long it's been there?"

Nate excuses himself and heads after Brody as Alex pulls his glasses off and wipes the steam and rain away using his damp sweater. "There's damage to the bumper—sorry, fender—over the front left wheel that would suggest either that the car was hit by another vehicle with enough force to push it off the side of the road, either accidentally or on purpose, or that the driver temporarily lost control and hit some trees on the way down. The absence of skid marks on the road makes it difficult to work out what happened."

"So you can't tell whether it was deliberate or not?"

"Hard to say at this point. I'll have to check everything thoroughly before I know for sure. I've taken swabs from the blood and some other trace evidence such as hairs and fibers, but with it being a rental, there's more of those than usual, like the fingerprints. So it will take time to process everything. The outside of the car has no obvious prints because the rain has washed them away." He slides his glasses back on. "There's no way of knowing how long the vehicle's been here, I'm afraid."

"I would think it's only recently come off the road, though, because someone else would have spotted it before me if it had happened yesterday."

"True. Was the engine still running when you found it?"

"No. The headlights were off and the engine was cold." She had made sure to feel the hood for heat.

He sighs. "Well, when you find the keys, bag them up and let me have them asap. I'll see what I can pull off them."

She looks at the ground. "Do the footprints around the car give any clues?"

Alex shakes his head. "Not on a day like this. They were the first thing I looked for, but the scene already had too many people come and go and the ground has turned to mud."

"Is there anything in the trunk?"

"Yes. I managed to force it open and found a travel bag containing a set of spare clothes for a male. I'll take it with me to check everything over."

She stops him. "Men's clothing? Any female belongings?"

"No, none. Nothing to suggest a woman was in the car. Not until I process the evidence, anyway."

"Huh." With the baby, and the woman's sneaker being found she had just assumed the driver was a woman, but it could've been the father of the child. Or perhaps both parents.

Alex smiles. "You have that glassy stare that detectives get when they're making important links, so I'll leave you to your thoughts." He takes the sneaker from her hand and bags it up as he walks away.

She watches him stumble through the undergrowth. Suddenly the rain starts again, and it's coming down harder than ever. She pulls her coat tight, zipping it up. Her thoughts are in overdrive. Why was the driver only travelling with overnight clothes for him? Where are the baby's spare clothes, diapers and formula? And who does the woman's sneaker belong to?

A darker thought crosses her mind. Perhaps the male driver of the car was in the process of abducting the child when he went off the road. That would explain why he was unprepared; it could have been an opportunistic grab. Maybe that's why the car has damage on the driver's side; perhaps someone was trying to stop him from driving off with the baby. But then why didn't they take the baby after they'd stopped him? Why didn't they call the police? Something must have happened to them.

Once she has the baby's ID, she can find out who the parents are and whether they were battling each other for custody. Because it's becoming clear that what at first appeared to be an accident is now looking more sinister.

CHAPTER EIGHT

After six hours searching the woods with five uniformed officers plus Nate and Brody, nothing else has been found. The rain has persisted throughout, making it harder for everyone to stay positive. Madison's boots are covered in mud and her jeans are sticking to her thighs, so when she sees a bright flash go off nearby, her heart sinks. She looks up at the road above and sees a man snapping photos of the scene, and of her. "Perfect," she mutters. She turns away from him to limit the damage.

Her phone vibrates in her back pocket. With damp hands she retrieves it and sees Kate Flynn's name. Kate's one of the local TV news reporters, and an old high school friend. Madison pauses before she answers. Kate may be a friend, but she's ruthless when it comes to finding a headline. "Hey, Kate."

"Hi. I hope this weather isn't foreshadowing how your career as LCPD's newest detective is going to play out." Kate laughs. It sounds like she's driving.

Madison groans. "I hope not. Hey, do you have a reporter at the scene? Some guy's taking unflattering photos of me."

"That'll be Gary Pelosi, from the *Lost Creek Daily*. He gets around almost as much as me."

"Just what I need." Madison stays facing away from him. "So I guess you're calling for an update on the car that crashed?"

"On the driver, yes. Whose car is it? The make and color were shown on the early bulletin, but no one has called the news desk to identify it."

It's a sad fact that more people will phone the local news desk with a lead than the local police. Madison's never been able to figure out why.

"Do you have the driver yet?" asks Kate.

"Not yet. I can't tell you anything because there's nothing to tell. We're still searching."

"There's talk about a baby being found in the back of the car. Is that true?"

Madison rolls her eyes. That's the problem with a town this small: news spreads too fast. She tries to think whether confirming the baby's presence is a good or a bad thing at this stage. She wouldn't want to alarm anyone who's left their baby with a partner overnight, but it could help them identify who the baby and the driver are. She decides to go with it. "That's right. She's around a year old and completely unharmed."

"So she was left alone?"

"As far as I can tell." She pushes her hair out of her eyes. "I can't imagine who would have abandoned her. She's adorable." Although Douglas is overseeing the baby's care at the hospital, Madison intends to visit her as soon as she can.

"So it wasn't voluntary. What are you thinking: the parents were abducted?"

She smiles. Kate's job is similar to her own: they both spend their days searching for answers and helping to find missing people. They just go about it differently. "At the moment, I can't comment, because I genuinely don't know. If I don't have identities or bodies within the next few hours, I'll get search and rescue in."

"Will you be holding a press conference?"

Her stomach flips with nerves at the thought of it. She always dreads public speaking. "I'll leave that up to the chief to decide, but if she wants to go down that route, I'll let you know."

"Thanks," says Kate. "Talk to you soon."

Madison pockets her phone. The media can be both a curse and a blessing in this job. Most of the local press annihilated her character during her trial, and her friendship with Kate was non-existent by the time she was convicted. They're slowly repairing that now that Madison's back in town, and if Kate can help her locate the baby's family, then she'll gladly swap information. The victims will always be her first consideration.

Shelley approaches her and holds out her portable radio. "It's Stella from dispatch. Says she needs to talk to you."

Madison takes the radio and watches as Shelley tries to dry the rain from her face. "Hi, Stella."

"Hey, Detective. I have a caller on the phone who wants to report a missing woman, and I thought you might want to hear what he has to say considering this morning's incident. Can I put him through to your cell phone?"

Excited at the thought of a lead, Madison agrees. "Sure. Got a name?"

"Vince Rader, from Ruby's Diner."

Her heart sinks. She knows Vince. He had just moved to town with his wife Ruby the year before she was arrested. She'd spoken to him a few times back then and he seemed perfectly fine, but since her return to Lost Creek, she's heard rumors that he's turned into some weird conspiracy theorist. She hasn't eaten at the diner yet—she prefers the modern coffee shop in town where your breakfast doesn't arrive swimming in grease—so she doesn't know if the rumors about him are true. "Put him through." She hands the radio back to Shelley, who returns to the other officers still searching the woods.

When Madison's phone rings, she answers it right away. "Mr. Rader? Detective Harper here. I understand you'd like to report a missing woman."

She's greeted with silence, before: "I'm glad to see you back at LCPD, Detective. I hope the years since we first met haven't caused you too much damage."

She frowns. That's a strange thing to say. She figures the rumors are true; something's happened to Vince to make him a little crazy. "Thanks. What doesn't kill us makes us stronger, right?" He doesn't laugh. "Can I have the details of your missing person?"

"You can. Got a pen handy?"

She rolls her eyes. "I'm in the middle of a downpour in the woods, so no, I don't currently have a pen, but go ahead, I'm sure I'll remember the pertinent details." She covers one ear with her cupped hand to hear Vince over the rain. The tree she's standing under provides some shelter.

"Her name's Kacie Larson. Nineteen years old. She's a waitress in my diner who's been with me about six months."

"Okay, and how long has she been missing?"

"Eight hours so far. That I know of, anyway."

Trying not to sigh, she says, "That's not really long enough to be considered missing, Mr. Rader."

"She's an attractive young woman who didn't report for work at six a.m. She was down for the breakfast and lunchtime shifts, which are now over. I'm sure I don't have to tell you how suspicious that is. Besides, I went to her apartment, but she's not answering the door. And I've driven around town looking for her, but she's nowhere to be found."

Madison considers it. Then thinks of the baby she found. Figuring it's a long shot but still worth asking, she says, "Do you know if she has any children?"

"Sure, she has a baby."

Madison is immediately alert. "Tell me about her baby: age, name, et cetera."

"She's just celebrated her first birthday, and her name's Ellie. Kacie lives above the hair salon over on Delta Lane, and sure, she can be a little unreliable, but she's never been this late. And she always answers her phone."

The missing woman's daughter fits the description of the girl found in the car, but Madison has to be sure. "Has Kacie recently hired a rental car? A red Ford Fusion?"

He doesn't answer at first. "You think she could've been involved in that accident from earlier today? I saw it on the news."

She pulls her hood up and steps further under the tree, trying to dodge the worst of the rain, which is now coming down sideways. "You tell me."

"I can't imagine why she would. She's not talked about leaving town for any reason. I believe she has a driver's license, though."

"Is Kacie married or living with a partner?"

"Negative on both fronts."

She tries to think. If it *was* Kacie in the car, who do the men's clothes belong to? "Who's the father of her baby?"

"Good question. All Kacie has ever said about him was that he was a deadbeat."

It's going to be difficult to track down the baby's father at this rate. Madison asks, "If I give you my cell number, could you text me Kacie's phone number and address? I'll check it out."

"Of course. I wouldn't waste your time with this if I wasn't concerned, Detective. I like to look after my employees."

She shudders. She's not sure if it's just because of the cold, but for some reason she finds Vince a little creepy. "Thanks for calling it in. If you hear from her in the meantime, let me know."

"Of course. Before you go, I'd like to ask if you could drop by my diner sometime this week. I have a proposition for you."

She hesitates, not sure what he means, but to get him off the line she says, "Sure, I'll try."

Shelley approaches her as she pockets her phone. "There's definitely no one out here, Madison. Other than the car and the sneaker, we haven't found a thing."

Madison nods. "Okay. Time to call it a day until we have more information. I'll tell everyone to pack up for now." They're already losing daylight anyway. The heavy dark rain clouds don't appear to be in a hurry to disperse.

Nate and Brody approach, both soaked to the skin. Brody's panting but obviously happy to be of service. With gusto he shakes the rain off his thick brown and cream coat, spraying Nate, who rolls his eyes. "I guess I should be glad he's not doing it in the car." He wipes his face. "Did I hear you say you're stopping the search for today?"

"Yeah. I need to get back to the station and brief everyone, as I think I know who we're looking for now." Madison touches his arm. "Thanks for your help today. I appreciate it."

"No problem. If there was someone in this part of the woods, I'm pretty sure Brody would have found them by now. If you need anything else, just say the word. It's not like I have anything better to do."

"Sure." She smiles. "I'll bring some takeout home with me later."

Nate says goodbye to both of them and heads back up the embankment with Brody. Shelley's giving her a bemused look, which Madison chooses to ignore. She doesn't want to feed any rumors about her and Nate. Instead she says, "Would you arrange for the car to get towed to the station and then check in with the businesses along this route to see if anyone has security cameras? If it was caught on camera driving past, we might be able to zoom in on the driver's face, or maybe we'll catch someone walking around disoriented." It's a long shot, as there aren't many businesses out this way, but perhaps they'll get lucky with one of the gas stations.

"Sure thing."

"Thanks." Just as Shelley's about to walk away, Madison asks, "Do you know Kacie Larson?"

Shelley raises her eyebrows. "Kacie from the diner?"

"That's her. Vince Rader just called in to report her missing. Well, I'm not sure she's actually missing, but she's not turned up for her shifts today."

Shelley puts two and two together. "You think our baby could be Kacie's?"

"Could be."

Madison thinks of Chief Mendes and how she's expecting her to find the driver by the end of the day. But her stomach is growling with hunger. Breakfast was a rushed bowl of cereal almost eight hours ago. She thinks of Vince at the diner. Maybe she could kill two birds with one stone and in the process find out just how strange this guy is now.

CHAPTER NINE

When Madison walks into the diner, some of the locals stare at her. Since she arrived back in town, she's been trying to get used to the sneaky side glances everywhere she goes, but it's annoying, which is why she avoids places like this, full of characters who once they have an opinion about you rarely change it.

She walks up to the counter, where Carla is serving a bowl of pumpkin soup. Carla has been working here long before it was called Ruby's. She's worn her long chestnut hair up in a bun every day for years, from what Madison can tell. When she looks up, Madison says, "Hey."

"Hey yourself. Oh my God, you're soaked to the bone." Carla hands her a clean dish towel. "Here, dry your hands and face."

"Thanks." Madison does as she's told.

"How come we don't see you in here ever?"

She shrugs, not wanting to get into it. "I've been busy."

"So we heard," says Cole Knox, a guy sitting to her left pretending to read the local newspaper. She remembers him; he lives out by the railroad tracks and likes to steal people's dogs. She's arrested him more than once in the past.

She ignores him. "I'd love a bowl of chili with some bread on the side when you have a minute. The weather is brutal today and I'm freezing from the inside out."

"No problem. Go take a seat and I'll bring it over."

Before she turns, she says, "Is Vince around? He asked me to stop by."

"I'll go get him."

"Before you go…" Madison nods to the end of the counter, indicating she wants to speak to Carla in private. Carla follows her and Madison lowers her voice. "I wanted to ask about Kacie Larson. Vince told me she didn't show for work today. Is there anything I should know about her? Any reason why she might not turn up?"

Carla studies her face. "You mean does she have a liking for bad boys or drugs?"

Madison nods.

"No, not Kacie. She's just a hard-working single mom. She's a little unpredictable, I guess, what with her only being nineteen."

"What do you mean by unpredictable?"

"Oh, just a little up and down with her moods. Some days she's nice as pie, and then the next she can be fighting the black dog like most of us. She looks young for her age, so some of the customers flirt harder with her than they would the rest of us, but she doesn't take any crap from them. I don't think she's dating anyone. Of course, I don't follow her around town, so who knows what she gets up to in her spare time, but I've never heard of any trouble she's been involved in."

Madison was hoping for some clue as to what could've happened, but it doesn't sound as if Kacie is involved in any drama. "When was the last time anyone saw her?"

"Vince grilled us earlier about that. She was on a late shift here last night and left just before nine."

"And has she appeared upset or secretive about anything lately?"

"No, not at all. I left at eight and it sounded to me like she had somewhere to be after her shift. Something she was looking forward to."

"But you don't know what?"

Carla shakes her head.

"Would anyone else here know?"

"No, the girls and I have been talking about it, but she didn't tell anyone where she was going."

"Was that intentional, do you think? Or does she always keep her private life to herself?"

"Kind of. She's quiet as a mouse until you get to know her, but even then she doesn't tell you much. She prefers it when we talk about her daughter. It's like she hates being the center of attention herself."

Sounds like Kacie has low self-esteem. Madison tries to think. Maybe she had agreed to meet a new boyfriend. Perhaps someone she met online. "Does anyone know who the father of her baby is?"

"No. She's never disclosed it to any of us and no guy has ever come in here to talk to her about Ellie, so we assumed she left him behind when she moved here."

"Did she start working here as soon as she arrived in town?"

"Yes, more or less. About six months ago. Vince took her on without knowing much about her. I think it was because she came in with her baby and it was obvious she was desperate for work. He found her the apartment, too. He's friends with the landlady, Diane."

Madison chews her lip. Why has Vince gone the extra mile for Kacie?

"Can I ask you something?" says Carla, leaning in.

"Sure."

Concern is spread across her face. "It's just that Vince says the baby found earlier might be hers. Is she okay?"

Madison knows she has to be careful. Although Carla means well, it's easy to let things slip working in a place like this, where everyone's consumed with catching up on the latest news and gossip. She has to assume that whatever she tells Carla will soon spread to the customers. "It's too early to know if she is Kacie's daughter, but yes, the baby's fine. She's being checked out at the hospital, but she has no injuries."

Carla looks relieved.

"What kind of mother is Kacie?"

"Wonderful. Little Ellie just adores her. They're the kind of mother and daughter people stop in the street to admire. Know what I mean?"

Madison nods. People used to stop her when Owen was a toddler. They'd tell her what an angel he was, with his blond hair and cheeky smile. He'd smile at just about anyone. He's not been doing that so much lately, at least not for her. She just has to hope Nate's right and time will heal their bond. "I'll be keeping a close check on the baby, don't worry. I'll do everything I can to reunite her with her mother."

Carla smiles sadly. "I just pray Kacie's safe and we hear from her today. I can't handle another person going missing." Before Madison can ask her what she means, she has turned away. "I'll go get Vince for you."

Madison frowns. Maybe she needs to check on local missing people to see if Lost Creek has itself a problem. She's reminded of the declaration on the town's welcome sign. It proudly boasts that Lost Creek is *Where the lost are found*. That tickled Nate when they first arrived in town together four months ago, because it was ominous and kind of ridiculous if you thought about it. Lost Creek isn't a transient community or a resort town. It's so remote that it's mostly made up of people who were born here, so it's a strange thing to declare on the welcome sign.

As she slides into a booth, she hears Cole talking to a couple of other guys at the counter. He nods in her direction occasionally. It irritates the hell out of her, but she's mindful of what Chief Mendes said earlier, so she has to let it slide. Assholes like that aren't worth her time.

She looks around for Ruby, Vince's wife, but she's not in. Come to think of it, she hasn't bumped into her at all since she's been back. As she waits for her food, she wonders if they split and maybe that's what sent Vince a little strange. Then she notices the scary, pained expressions carved into the pumpkins that are dotted around the diner, and wonders what kind of weirdo was in charge of creating those.

CHAPTER TEN

Madison senses someone has approached her booth, and when she looks up, she finds Vince looming over her. He's a tall guy and he's looking a lot older than when she first met him. His face is heavily lined and he looks like he doesn't get a lot of sleep.

"Mind if I join you?" He doesn't smile.

"Go ahead."

He slides in opposite her. "I'm glad you came so quickly. I've just tried calling round to Kacie's apartment again, but there's still no answer, and the staff from the hair salon below haven't seen her at all today, or heard her baby cry. Kind of odd, don't you think?"

She nods, but she doesn't want to fuel any fire without the facts. "I'll head to her place next. I just need something to stop me from passing out with hunger first." She smiles. "Can you give me a description so I know who I'm looking for?"

He pulls out a photo. "This was Kacie on her first day at work, back in February."

She's wearing a white shirt with her name embroidered across the single breast pocket. She has long, straight dark brown hair and green eyes, and she's wearing more makeup than necessary. It's obvious where the foundation stops, because her skin is pale underneath. Her blue eyeshadow is badly applied, making her appear younger than nineteen. Madison is quickly overcome with sadness. Kacie is young and pretty, making her a perfect target for a predator. She has delicate features and looks to be petite. Her smile is bright and warm, showing slightly crooked front teeth. It's clear why the diner customers would like her.

She looks up. "You take a photo of all your staff?" It seems a little odd to her.

"On their first day, yes. The staff—male and female—enjoy looking back at the photographs when they eventually move on."

Kacie's feet aren't visible in the photo. "What kind of shoes does she normally wear to work?"

"Sneakers. Yesterday she was wearing her white Converse. They have a black line around the base and red laces that she added herself. She likes to customize her clothes. She was dressed in this white shirt and black skinny jeans."

He's watching her closely for a reaction, so she masks her dismay. The sneakers sound a perfect fit to the one found in the woods earlier, so Kacie was highly likely at the scene, which means the baby is her daughter. "You're incredibly observant. I don't know if I could tell you what shoes *I* was wearing yesterday, never mind someone else's."

He doesn't avert his gaze; instead he appears to be flattered. "I notice everything, Detective. Perhaps it's my interest in true crime."

She nods to the photograph. "Mind if I keep this for now?"

"Not at all. It's a good one to share with the media, as she's looking directly into the lens and it's not too old."

When conversation runs dry and Vince doesn't make any move to get up, she asks, "Where's Ruby today?"

His face immediately clouds over and he looks away. It confuses her. Carla appears and places a coffee in front of her. "Chili's coming."

Vince watches the waitress walk away. "I don't know where Ruby is." He pauses before turning back to Madison. "I haven't seen her in six years."

Madison frowns. "You split up?"

He slowly shakes his head. "No. She vanished. Presumed dead."

Her mouth opens but she doesn't know what to say. It's the last thing she was expecting to hear. "I'm so sorry, that must be devastating." She wishes someone had told her, to stop her putting her foot in it. That must be what Carla was referring to earlier. "Did Detective Douglas investigate?"

He nods. "Along with your friend, the late Detective Mike Bowers."

She tries not to think of Mike. He was her sergeant last time she worked at LCPD, and was promoted to her role when she was arrested. Vince is right: they were friends. But he's gone now. She gets a flashback of the last time she saw him. Of his final moments alive.

"And what did they conclude happened to her?" she asks. Carla interrupts by sliding a fine-looking bowl of chili in front of her that smells deliciously spicy. Madison pulls apart a crusty white roll, her mouth watering in anticipation. "Do you mind?"

Vince shakes his head, so she starts eating.

"They were at a loss to explain her disappearance because they didn't find her body. Detective Douglas insisted it was possible she was having an affair and her disappearance meant she'd chosen her lover over me." He looks indignant. "There's no love lost between Douglas and me. The guy is a goddam idiot who wouldn't know the truth if it bit him in the ass."

That's how Madison used to feel about him, and she's hoping he'll prove her wrong. "Is that why you asked me here? You want me to reopen Ruby's cold case? Because that's not really up to me, I'd have to ask Chief Mendes—"

He holds his hand up, cutting her off. "I already petitioned the new police chief the minute she took over from Chief Sullivan, but she's having none of it. Not unless I can provide some kind of evidence that my wife was abducted and murdered. No, I asked you here because I'd like to interview you for my true-crime podcast."

Madison drops her spoon, splashing brown sauce down her pale blue shirt. "Dammit." She wipes it with a napkin but it just makes things worse. She doesn't know what's more ridiculous: that Vince runs a true-crime podcast or that he'd ask her to be on it.

"I've followed your case closely, what with you being a local," he says. "And you'd be a good interviewee, especially now you're back on the force. I mean, you've experienced both sides, defendant and detective. And you must have all kinds of stories from your time in prison."

She shakes her head, trying hard not to laugh. After what he just told her about his wife, it would be inappropriate. Ruby's disappearance does explain his intensity, though. "I'm sorry, Mr. Rader—"

"Please, call me Vince. Otherwise I feel like some kind of suspect."

She raises an eyebrow. That's a strange thing to say. She wonders then whether he *was* ever a suspect in his wife's disappearance. He must have been questioned more than once. The husbands always are. "Vince, I have to decline your invitation. It wouldn't be appropriate in my current role and it would just stir up bad feeling in the community for me to discuss Officer Levy's murder. Some people still think I'm guilty, despite the fact his real killers were caught."

He leans back. "That's a shame. Your friend Nate Monroe wasn't keen on discussing his experiences either. Perhaps when you've both settled into your new lives here, you might feel differently."

He must have spoken to Nate this morning. She changes the subject back to their missing person. "Did you see Kacie leave here after her late shift last night?"

"No, I was upstairs preparing for my latest episode. I had a special guest arriving at midnight."

She frowns. "Midnight? Why so late?"

"He requested anonymity. He's a famous crime writer, so instead of recording his interview live as usual, I agreed to pre-record it and keep his visit quiet in order to secure him."

Madison pulls out her pocket notebook. "What's his name?"

"Why?"

"Maybe he saw Kacie out and about before or after his interview."

He shakes his head. "I don't see why she would have come back to the diner at that time. She certainly wasn't around when I let him into my apartment. And he didn't leave until after two a.m. I can't tell you anything else about him, because I'd be breaking his trust. But I agree it's worth asking him if he saw anything. I'll give him a call and let you know what he says." He stands up. "Keep me updated, Detective. I don't want Kacie to turn into another sad statistic, so if there's anything else I can do, just ask."

She nods and watches him walk behind the counter to talk to the cook. Her gut is telling her something is off about this guy. His wife is presumed dead and his youngest staff member has gone missing.

As a result, Vince Rader just became Madison's first suspect.

CHAPTER ELEVEN

Hi,

The agency passed me your letter. So you're a fan of mine, huh? I always like to hear from fans. I get a lot of letters and emails but I don't reply to all of them. I think the photo you included made yours stand out. I like the bunny ears filter you used.

Some of the fans who write to me are a little crazy, so I have to be careful who I reply to. Your letter made me think you're not like the others. You seem genuine. I like making genuine connections. You might think you know everything about me because of what's out there in the media, but trust me, there's more to learn. I'm not as one-dimensional as they make me out to be.

And no one but the media uses my real name; my friends call me Ace. I'm going to call you Bunny.

Write again, Bunny. Tell me more about you.
Ace

Dear Ace,

I've been a *huge* fan of yours for ages, so I can't believe you wrote back to me! I know you've had a hard life, but you inspire me every single day because I've not had the easiest life myself. I get really down some days because certain things have happened that I can't tell anyone about. No one would understand. No one except you.

Where did the nickname Ace come from? I've enclosed another photo, taken at New Year. What do you think?

I read there's a new documentary being made about you, about how you got to be even more famous because of the bestselling book. Did they get permission for this documentary? I'm wondering if you're actually going to be in it or whether it's just another one cashing in on your fame. I would be mad if someone used my life story without my permission and they actually profited from it. How does it make you feel?

I can't wait to hear from you again.

Love, Bunny

CHAPTER TWELVE

As the rain finally pauses, Madison arrives at Kacie Larson's address. She's on the phone to the station while Steve runs a criminal background check on Vince Rader for her.

"No arrests or convictions," says Steve. "And I can't say I remember anyone ever having any complaints about the guy, so he's not a known troublemaker."

"Okay, thanks. I just wanted to check."

"No problem."

She gets out of her car and takes a good look at where Kacie lives. Her apartment sits above a row of three business units: a hair salon, a tattoo parlor, and a drugstore. As Madison climbs the external steps to reach the apartments above, it feels like the rotten wood is about to give way under her feet. This isn't the worst part of town, but it's a little run-down. Each of the three businesses below has a separate apartment over them, and Kacie's is the first you reach at the top of the stairs. Madison bangs on the front door and announces herself, then waits for a response.

There's no sound or movement from inside. Having phoned ahead to the landlady, she'd arranged to pick up the spare key on her way over here. She slips on a pair of latex gloves and shoe covers to preserve any evidence, and then tries the key in the lock. The door opens. It's dark inside, with just a table lamp casting a dim light around the living room. The drapes are closed, possibly still from last night. Madison suddenly wishes she'd brought an officer with her for support, in case someone decides to jump out at her. But she's here now and she doesn't want to wait.

With her right hand hovering over her gun, she steps inside, leaving the front door open behind her.

"Kacie? Are you in here? I'm a detective with the Lost Creek Police department." She listens, but there are no sounds other than the wind outside. After a minute of silence, the front door slams shut behind her, making her jump. "Jeez." She takes a deep breath.

The living room is small, adorned with Halloween decorations and uncarved pumpkins. The stillness is unnerving, but she can't see anything that indicates there was a struggle in this room. And it certainly doesn't smell of blood or a decaying body. It smells of burnt-out candles and autumn spices. Madison carefully works her way through the small apartment, switching the lights on and off as she goes. The baby's crib is in the only bedroom, situated next to a single bed. Clothes are strewn around and there are toys everywhere. It's bone-chillingly cold in here, suggesting no one has been home today.

Kacie owns plenty of books, but there's no cell phone or computer lying around. The kitchen is about as tidy as you could hope for with a small baby, but that's good, because it doesn't look overly clean, like someone's covered anything up. She glances at the calendar on the wall above the sink. There are a few doctor's appointments for baby Ellie listed throughout October, and Kacie's work schedule is pinned next to the calendar. A closer look at yesterday's date on the calendar shows she's drawn a red star in the corner of the box, but there's no explanation for it.

"Hmm. What were you up to last night, Kacie?" Madison mutters. She pulls her cell phone out and snaps a photo. Then she tries calling Kacie's cell phone again. Last time, on the way here, the call didn't go through; she was immediately cut off after a few warning beeps. Now the same thing happens again, suggesting the phone could be out of reach of cell service, or the battery has died, or it's switched off and no voicemail is activated. Or, more worryingly, maybe someone's destroyed it.

She spots a tan-colored purse resting against the couch, on the floor. Owen has a similar habit with his backpack. Every single time he gets home from school he dumps it either by the stairs or the couch. It drives her mad because she's usually the one who trips over it. She kneels down and opens the purse. There's nothing unusual inside: a lip gloss, a compact mirror, tissues, two pacifiers, a small wallet with some cash. But no cell phone. This isn't good. Not many people leave home without their wallet.

She stands up. She's convinced now that Kacie is in danger. Whoever was driving the Ford Fusion must have abducted her. But she keeps coming back to the same question: why would they leave the baby behind? The kind of man who would abduct a young woman is highly likely to be capable of hurting a baby. But he left Ellie alive, suggesting he might care about her. Does that mean he's the baby's father?

Satisfied the apartment is empty, she locks up and removes her protective gear. Although she doesn't think Kacie was harmed in the apartment, it could provide some much-needed clues about what happened last night. She needs to get Alex in to check it out. For now, she heads next door, where she bangs loudly.

A shirtless young man with long hair opens the door and squints as if it's bright out, even though it's not. "Help you?"

She shows him her badge. "Detective Harper from LCPD. And you are?"

"Justin." He pushes his hair out of his face and lights a cigarette.

Trying to ignore the intoxicating smell of nicotine, she says, "Can you tell me anything about the person who lives next door to you on this side?" She points to Kacie's apartment.

He rubs his eyes and she can smell pot. "Her name's Kacie, she works at the diner. Some nights she brings me leftovers." He smiles. "She's cool."

"Have you seen her today? Or heard her coming and going from the apartment?"

He shakes his head, and his expression changes from bemusement to concern. "Nah, I've only just woken up. Why? She okay?"

From his relaxed demeanor, he doesn't appear to be hiding anything, but she wonders why he's only just woken up at almost four in the afternoon. Could he have been up late last night kidnapping a young mother? "What do you do for work?"

He smiles proudly and she thinks he's about to say he's a firefighter or a doctor. "I'm in a band. We gig three nights a week, so my sleep pattern's out of whack. I work in the tattoo parlor downstairs part-time too."

Madison sneaks a look over his shoulder and can see his living room is full of guitars and Marshall amps. "Were you home last night? Did you see her return from work? Or did she drop off any food?"

He takes a deep breath, like it's an effort to remember that far back. "She definitely came home from work, because I heard Joely leave."

"Who's Joely?"

"Her friend. They take turns looking after each other's kids while they're at work. And Joely has this crappy car that backfires whenever it starts up. So I heard her leave. After that, I heard Kacie's TV go on, but then I put my stereo on so I didn't hear anything else."

"Do you know where Joely lives or works?"

"Sure, downstairs in the salon. But it closes at two today, so you've missed her."

Madison makes a note of the details. She knows from experience that when someone's missing, the most important people to speak to first are their partner and their best friend. They often have important insights into the missing person's lifestyle that no one else does. "Okay, thanks. If Kacie comes home or you spot her anywhere at all, call LCPD so we know she's safe, okay?"

"Sure."

She heads to the final apartment in the row, but Justin shouts, "It's empty. The old tenant left about a month ago and there's been a burst pipe so the landlady can't lease it until she gets it cleaned up. But knowing how tight she is, that'll be never."

She keeps going regardless. "Okay, thanks." An overwhelming odor of sewage hits her as she draws closer, even with the door and window closed. She can't imagine anyone would be inside. There's no answer to her knocks, and the front window is obscured with drapes that are pulled closed.

She turns back and heads to her car. It's time to officially register Kacie Larson as a missing person.

CHAPTER THIRTEEN

After taking a steaming-hot shower, Nate's making himself a coffee and thinking about Vince's offer. But he can see no reason to go on the guy's podcast or give interviews to anyone about what he went through. Maybe he'll feel differently once he's caught Father Connor. Maybe then he'll want to scream it from the rooftops so everyone knows what a hypocrite the guy is, and what he put Nate through.

Brody joins him on the couch in the living room. Until the summer, this house belonged to Stephanie Garcia—Madison's ex-girlfriend—but she was brutally murdered in this very room. Nate cleaned up the crime scene so that Madison didn't have to. He notices that she's had the carpet removed in his absence and replaced it with hardwood flooring. The smell of dried blood is gone, so much so that Brody doesn't stop to sniff it like last time he was here. Being a former cadaver dog, he's always hot on that scent.

His phone buzzes. He pulls it out of his pocket and sees an email notification from a pseudonym he recognizes. It's been months since he last received an email from Father Connor. He and Rex discussed the absence of contact recently, and Rex was convinced it was because the priest must have passed away. He pointed out that the guy would be seventy years old now and had been on the run from the authorities for years. That had got to be stressful. But Nate wasn't convinced. Evil has a way of outliving everyone else.

He opens the email.

I have a surprise for you, Nathaniel. You're finally about to pay for what you did to my beautiful niece. I'm ready to expedite your journey to hell.

That's it. They're always short and delusional. But they have a big impact on Nate's mood. His heart rate has already quickened and he's holding his cell phone too tight. His other hand unconsciously feels for the rosary under his T-shirt. He's not even sure why he still wears it. It was Stacey's, but he can't do anything for her now. And he doesn't even know whether he still has his faith.

An unexpected bang at the front door makes him jump. Brody leaps off the couch and barks aggressively as he runs to the hallway. Nate checks his watch. It's almost five o'clock already, and the living room is in darkness thanks to the approaching sunset. He hadn't noticed until now.

"Brody! You're back! Hey, boy." Madison's son is home from school.

Nate stands and switches on some lights while Owen leads the dog into the living room, dumps his backpack and basketball on the floor and grins at Nate. "I didn't think you'd come back."

Nate hugs him briefly. "How could I resist the allure of Lost Creek?"

Owen takes a seat on the arm of the couch. He looks good; less stressed than when they first met four months ago. Nate was at the police station when Owen and Madison were reunited after seven years apart. Owen's had to deal with a lot more stress than other kids his age: losing his mom to prison, his girlfriend to murder and his dad to… well, Nate wasn't present for that death, but he knows it was gruesome.

Owen pulls a bag of potato chips out of his coat pocket and starts munching. "How was San Diego?"

Nate thinks of Rex and the hospitality his friend showed him. "It was good. I was force-fed home-cooked meals and put to work with the animals. I mean, I went there for a break, but it was more physically demanding than being a PI." He smiles.

"Mom said you were going to leave Brody behind with Rex. How come you didn't?"

The dog has retrieved his ball from the kitchen and he drops it at Owen's feet. Owen rolls it along the floor and Brody dives after it, almost knocking over a table lamp.

"Let's just say he wouldn't let me." Nate smiles. "Anyway, how's things with you? Are you both doing okay?"

Owen takes a deep breath. "We're okay, but we keep arguing. Mom's constantly checking in on me and treating me like a child. I'm trying to bite my tongue, but it's driving me insane. She always asks questions at exactly the wrong time, you know?"

Nate feels for him, but he knows first-hand what Madison went through to get him back. "You just have to remember you *were* a child last time you lived together. She must still picture you that way. But she'll adjust eventually. Just go easy on her." His phone buzzes. It's another email from Father Connor, but he doesn't want to read it in front of Owen. Two emails in one day is unprecedented, never mind in one hour. The guy is clearly getting worked up.

"What's the matter?" asks Owen.

Nate shakes his head and pockets his phone. "Nothing."

"It's that priest guy, isn't it? The one who framed you for murder."

He raises his eyebrows. "You know about him?"

"Yeah, Mom told me some stuff about you but she wouldn't say too much, so obviously I googled you. She said the priest is taunting you about your fiancée's murder." He pauses, as if he's considering whether to ask something. Sheepishly, he says, "What was it like being on death row?"

Nate smiles sadly. He wondered how long it would take Owen to ask about that. Teenagers are naturally inquisitive, but he trusts Madison's son. Before Nate left for San Diego, he spent almost two months living with them straight after their reunion. Owen confided in him what it had been like for him after Madison's arrest. How bewildered he had been when, at just ten years old, he was forced to live with complete strangers. The teenager Nate sees in front of him now appears more at ease with himself. Perhaps he's finally moving on. "I was known as death row inmate #1109876. A number I'll never forget."

"Did they tattoo it on you?"

"No, thank God. Although I wouldn't have put it past them. Death row was a strange experience." He's back in his ten-foot-by-six-foot prison cell, thinking of the mind-numbing boredom he experienced every day for seventeen years. That was even worse than the fear of execution and being alone with the constant flashbacks of finding Stacey battered to death on the floor of her garage. "I don't even think I can put it into words, to be honest."

Owen appears to understand, because he nods thoughtfully. "How many people did they execute while you were there?"

Nate looks down at Brody, who's happily chewing his ball to bits. He leans forward to stroke the dog's thick fur. "Well, you have to understand I was unlucky enough to be in Texas, which has the most active execution chamber in the US. I don't know the official figure, but my guess would be about three hundred people."

Owen's mouth drops open. "What the hell? I thought you were going to say five or six!"

He's not surprised at the boy's shock. "How I ever got out alive is something I still wonder to this day." It usually brings him out in a cold sweat, and he still has nightmares about waking up in the death chamber, about to receive his lethal injection. It can be difficult to shake that off. "I was released just three months before my final execution date."

"Holy shit." Owen has gone pale. "I can't believe how close you came. What if they'd executed you before finding out you were innocent?"

"Believe me, it happens." Too often.

"Did you know anyone who was executed?"

Nate nods slowly. "Several of my cell neighbors. Others avoided it for as long as possible by pretending to be sick."

Puzzled, Owen says, "Why would that postpone it?"

Nate looks him in the eye. "Because on death row you have to be fit in order to be executed."

"That's insane. How is that even legal?"

He shrugs. He doesn't know how to explain half the things that went down on death row.

"Mom said that it was some woman who got you out of there."

Kristen Devereaux's face flashes before him. Talking about her makes him anxious. He has so much guilt. "Kristen worked at the University of Texas school of law. She would use real case studies in her classes, getting her students to examine trials that may have been mishandled. They'd find the weaknesses. Rex recommended my case to her—that's how I met him—and they could tell almost immediately that something was wrong with my conviction. Kristen and her students basically got me off death row." What he doesn't say is that the process took years, and she wasn't around to see him leave prison a free man. She disappeared off the face of the earth just months before his exoneration. Nate has always suspected that Father Connor had her killed in order to sabotage her efforts in securing his release. He just needs to prove it, which is what Rex is trying to help him with; he's keeping an eye on sightings of Father Connor whilst looking into Kristen's disappearance. But the trail has gone cold on both counts. "To cut a long story short, she was able to get some DNA tested that eventually proved my innocence."

"So if Stacey Connor was actually killed by her uncle, how come he's not in prison?"

"Because he went on the run with his sister, Stacey's mom." Deborah Connor refused to believe her brother could have had anything to do with her daughter's death and instead blindly followed Father Connor into accusing Nate, knowing full well he could never have harmed anyone.

"That's so messed up," says Owen. "So why does he keep contacting you if he got away with murder? I mean, I'd be living abroad somewhere with no extradition treaty, using a fake name and wearing a wig."

Nate doesn't smile. "Because he's a hypocrite. The worst kind, actually. One who pretends to live his life by the Bible whilst breaking every single commandment." He takes a deep breath and tries not to go on a rant. "He blames me for Stacey's murder because he thinks I turned her into some kind of sex-crazed alcoholic. He tells himself that she was some angelic little girl until she met me and then all of a sudden she was a sinner. He couldn't have a sinner in his house, not in his position as parish priest, so he killed her. The reality is that Stacey and I never slept together—we were waiting until we were married—and she had turned to drinking to deal with something in her private life. Something she never disclosed to me." He used to wonder what that was, but after all this time, he realizes it doesn't matter anymore. She's dead and her killer won't accept responsibility. That's something Nate intends to help him with. "Anyway, don't tell your mom we've discussed all this sordid stuff." He grins. "I wouldn't want to get on her bad side."

Owen stands up. "Sounds to me like we need to find that guy so he can be locked up."

Nate nods but remains silent. When he finds Father Connor, he won't be giving him to the police.

Owen grabs his bag. "I've got homework to do before Mom gets home. Catch you later."

Nate watches Brody run upstairs after him. As he sits alone in the living room, he wonders how he'll fill his days now that Madison doesn't need his help anymore and he has no active investigation to work on. When he can't think of anything else to do, he opens his laptop and googles his favorite subject. Father Connor.

CHAPTER FOURTEEN

The sun has set by the time Madison arrives back at the police station. She's finding these short fall days depressing. She looks around to see who's in. Detective Douglas is back from the hospital. He's holding a coffee and shooting the shit with Steve. When she approaches them, Steve looks amused by how wet and windswept she is. It irritates her that they're standing around chatting while she's been working her ass off all day. "I need to update everyone on our missing person. Is the conference room free?"

Douglas looks to Steve, who says, "Sure is. I'll rally the troops."

She pulls her damp coat off and throws it across her office chair. "Stella? We're having a quick briefing. Shouldn't be more than fifteen minutes. If anyone calls in about Kacie Larson, come get me. She's now officially a missing person."

Stella shakes her head. "Dammit. Not Kacie." She clearly knows her and wants more information, but when the phone rings, she immediately answers it.

Madison pours herself a water from the cooler and then waits in the meeting room as Detective Douglas, Sergeant Tanner, Alex from forensics and three uniformed officers walk in. Chief Mendes arrives last and joins her at the front of the room, saying, "This is everyone who's currently available."

Madison nods. Everyone's looking at her expectantly and she wonders if any of them are so loyal to Douglas that they're hoping she'll make a fool of herself with this investigation. "Okay, guys, this is what we've got: a red Ford Fusion was found abandoned at six thirty this morning in the White Woods with a baby girl inside. She's unharmed. Don? Is she still at the hospital?"

Detective Douglas straightens up. "Yes. She's been given the all-clear from the doctor, but child services are struggling to find a foster home for her somewhere local." He pulls out his cell phone to check the details. "Her assigned social worker is Maya Smith. We're to let her know as soon as we identify the child so she can contact any relatives and find a long-term solution. Just in case the worst happens."

Madison's stomach leaps. Maya Smith was the social worker Owen was assigned to immediately after her arrest. She withheld information from Madison, making the ordeal worse than it had to be. "I believe I now have an ID for the baby: Ellie Larson. She's twelve months old. Would you text me Maya's contact details so I can let her know?"

"Sure." He does it there and then.

"Her mother is nineteen-year-old Kacie Larson. And Kacie is currently missing."

Chief Mendes looks at her. "How do you know?"

"Her employer notified us this afternoon. She didn't turn up for her shift at Ruby's Diner today."

Officer Dan Goodwin shares a skeptical look with the guy next to him and shakes his head.

Madison notices. "What's the matter?"

"Sorry, Detective. It's just that Vince Rader calls us with something every week. Considers himself an armchair detective because of that lame-ass podcast of his. I'd take anything he says with a pinch of salt."

Although Madison has her own thoughts on Vince Rader, she has to hide her annoyance that Dan's not remaining open-minded. Sure, Vince probably is a classic busybody, but it's observant people like him who give the police their best leads. While he's curtain-twitching, everyone else is walking around oblivious, making it easier for perpetrators to get away with their crimes. "I've been to Kacie's apartment this afternoon. It's empty, but there are no signs of a struggle or of a clean-up. Her cell phone is unresponsive and the diner staff haven't seen her since she left her evening shift last night, just before nine o'clock. Her neighbor says she definitely arrived home, but we don't know what happened after that."

Steve clears his throat before asking, "Do you believe she was driving the car when it went off the road?"

"Possibly. I mean, her baby was in it so it's likely she was too at some point, unless the baby was being abducted. We need to locate the child's father and check whether there was an ongoing custody battle or any other issues, because Alex believes it's possible the vehicle could have been forced off the road."

Douglas says, "I'll look into it."

Alex chimes up. "Apart from the baby, and the blood in the front of the car, the only other item found was a bag containing a man's overnight things, which don't include anything significant or out of the ordinary. The car keys still haven't been found."

"What about the sneaker?" Madison asks. "Anything useful there?"

"I've taken swabs of the blood and will send it to the state crime lab for them to analyze," says Alex. "Results will take a few days."

Officer Goodwin adds, "We haven't found the matching shoe, so it's likely still attached to the missing woman."

Madison turns to Douglas. "Did the hospital have any women come in overnight who might have been involved in a car accident?"

"None. I'll track down both mother and daughter's birth certificates when I get a minute. I checked with Dr. Scott too, but no Jane Does have turned up at the morgue."

"Is Dr. Scott the medical examiner?" she asks.

"Right."

Last time Madison worked here, Dr. Phillips was the ME. He was nearing eighty, and always promised to keep working until the day he died. Maybe he kept his promise. It's a shame he's gone; he was a nice guy. She holds up the photo of Kacie that Vince gave her. "I'm sure some of you already know Kacie because of where she works, but I've emailed everyone her description. Vince Rader gave me this photo, taken earlier this year. We need to get some missing person posters pinned up around town."

Mendes takes the photo from her. "Leave that with me." She looks closely at the photo. "I recognize her now." Turning back to Madison, she says, "Good work so far, but until Kacie's back home with her baby, you need to prioritize this case. It won't be long before it makes front-page news."

Madison feels all eyes on her. There's nothing like starting a new job and being thrown in at the deep end. "Understood."

CHAPTER FIFTEEN

After making a call to the head of the county's child services department, Madison takes a detour to the hospital before heading home.
She wants to check in on baby Ellie and make sure she's being
properly cared for. Her head is buzzing with everything she still
needs to do, but for her first day on the job, she's done as much as
she can. The temptation to work into the night to prove herself and
find Kacie sooner is strong, but she's no good to anyone exhausted.
She's left Detective Douglas instructions to start following up leads.
Plus, the uniformed officers will have flyers to hand out door-to-
door as they canvass the area. When she gets home, she's looking
forward to a hot bath. Her feet are killing her and her bones are
chilled from all the time spent outside in the rain.

At the hospital, she tracks down Ellie Larson's room and gets
permission from the nurse in charge to go in. She recognizes the
woman sitting next to the crib. Maya Smith. Maya doesn't notice
her at first; she's texting someone. The sight of the woman after all
this time makes Madison tense.

She glances at the baby, who's standing up and bouncing on the
mattress, holding on to the side of the crib with both hands. When
she spots Madison, she points and smiles, making Madison's heart
melt. That's when Maya looks up. It takes a couple of seconds for
recognition to dawn.

"Ms. Harper. So nice to see you." Her face doesn't agree. She
stands up, phone forgotten.

"It's Detective Harper." Madison's trying not to be petty, but this
woman treated her terribly after her arrest. She wasn't allowed any

contact with Owen unless it was supervised by the social worker, which was understandable, but Maya appeared to get off on the power she had. She implied more than once that Madison was a threat to Owen, and that he was better off not visiting her anymore, and that was *before* she was even found guilty. Maya should have helped her maintain contact with her son after her conviction, by letter or even just by official updates through child services, but the trail went cold immediately. Maya refused to return any of her calls from prison, and Madison couldn't afford the lawyer's fees to fight for information. She suspects Maya was being influenced by the people who framed her for murder, but she has no proof.

She knows that not all social workers are like this one, because she's worked with some of the best. That was what made the whole situation a bitter pill to swallow. Now, she has to try not to let her contempt for this woman affect how she interacts with her. Because this is about Ellie, not Owen.

"There's really no need to visit the baby," says Maya. "She's safe with me."

Madison goes to the crib and picks Ellie up. She's a comforting weight in her arms and she finds herself automatically bouncing gently. The baby immediately grabs some of her hair and starts sucking on it.

"I don't think you should be doing that."

Maya is clearly irritated by her. Is she worried Madison will report her for what happened between them? She hopes so. Because she just did. "I know her name now. It's Ellie Larson. Her mom is missing, but I'm hopeful I'll find her fast and they can be reunited. Which means that under no circumstances should you even be thinking about trying to convince your team that Ellie should be adopted."

Maya crosses her arms. "I don't take my orders from you, *Detective*."

"I know. Which is why I've had a conversation with your manager and made her aware of the situation. Patricia was in agreement that the best thing for Ellie would be for me to take her home tonight until her extended family can be traced."

Maya's face clouds over. "What? Why on earth would *you* care for her? You can't even care for your own son!"

It takes every bit of self-control not to react to that. Madison doesn't want to show that what Maya did back then affected her deeply. She doesn't want to give her that power. It's obvious that Maya's in the wrong job and should be nowhere near vulnerable children and parents, which is what Madison explained to Patricia. "Ellie's staying with me until your manager collects her from my home in the morning. If we don't find any family members to care for her, Patricia has a foster family in mind."

Maya turns white. "I can't believe she would agree to that without even consulting me." As she puts two and two together, a look of realization crosses her face. "You've bad-mouthed me to her, haven't you? You've lied about me. All because you blame me for losing your son."

Madison can feel her blood boiling. "I didn't *lose* my son, Ms. Smith. You kept him from me." She pauses. "Tell me something. When you saw the news about my conviction being overturned, did you ever consider reaching out and apologizing for the way you treated me? Did you ever check in on Owen after you placed him with those criminals?"

Maya remains silent, a look of defiance on her face.

"Do you ever feel guilty for your part in me missing out on seven years of my son's life?" She can feel tears building in her eyes and hates how her anger makes her visibly upset. She won't shed tears in front of this woman. "Are you planning on doing the same to this little girl and her mother?"

Maya grabs her purse. "Mothers like you are the problem,' she spits. 'Not me."

On her way out of the room she tries to take a child's car seat with her, as well as a bag of supplies she's obviously brought from the office. Madison can see diapers, formula and some toys. "You can leave those behind. Ellie will need it all."

Maya stops. She looks like she wants to say something, but thinks better of it. She brushes past and is gone.

Madison looks down at Ellie and strokes her soft fine hair. The baby peers up at her with the same beautiful green eyes Madison saw in Kacie's photograph. "I'm going to find your mommy. I promise."

CHAPTER SIXTEEN

With Ellie safely secured in the car seat, Madison drives home. The baby is sleepy as they pass the pumpkins and elaborate horror decorations on people's front lawns. This year has gone by so fast; she can't quite believe it will be Halloween in three days.

She started the year as an ex-felon living in a halfway house in California, waiting tables cash-in-hand and carrying an illegally bought gun in order to protect herself. She was only two months out of prison and she had no money, no son and no hope. When she realized she couldn't live that way anymore, she became determined to clear her name and find her son. And for that she sought out Nate Monroe. She had never met him before, but she had followed his case closely while she was incarcerated. All the inmates had. His last couple of years on death row were played out on TV as Kristen Devereaux fought hard for his release. When it finally happened, Madison was pleased for him, and when she learned he'd become a private investigator after his release, she took a gamble that he might be the best person to help her find out who'd framed her. She was right.

She smiles as she remembers their first meeting. It didn't go well. The minute he found out she was an ex-cop, he wanted to walk away and never look back. It had been a crooked detective who had helped Father Connor frame Nate for his fiancée's death, so he didn't want anything to do with the police. Somehow Madison had managed to convince him to give her a job as an unlicensed PI. Although they found it difficult working together at first, they soon learned to trust each other. Once they'd finished their first investigation up in Shadow Falls, California, Nate agreed to travel to Colorado with her to work on her own cold case.

The sky is pitch black by the time she pulls up to her driveway, the stars hidden behind rain clouds. She switches the car's engine off, excited to catch up with Nate properly, then remembers she was supposed to bring takeout home with her. Her shoulders slump. She looks at Ellie, who is more alert now the engine has stopped. "You're going to have to distract them for me so they don't realize I forgot dinner."

Ellie smiles at her, drooling a little.

Slamming her car door closed, she pulls her hood up and runs through the rain to the passenger side. She unclips the child seat and lifts it out of the car. Her porch steps are suddenly illuminated by the light from inside the house as someone opens the front door. Owen is waiting for her.

She runs inside and places the child seat on the floor while she removes her raincoat. "Hey." She hugs him briefly but doesn't get much of a response. He's looking at the baby but he doesn't ask a single question. "Where's Nate?"

Brody suddenly appears and barks softly at her whilst wagging his tail. She knows he's good with kids because of where he lived before meeting her and Nate: at a summer camp with children of all ages. Even so, she thinks it's best he stays clear of Ellie. Just in case the baby spooks him. "Could you let Brody out into the backyard for me?"

Owen leads the dog through the kitchen while she retrieves the baby from the car seat. Ellie's eyes are wide as she takes in her new surroundings from Madison's shoulder. Nate is in the kitchen and Madison can hear sizzling coming from a pan. The smell of sweet-and-sour sauce reaches her and her stomach growls in anticipation.

"We knew you'd forget takeout," says Owen. He's not smiling.

She ignores his attitude. "Working a thirteen-hour shift will do that to you. I'm sorry." She walks to the stove to see what Nate's cooking. "This smells amazing."

Nate looks up, wiping his hair from his eyes with his forearm. "How was your…" He pauses. "Hey, who's this?"

"This is Ellie. She's just staying with us overnight." Then, lowering her voice even though the baby can't understand her, she adds, "Her mom's missing."

Nate raises an eyebrow whilst letting Ellie grip his finger.

"You're not adopting her or anything, are you?" says Owen, only half joking.

"Of course not. I'm going to find her mom and get them reunited as soon as possible. Don't worry, your position as my favorite child is safe. For now." She grins, but he just rolls his eyes at her. It wipes the smile off her face. He won't let his guard down around her for some reason. Is he scared of losing her again? She doesn't think so. It's more likely resentment at losing her in the first place.

Nate strokes the baby's cheek. "What does she eat?"

"I have formula and some jars of baby food. She's fine for now, though." The nurse at the hospital had fed her before Madison brought her home.

He stirs the vegetables in the pan. "So how was your first day back?"

She takes a seat at the breakfast bar next to Owen. Ellie reaches for his hair, and he surprises Madison by taking the baby from her and making silly faces. Ellie loves it. Madison uses the opportunity to wash her hands and tie her messy hair back before taking her seat again. After a deep breath, she says, "It was exhausting. I got thrown in at the deep end, though in a way that's a good thing, because I didn't have time to worry about what anyone thought of me."

"We watched Kate Flynn on the news earlier, talking about the accident," says Nate. "Has anyone come forward about the abandoned car yet?"

"No, but I think Ellie's mom was in it." She doesn't want to talk about work now she's home, so she turns to Owen. "How was school? Did you find your chemistry books in the end?"

"Yeah." He looks away, embarrassed.

"Let me guess: they were in your room all along?"

He doesn't reply. He passes the baby back to her instead, as Nate brings the food over.

Madison balances the baby whilst eating. Owen tells them about a kid at school who broke his fibula during this morning's basketball practice and Nate asks questions about the injury. Owen's much more talkative now that Nate's back; normally he'd be upstairs in his room all evening. It's going to be nice for her to have another adult in the house to talk to. "So what are your plans now you're back?" she asks Nate. "Will you be looking for a new investigation to work on?"

"Maybe. I haven't really thought about it."

She thinks about Vince Rader. She'd like to learn more about him, and Nate could help her with that. "I have someone you could look into."

He smiles. "Already?"

"Vince Rader, owner of Ruby's Diner."

"I met him earlier. He's an interesting character."

"What were your first impressions?"

"He's a little intense. A true-crime buff, from the sounds of it. Even has a podcast."

She rolls her eyes. "I heard. Ellie's mom, Kacie Larson, works for him and he's the one who notified us she's missing. Plus, his own wife went missing six years ago."

Nate lowers his fork and sits back. "Shit. Did she ever get found?"

She shakes her head as she takes a mouthful of chicken before Ellie can grab it.

"So you think he could be involved in this latest disappearance?"

"I don't have anything to suggest that at this stage. But seeing as you have time on your hands, perhaps you'd like to do a little digging for me. Maybe speak to the locals and find out what people think happened to Ruby Rader six years ago, and whether anyone has reason to suspect Vince was involved. He doesn't have a criminal record, but it would be good to have someone who isn't me asking questions about him. I get the impression the locals might not open up to me just yet. You can dazzle them with your Kansas charm."

He smiles again, and she can tell he's happy to have something to work on. But before he can say anything, his phone rings. "Excuse me for a second." He stands up and walks to the sink as he answers. "Hello?"

She watches as his expression changes.

"Hey, Arlene. Is everything okay?" He looks at Madison and whispers, "Rex's neighbor." As he listens, he turns deathly pale. "What do you mean? Why are the cops at Rex's place?"

Madison puts her cutlery down and joins him at the sink, balancing Ellie on one hip. As she leans in, she can hear the woman's voice.

"My horses got spooked, so I went out to check on them," Arlene is saying. "I heard Rex's dogs barking non-stop in the kennel, then came the police sirens, so I drove over to take a look at what was going on. The police have been inside for so long now that I'm considering going home, but I thought I'd better let you know something's up."

"Can you see Rex? Is he with you?"

Madison hears the woman say, "No, he's not with me." Then, "Oh my God."

She can see Nate's hands trembling. He closes his eyes. "What is it, Arlene? What's happening?"

"Nate, the coroner's van just showed up."

He runs his hand through his thick brown hair. "Call me back as soon as you know anything." He ends the call and looks at Madison with frightened eyes. "Something's happened to Rex. That son of a bitch has killed him. I just know it."

Madison is lost for words. She knows who he's referring to. But would Father Connor really go that far?

CHAPTER SEVENTEEN

Detective Christine Russell from the San Diego Police Department walks through the darkness, past the kennels and stables filled with barking dogs, angry cats and agitated horses. They clearly don't appreciate the team of police vehicles that have interrupted their evening, or the officers who are looking in on them with flashlights. At first she thought this was some kind of illegal puppy farm, but she's been assured all the animals are fit and healthy, and there's more than enough food and water out for them. In fact, the living conditions appear better than her own small, cramped apartment. Still, the constant barking from the dogs threatens to make her headache worse. She missed dinner tonight and is irritable enough as it is.

She walks right up to the uniformed officer stationed outside the front door of the victim's home. He's scrolling on his phone instead of paying attention. He doesn't even hear her coming, he's so engrossed with his screen.

"You on a break, Officer?" she asks.

He looks up, and when he sees who's addressing him, he straightens and slips his phone in his pocket. "No, Detective."

"So what's to stop me shooting you dead while you're checking out photos of, what, hot chicks? Hot guys? I mean, Christ, Bradley, I could be the killer returning to the scene of the crime and I could have easily walked past you with absolutely no resistance. You think I want someone as uninterested as you on my team?"

He swallows. "You're right, I'm sorry. But it was a text from my kid's babysitter. He's sick and needs collecting, so I'll have to organize something with my girlfriend, who's at work."

She rolls her eyes. "I don't give a shit about your personal life. If you're not one hundred percent present, you're a danger to my team. Now get out of here and find me someone who actually wants to be a cop." She pushes past him into the dark hallway of the house. The foul aroma of stale vomit greets her, followed by the putrid smell of death.

Her partner, Detective John Purdue, sees her coming and smiles. "You making grown men cry again, Christine?"

She laughs. "You better believe it." She glances down at the guy sprawled on the floor. He looks to be in his late forties, maybe early fifties. His eyes are bulging and there's dried vomit, blood and saliva around his mouth and throat and down his pale blue T-shirt. Unfortunately, the flies have already moved in, and one pops out of his mouth as she stares. She's suddenly glad she skipped dinner. Kneeling down to get a closer look, she covers her mouth with her sleeve but can still smell a strange garlicky odor. "So what happened here?"

Purdue takes his usual deep breath before launching into the details, then regrets it immediately as he gags. "Jesus. I'll never get used to that smell." He composes himself and says, "At first I thought he'd choked on something and there was no one around to help him. I mean, that's *my* worst fear, what with living alone and all. But the medical examiner took one look at him and suggested poison."

Russell raises her eyebrows and looks up at him. "Any sign of a needle or a bottle? A glass of water or soda? Something that may have residue in it?"

He shakes his head. "No. The ME will check for puncture marks on his skin during the autopsy. As you can see, the place is a mess, so he must have tried to resist his killer."

"Get his garbage bagged up for evidence. How long has he been in here like this?"

"The ME wasn't sure exactly—you know how they like to wait for the autopsy—but he offered a guess of at least twenty-four hours."

Christine stands up and looks around. "Anything obviously missing?"

"Not that we can tell so far. His car and valuables are still here."

They're in what looks like the guy's study; there's a huge oak desk with a computer on it. His chair is overturned, along with a large bookcase, its entire contents spilled all over the place. She's surprised the house doesn't smell of animals, considering there are two kittens running around and one more hiding on top of a second bookcase. It's black, with yellow eyes, and can be no older than a couple of months. She's not tempted to coax it down, because cats hate her. She always gets scratched.

"I've called animal welfare," says Purdue. "They'll be along shortly. And I spoke to the neighbor from the next ranch over—Arlene Simmons. She identified our victim as Rex Hartley. Said he lives here alone, and the only other recent visitor, besides her and his attorney, was a Nate Monroe, but she doesn't have an address for him, just a cell number. She doesn't think he lives in California. But get this: apparently Mr. Monroe had been staying with the deceased as a house guest until yesterday."

She gives him *that* look. "I'll bet you fifty bucks he's our guy."

He laughs. "No way. I'd just be giving it away."

She hopes Monroe *is* their guy. It means less work for them, which would be awesome considering she has five other homicides on her caseload this week. The rest are boring domestic cases, but they still need closing fast if she's to keep the captain off her back. "Nate Monroe. Why does that name sound familiar?" she mutters. Walking over to the computer, she pulls on some gloves and shakes the mouse. The monitor comes to life. Expecting a password warning, she's surprised when the screen shows a security video playing on a loop. The same thirty-second shot over and over again. Was Rex Hartley trying to tell them who his killer was? "Take a look at this."

The images are of a car pulling out of the long driveway in daylight. The security camera clocked the time as 3.58 p.m. She can make out one person inside, a male. She makes a note of the brand—a Jeep Grand Cherokee—and the license plate. "Run a check on this, would you?"

Purdue takes the piece of paper from her and gets on his cell phone as he wanders out the front door, presumably for some fresh air.

In the meantime, Russell uses her phone to google Nate Monroe. The headlines that appear on her screen make her mouth drop open. *Killer priest released after seventeen years on death row.* She chooses one to click on and reads the gory details of Stacey Connor's brutal murder back in 2000. Monroe was on a path to priesthood before he gave it all up for the victim. There's a photo of the smiling young couple in happier times. The question that springs to her mind is: was he freed because he was innocent, or was he, like so many others, only released on a technicality? An error made during his trial that had nothing to do with his guilt or innocence? She needs to dig deeper.

Detective Purdue reappears. "Bingo! The Jeep is registered to a Mr. Nathaniel Monroe."

She smiles widely. "What a stupid son of a bitch."

CHAPTER EIGHTEEN

Madison rubs her eyes as she feeds Ellie some puréed apple and waits for her morning coffee to kick in. She managed just four hours' sleep last night. She couldn't stop running through possible scenarios for Kacie Larson's disappearance, and at two in the morning, she heard Nate go out. She tried to catch him to see if he'd heard back from Arlene, but he sped off before she could get out the front door. It's only now she's properly awake that she realizes he took Brody with him. He isn't answering his phone, so she can only hope he went out because he couldn't sleep and not because he's driving back to San Diego.

Sitting in the kitchen, she listens to Owen banging around upstairs, getting ready for school. She wonders how one teenager manages to sound like a herd of elephants. She tries to enjoy her time with the baby. Ellie was unsettled overnight, probably wondering where her mom was, but she's content as she eats breakfast. It helps that she's playing with Madison's cell phone. They're currently running through every single ringtone option, Ellie laughing at the more outlandish ones.

Madison leans back as she realizes this will probably never happen for her again: having a baby. She's been single ever since she split up with Stephanie Garcia, which was ten years ago now. It's not that she doesn't want a partner, but she can't imagine anyone would want her, thanks to her sordid history. She thinks of Nate. His past is even worse than hers. She doesn't know if he'd ever date again, given what he's been through. She's never heard him talk about meeting someone or starting a family. Maybe he'll return to the church one day.

Ellie drops the cell phone and it rings as Madison picks it up. It's Detective Douglas. "Hey, Don."

"Hi. Is Nate Monroe with you?" he asks.

"Not right now, but I think he'll probably be back soon." She wonders why Douglas would ask for Nate. It's not like they're friends or anything. "What's going on?"

Douglas sighs heavily. "Okay, don't shoot the messenger, but I got in early this morning to make up some time and I just took a call from a detective in San Diego. She asked a lot of questions about your friend."

"What? Why would she be interested in Nate?"

He hesitates before answering. "She wants us to arrest him as soon as possible."

Madison's heart starts racing. Then she laughs. "What the hell? You almost had me there for a second, Don. I thought you were serious."

He doesn't laugh. "I am serious, Madison. She and her partner will be coming here as soon as they get their captain's agreement. They want to question Nate for the murder of some guy called Rex Hartley."

She inhales sharply and a wave of dread sweeps over her. "Rex is dead? Please say that's not true. Could you have misheard them?"

"You know the victim?" he asks.

"Yeah, he's Nate's closest friend." His only remaining friend other than her and Owen. She leans back against the kitchen counter. Owen appears in the doorway. He dumps his backpack on the floor and looks at her questioningly. She realizes that must be why Nate left the house without telling her where he was going. He must be driving back to San Diego. Straight into an arrest warrant. She has to swallow back her alarm. "How did he die?"

"I don't know. She wouldn't give me many details. She asked what I know about Nate, and whether he's been in any trouble since he's been in town."

Madison is struggling to think straight, and her arms are covered in goosebumps. "But how would the San Diego police even know they were friends?"

"I don't know. All she told me was that their victim was killed sometime the day before yesterday. Do you know where Nate was that day?"

She slowly shakes her head—not that Douglas can see. Her eyes lock onto Owen's. "I assume he was with Rex in San Diego until he left to drive home, but I don't know what time that was."

Douglas is silent. She knows from experience that he'll be keen to find Nate himself and drag him into the station. He's a shoot-first-ask-questions-later kind of cop. Finally he says, "You need to convince him to come to the station. If he has nothing to hide, we can clear this up and they can move on to finding Rex Hartley's killer. But if he goes on the run and becomes a fugitive, well, you and I both know that'll look bad for him."

Madison feels like she might vomit. Her appetite for breakfast has vanished. "I'll find him."

She ends the call. Her stomach flutters with dread at the thought that Nate might already have done something stupid to himself. Death row had a devastating impact on him that he's never been ready to admit, and he's good at hiding it most of the time. She immediately tries calling him, but there's no answer.

"Nate's friend is dead?" asks Owen incredulously.

"Apparently. And the cops think Nate killed him."

His eyes widen even more. "No way. Does that mean you have to arrest him?"

She closes her eyes against the thought. "I seriously hope not."

CHAPTER NINETEEN

The wind is rocking Nate's car as the rain lashes down on the windshield. He's parked under some trees near Fantasy World amusement park on the edge of town. He's trying to stay out of view. No passing cars will spot him here without his headlights on, not on a dark morning like this.

Wiping his eyes, he leans his head back and waits for the cocaine craving to pass. Since leaving Madison's at 2 a.m., he's been fighting the almost overwhelming urge to use. He's numb and nauseous, unable to plan what comes next. Unable to think clearly. Brody is whining next to him, but not because he wants to be let out of the car. He can see Nate's not doing well. He should have left the dog at Madison's place, but he wasn't thinking straight, and the minute he opened the front door, Brody ran ahead to his car. The dog has become his constant companion, which makes him feel even crappier, because Brody deserves better.

Nate was clinging to the hope that Arlene was wrong, and when she called back to say someone had been taken away in a body bag, he hadn't wanted to believe it. He tried calling Rex, but Rex wasn't answering his phone. Now he brings himself to try one more time anyway.

After three rings, someone picks up. "Hello?"

It's a guy, but it's not Rex. "Can I speak to Rex Hartley?"

There's no answer for a minute, until: "Who is this?"

Nate closes his eyes and ends the call. That was clearly a cop. Which means Rex really is dead. The guy who helped Kristen secure his release from prison has been murdered. It was Rex who greeted him outside the prison gates. There were no family members or childhood friends waiting for him. Just Rex. Kristen would have been there if she hadn't gone missing earlier that year. Without Rex, he has no one in this world.

He thinks of Madison. Now they've cleared her name and got her job and son back, she doesn't need him anymore. No one does. He's not sure what he's supposed to be doing with his days. He doesn't have a purpose when he wakes up in the morning. And it's not a nice feeling. He thinks of her request to look into Vince Rader. How can he concentrate on that now?

He rubs his jaw and stares at himself in the rear-view mirror. His hair is messy and he needs a proper shave. His eyes look empty. He can't understand why God keeps him alive just to be tortured over and over.

His phone rings. It's Madison. He doesn't answer. He wonders if she's heard about Rex. Maybe it's all over the news. His heart skips a beat at the thought of the San Diego police already looking for him.

It rings again. She's persistent, so he answers it this time. "Have you heard what's happened?" he asks.

"Nate, I'm so sorry." She sounds genuinely upset. "Where are you? Please don't do anything stupid."

He scoffs. "Do you know how many times you've said that to me in the short time we've known each other?" Too many times. Because his immediate reaction to stress is to get high and try to block everything out. Prison robbed him of any other coping mechanisms he'd once had.

"Listen," she says. "I don't care how high you are or what you've done to cope with the news about Rex. Just get your ass to my house right now. I'm here for you, Nate."

"We both are." Owen speaks up behind her.

Nate smiles sadly. "Have you been told to bring me in yet?"

She hesitates. "Yes. But you know me, Nate. I'm not going to. I know you didn't hurt Rex, and I'll make them see that. Besides,

I really need your help looking into Vince's background. Don't leave me high and dry."

He rubs his jaw. "I've been framed once before, Madison. I'm not going to let it happen again. I'd rather die than go back to death row." His voice catches at the end and he hates himself for being weak. If he could trust law enforcement, he'd turn himself in and answer their questions. But he can't risk his freedom in the hope that the San Diego police are less corrupt than the Texas police who took a bribe from Father Connor all those years ago.

"Nate, if you disappear, I'll never forgive you," she says. "If you won't come here, then at least find somewhere safe in town to lie low until I can get this figured out. But for God's sake, you better stay in touch with me. Do not put me through any more sleepless nights." She attempts a laugh, but it sounds desperate.

He takes a deep breath. "If I stay in touch, they'll track my phone. I have to go off grid for a while, Madison. You do what you need to do in order to keep your job. I'll do what I need to do to end this."

She tries to protest, but he cuts her off and pulls the battery and SIM card out of his cell phone. He'll throw them both away, separately, so his location can't be traced. As he looks up at the sky, he thinks about Rex.

Nate knows his friend didn't die from a heart attack or a stroke, otherwise he wouldn't have been found so soon. He lives alone with his animals. Arlene pops by every now and then—she joined them for dinner a few times while Nate was visiting—but from their earlier conversation, it's clear she wasn't the one who called the cops.

No. It was Rex's killer who called the cops. They wanted him found. They wanted the cops to know he died while Nate was in the vicinity. They probably staged the crime scene and planted false evidence to make him look like the killer. Which means it was Father Connor.

Nate starts the engine and speeds away from the park.

CHAPTER TWENTY

When Madison arrives at the station, still flustered after her call with Nate, she heads straight to her desk, where Douglas is talking to Stella. Keen to focus on finding Kacie, she asks, "Any update on Kacie Larson? Or have any tips come in?"

"No sightings, no," says Douglas. He nods to Mendes's office. "And the chief looks pissed."

"She never looks happy, though, let's be honest," says Stella behind them. "Unfortunately, I've had no tips about Kacie come in overnight—well, not if I discount the psychics and the drunks, which I always do. How's her baby doing?"

The thought of Ellie makes Madison smile. "Surprisingly well considering her routine's been changed and she's not seen her mother for a while. She spent the night with me, but child services have found her a foster family, so she got picked up before I left for work." She switches her computer on and asks Douglas, "Did you check out who hired the rental car we found yesterday?"

He sips his drink before answering. "I tried, but they wouldn't tell me anything unless we have an open criminal investigation. I'm waiting on a callback from a supervisor. But now that we know we definitely have a missing person who needs to be located fast, they might be more inclined to help, so I'm about to put some pressure on them. By the way, the officers who were handing out flyers last night reported that the only sightings of Kacie they were told about occurred while she was working her late shift in the diner or walking home alone afterwards, along Delta Lane, at about nine. It appears no one saw her after that."

Disappointed, Madison nods. "Okay. I've got some leads to follow this morning. And I'll ask Chief Mendes to hold a news conference so we can get the press and the community searching for her."

Mendes appears behind Douglas. She's wearing another sharp pant suit, this one navy. Madison wonders if she has a whole closet full of them and nothing else. She certainly can't imagine her in jeans and sneakers. Madison's keen to get out chasing leads, but Chief Mendes motions them over to her office. The look on her face would suggest Madison's in trouble. She glances at Douglas, whose expression gives nothing away. He's a tough nut to crack, and she wonders if she'll ever get to know the real Don Douglas.

Once inside, Chief Mendes closes the door behind them. "So, Madison, we need to discuss your friend Nate Monroe." She crosses her arms and perches on her tidy desk. "Is he a killer? Because I looked into his history and I can't figure out what to believe. Was he framed, or did he only get off death row on a DNA technicality? Because we all know that happens and I'd really like to believe you wouldn't be associating with a killer."

Madison bristles. "Listen, Nate's the most honest person I've ever met. There's no way on earth he killed Rex Hartley. Rex was his friend. There was no tension between them whatsoever, so it's completely ridiculous to even entertain the idea that he would hurt him. I mean, there's not even any motive."

"So why do the San Diego police want to arrest him when they arrive?"

Her mouth goes dry at the thought of it. "My guess? Because he's an easy suspect. He'd been staying with Rex for the last two months, but if he was going to kill him, do you really think he'd wait until his last day there? I mean, he's not stupid." She's met with a blank stare, so she says, "How did Rex die?"

Mendes checks her notes. "They think he might have been poisoned. The substance is yet to be determined, because the autopsy isn't scheduled until tomorrow morning, but he had vomited a lot of blood and saliva. There are clear signs of a struggle in his home. The police believe that whoever attacked him stayed to watch him die."

Rex's final moments must have been excruciating, and Madison prays Nate never finds out the details. "It wasn't Nate. He's not capable of that. You have to trust me on this."

"So where is he?" asks Douglas.

She crosses her arms. "I don't know. I spoke to him on the phone briefly before coming here, and he sounded devastated. He's more than likely gone on the run, because he doesn't trust cops."

"Well that's not strictly true," says Mendes, raising an eyebrow. "He trusts you."

She doesn't know what to say. How does she explain what they've been through together? How hard it was to gain his trust? "We need to be looking at Father Jack Connor for Rex's murder."

Mendes considers it. She obviously read about Father Connor when researching Nate. Their names are forever linked. "You think this is some kind of revenge for Nate getting off death row?"

"It's a strong possibility. Connor's been taunting him with crazy emails for almost two years, talking about seeing him in hell and reaping the repercussions of his sins. The guy's a nutjob!" She's getting worked up, so she takes a deep breath. "Without knowing all the details around Rex's death, I can't suggest anyone else. Maybe once I've spoken to the San Diego police and seen the crime-scene photos…"

Mendes is shaking her head. "No way. You can't be involved in the case; you're friends with the main suspect. I'm assigning it to Douglas." She looks at him. "I want you to liaise with the San Diego PD once they're here. I don't know exactly when they're flying out, but the detective I spoke to—Christine Russell—said she's hoping to arrive either tonight or tomorrow. You should be the one to bring Nate Monroe in for questioning, and no leaking any details to your partner here, otherwise we could all get it in the neck from whoever prosecutes this case." She turns to Madison. "Hard as it is, we all have to remain objective."

Madison is annoyed. "But Douglas won't look beyond the evidence. He doesn't even know Nate well! And no disrespect, Don, but look at what you did to me! You jumped to the most obvious conclusion in that case, falling for someone's plan and landing me in prison."

Douglas eyes her sternly. "I made a mistake. You're never going to let me forget it, are you?"

Chief Mendes takes a step toward her. "That's enough. You need to focus on finding Kacie Larson before the DA starts breathing down my neck and the press make us look incompetent."

Madison shakes her head. "That all you care about, Chief? How we look to the media? Shouldn't we be finding Kacie because she's worth finding?"

Mendes's eyes burn with fury. "If you meddle in this other case at all, I'll suspend you without pay. You don't question my orders, Detective Harper. Not now, not ever. Are we clear?"

Madison wants to storm out and slam the door shut behind her so hard the glass shatters, but she has to remain professional. She glances at Douglas, who, from the expression on his face, has put his wall back up. Which probably means he's going to go in heavy-handed to track Nate down. He's going to throw him under the bus in order to look good to Chief Mendes.

She leaves the office cursing them both under her breath.

CHAPTER TWENTY-ONE

After driving away from the station, Madison tries to put Nate out of her mind and focus on finding Kacie, but it's not easy. She finds herself constantly checking her phone in case he gets in touch. Finally, realizing that Kacie needs her more than he does, she slips her phone in her pocket and concentrates on solving her current case as fast as possible.

Although it's still early in the day, the hair salon beneath Kacie's apartment is already busy, and when she steps inside, the combined smell of ammonia and perfume make her cough. The decor is like any other salon, with framed photographs of models of all ages lining the wall. Their hairstyles look dated to Madison, but as someone who learned to trim her own hair out of necessity, she shouldn't really judge.

The young receptionist is chewing gum and scrolling the internet on her phone, paying no attention to any potential customers. Madison is admiring her intricate rainbow-colored dye job when she finally looks up and greets her. "Good morning."

"Hi. I'm looking for Joely," she says.

The receptionist smiles broadly. "Are you her nine thirty?"

"No." Madison flashes her badge. "I need to ask her some questions."

The girl's eyes widen and she looks around the salon. "Joely?" she yells. "This cop wants to talk to you."

A slim black woman of around twenty years old makes her way over. The look on her face is one of worry. "Is everything okay? It's not Aaron, is it? I just dropped him at kindergarten."

"No, nothing like that. I'm here to ask you about Kacie Larson."

Relief that her son is safe washes over Joely's face. When a loud hairdryer bursts into life and drowns out all other noises, she suggests they step outside, where she lights a cigarette. Madison retrieves her notebook and tries to ignore the urge to smoke. The rain clouds have finally cleared and the sun makes an appearance overhead, but it's still cold. "Would you tell me when you last saw Kacie?"

"Sure. It was the night before last. I was babysitting for her." Joely frowns. "Is she okay?"

"We're not sure. Her boss has reported her missing."

Joely drops her cigarette in shock. As she stoops to pick it up, she says, "Oh my God. Wait, but where's Ellie?"

"The baby's completely safe, don't worry. She's with a foster family for the time being. I really need to know what happened that night. Can you tell me what you talked about and what time you left her apartment?"

There are tears welling in Joely's eyes. "Ellie's with a *foster* family? I can look after her. Don't give her to child services, please!"

Madison understands her concern, but she can't tell her that. "I'm sorry, but unless you're a blood relative, you won't be allowed to care for her. But you can help her by telling me everything that happened last time you saw Kacie. It's important."

The young woman runs a hand over her hair as she tries to think back. "She was working at the diner that evening, so she got home after nine. I didn't stay long once she was back, because Aaron was sleepy. I must have left by nine fifteen, maybe nine thirty."

"And how did Kacie seem to you?"

She looks surprised by the question. "The same as always."

"She wasn't upset or excited about anything? Did she do anything out of the ordinary?"

"No. She said she had stuff to do so she didn't want to chat for long. Sometimes she offers me a drink and we watch TV together, but she seemed a little distracted."

"Did she say what it was she was planning to do after you left?"

Joely shakes her head. "No. I didn't ask. I assumed she meant she had to bathe Ellie and tidy the apartment. I mean, it was late, plus it was cold and dark out. What else would she be doing?"

Good question. "Does she have a boyfriend or anyone else in her life? Or any family nearby?"

"She wasn't seeing anyone, no. Not since her and Justin split up. You know about him, right?"

Madison is surprised. Justin didn't tell her that he and Kacie had dated. It rings alarm bells. "He's her neighbor?"

"Right. I think it was just a relationship of convenience for both of them, though, so it didn't last long. He's not her normal type; he's a stoner, and she didn't want weed around Ellie. They argue about the smell coming from his place all the time, and don't even get me started on his crappy loud music. He always times it with Ellie's naps."

Interesting. She wonders if their arguments might have escalated to the point of him harming Kacie after she got home that night. He did say he'd heard Joely leave after Kacie got home, so he was clearly around. "Do you know Justin's last name?"

"Carmichael."

She makes a note so she can run a criminal record check later. "What about Kacie's family? Do you know them?"

Joely frowns. "No. She doesn't talk about them at all. Ellie's only daycare was me or one of the waitresses from the diner. I never met Kacie's parents or any brothers or sisters. All I know is they don't live in Lost Creek."

"So who would you say I should contact as her next of kin?" Joely suddenly looks horrified, and Madison realizes she needs to minimize alarm. "I'm not saying she's going to be found dead. I just need someone I can notify about her disappearance and to check whether she's been in touch with any of her family."

The young woman relaxes a little. "No one springs to mind, sorry. Maybe if you find her cell phone, you can see who's listed?"

Madison's heart sinks. How does someone so young survive with no family around them, especially with a young baby to care for? "Do you know if she's on social media? Facebook, maybe?"

"I only follow her on Insta, but she just uses it for messaging mostly." Joely pulls out her cell phone, opens Instagram and finds Kacie's profile. Madison leans in for a look as she scrolls through the photos. They're mostly of Kacie and her baby dressed up for Halloween and laughing together. Ellie looks well cared for in clean, warm clothes, and Kacie's affection for the child is obvious. The last post was published five days ago. "Did you take these?"

"Yeah, we took the kids to the pumpkin patch up at Fantasy World."

Madison knows the Fantasy World amusement park better than she'd like. It was the location of a murder back in the summer, and she and her son will forever be linked to the victim.

She leans in to study the most recent photo of Kacie and spots a small tattoo on her wrist. It looks like a semicolon, which isn't something she's seen as a tattoo before. "What does this mean, do you know?"

Joely tries to think. "She did tell me. It was something about mental health, but I can't remember exactly." She quickly googles it. "Oh yeah, it's instead of a period. She reads out the explanation: *A semicolon is used when an author could've chosen to end their sentence, but chose not to. The author is you, and the sentence is your life.*" She looks at Madison. "Kind of sad, really."

It is. "Did she seem suicidal to you?"

"No, not at all. She wouldn't leave Ellie motherless, there's no way."

"Did Justin tattoo it on her?"

"No, she already had it when she first moved here."

Making a note of that and Kacie's Instagram username, Madison says, "I take it Kacie likes Halloween."

"Yeah, it's her favorite time of year. I'm supposed to dye her hair tomorrow, ready for a party this weekend. She's going jet black with red tips and has been saving for ages to get it done." Slipping her phone away, she asks, "Do you think she'll turn up for her appointment?"

Madison tries to be optimistic for her. "I really hope so. If you see or hear from her, or if you hear anyone in the salon talking about what might have happened, please let me know. Just call the station and ask for Detective Harper, okay?"

"Sure. But be honest with me, do you think she's been, like, abducted or something?"

"I don't know yet. Hopefully she'll just turn up completely oblivious to the worry she's caused."

Joely looks doubtful. "There's no way she would leave Ellie alone on purpose. You have to know that she's a wonderful mother considering her age and how little support she has."

Madison smiles and puts a hand on the young woman's arm. "Don't worry. I'll do everything I can to find her."

CHAPTER TWENTY-TWO

Before Madison can drive away from the salon, a shadow blocks the weak morning sunshine. She glances up and finds Vince Rader peering down at her. He's holding a boxed security camera and is looking a little sheepish, like he's been caught red-handed at something. Wondering what he's doing near Kacie's apartment, she gets out of the car. "Morning."

"Detective." He nods. "I expect you're wondering what I'm doing here."

"You could say that."

He looks up the steps to Kacie's front door. "I thought about putting surveillance cameras out front. In case Kacie returns or someone starts snooping around, perhaps to cover their tracks."

Madison raises her eyebrows. "Come on, Vince. You can't be doing things like that. Every time you go near Kacie's apartment, you're leaving DNA behind and possibly destroying someone else's. You need to let *me* work on finding her." She really can't tell whether he's a concerned boss or a stalker.

His cheeks redden. "I'm sorry, I just find it hard to sit back and do nothing. This whole situation has echoes of when Ruby went missing." He looks away. "But I guess you're right, it was a stupid idea."

She crosses her arms. "Did Kacie give a next of kin on her job application when she applied for the waitressing job?"

"She must have. I would have noticed if she'd left anything blank. Perhaps I should have called them before notifying you she was missing."

"I think it's best done in person, and by me. They'll no doubt have a lot of questions."

"You're probably right. I'll fish out her application when I get a minute."

"Thanks. I'll need her bank details too. I can check whether there have been any transactions on her account since her disappearance, and whether the father of her baby pays her child support." She doesn't tell him she suspects it could be Ellie's father who ran the car off the road.

"You might struggle with that. She didn't have a bank account when she moved here."

"No? So how do you pay her?"

He hesitates. "Cash. It was supposed to be temporary, until she got herself sorted and opened an account."

Madison sighs. How does anyone get by without a bank account these days? Perhaps Kacie had one but she fed Vince a line in the hope of avoiding tax. "Fine. Did you get in touch with your podcast guest to ask if he saw anything the night he was at yours?"

"I tried. He's not answering the phone and he hasn't replied to my email yet."

She's surprised. "Is he usually easy to get in touch with?"

Vince nods. "He is."

Her instinct kicks in. "So you haven't heard from him since he left your apartment, and that was the same night Kacie disappeared?"

"I guess that's right." He appears to realize the implication. "Are you suggesting he could have been involved?"

Either he was involved, or this is yet another person linked to Vince who has gone missing. She pulls out her notebook. "I'm going to need his name and contact details. I want to speak to him myself."

Vince hesitates. "He's not going to be happy with me for giving you this." He pulls out his phone anyway and shows Madison the name and number he has listed.

"Shane Kennedy?" She's taken aback. "When you said he was famous, I assumed you meant locally. Didn't this guy have a big-budget movie adapted from one of his books a few years back?"

"That's right. And everyone's eagerly awaiting the follow-up, but he told me he's turned his back on fiction for good and is focusing on true crime now."

"Why would he do that?"

He rubs the back of his neck. "Shane had a run-in with the law a few years back and got a taste of what it's like to be falsely accused of something heinous."

Interesting. She needs to check out what Shane Kennedy was accused of and how far the charges were taken. If the allegations relate to young women, he could have something to do with Kacie's disappearance.

Her phone rings. When she sees Douglas's name, her heart skips a beat. Has he found Nate? "Excuse me a minute, Vince. I have to take this. Don't go anywhere just yet."

He nods and wanders over to the salon to peer through the window.

"Is everything okay?" she asks Douglas.

"I've managed to get the name of the person who hired the Ford Fusion." There's a hostile edge to his voice; he clearly hasn't forgiven her for their heated exchange earlier. "I'll text you the details, but she's called Veronica Webb. She lives in Utah."

Madison frowns. "Utah? Then what was she doing here? And why was she driving Kacie Larson's baby?"

"No idea. Do you want to call her, or should I? I have physio in an hour, so I could do with leaving soon."

"Fine, leave it with me. Any luck getting Kacie or Ellie's birth certificates?"

"Not yet. I've got to go." He ends the call without saying goodbye.

She rolls her eyes, then looks around to see Vince chatting to someone from the tattoo parlor.

He walks back over to her. "Paul says he hasn't seen Kacie for a few days, which is unusual, as he normally sees her coming and going when it's quiet."

Crossing her arms, she says, "You know you're not a detective, right? I should be the one asking those questions."

He raises his eyebrows. "I'm just trying to help."

She feels like he's getting a little too involved in Kacie's disappearance. He's the girl's boss, not her father. It makes her want to check his alibi a little more closely. "Just run me through the exact details of that night. You said you were with this crime writer."

"Right. From eleven forty-five until just after two a.m."

She frowns. That would have given him between nine fifteen—when Joely left Kacie's apartment—until around eleven thirty to abduct Kacie and do what he needed to do before getting back to the diner for his interview. "You know, it's not uncommon for perps to insert themselves into police investigations, to hide in plain sight, as it were."

He waves a dismissive hand. "Oh please, that's way too amateur. If I'd taken Kacie, I would never have struck up a conversation with the lead detective to begin with, and I certainly wouldn't have invited you into my diner, knowing full well you normally steer clear. No, I would be trying to blend in unnoticed."

He's so blasé about it that it bothers her. "So where were you during the hours between Kacie leaving work and Shane Kennedy arriving for his interview?"

He smiles, as though he's enjoying being challenged. "I took a nap, knowing I'd be up late with Mr. Kennedy. When you get to my age, you need all the sleep you can get. Unfortunately, I don't have anyone who can corroborate that, but you also won't find any witnesses who can claim I left my apartment between those times.

My cell phone was on and a quick call to the service provider will confirm it never left my side."

She narrows her eyes. "Perhaps, knowing we'd check that, you left your phone at home whilst abducting her. To muddy the waters. Let's face it, you know more about crime and forensics than the average Joe, what with your podcast and your experience with the police after Ruby went missing."

The mention of his missing wife makes his face cloud over with pain. She regrets it instantly.

He starts walking away from her. "Just find Kacie soon, Detective. I'm sure I don't have to tell you it's already reaching the point of no successful return."

She watches him go and feels like an asshole. But is he messing with her?

CHAPTER TWENTY-THREE

Dear Bunny,

Thanks for the new photo. You look great, much younger than your age. In answer to your questions: no, I'm not officially in the new documentary that's being made. It's another hack job from someone who wants to cash in on my name and fame. I'll be putting out a statement the week it airs to make sure viewers know.

Anyway, tell me more about you. Do you have a boyfriend? You must do, you're gorgeous. I'm single right now. I'm glad my story inspires you. Those of us who get dealt a bad hand have to make our own luck, and that's what I've always done. We can't rely on other people to help us out. There are so many con artists waiting to exploit us. It's best you keep our correspondence secret. I wouldn't want people to get the wrong idea.

I'm thinking you and I should stick together. Keep writing to me. I want to know more about you. And send more photos.

Your hero, Ace

Dear Ace,

I was so excited when you sent another letter! I like corresponding this way, it's exciting getting actual post as opposed to junk mail. And I love writing instead of emailing or messaging. It's like having a pen pal like I did in high school. She was Japanese, and we fell out because she took offense at something I wrote that didn't translate well. Hopefully that won't happen with us!

What's it like to be famous? Do you get sent free stuff all the time? Maybe if I sent you my favorite book, you could sign it for me. I'd gladly pay for postage and I wouldn't sell it on eBay or anything, even though it would probably be worth hundreds of dollars. I won't tell anyone that we write to each other, especially not the press. I'm not stupid. I know you hate them. And don't worry, I don't believe the lies about you. I think people are just trying to make money out of your fame.

You wanted to know more about me—I live alone with no family nearby. My mom died when I was thirteen, which was tough. I don't have any brothers or sisters. I'm pretty much alone. I love reading all kinds of books and watching horror movies. What else do you want to know? Tell me more about you!

Can't wait for your next letter.

Love, Bunny

CHAPTER TWENTY-FOUR

Nate's first instinct after hearing of Rex's death was to drive straight back to San Diego and investigate it for himself in the hope of finding something that would clear him and convict Father Connor. But it didn't take him long to realize that was the worst thing he could do.

The police will be crawling all over the crime scene, and now that Madison has confirmed the San Diego cops are considering him as a suspect, he needs to stay well away from California. He has it on good authority that the sunshine state houses the worst death row in the US—San Quentin prison—and he has no doubt that's where he'll end up if Father Connor is successful in framing him for Rex's murder.

Instead, he and Brody drive south to New Mexico, where he sells his Jeep ridiculously cheap to a used car dealership and purchases a second-hand Chrysler Pacifica. A minivan, essentially. It should help him blend in wherever he goes, plus the seats flatten in the back so he and Brody can comfortably sleep in it for now. He didn't want to give up the Jeep, because it was the only big-ticket item he'd bought with his wrongful conviction payout, but he has to assume the police will soon have an APB out for it, so it has to go.

After swapping the car, he heads back to Colorado with the intention of lying low for as long as possible while he plans his next move. He and Brody spend the night at an abandoned campsite twenty miles out of Lost Creek, surrounded by woods. With it being the end of October, there's no one else here, so he has privacy.

It's bitterly cold overnight, and the sleeping bag he purchased doesn't keep him as warm as the heat coming off Brody, who sleeps alongside him in the back of the car. The woods offer shelter from the wind and most of the rain, but he can't stay here too long without freezing to death. At some point he'll have to risk a motel room. But if his name and image are released to the press and the cops figure out he's travelling with a dog, he'll be an easy target.

He sits on a fallen tree trunk overlooking a small lake. Brody's wolfing down a pack of hot-dog sausages Nate heated up for their lunch. He stocked up on food and camping goods at a grocery store in New Mexico. He also bought some burner phones as well as a baseball cap, sunglasses and a couple of padded plaid shirts to wear over his sweaters in the hope of blending in with the locals and travelling around town anonymously for as long as possible.

Brody looks up at him, licking his lips, and Nate wonders if the dog will be his downfall. He'll make it easier for the public to recognize him. He curses himself again for not leaving him at Madison's place, but at the same time it's comforting to have him for company.

He sighs. There's nothing he can do about Rex's murder right now. Not until he's cleared as a suspect. And he can't just sit around here doing nothing until then. He decides to help Madison by looking into Vince Rader. It's a welcome distraction. He starts with Google, and finds Rader's *Crime and Dine* website. The "About Me" section doesn't offer much; just the basics. It seems Vince moved to Colorado with his wife Ruby eight years ago. It mentions he had a long career in the US Navy, followed by a stint as a commercial diver. Running a diner is a strange career move. Perhaps his wife was the driving force there until her disappearance. Maybe he keeps it open in the hope she'll return one day.

The fact that he was in the navy gives Nate a good place to start. He knows an independent military researcher from a previous case he worked with Rex, one who has contacts on the inside. Maybe he could look into Vince's military background and find out if he ever got into any trouble. He doesn't have the guy's number now he's changed cell phones, so he googles his place of work and manages to track him down through the switchboard.

"Marcus Alexander."

"Hey, Marcus. It's Nate Monroe, Rex Hartley's friend."

"Nate. Good to hear from you." Marcus pauses. "Let me call you back on my cell."

He doesn't want his workplace recording this call. That's understandable. Nate gives him his new number and waits for the callback, which is quick.

"How's Rex these days? It's been a while since he's needed my services."

Nate doesn't have the heart to give him the news, nor the energy to explain it. "He's fine. I'm actually after your services now, if you're still doing the freelance military research. I'd obviously pay you for your time."

Marcus hesitates before answering, his voice hushed. "Sure, as you're a friend of Rex. I take it this is for a criminal suspect?"

Nate doesn't know how Rex made so many contacts willing to break data protection laws, and he's always surprised when they agree to it. He must have made a lasting impression on them. "It is. I don't know anything about him yet, and thought his military record would be as good a place to start as any."

"Let me grab a pen. Okay, I need name, DOB and rank."

"His name's Vince Rader and he was in the navy. Since then he's worked as a commercial diver, but I don't know where. For the last seven-eight years he's lived in Lost Creek, Colorado. I don't know his DOB, but I'd say he's between fifty-five and sixty. I don't even know what he did in the navy, sorry."

Marcus laughs. "That's more detail than Rex ever gives me. I take it it's urgent?"

"Afraid so. There's a missing woman involved."

"Understood. Let me see what I can find. Is it safe to text you the information?" Marcus will know Nate's using a burner phone for this research.

"It is. Thanks for this, I appreciate it."

"No worries. Say hi to Rex for me, would you?"

Nate smiles sadly. "Sure thing."

Trying hard to ignore his grief before it takes hold, he gets into the minivan, followed by Brody. He tries to think who he should approach in Lost Creek to discreetly ask about Vince. He figures everyone in town will know him, seeing as he runs the diner, but he has to be careful not to bump into Madison or Detective Douglas.

He slips on a baseball cap and starts the engine.

CHAPTER TWENTY-FIVE

Vince has sent Madison the name and address of Kacie Larson's next of kin as listed on her job application: her parents, Emma and Pete Larson, from Prospect Springs. She arranges for Officer Shelley Vickers to come with her, as she doesn't know what to expect when the couple hear the news their daughter has gone missing.

It takes just under two hours to drive there, and by midday, Madison passes the welcome sign for Prospect Springs. Shelley's talking about the guy she's currently hot for: Jake Rubio, the EMT who took Ellie to the hospital. Shelley's only thirty and still very much looking for someone to settle down with, but at the moment, she's trying to convince Madison she wouldn't date Jake even if she could. "He's the kind of guy everyone lusts after. You can't be safe with someone like that, because if women are throwing themselves at him, of course he's going to cheat. What man wouldn't?"

Madison's amused. "I've dated both men and women like that, so it's not just a male thing. But give him some credit: just because he's hot doesn't mean he's an asshole."

Shelley gives her a look. "Come on, Madison. I was a cheerleader. I know exactly what men are like."

"So are you saying you wouldn't sleep with him if the opportunity arose?"

"What are you, crazy? Of course I would! Even one night with Jake would be worth it."

Madison shakes her head, laughing.

"What's going on in your love life these days?" asks Shelley. "Are you dating Nate Monroe? Because he's something else."

"What do you mean by 'something else'?" Madison keeps her eyes on the road.

"Well, he's tall and handsome, and he's got that haunting back-story of a lost love and an uncertain future. Plus, wasn't he almost a priest at one point? I mean, who wouldn't want to give him a go?"

Madison laughs, "My God, Shelley, you have such a way with words. But no, we're just friends. He's a great guy, but he's in trouble at the moment. His closest friend was found murdered last night in San Diego, and the local cops think Nate might be the killer."

"That's terrible. He can't catch a break."

Madison nods, but doesn't explain further. "Put the zip code in, would you?" They might have reached Prospect Springs, but she doesn't know where she's going. Shelley punches the zip code into the sat nav, which tells them they're only two blocks away from the Larson house. Madison's stomach flips at the thought of what awaits.

"I don't know anyone who enjoys this part," says Shelley, shifting her weight in the seat beside her. She's sipping a takeout coffee they stopped for on the way.

"Tell me about it. But let's hope Kacie is sitting in their living room completely oblivious to the trouble she's caused." Even as she says it, she knows it's not going to happen. From the sounds of it, Kacie wouldn't voluntarily leave her baby unattended.

"I wonder how her parents will react."

"Depends how close they are. She must have left home at a young age for a reason, so they can't be super close. And they can't know she's missing, because they haven't filed a missing person report. Keep an eye on their body language. You never know, they could have been involved in her disappearance."

"You think? Surely not?"

Shelley's naïve reaction reminds Madison of when she was in charge of mentoring the young rookie straight out of the academy. Back then, Shelley believed that most people were inherently good and the bad guys were few and far between. But Madison knows better. Shelley should know that too by now. "Anything's possible. Maybe they weren't happy she got pregnant so young."

When they reach the house, Madison switches the car's engine off and looks at Shelley. "Ready?"

Shelley takes a deep breath. "Honestly? No."

"If you want to be a detective one day, you need to get used to this kind of thing. But remember: we're not here to tell them their daughter is dead. Just that she's missing. And they may be able to help with leads."

Shelley nods.

The house is a large white colonial style, with a landscaped front yard and a double garage. The Larsons clearly have money. It makes Madison wonder how they can let their daughter and grandchild live alone in that tiny apartment in Lost Creek with no financial support. She approaches the front door, where a dog is yapping so loudly at their approach that she doesn't need to ring the bell. It takes just a minute for the door to swing open. A glamorous woman holding a noisy white Pomeranian looks at them. The color drains from her face when she spots Shelley's police uniform.

Madison flashes her badge. "Hi, I'm Detective Madison Harper from Lost Creek Police Department, and this is Officer Shelley Vickers. May we come in?"

The dog starts growling at them as the woman's smile drops. "What on earth for?"

"We just need a moment of your time." Madison doesn't want to discuss it on the doorstep. The woman must realize they're here to deliver bad news, because she moves aside with a look of trepidation.

Madison and Shelley step into the spacious hallway, where a smartly dressed man appears. She wonders why the couple are at home during the day, but then spots a home office off to the left. "What's going on?" he asks.

"I don't know," says his wife. "They're police officers."

Madison speaks up. "I'm here about Kacie Larson. Am I right in thinking you're her parents?"

"Oh my God." Mrs. Larson drops the dog, which runs off to the kitchen. "What's wrong? Is she okay?"

"We're not sure yet. I'm afraid she's been reported missing and I've been asked to find her. Perhaps we should take a seat."

The look of confusion on their faces is heartbreaking. Before she arrived, they were going about their everyday routine, completely oblivious to what was about to happen. She leads them to the couch in the living room and they automatically sit down next to each other, but they're too shocked to speak. The room is as neat and well maintained as they are, with a fire burning in a large hearth. The heat it gives off feels good, but Madison's hands remain cold at the prospect of delivering bad news. "We've found what I believe is Kacie's shoe, and I'm sorry to say it was bloodstained."

Mrs. Larson looks close to tears. "This can't be happening!"

Her husband puts his arm around her. "This must be why she didn't message you back."

Madison gives them a second to absorb the news while she glances at Shelley, whose face is unreadable. Turning back to the couple, she says, "Of course, it could just be that she's injured and unable to ask for help, but I need to piece together a timeline of when everyone last heard from her."

Mr. Larson nods, but he's clearly struggling. He appears to have many questions, but none of them make it out of his mouth. To Madison, neither of them looks like they could be involved in their daughter's disappearance. He takes a deep breath, and she notices that his hands are shaking. "I'm sorry, I'm drawing a complete blank. It's like my mind has switched off."

Madison nods. "That's perfectly normal. And I want to reassure you that Kacie's baby is completely fine and being cared for by a foster family. She's healthy and unharmed."

Mrs. Larson looks up through her tears. "What?"

"Ellie's with a foster family, so—"

"Kacie doesn't have a baby. Why would you think that?"

Shelley looks as confused as Madison feels. What the hell is going on? Did Kacie have the baby without telling them? Was that why she moved out of home? Or is the baby not really hers?

"I'm sorry, I was told Kacie has a baby girl. Ellie? She's twelve months old."

The Larsons look at each other, bewildered. Then the dog starts yapping loudly again and runs to the front door. As it swings open, they hear a female voice: "Sammy!"

Madison walks toward the hallway as the Larsons stand up. A teenage girl appears. She drops her backpack on a chair by the front door and picks up the excited dog. When she sees Madison, she frowns. The couple rush over to her. "Kacie! Where have you been?" demands Mrs. Larson.

Kacie pulls away from their attempts to hug her. "What's going on?" she asks.

Madison's heart drops into her stomach. It's clear she's made a terrible mistake.

CHAPTER TWENTY-SIX

All Madison can do is watch the scene play out in front of her with a creeping feeling of dread.

"Where the hell have you been?" yells Kacie's dad. "The police just told us you were missing. Have you been skipping school again?"

Kacie looks mightily pissed off at the accusation. "I don't know what you're talking about. I've been there all morning!"

Shelley approaches Madison and says quietly, "What's going on? Did we locate the wrong Kacie Larson?"

Madison shakes her head. "This is the address our missing woman put on her job application." She closes her eyes as she realizes her Kacie Larson must be living under a false identity.

"What's going on, Detective?" Mr. Larson approaches her looking rightfully angry. "Why did you come here if our daughter's not missing?"

Madison swallows. She's already thinking about how much heat she's going to catch from Chief Mendes for unnecessarily upsetting this family. "I'm so sorry. There's obviously been a terrible mistake." They're staring at her for answers, but her mouth has gone dry. "I've obviously been misled. We're looking for a nineteen-year-old woman from Lost Creek, and for some reason she's taken your name." She looks at Kacie before turning back to the parents. "And she gave your names and address as her next of kin."

Mrs. Larson takes a deep breath as her hand rests on her throat. "I'm just so glad it isn't our daughter you're looking for."

Kacie is shaking her head in disgust. "Why would someone do that? It's creepy. Do I have to change my name now?"

Madison tries to think fast. "Could it be one of your friends? Because the young woman who's gone missing must know you and your parents in order to have used your details."

"I don't hang out with anyone that age," says Kacie. "My friends are all the same age as me: seventeen. And I don't invite weirdos like that into my life."

Madison pulls out one of the missing person flyers and shows it to the girl, who's moved away from her parents and is leaning against an armchair. "You don't recognize her at all?"

Kacie takes it from her and studies it. "No."

"Could she have gone to your school?"

"If she did, she's not in my crowd. She could be one of the losers, I guess. I mean, look at her makeup, it's awful!"

"Kacie!" her mom scolds her.

"What? I'm just saying. I don't recognize her anyway."

Mrs. Larson says, "This is crazy. I really wish you hadn't scared us like that, Detective. I think I need a brandy."

Her husband goes to their drinks cabinet and prepares them both a shot. After downing his, he says, "You should have got your facts straight before coming here. What if one of us had reacted terribly to the news and done something stupid? I mean, my God, the thought of your child going missing is every parent's worst nightmare, and now, thanks to you, I know what that feels like."

Madison nods. She deserved that. "Again, I'm sorry. I'll make sure never to repeat this mistake. We'll get out of your hair now."

But Mr. Larson isn't prepared to let her off so lightly. "An apology won't cut it. I want to make a formal complaint. Because that was really messed up coming in here and scaring us like that. I bet the local news would like to hear about it."

Madison can't tell if he's seeing dollar signs at the thought of suing the department or whether he's genuinely upset. She feels shame burning her cheeks. "I can understand why you would feel that way, but I didn't set out to upset you; it was a genuine error as a result of the missing woman giving false details. But if you'd like to make a complaint, just contact my department."

He doesn't hesitate. "Are you going to leave your card?"

"I'm sorry, I only started working in the department yesterday, so I don't have any cards made up yet." She couldn't be more embarrassed.

Mr. Larson rolls his eyes. "That explains it. Your chief sent a rookie to deliver bad news to the wrong family. They should be ashamed of themselves."

Shelley steps forward and pulls out her pocket notebook. "Here." She scribbles down the station's contact details and tears off the sheet of paper, handing it to him. "We apologize for the mistake and I'm glad you have your daughter safely with you, but we came here to help someone else find *their* daughter. At least you get a happy ending, Mr. Larson. Because the parents of the missing woman might not, and it'll be us who'll have to deliver the bad news to them." She looks at Madison and nods to the door. "Let's go."

Madison follows her out of the house, quietly closing the front door behind her. She doesn't speak until she's driving away. She's too mad at herself. "That was a shit show. I can't believe I screwed up."

Shelley's shaking her head. "You followed the evidence. Anyone would've made the same assumption that they were our missing woman's parents. Don't be so hard on yourself."

Madison suddenly wishes she was back working for Nate as a PI. At least they'd been partners. With Detective Douglas not being back to full health, she's been left high and dry with no one experienced to partner with. She wonders then whether Chief Mendes is setting her up to fail so that she can pretend she gave her a try before firing her.

"The main thing we learned from that," says Shelley, "is that our missing woman is living under a false identity."

Madison nods and tries to concentrate on the case rather than on what just happened. "There's got to be a reason for it. I need to find out who she really is, but until Douglas gets the baby's birth certificate, I'm relying on the public helping us."

"Hopefully she didn't use a fake identity on that too." Shelley sighs. "The fact that she felt she had to change her name suggests she must have been running away from something."

"Or someone." Madison is determined to get to the bottom of what's going on. "Wait until Mendes finds out I upset that family for no reason. She'll probably fire me."

"Does she need to know?" asks Shelley. "I mean, Mr. Larson probably won't complain once he's had a chance to cool down, and I'm happy not to tell her."

Madison is grateful for the support, but she doesn't think Mr. Larson will calm down. With embarrassment weighing heavy on her, she drives the rest of the way home in silence.

CHAPTER TWENTY-SEVEN

Shelley was wrong about Mr. Larson calming down. When they arrive back and walk past Mendes's office, the chief is fuming. "In here, now."

Shelley follows Madison in, but Mendes doesn't want her here. "Not you, Officer. I'm sure you have somewhere else to be."

Madison wishes she could swap places with her as Shelley walks away. She steels herself for what's to come, and then notices that Douglas is in the room too.

"What the hell just happened?" says Chief Mendes, hands on her hips. "In all my time working in law enforcement, I've never heard of a detective giving bad news to the wrong family. What were you thinking?"

"Those were the contact details our missing woman provided to her boss," Madison says weakly.

"You could have done what Detective Douglas did and secured the baby's birth certificate first, to check who her mother really is."

Madison turns to him. "I asked whether you had it before I went, but you said you didn't."

"I received it by email just after we spoke."

Incredulous, she says, "So why didn't you forward it to me, or call me straight back?"

"I was busy."

She shakes her head. "I get it. You set me up."

"What? Stop being paranoid, Harper." He looks away.

The chief holds up a copy of the birth certificate. "The baby found in the car yesterday is called Ellie Stuart, and it clearly states that her mother is Ashlee Stuart, not Kacie Larson. The date of birth given for Ashlee makes her seventeen years old, not nineteen. She's clearly been misleading everyone since she arrived in town."

Madison is shocked. If their missing woman is only seventeen, she's officially a child, and the case needs to be handled even more carefully. She leans in to look at the birth certificate. "Are we sure our missing woman really is the mother of this baby?"

Mendes gives her a blank stare. "That's your job to find out."

Her mind is suddenly in overdrive as the various possibilities run through her head. "The father's name isn't listed."

Douglas stands up. "No. It just says 'father unknown'."

Chief Mendes shakes her head, clearly frustrated. "We don't have time for this right now; everyone's here for the press conference. Think you can handle that without screwing it up?"

Madison has to bite her tongue. She doesn't deserve to be spoken to this way. Sure, she made a mistake, but she's only two days into the job, with a part-time partner she can't trust, and she was acting on false information. "Yes. Do you want me to reveal this latest information about her real name and age?"

"Not until you've confirmed it. For now, we have no choice but to run with the name she was living by, as that's how locals here will know her. Don't give the press too much information yet, just the basics. The aim of this conference is to find our missing person as soon as possible by bringing in leads and sightings. If the press finds out at this stage that she's not who she said she is, they'll turn against her, and public interest in finding her will wane." Mendes opens her office door and speeds ahead of them both.

Douglas turns to Madison. "See how easy it is to make mistakes? Maybe now you'll appreciate the kind of pressure I was under when I arrested you."

Madison remains silent, not trusting herself to speak.

In the conference room, she and Mendes position themselves at the front while they wait for the news teams to get settled. She has to try not to let any of this latest stress show on her face while she's being filmed, but she'd give anything for ten minutes to regroup in private. She glances at her cell phone. Nothing from Nate.

Looking around, she spots Kate Flynn already seated, and they share a nod. Kate is sitting next to Gary Pelosi, the newspaper reporter who was snapping unflattering photos of Madison in the woods yesterday. She doesn't recognize the other people here. She sees Shelley and Steve slipping in at the back of the room, where they stand next to Douglas. Shelley gives Madison a reassuring thumbs-up.

When it appears no one else is going to arrive, Chief Mendes steps forward to the four mics positioned on the podium in front of her.

"Good afternoon, everyone. For those of you who don't know me, I'm Chief Carmen Mendes from the Lost Creek Police Department." The murmuring dies down and everyone settles. "We've called this press conference because a local woman has gone missing and it's vitally important we locate her as soon as possible. Not only are we concerned for her safety, but she's a young mother and her baby needs her to come home. We're hoping that by releasing details, we can help raise awareness and bring in much-needed sightings." She turns to the wall behind them as Madison switches on a projector.

Kacie's face appears enlarged on the wall. It's the photo Vince gave her.

"This is nineteen-year-old Kacie Larson. You may recognize her from Ruby's Diner, where she has been waitressing for the last six months." Mendes pauses as the news teams type frantically. "Detective Madison Harper is the lead investigator in this case and she will now detail the timeline of events."

As Madison steps forward, she can feel her hands sweating with nerves. She's never given a press conference before and she's acutely aware of the mics and cameras aimed at her. If she screws this up, it will forever be available to replay on YouTube, and Owen will probably accuse her of embarrassing him. She blocks all that from her mind in order to get as many people as possible looking for Kacie.

CHAPTER TWENTY-EIGHT

Madison clears her throat and decides to look directly at Kate as she speaks. "Kacie was last seen at around nine thirty on the evening of October twenty-seventh. She worked her evening shift at the diner without incident and left just before nine p.m., walking the short distance home alone. She lives above the New You hair salon on Delta Lane. She arrived home at just after nine to a friend who was taking care of her twelve-month-old daughter, Ellie."

Gary Pelosi raises his hand and asks a question without waiting for permission. "Just to clarify; the baby isn't also missing? There've been conflicting reports."

Madison ignores his rudeness. "The baby is unharmed and currently being cared for by a foster family. We don't know the identity of Ellie's father at this stage, but if anyone does, they're urged to get in touch with us as soon as possible."

She clears her throat again. "Kacie's friend left her apartment by nine thirty and said Kacie didn't appear worried or upset. One waitress in the diner actually thought she was looking forward to getting home, so it's possible she had something planned for that evening. There was a star marked on her kitchen calendar for that date, but with no explanatory note." She pauses and takes a sip of water. The room is deadly silent apart from the tapping of keys on laptops and smartphones. "What complicates issues is that Kacie's daughter was the baby found in the abandoned car in the White Woods yesterday morning. We have no idea why Ellie was in the car, as it isn't Kacie's vehicle. What we need is for anyone who saw

Kacie after nine thirty on October twenty-seventh to call in and tell us what they saw. Equally, if you witnessed the car crash in the early hours of October twenty-eighth, call us." She clicks her remote and the photo projected onto the wall changes to the red Ford Fusion.

"Could Kacie have been taken from her apartment?" asks Kate.

"We don't believe so, but of course, we'll consider all possibilities."

"Who is the owner of the red Ford?" Kate again.

Madison takes a deep breath. She hasn't had a chance yet to contact the person who hired the vehicle. At this stage, she doesn't know if Veronica Webb was in the car and is missing herself, or whether she had hired it for someone else. "It's a rental car, but I won't be disclosing the name of the person who hired it yet. I can say there is no obvious link between them and Kacie Larson. I should know more about that in the coming days."

"What was Kacie wearing when she was last seen?" asks Kate.

"Her diner uniform: a white shirt with her name embroidered across the front, and black skinny jeans with white sneakers. Any more questions?"

A guy she doesn't know raises his hand. "Is it true you found a woman's sneaker at the scene of the car crash?"

Shit. How does he know about that? "I can't comment on that at the moment."

The journalists start getting excited as they realize the implications.

He continues. "Are you investigating the link between the missing girl and her boss, Vince Rader?"

She shifts position. "What do you mean?"

"Well, everyone in town knows Mr. Rader's wife and four-year-old grandson mysteriously vanished a while back and he was the main suspect."

Vince never told her his grandson also disappeared. Why would he keep that from her? She frowns just as someone's camera flash goes off, dazzling her.

"They were never found and are presumed dead," the reporter continues, "and now one of his waitresses has disappeared too. Isn't that too much of a coincidence?"

She has to choose her words carefully, because this guy linking the two cases during a press conference is unprofessional and could hurt Vince's livelihood and reputation. "There is no evidence to suggest Mr. Rader was involved, and we haven't brought anyone in for questioning yet."

Gary Pelosi takes another turn. "How hopeful are you of finding Kacie alive?"

She doesn't hesitate. "This is still very much a missing person investigation, not a homicide investigation. We will do everything we can to find her. As a result, you'll see an increase in law enforcement activity in the town over the coming days. The safety of our community, including Kacie, is our main objective."

"Does that mean there will be a full search of the town?" asks Kate.

Chief Mendes moves forward. "We'll be discussing next steps as soon as this conference is over. Okay, we only have time for one more question."

The reporter again. "Chief Mendes, how confident are you that Detective Harper has the experience needed to be the lead investigator in this case? I mean, this is her first week in the job after spending time in prison for manslaughter, and I've got to be honest: if I was related to Kacie, I'd want Detective Douglas leading it instead."

Madison shakes her head in annoyance. What a dick. Why does this guy have it in for her?

Mendes is more professional. "We work as a team here at Lost Creek PD, and all of us will be working hard to find Kacie Larson alive." Wrapping up, she says, "As soon as we have more information, we'll release regular updates. I'd like to finish by stating that if anyone watching this has any relevant information, please get in touch with us immediately in order to help us bring Kacie Larson home."

Kate stands up. "I have more questions."

Mendes is already heading for the exit. "I'm sorry. That's all we have time for right now."

Madison and Douglas follow her back into her office. Mendes sits at her desk and checks her cell phone screen. "Vince Rader reported her missing, right?"

"Right."

"So is there any chance he could have harmed her? He would know her shift patterns, he had a photo of her ready to go, plus I've heard rumors he found her an apartment as well as being quick to offer her a job when she first moved here. I just feel like he's being a little too helpful."

"I agree," says Madison. "I've checked if he has any prior offenses, but he's clean. Doesn't mean I can't do some digging, though. Maybe he's got an angry ex who could tell us more about him." She doesn't tell them she's asked Nate to see what he can find too.

"Want me to question him?" asks Douglas.

Madison looks at him. "If anyone's going to question him, it should be me. But not until I have something concrete to work with. He knows he's an obvious suspect, so he would have been careful, and he needs treating delicately. The minute we bring him in, he'll clam up and we'll lose our chance to work him."

Mendes chews on her lip for a second. "Fine. In the meantime, we need a full search of the woods and surrounding areas. I'll contact the search-and-rescue volunteers. Don, you oversee that. Madison, I assume you have plenty of leads to chase up in the meantime?"

"Yes."

"Good." As Madison turns to leave, Chief Mendes says, "Has your friend Nate turned up yet?"

She turns back. Douglas is watching. "No. I haven't heard from him. To be honest, I don't think I'll be seeing him again." She can't tell if Mendes believes her or not, but she doesn't care, because she's telling the truth. "When are the San Diego cops arriving?"

Mendes looks at Douglas, who says, "They'll be here tomorrow morning. The detective in charge keeps asking me whether I've arrested Nate yet. She's determined to see him charged for his friend's murder."

Madison tries not to react as she leaves the office.

CHAPTER TWENTY-NINE

Nate is back in Lost Creek, seeking information about Vince Rader. He spots an old-fashioned barber's shop called Big Daddy's Cut 'N' Shave. A sign in the window states walk-ins and dogs are welcome, and he considers whether to stop. As he slowly approaches, he spots several old guys chatting inside, and that decides it for him. He hasn't had a haircut in a while and he knows places like this can be a valuable source of information, depending on how the customers take to him. He turns to Brody. "Think you can charm them for me, boy?"

Brody barks an affirmative and starts panting at the thought of working undercover.

Nate pulls into an empty parking space outside and wanders in. The four men look up at him, then at the dog, their coffees forgotten. They're all gray-haired, except for the muscly bald barber.

Nate smiles widely. It's the last thing he feels like doing, but he needs to stay focused. "Hi. I saw walk-ins are welcome and, well…" he runs a hand through his unruly hair, "it's been a while since I got a decent haircut." The truth is, he's only had four haircuts since his release from prison: two from Rex, one from Arlene—Rex's neighbor—and one from Madison before he left for San Diego. He was hoping she'd be better at it than Rex, but that proved not to be the case. Luckily, he doesn't mind his hair a little long.

The barber stands up and wipes the tan leather chair in front of him clean of cuttings. "Take a seat."

"Appreciate it." Nate climbs into the ancient chair whilst Brody takes turns visiting each guy. They fuss him, instantly taken.

"I'm Big Daddy, and this is Pete, Charlie and Joe."

Nate nods to them in the mirror.

"What do you want me to do with this?" The barber runs his hands through Nate's hair to judge how overgrown it is. Nate tries not to flinch at his light touch. Seventeen years on death row with almost zero physical contact made intimacy in any form difficult.

"Just neaten it up. And maybe a shave, too?" He gets the impression a haircut will take this guy two minutes, not long enough to glean information.

"Sure thing."

As Big Daddy sets to work, Charlie asks, "What is he, German shepherd cross?" He's brushing Brody's back and pulling the fur from the brush, dropping it onto the floor. Brody's loving every minute of it.

"We think he's crossed with a Siberian husky, but that's just a guess, since he's a rescue. His previous owner was a cop."

That raises eyebrows. "Are you a cop too?" asks the same guy. The mood changes.

Sensing they're not fans of law enforcement, Nate says, "God, no. I've never met a cop who wasn't crooked."

They all laugh, including Big Daddy, who asks, "You new in town? I don't remember seeing you around."

"Yeah, I'm just visiting a friend for a few weeks. Is there anywhere you can recommend for food? I drove by Ruby's Diner earlier; what's that like?"

Joe speaks up. "I eat dinner there every night since I lost my wife. Carla's real friendly and always gives me the biggest slice of pie for dessert."

"Good to know," says Nate as he feels his hair fall onto his hands. "Is Ruby the owner?"

They all share a glance before Charlie says, "She owned it with her husband, Vince. But she's not around anymore; went missing some years back. Vince runs the place on his own. I doubt he'll ever remarry."

"That's a shame. Did she just take off?"

"No one knows. Vince was even the main suspect for a while. The cops thought he'd murdered her and their grandson and hidden the bodies. Goddam assholes. They always blame the husband."

Nate knows that's because it so often turns out to *be* the husband. Or someone related to the victim. He doesn't say that, though. "It's the easy option, that's why. Means they get to do less work." The men all nod in agreement. "Did they have any reason to suspect him? Has he got a shady past?"

Pete chimes in. "Nah, he's a navy vet and a stand-up guy. I don't believe for a second he had anything to do with Ruby's disappearance. The waitresses all love him. My granddaughter works there on weekends. She's never said a bad word about him. He gave her a big advance on her earnings so she could afford a car."

"Let's be honest, though," says Big Daddy. "He can come across as weird until you get to know him." He starts lathering Nate's jaw. "But that's because he doesn't trust people easy. I mean, why the hell would you when your wife vanishes and the police are hell-bent on blaming you, right?"

Nate knows how that feels. He probes a little further about Vince, but the men don't reveal anything interesting, so he lets them move on to gossiping about other people. Unless Marcus comes back with something incriminating from Vince's navy career, it's looking like Madison should be focusing her attention elsewhere.

When Big Daddy has finished, Nate studies his reflection in the mirror. He looks clean-cut and respectable. Maybe it will buy him some time before he's recognized by Detective Douglas or the San Diego cops, assuming they're in town already.

Once he's paid and said his goodbyes, he and Brody drive to a more secluded spot. Knowing that Madison will be frantic with worry at a time when she should be focusing on her new job, he wants to check in. But he can't risk contacting her, even with a burner phone. When the San Diego police realize she's a friend of his, they'll watch her closely, and he wouldn't put it past them to check her phone records. Keeping an eye out for any passing patrol cars, he decides to call Owen instead. It's less risky.

Madison's son picks up on the second ring. He sounds wary when he answers, because he won't know this new number.

"Owen, it's Nate. Are you alone?"

"Yeah, I'm at school, but between classes. Where are you?"

"Listen, I can't talk for long and you have to promise me you'll ditch your phone if any cops try to take it from you. They can trace me through phone records, and if they find me…" He hesitates. "If they find me, I'll be going back to prison. Do you understand what I'm saying?"

Owen is silent while he digests the implications. Finally he says, "Got it. I won't tell anyone you called."

"You can tell your mom when she gets home tonight, but don't text her about me. Put nothing in writing, okay? Keep it verbal."

"So you mean act like a criminal?" He sounds amused.

Nate smiles. "That's right. Try to stay one step ahead of the cops at all times. I'll replace your phone if you have to dump it. I might even get you that new one you've been pestering your mom for."

"Cool. I might ditch it anyway then." Owen laughs. "Just kidding. Mom will be pissed when she finds out you called me instead of her. You know that, right?"

He does. "Just tell her she doesn't have to worry about me. I haven't done anything stupid and I'm not going to San Diego."

"Sure. Is Brody okay? You're not going to abandon him somewhere, are you?"

"Of course not. He loves living on the run. He's had four sausages already this morning."

Owen laughs. "When will we see you again?"

Dread fills Nate's chest. If he gets caught, the answer will be never. Not outside a prison, anyway. "I don't know. Just tell your mom to trust me, and make sure you don't tell the San Diego cops anything about me if they ask. They'll figure out pretty quickly that your mom and I are friends and they'll suspect she'll be helping me, so they might target you instead. Probably turn up outside your school when she's not around. Just give no comment answers to everything they ask. Do you know what I mean by that?"

"Of course. I was arrested for murder back in July, remember? I've given tons of police interviews."

Nate finds himself smiling, because Owen only had two interviews for that charge before being swiftly released. "Oh yeah. I forgot you're a real pro at keeping out of jail." He checks his rear-view mirror, watching a car that's pulled up behind him. The driver gets out and walks away. "I've been looking into Vince Rader for your mom. Tell her I've got someone checking out his navy career for any warning signs, but I think she might be heading down the wrong road with him. Tell her to keep an open mind for now and I'll carry on digging."

"Okay. I asked around at school, and everyone who eats at the diner said he's cool. I haven't managed to find anyone who's got anything bad to say about him."

Nate knows that doesn't mean Vince isn't hiding something, but it's a good sign. "I should go. Look after your mom, Owen, she's under a lot of pressure right now. And don't try calling me unless it's an emergency."

"I'm glad you got in touch. Be careful."

He ends the call. He feels bad bringing Owen into this, but he doesn't want him or Madison to worry about him more than they have to.

He opens the web browser on his phone and starts scrolling news websites to see whether he's been announced as a wanted man for Rex's murder yet. There are plenty of reports about Rex's death in the Californian press, with headlines such as *Local man found poisoned at home—killer still at large.*

He finds no mention of his name. Well, not linked to Rex's murder, anyway. Maybe the detective in charge is keeping an open mind. Or maybe they're just keeping their cards close to their chest until Nate's been arrested. He considers whether to hire a lawyer, just in case. Maybe Richie Hope, the guy who helped Madison and Owen out of a tough spot over the summer. At least Richie could find out what evidence the cops think they have on him. He decides against it for now. He wants one last chance to fix his own problems before hiring an attorney becomes a necessity. Because by that stage, he's already screwed.

He opens the last email he received from Father Connor. Ignoring the deplorable content, his finger hovers over the screen. He knows what he has to do, but he's still hesitant. Because for the first time ever, he's going to reply to Stacey's killer.

CHAPTER THIRTY

Madison watches from behind her desk as Detective Douglas rallies all available officers to join the search party. He's barking orders whilst handing out the department's stash of high-vis vests. She can tell he's in his element.

"Don't read too much into it," says Shelley as she watches him. "Let Douglas do the legwork while you get to stay in the warm and use your brain."

Madison smiles at her. "Thanks. Are you going out with them?"

Shelley nods. "I've been told to pick up a large order of coffee on my way for the volunteers. I think Chief Mendes is punishing me for our little trip earlier." She rolls her eyes. "By the way, I'm waiting on the surveillance footage from the gas station out near the White Woods. The owner is on vacation and the employee doesn't have the authority to hand it over. He wouldn't give me the owner's cell number either. Thinks he'll be fired for giving out personal information."

Madison sighs with frustration. "Do we know when the owner is due back?"

"Either tomorrow or the next day."

"Okay, thanks." She watches Shelley walk away, then checks her phone. Still nothing from Nate. She feels bad that she can't do anything for him while she's busy with this investigation. She can't even let him know when the San Diego detectives arrive. He should have stayed put until then. Together they could have come up with a plan.

Douglas approaches her. "Before I head out, I wanted you to know I looked into whether there were any custody issues with regards to the baby, like you asked. I just heard back, and there's no history of any court proceedings. I think it's safe to assume the father of the child doesn't know or care he's a dad. Maybe our missing girl ran away when she got pregnant."

Madison considers discounting the anonymous father of the baby as a potential suspect, but decides it's too early to rule anyone out. "I need you to find out who Ellie's father is. The clothing found in the car suggests a man was involved, so until I know who those clothes belong to, I'm not going to dismiss him as a suspect."

He nods. "I can ask around."

"I've got hold of Ashlee's birth certificate now, and like Ellie's, it only lists her mother's details, no father. But death records show her mother died in 2015 of liver failure. So we still don't have a next of kin for her."

Douglas looks keen to get the search started, but before he goes, he says, "Listen, don't let Mendes pit us against each other. The fact that I can't work my usual hours right now is obviously causing communication problems—like with the baby's birth certificate—but it wasn't intentional. We're going to have to trust each other if we're going to work together long-term. And sure, you screwed up earlier with the Larsons, but I guarantee you won't make that mistake again."

She tries to work out if he's being sincere. "Thanks. Good luck with the search. Call me the minute you find anything."

He nods before leaving.

She sighs as she tries to figure out where to start. Douglas might be on to something when he suggested Ashlee could be a runaway. She might actually have been reported missing by whoever she went to live with after her mother's death. They know now that she's only seventeen, which would mean she was just thirteen when she lost her mother.

She brings up the missing persons database on her computer and searches for Ashlee Stuart. There are no positive hits. For now, her best hope of tracking down Ashlee's wider family is for the public to watch the press conference and phone in with tips. Perhaps old school friends will recognize her. In the meantime, she'll try to figure out a motive for Ashlee's abduction. With that in mind, she thinks about other potential suspects. They have confirmation that Ashlee made it home that night, so the last known person to see her alive is her friend Joely. But Madison doesn't consider her a suspect. She was shocked and upset when she heard her friend had gone missing, and she had her own child to take care of.

The only other person she knows for a fact was around that night was the neighbor, Justin. She types his name into the police database and sees he has a few speeding tickets but nothing else. He didn't seem the type to muster enough energy to hurt someone, but it's always worth checking. She'll spring a surprise visit on him later to see if he'll let her look around his apartment without a warrant. While she's searching the database, she tries Ashlee's real name too. There are no hits. She didn't think there would be, but it's always worth checking in case she's been arrested for prostitution or drugs offenses. Because if she has been, there are more potential suspects to look into for her disappearance: johns and drug dealers for a start.

She locates the email Douglas sent her containing the contact details of the woman who hired the crashed car. Using her desk phone, she calls the cell number listed, not knowing what to expect.

"Veronica Webb," says an impatient voice.

Madison is surprised. She half expected the woman to be missing. "Hi. I'm Detective Madison Harper from Lost Creek Police Department in southern Colorado. I understand you recently hired a car from Voyager Rent-A-Car?"

"That's right," says Veronica. Slowly she adds, "How do you know that?"

"Because the car has been involved in an accident here in town."

"Oh crap. It's my name on the rental agreement. What's he done now?"

Madison frowns. "So you weren't driving the car yourself?"

"No, I hired it for my boss. I'm a virtual assistant for a couple of authors. I hired that one for Shane Kennedy." She pauses. "Is he okay?"

Madison is shocked Shane Kennedy was the driver. She tries to think. What was Vince's podcast guest doing with Ashlee's baby in his car? And where is he now?

"Hello?"

"Sorry," she says. "I'm not sure how Shane is, because he's not been seen since the night he gave his interview to Vince Rader. I assume you arranged that for him?"

"That's the *Crime and Dine* host, right? It was supposed to be a quick in-and-out job under cover of darkness."

"Has Shane contacted you since then?"

Veronica sounds unfazed. "No, but he's always going AWOL on me. He's a little paranoid and thinks everyone's out to sell a story about him. You have to understand: writers are weird, and he's become a real recluse over recent years because his fans can be somewhat psycho. Why don't I try calling him and get back to you?"

Madison wants to speak to him herself. "I'd rather take his number. It's important I speak to him as soon as possible."

"Why? Because of the car? Oh God, he didn't hit someone, did he? Because that would mean he's probably drinking again, and I can't work with him when he's in that state."

"No, nothing like that. Can you give me some contact details for him? I have his cell number but that's all."

Veronica hesitates. "I don't know…"

"I have to insist, I'm afraid."

Finally the assistant agrees. "He's going to kill me for giving this out."

"You can say I told you it was an emergency." Madison confirms the cell number she has for him and takes a note of his email and home address. Turns out he resides in Nevada. When she has everything she needs, she says, "Please get in touch with me if you hear from him. If he's as paranoid as you say, then he won't want the media getting wind of what's happened down here."

"Would they care about a car crash with no injuries?"

Madison decides against telling her about the baby found in the car, and the missing girl. "If his name is linked to it, they might. Thanks for your time."

She ends the call and immediately dials Shane Kennedy's cell number. The line is completely dead. She tries again to be sure. The call doesn't go through. "That's not good."

Has he destroyed his phone to avoid being traced? She remembers Vince mentioning that Shane had been in trouble with the law a few years back because of a 'heinous' allegation. Is he a sexual predator who once got away with his crimes? Her adrenaline kicks in as she realizes she now has a new suspect.

CHAPTER THIRTY-ONE

Dear Bunny,

Thanks for sticking with me despite everything. I keep all your letters to read when I'm going through a period of self-loathing. It doesn't help that it's summer right now. I hate summer more than any other season. It gets way too hot here and there's absolutely no reprieve from the rising temperatures.

We've been writing back and forth for almost a year now, and I think it's time we met each other in real life. Would you come here to visit me? Or are you too scared? Ha! Just kidding. I just want to see you with my own eyes. I want to listen to your voice and ask you everything I keep forgetting to ask in my letters. What do you say? I'll even tell you how I got my nickname, and that's a closely guarded secret.

I can't write more at this time, I have to work. But I'm including a present for you. You clearly love books, so I hope you like it.

Yours, Ace

No reply sent.

CHAPTER THIRTY-TWO

Steve has offered to track down the cell phone records for both Shane Kennedy and Ashlee Stuart, giving Madison time to dig into Kennedy's criminal record. She doesn't know at this stage whether he was the person who took Ashlee or whether he's a missing person himself, and she doesn't have either of their cell phones for Alex to perform a full forensic analysis.

She checks her watch; it's 4.30 and already dark outside. That will slow down Douglas's search-and-rescue efforts. As she stares at her tired reflection in the window next to her desk, she notices Stella approaching. She's early for her night shift.

Stella places a cup of chamomile tea in front of her. "Here you go, sweetie. I watched your news conference. I thought you did well for your first time. I could tell you were nervous because you were fiddling with your pen, but that's only because I know you so well." She smiles. "I'm hoping my phone is going to light up with tips this evening."

"Me too. Thanks for this." Madison takes a tentative sip; it's just the right temperature. Taking a break from her screen helps her relax a little. "What's your impression of Ashlee Stuart? Did you interact with her much in the diner?"

"Oh, sure. She's the kind of girl you just want to mother, you know?" Stella takes a seat at her desk. "Ever since I met her, I felt like she'd been abandoned by someone. I don't know why, but I always feel compelled to give her a hug before I leave the diner. I'm sure she thinks I'm a senile old woman, but she always lets me do it."

Madison nods. So many young people are let down by their parents and wider families. Perhaps Ashlee was one of those. "When was the last time you saw her?"

"Over a week ago. I've been trying to stay away from the diner because of their banoffee pie. I just cannot resist it, no matter how hard I try." Stella chuckles to herself before turning serious. "But I'll tell you one thing, Madison. If I'd known that was the last time I'd see her, I would have made her come and live with me. Her and the baby. I have four licensed weapons at home, and anyone who wanted her would've had to come through me and Bertie." Bertie's her dog.

Madison smiles. "Hopefully that wasn't the last time you'll see her."

Stella's phone rings and she slips her headset on.

Madison turns back to her computer and thinks about Shane Kennedy. "Why on earth would you be driving Ashlee Stuart's baby out of town?" she mutters. She types his name into the database to see if Vince was right about his previous run-in with the law, but the system freezes. She waits a few seconds, but nothing happens, no matter what she presses on her keyboard. She looks over her shoulder just as Stella hangs up on the caller. "Hey, Stella? You having any problems getting into the database?"

"Yeah, it goes down at least five times a day. Whenever I report it to Roy in IT, the little shit tells me patience is a virtue, so I don't bother anymore."

Madison rolls her eyes. "Dammit."

She googles Kennedy instead. He definitely has an arrest record, because his mugshot appears. She realizes that although she's heard of his name, thanks to the press surrounding the movie adaptation of his book, she's never actually seen what he looks like. He's handsome with his dyed jet-black hair, hazel eyes and designer stubble. He doesn't look happy in his mugshot, but he doesn't look smug either. The news article says that at the time of his arrest in 2016, he was thirty-two years old, five foot eleven, weighing one hundred and eighty-two pounds. Her eyes search for the charge: sexual assault. She sits back for a minute. "Bingo."

Leaning in again, she reads about the allegations. It seems that a teenage girl claimed she met him at a book signing event and he invited her back to his hotel room, where he tried to sexually assault her. It's one of those he-said-she-said claims that are so hard to prove either way in court, but that doesn't mean it didn't happen. A later article tells her the girl withdrew her allegation after four months, and she wonders whether Kennedy bought her silence. By then, though, the damage had already been done in the eyes of the media. She scrolls through the other headlines and winces. Almost every single one is negative. Rightly or wrongly, the allegations and subsequent media coverage have ruined Shane Kennedy's reputation.

She wonders how long it will take Steve to get Kennedy's phone records. They would show any potential link to Ashlee. She needs Alex to prioritize the full search of Ashlee's home. They might find her cell phone hidden somewhere. She tries calling him, but there's no answer. He might have already left for the day. She sends him a quick email.

I'll need your help at Ashlee Stuart's apartment first thing tomorrow for a full forensic search. Also, see below for a link to her Instagram account. Is there any way of accessing her private messages? If not, can you search through her posts and see if there's any link to a Shane Kennedy, crime writer? Thanks.

She continues scrolling websites about Kennedy. Despite the negative press and the allegations, he clearly still has a huge fan base. Judging from the comments across social media, it consists mainly of teenage girls, and they're all eagerly awaiting his next book, the sequel to his bestseller, *Bitter Road*. But another quick search shows he hasn't published anything since the year of his arrest.

Vince said Kennedy was focusing on true crime now instead of crime fiction, which was why he was interviewing him for the podcast. Madison wants to listen to that interview to see what it reveals about him. Grabbing her raincoat, she heads out of the station.

CHAPTER THIRTY-THREE

Back at the empty campsite, Nate sits in the driver's seat of his minivan and looks out over the water without really seeing. His thoughts keep taking him to Rex's murder, and as a result, he's sinking into the abyss that haunted him on death row. The feeling of powerlessness has returned.

He checks his phone. Father Connor has yet to respond to his email. His reply to the priest made it clear that it was time for them to meet face to face and settle this mess once and for all. Father Connor's silence speaks volumes: he's a coward. He'd rather blame Nate for Stacey's murder than admit he killed his own niece for some screwed-up reason known only to him.

Nate's thoughts turn to Stacey's house, which is frozen in time for him. He'll only ever remember the home she shared with her mom and uncle as the crime scene it was when he walked in that night almost twenty years ago; with Stacey's body stretched out on the floor of the garage, her head a battered mess and her blood dripping off the walls. She had been beaten to death with a hammer. The same hammer Nate had been using to fix up the house at her mom's request. Was Deborah preparing to set him up then? Had she been blindly following her brother's instructions? No. He doesn't think she would be complicit in her daughter's murder. She had loved Stacey, that was obvious. So had he. He closes his eyes against the last image he has of his fiancée.

He can't understand why Father Connor killed her. There's no logical reason for it. They had a good relationship as far as he could tell. Stacey was a positive, funny and loving person. Sure, she had been drinking in the weeks leading up to her death, a result of finding out something she never got the chance to disclose to Nate. And while her uncle didn't appreciate her drinking, she still did everything he demanded of her: she attended church, she helped out with Sunday school, she was in college, and she had taken her relationship with Nate slowly; they both had, out of respect for the priest. They didn't keep it a secret, but they never even held hands in front of him. And they had kept all desire for a sexual relationship in check, preferring to wait until they were married. Because they both tried to live by the guidance of their faith.

Nate hadn't intended to fall in love. He was happy progressing along the route to becoming a priest. His calling had started as a teen and he had taken it seriously. He'd moved from Kansas to Austin, Texas, to study philosophy at university. Father Connor became his mentor almost from the minute Nate stepped through the door of his church. He didn't fall in love with the priest's niece on purpose, and he didn't act on his feelings for months, battling the decision of whether to give up the priesthood and marry Stacey instead. It had been the hardest decision of his life. But he suspects Father Connor thinks Nate showed him the ultimate disrespect. And back then Nate hadn't appreciated how fanatical the priest was.

He shakes his head and takes a deep breath. With another lonely evening drawing in, he wishes more than ever that Rex would call with a new investigation for him, and that his murder was all a terrible mistake. Rex was a people person. He'd listen to people's problems and then point them in Nate's direction if they needed help with something. Most of Nate's cases were small-time: cheating partners, stolen pets, fraud. But the last two had tested his abilities, and he was glad to have met Madison and taken her on as an investigator until she could return to her real job. They'd found the missing girl in Shadow Falls, California, and discovered who had framed Madison for murder. They worked well together.

But with Madison now settled, and Rex dead, that leaves Nate with nothing to focus on. Looking into Vince Rader's character isn't enough to keep him occupied.

He thinks about Kristen Devereaux. Rex was trying to find out why she'd vanished the year before Nate's exoneration. Maybe that's something he could start investigating himself to distract him from his current mood. He googles her name and her image appears—a staff photo from the university where she worked—attached to several headlines about her disappearance. She showed him respect and patience during her visits to him on death row. Once she was convinced of his innocence, she and her students stopped at nothing in their efforts to get him cleared. But then she vanished before finding out she'd been successful. He was unable to look for her whilst locked up, but his lawyers told him that her home was untouched, showing no signs of a struggle. She just vanished. And Father Connor is the only suspect that makes sense.

Nate realizes his fists are clenched. He's already confided in Madison about what he'll do to the guy once he has the answers he needs. He just has to do it in a way that doesn't land him back on death row.

His phone buzzes with a new email and he stops breathing. But it's not Father Connor or Marcus Alexander.

Mr. Monroe, I'm Rex Hartley's lawyer. He gave me your contact details in case of his death, but I've been unable to reach you by phone so I'm hoping this email account is still active. I have some documents for you. Please get in touch using my private cell number below. This isn't about handing you to the San Diego police. I was a close friend of Rex and I know you had nothing to do with his death.

Yours,
Henry Collins

Nate swallows. He wonders what documents Rex left for him. It must be related to his estate. Perhaps, as Nate was the rescue center's biggest donor, Rex wanted him to take care of the animals, make sure they all found good homes. But it could also be a scam by the police to track him down. He rereads the last two sentences.

This isn't about handing you to the San Diego police. I was a close friend of Rex and I know you had nothing to do with his death.

He looks across at Brody, who's resting his head on his paws, but when Nate makes eye contact, the dog looks up and his tail begins thumping slowly against the seat. "What do you think, boy? Should we trust this guy?"

Brody barks, and Nate's inclined to agree. He knows Rex wouldn't have passed his contact details to just anyone.

CHAPTER THIRTY-FOUR

It's dinner time at Ruby's Diner, and the smell of roasted meat and lasagne makes Madison's stomach growl with hunger. She isn't here to eat this time, though. When she spots Carla, she walks over. "Evening, Carla. Is Vince around?"

Carla jumps and then looks embarrassed. "Sorry, I'm a little jittery today. He's upstairs on a call. Shouldn't be too long."

Madison notices the puffiness of her eyes. She's clearly been crying. The mood in the diner feels different too. Solemn. A lot of the customers are staring at the TV above the counter, which is switched to the local news channel. Kate Flynn is discussing the case. Madison realizes they would have all watched her earlier press conference.

She spots the flyer that was printed before they knew their missing girl wasn't really called Kacie Larson. It shouldn't matter too much at this stage because that's how the locals know her. It's pinned to the noticeboard and there's a stack on the counter for people to take away with them. She nods to it. "I imagine everyone's pretty upset about her disappearance?"

Carla nods, trying to hold back tears. "She may not be from Lost Creek originally, but she's one of us. The thought that none of us are safe and her poor baby might be motherless is too much." She raises her hand to her mouth.

Madison thinks of Ellie, who she knows has settled well with her new foster family. She's determined to do whatever it takes to reunite her with her mother. She slips an arm around Carla's shoulders. "I know. Try not to worry about Ellie; she's being well cared for and probably won't remember any of this when she's older. We just have to try to stay positive, because we don't know anything for sure yet." She thinks of the bloodstained sneaker found near the car. She didn't want to confirm it when the reporter asked about it at the press conference because she doesn't want people to give up hope of finding Ashlee alive. When they lose hope, they stop looking. "Detective Douglas has a whole team out searching. Hopefully we'll find her walking around confused from a concussion."

Carla nods. "Is it true Kacie wasn't her real name?"

The question takes Madison by surprise. "What makes you say that?"

Carla glances at Kate on the TV. Madison listens in.

"Of course, if the birth certificate is to be trusted and the missing woman's name is actually Ashlee Stuart, then that would mean the Ruby's Diner waitress is just seventeen years old. This, then, becomes a missing child case the police have on their hands, and unfortunately it's well known that if a missing child is not located within seventy-two hours of their disappearance, they're much less likely to be found alive."

Madison shakes her head. Kate got herself a copy of the birth certificate. Of course she did. It's not like Madison was going to keep it a secret but it might put people off looking for someone they feel has lied to them. "We've only just found that out, but yes, it's looking like she was living under a false identity."

Carla nods, trying to remain composed. "I always thought she seemed younger than nineteen. But it doesn't matter to me." She takes a deep breath. "You know, it's so ironic that she's on the news."

"Ironic?"

"Yeah, because she hates watching it. She always switches channels no matter how much the old boys kick up a fuss. They just love to listen to it on repeat the whole time they're in here. Gives them an excuse to get on their soapboxes and moan about something. But Ashlee's a sensitive soul. She doesn't like to know about all the bad things that are going on in the world. I guess now she's experiencing it for herself." She wipes her eyes. "The other waitresses and I are holding a midnight vigil outside the Baptist church tonight. Hopefully that will reinforce the fact that her life is worth saving no matter what her name is."

Madison smiles. "Let's hope so." Vigils are good for raising awareness of a missing person, and who knows, maybe the perp will show up to get off on the pain he's caused. "I'll be there."

"I bet you're hungry, aren't you? Detectives never eat properly. Here." Carla slips her a piece of pumpkin pie with cream. "Eat this while you wait for Vince." She fills a coffee cup for her too.

The smell of the cinnamon and pumpkin spices fills Madison's nose, while her stomach growls with gratitude. She's reminded that Ashlee's apartment was full of Halloween decorations. "Did Ashlee have something planned for Halloween? A party, maybe?"

One of the younger waitresses suddenly rushes past them, sobbing.

"Becky?" Carla turns to Madison. "She's scared someone's going to hurt her next. Vince has bought us all pepper spray to keep us safe. And the customers are telling me how they're getting security tightened in their homes. This has really shaken people up." She follows Becky, leaving Madison to find an empty booth. It's sad that the community is feeling anxious, but good that they're starting to take their safety more seriously. It could stop this from happening to someone else.

The pie tastes wonderful, just what she needs to fill the gap until dinner, and the coffee complements it beautifully. She could do without the disapproving glances from the other diners, though. She can't tell if they're judging her for taking time out of her investigation to eat something, or if it's because they still think she killed her co-worker seven years ago. Staring back hard at them does the trick. They look away in disgust. Perhaps if she manages to find Ashlee Stuart alive, they might change their minds about her. Then again, probably not.

While she waits for Vince to appear, she calls Owen to check in on him.

"Hey," he grunts.

"Hi. What are you up to?"

"I watched you on TV. My friend says you're hot, so I won't be speaking to him ever again."

She laughs. "Maybe he needs glasses. Did I do okay? I didn't embarrass you?"

"I'd rather you left the TV appearances to someone else, but what can I do? I recognize Ashlee from the diner. I didn't know she had a baby, though. Is there really no sign of her, or are you holding back information?"

"I don't have many leads, but there are a few. Is there any sign of Nate?"

He doesn't reply.

"Owen?"

"That depends. Have the San Diego police arrived yet?" He sounds wary.

She frowns. "That's a strange question."

"Humor me for a minute."

"They're not here yet, no. I'm not allowed to speak to them even when they do arrive; my boss has made Don Douglas the liaison. Why, Owen? You're worrying me."

He answers slowly. "So would you say it's unlikely your phone is tapped yet?"

She rolls her eyes, annoyed at his games. "Owen, just tell me whatever you want to say. No one is tapping my phone; this isn't a movie."

He hesitates, and she can almost hear him thinking. Finally he says, "He called me earlier today."

Her shoulders relax with relief. She has so many questions. "Thank God. Is he okay? Where is he?"

"He's fine. I don't know where he is, but he did tell me to make sure you know he hasn't done anything stupid. He said the San

Diego police are going to want to arrest him, so they might start following you and possibly me once they realize we're friends with him. He said we have to stay tight-lipped and I'm only supposed to call him on his new number if it's an emergency."

Madison sighs. There's so much she wants to say to Nate. Not that she can offer him any reassurances now Douglas will be liaising with the San Diego police. But she might be able to talk him out of making any hasty decisions. "I wish he'd called me instead."

"He knows they're more likely to check your cell records than mine, you know, to trace his calls. I think he'll keep in touch with me. But for now, we have to trust that he knows what he's doing." Owen sounds excited to be involved in this mess.

"I wish I could. But when that priest is involved, there's no telling what Nate's capable of."

"He said he's got a guy looking into Vince's military background, but he thinks you're barking up the wrong tree with him. He wants you to be open-minded."

So Vince was in the military. She spots him approaching. "Thanks for telling me. Are you okay to fix yourself dinner? I'll be another hour or two."

"I'm going to Stu's house. His dad's ordering in."

She feels guilty that he's eating somewhere else; her plan of having them sit down to eat together every week night isn't going as she would have hoped. "Okay, bye." She wonders if he'll want to come to the vigil for Ashlee. It will probably remind him too much of Nikki Jackson, the girl who died at Fantasy World this summer. He's still dealing with his own grief for her. She slips her phone away as Vince steps forward.

"You wanted me?"

She stands up and keeps her voice low. "I need to listen to your interview with Shane Kennedy."

Vince takes a deep breath, mulling it over. "I take it you've not been able to find him?"

"That's right. And it turns out he was driving the car we found baby Ellie in."

He raises an eyebrow. Realizing the implication, he nods. "Follow me."

CHAPTER THIRTY-FIVE

Vince's apartment is tidy and surprisingly tasteful. His oak furniture looks like it could have been lovingly passed down through generations. The living room is large and spacious, and now that the sun has almost completely set, the warm orange glow from the expensive-looking table lamp illuminates the room. One wall is completely filled with floor-to-ceiling shelves stacked full of books. She doesn't get a chance to read their spines, as he quickly offers her a bourbon.

"No thanks. I'm on duty, so I shouldn't."

He pours her a lemonade instead. "Take a seat."

She chooses a leather armchair and waits as he places his laptop on the coffee table and takes a seat opposite her on the couch. After a sip of her drink she asks, "So have you heard about Kacie's real identity too?"

He nods. "I can't say I'm surprised."

"No?"

"When a young woman arrives in town with no family and begs for a job waitressing in order to feed her baby, it's pretty obvious she's running from something. I didn't suspect she was using a fake name, though."

"You really think she was running away from something?"

He sips his bourbon. "She was jumpy when she first started working for me. Every time the door to the diner opened, she'd look up and check who'd entered. That lasted for a couple of months, until her confidence grew. She was quiet as a mouse with the customers at first, but it didn't take long for her to give as good as she got."

Madison thinks about it. It's beginning to sound like Ashlee's past might have caught up with her. "You never asked her why she moved here?"

"Oh, sure. All she'd say was that she wanted her independence. I didn't push it. But now I wish I had." He smiles sadly. "Hindsight's a bitch."

She agrees. "How long exactly was Shane Kennedy here that night?"

"About two hours. The diner was obviously closed by the time he arrived, so I let him in the side entrance to the building, which comes straight up here. He drank a couple of coffees during his visit and we discussed the case he's currently writing about. He's still in the research phase." He hovers his hand over the laptop. "How much of the interview do you want to hear? I'm guessing not all of it."

She doesn't want to be here for two hours, so she says, "Just the first few minutes and the last few for now, but I'll take a copy of the full recording away with me so I can listen when I get time."

He hits the play button, and Madison leans in, even though the volume is loud and clear when Vince's voice starts. Mainly because she wants to listen for any signs of a female being present: a cough or a laugh in the background. If Vince or Shane were involved in Ashlee's disappearance, she might have been present for some or all of the interview.

VINCE: Today I'm pleased to welcome someone who has been requested by my listeners numerous times. No one knows I've secured this interview, so it may come as a pleasant surprise to learn that Shane Kennedy, author of the hugely popular crime novel *Bitter Road*, is joining me. Shane, it's a pleasure to have you here.

SHANE: It's a pleasure to be here. That book's always going to follow me around, isn't it? [Laughs good-naturedly]

Shane's voice is confident and Madison can hear hints of a Brooklyn accent, although it's not overpowering. She wonders why he left New York to live in Nevada. Maybe he's a gambling man and wanted to be closer to Vegas. She pictures the black-haired, hazel-eyed writer from his mugshot as he talks.

VINCE: Probably, yes, but I'm sure the royalties help soften the blow.

[Shane laughs]

VINCE: Now, getting you here wasn't easy, and I'm not going to rake over old ground as that's not what we're here to discuss, but would you like to explain to your fans why they haven't heard from you in a while? I understand you're leaning in a different direction these days, writing-wise.

SHANE: That's right. I enjoyed writing fiction, but I think the unexpected success of *Bitter Road*, especially once made into a movie, was a little unnerving for me. The instant fame threw a lot of unwanted attention my way. The first time you get recognized is cool, but the millionth time is tiresome. That's not to say I don't appreciate the fans; I do. But some people feel like they own you just because they've read your book, or that you owe them something in return for them spending ten bucks on your novel. And when you don't give them what they want, they go a little crazy.

Madison raises an eyebrow. She's surprised a writer would openly criticize his fans, but knowing what he was accused of explains why he's jaded.

VINCE: Sounds scary. So your new direction has led you to researching true-crime cases, primarily cold cases. How did that come about?

She notices the hesitation before Shane responds.

SHANE: I wanted to see if I could put my talent for crime writing to good use. Because when you write a crime novel, you become the criminal, the victim *and* the detective. You have to solve the case for the reader. I thought that if I could do that without any police training, I might be able to solve some real crimes along the way. So when you got in touch—

Vince stops the recording. "Okay, let me skip ahead to the end, as he just discusses research for the next hour or so."

Madison waits patiently, a little annoyed that Shane thinks writing about a fictional criminal investigation is the same as investigating a crime in real life. She'd like to see how he'd cope in a shootout, or with telling a mother her child has been murdered. Actually, she wouldn't wish that on anyone.

"This is five minutes from the end."

VINCE: Thanks for making the long trip from your home to our small town, and for giving me an exclusive.

SHANE: No problem at all. If your listeners have any tips on this case, they can pass the information to me through you, if that suits?

VINCE: Of course. Well, that's it for this time, folks. I hope you enjoyed my first ever pre-recorded interview. Join me again on *Crime and Dine* on Friday, when I'll be back to the usual live shows. But until then, keep your eyes and ears open and your hands on that mace.

It sounds like Shane laughs, and then the interview appears to be over. Madison hears them stand up, and what sounds like a coat being zipped.

VINCE: Seriously, thank you for making the trip, I appreciate it.

SHANE: No problem.

VINCE: It's a cold one tonight. Can I make you another coffee, or any food to take with you?

SHANE: Better not. I could do without stopping for the restroom.

VINCE: Sure. Are you parked close?

Madison leans in. This could be important.

SHANE: Not far. I'm hoping to head straight out of town to drive through the night. I like night-time. It's a little less scary when there are fewer people around.

They say their goodbyes and then the recording ends. Vince closes his laptop and looks at Madison. "What do you think?"

"Do you always keep recording even after the interview?"

"Not normally, no. But I was a little distracted by what we were discussing, so I forgot to stop the recorder until after he left."

She takes a deep breath and sits back. "I still don't understand the link between Shane and Ashlee."

"Me neither," he says.

"Did your staff know Shane Kennedy was coming?"

"No. I made sure none of them knew; that was a condition of his interview." He pauses. "I did tell Carla, actually. Because she saw me reading *Bitter Road* and knew I had a top-secret interviewee. But she can be trusted. I specifically told her not to let on to anyone."

Thinking out loud, Madison says, "Why on earth would Ashlee's baby be in his car, and why have both he and Ashlee gone missing at the same time? Did you get any sense that the allegations against him could have some truth in them?"

"You mean do I think he's a sexual predator?"

"Well, yeah. I mean, you obviously know a lot about how criminals work, because of your interests. Did he say anything inappropriate while he was here? Were there any red flags?"

Vince takes a deep breath. "No. But I think sexual predators get away with abusing people because they're good at it; at the manipulation and grooming. I mean, just look at Ted Bundy. He was attractive, charismatic and charming, and he used those qualities to disarm his victims. That makes it difficult to tell the good guys from the bad. But honestly? I don't think Shane Kennedy is missing. He has a history of alcohol abuse, so perhaps he gave in to temptation and decided to have a couple of drinks before he left town, and then ran his car off the road. He wouldn't want that to get out to the press, so maybe he abandoned the car, called a cab or a friend, and now he's gone into hiding to ride out the negative press."

"I'll check if he stopped in at any of the bars in town on his way."

Vince shakes his head. "I've already done it. He didn't. But that doesn't mean he didn't carry a flask with him, or have a six pack in the car. He probably took the evidence with him to avoid DUI charges."

It's a possibility. After all, Veronica said he was a nightmare to work with when he was drinking, so that confirms he has a problem with alcohol. She'll get Shelley to check with the local bars in case Vince is misleading her. "That wouldn't explain why the baby was found in his car."

He looks away. "True. That is a mystery."

Something about the way he says it makes her wonder if he knows more than he's letting on. She realizes the significance of two people going missing within hours of being around Vince. Is he taking his interest in true crime too far? Is he staging disappearances now so he can be the one to solve them and gain notoriety for his podcast? She doubts it, but she has to consider all possibilities, despite Nate suggesting he isn't a good suspect.

Standing up, she says, "I better get going. Will I see you at Ashlee's vigil later?"

He looks surprised. "When's that?"

"Midnight at the Baptist church. I think Carla arranged it. She didn't tell you?"

He hands her a flash drive containing a copy of the interview, then leads the way to the door. "It probably slipped her mind." Before opening it, he turns to face her. "I know what you're thinking, Detective. At least I hope you're thinking the obvious."

She pulls her coat on. "What do you mean?"

"Well, if I were you, I would be thinking: here's this older guy whose wife and grandson went missing six years ago and are presumed dead; his youngest waitress has vanished overnight, and the famous writer who turned up to give him an interview is nowhere to be found. Plus, this guy runs a true-crime podcast and is clearly a little whacko. I've heard the rumors have already started up again about how I probably killed Ruby, and now I've killed Ashlee too."

She suddenly feels sorry for him. "Why didn't you tell me your grandson went missing at the same time Ruby did?"

He shrugs. "It hurts to think about him, never mind talk about him. My son and daughter-in-law moved away four years ago. They couldn't bear living in the town where Oliver went missing. I've not heard from them in two years and doubt I ever will again. That's my wife, my son and my grandson all lost to me. People don't realize there are far-reaching consequences behind every missing person."

She doesn't know what to say.

"I *should* be your prime suspect for Ashlee's disappearance, Detective Harper. If I were in your position, I would at least bring me in for questioning, considering there's almost three hours unaccounted for in my alibi, when I was home alone."

She smiles. "Are you telling me you want to come down to the station and answer some questions?"

"I'd rather not, but if eliminating me helps you find Ashlee, then I would go in a heartbeat. And I would take a polygraph test too."

Madison knows it's not unusual for guilty people to pull the old polygraph line, convinced they can beat it or that just claiming to want to take it will make them look innocent. But she doesn't think that's the case here.

She just hopes her instincts aren't wrong.

CHAPTER THIRTY-SIX

Bunny,

Why haven't I heard from you in forever? You haven't returned any of my recent letters. I don't like women who blow hot and cold. What are you, a tease? You should remember it was *you* who initiated contact with *me*, so don't play games with me.

This is my last letter and your last chance. If you don't reply to this, I'm done with you. But I want you to reconsider. So much has changed since you last wrote that I'm finally excited about something for the first time in years. It's time we met. Send me your address and I'll arrange something. You just have to promise me that our time together will stay confidential, because I don't want word getting out to the press. I don't need any more food for the trolls and I don't want anyone to know where I live.

You're no longer just a fan to me, Bunny; after almost two years of getting to know each other, I consider you my girlfriend now. I hope you feel the same way about me as I do about you. Remember, though: don't tell anyone, because other people won't understand what we mean to each other.

Love, your boyfriend Ace xxx

Dear Ace,

I'm sorry for my lack of replies. I've been busy with life and I got a little scared, to be honest. But I heard the good news—that's great for you! You can finally move on from the horrible allegations.

Okay, I'm going to put my trust in you. I want to meet up. I'm nervous, though. You're this famous person I've seen on TV and read about and who gets *actual* fan mail from all over the world, and I'm just this girl from a small town who's insignificant to everyone. I don't know why you're interested in me, I can't actually believe it, so you're right. We need to meet to see if our feelings are as strong in person.

I live in a small town called Lost Creek, in southern Colorado, but give me a couple of weeks to sort a date and time when I can get away without anyone missing me. Then I'll give you my full address. And don't worry, I won't tell anyone about you.

OMG this is really happening! It will be interesting to see if I'm what you're expecting. I know you'll be exactly what *I'm* expecting.

Love, your Bunny xxx

CHAPTER THIRTY-SEVEN

Owen is still out when Madison arrives home to a cold, dark house, so she makes herself a frozen microwave meal for dinner. While it heats up, she has a quick back-and-forth with him via text, just checking in and making sure he knows she'll be out at the vigil later. Then he tells her he's got to go because his friend is beating him at some video game. She feels a little sad that he doesn't need her as much as she expected, and there's a pang of sorrow as she considers all those years she didn't get to mother him.

She takes her dinner into the living room and puts the TV on low while she eats the rubbery mac and cheese. Being home alone quickly becomes depressing. It's already been a long day, but she can't relax and change into sweatpants just yet, because she still has to attend the vigil. She'd give anything for Nate to walk in now and give her that sheepish look of his. The one that tells her he knows he's been stupid by reacting too quickly and is now sorry for not listening to her. She hopes he isn't surviving on just cocaine and vengeance.

Even though Chief Mendes says Douglas is to be the liaison with the San Diego police, Madison has no intention of staying silent. She'll be taking them to one side in private and explaining what she thinks happened to Rex. They need to know Nate is no killer. But then his words come back to haunt her. He previously declared that if he ever managed to find the priest, he wouldn't be handing him to the police. She shudders at the thought of him going against everything he believes in to see his fiancée's murderer brought to justice.

He might have given up on the priesthood at twenty, and he might have doubted his faith while in prison, but she knows he still believes. And she has to hope he'll hold on to that when he finally tracks Father Connor down. She just wishes she could be there when it happens.

As the wind howls outside, Madison doesn't feel like waiting home alone. She calls Kate and arranges to visit her before they both attend the vigil. Kate will be filming it live for the news.

The roads are almost empty as she drives through the night. At eleven o'clock, she pulls up outside Kate's large home and jogs to the front door to keep warm. It takes more than one knock before anyone opens it.

"Oh my God, I'm so sorry, Madison! I didn't hear you." Kate leads her into the open-plan kitchen. "Sally's being a pain in the ass, so I've had to send Patrick up to try to get her to go to sleep. This one, on the other hand, is being an angel as usual."

Kate Flynn lives with her husband and two children, five-year-old Sally, and Ben, who is almost four. He's incredibly shy around anyone but his parents, and Kate has told Madison how he suffers with selective mutism at pre-school and in some other social situations. He's adopted, and they don't know much about his past. His anxiety doesn't mean he can't communicate at all; he just uses other means. Most kids would be asleep by now, but Ben struggles with night-time. He naps during the day instead, which Kate is seeking help for through various experts.

Madison's friendship with Kate is something she's worked hard to repair since she returned to Lost Creek. She understands that, as a local TV reporter, it was Kate's job to cover her murder trial, but it turned nasty when Kate was forced by her boss to report both sides of the story. She couldn't leave out the false rumors that were circling, and she couldn't ignore what the victim's parents were telling anyone who would listen: that Madison was their son's killer and needed to be executed. She was competing for headlines with other media outlets, and Madison knows the lure of a good scandal. But being on the receiving end was devastating, and she chose not to keep in touch with Kate during her incarceration. She needed time to calm down and put it all into perspective.

Over the last few months, however, they've got together several times to catch up and slowly move forward. Kate has a likable personality that's hard not to warm to, and her cynical sense of humor is refreshing. Her house is about three times the size of Madison's, and is decorated perfectly. Everything is white and modern, with barely any clutter apart from the kids' toys.

Madison sits next to Ben at the dinner table while Kate pours them hot chocolates. "Hey, Ben," she says. "Are you enjoying your game?"

Ben doesn't even glance at her. He's playing on his iPad, something he carries with him everywhere he goes. There's an app he can use to click on pictures to communicate spoken words when he's feeling shy or anxious.

Kate joins them at the table and places a hot chocolate in front of Madison. When Ben sees it, he hits the record button and starts filming as she blows on it. She smiles and looks at Kate questioningly.

"He's starting to film us a lot," says Kate. "Patrick thinks he might be the next Spielberg, but I think it's his way of remembering people. I've caught him playing back the videos later on and having conversations with the people in them. Almost like he's practicing what he should've said. Apparently he likes playing videos of me while I'm out at work too. I think it's a comfort thing."

Madison smiles. "That's adorable."

"I know, right? The doctors tell us he'll outgrow his mutism eventually, so I don't make a big deal about it. He's become a little clingier with me lately, and talks less to Patrick, but hopefully it's just a phase."

Madison can see Kate's love for her son.

"So, have you got an inside scoop for me about Ashlee Stuart?" asks Kate. "I hope you don't mind me revealing her real name, by the way. I had to beat the others to it."

"I wish I did have a scoop, but that would mean I actually have a decent lead to follow." Madison wonders whether to tell Kate about Shane Kennedy, but she doesn't want it getting out to the media that he might be involved somehow. That would bring more reporters to Lost Creek, and she could do without the added scrutiny. "No one seems to know who the baby's father is. Have you heard any rumors?"

Kate shakes her head. "No, nothing. And even though a lot of people know Ashlee by sight, because of where she works, I can't find anyone who went to school with her or who actually knows her very well."

"Yeah, I'm having the same problem. Her birth certificate shows she was born in Prospect Springs to a single mother. Unfortunately, her mom died in 2015 and that's where the family leads end. I'm hoping the news conference will bring in a flood of phone calls, because someone must be missing her."

Kate scoffs at that. "You'd be surprised how many young people have no one looking out for them. Maybe she's estranged from her wider family." She pauses. "Were you being honest at the press conference when you implied Vince isn't a suspect?"

Madison isn't surprised by the question. "Don't get me wrong, I can see why he makes a good suspect, but I have no evidence to suggest he had anything to do with it. Why? Do you think he's capable of hurting Ashlee?"

Kate sips her drink. "I don't know. That podcast of his is weird, though, don't you think? Has he asked you to be on it yet?" She laughs. "He tried to talk me into persuading you."

Madison rolls her eyes. "Why doesn't that surprise me? Yeah, he asked. And I declined."

"He told me the other day that he wants to get that guy from Denver on his show; the one who took an Alford plea last month."

"Which guy is that?"

"Cody Stevens." Kate lowers her voice so Ben doesn't hear, but he's completely absorbed in the iPad. It doesn't stop her from spelling out certain words, though, just in case. "He r-a-p-e-d two twelve-year-old girls back in 2012. They were friends, and were so traumatized by what he did to them that they k-i-l-l-e-d themselves."

Madison's mouth drops open. "That's terrible. How did someone like him get offered a plea deal?"

"One of the witnesses perjured himself at the original trial. The prosecution basically falsified evidence and they didn't even lose their jobs over it. Can you believe that?" Kate shakes her head in disgust.

"Does that mean he was innocent, then?"

"I guess we'll never know. He can't be retried now he's accepted that deal. Vince asked if I could use my contacts in Denver to track him down so he can invite him on the podcast. But Cody released a statement after his release saying he just wants to be left alone to move on with his life in peace. He's been spotted in Vietnam, probably because they don't extradite to the US. Vince was disappointed when I told him."

Madison shakes her head. "He is a little obsessed with crime. Do you think it's because his wife and grandson vanished?"

Kate smiles wryly. "Or is that what he wants us to believe? I mean, Vince didn't run that podcast while Ruby was alive, I can tell you that much. Could it just be a front to disguise who he really is and to garner sympathy so we all forget that he remains the most likely suspect in Ruby and Oliver's disappearance?"

Madison frowns, but before she can question Kate further, a weary Patrick appears from upstairs holding a wide-awake little girl in a ballerina outfit.

"Hi, Madison. Sally wanted to say hello." He rolls his eyes to suggest it's going to be the only way to get her to go to sleep.

Sally wriggles out of his arms and runs to Madison. "Look at my new teddy. He's missing an eye."

Madison laughs. "He's still very handsome, though."

Kate glances at the clock on the wall. "Shoot, we need to get going."

It's almost eleven thirty, and Madison knows Kate has to be at the vigil early to set up with her camera operator.

"Where are you going, Mommy?" asks Sally. Ben appears alarmed at their sudden rise from the table.

"I have to go to work, honey. But I won't be long, and Daddy's staying with you."

Sally's face drops and her bottom lip starts quivering. "But I don't want you to go to work."

Patrick and Kate share a look, and Kate turns to Madison. "Let's escape before the theatrics start."

Madison smiles, remembering Owen at this age. He hated her leaving for work, and she bribed him many times with promises of all the fun they'd have when she got home.

They grab their things and leave Patrick to deal with the crying children.

CHAPTER THIRTY-EIGHT

The mood outside the church can only be described as somber. The rain clouds have finally dispersed, leaving a clear night. Although the stars are glistening in the sky above, there's a chill in the air, and the darkness is only relieved by the candles in people's hands and the light spilling out through the church windows.

Madison can see her own breath as she walks toward the crowd, leaving Kate to discuss filming logistics with her camera operator and producer. She recognizes the waitresses from the diner and heads over to Carla, who's handing out candles.

"I'm glad you came," says Carla. She lights a candle for her. "Here."

"Thanks. There's a good turnout already." Looking around, Madison can see a lot of families, as well as older people who have come to show their support. Everyone is wrapped in thick hats and gloves, not letting the cold put them off. She spots Joely with her son and what could be her mother. She doesn't see Vince, though. "Vince didn't seem to know this was happening. Is there a reason you didn't tell him?"

"No, not really." Carla looks away.

Madison wonders if there's tension between them. "You sure?"

Carla turns back. "Yes. It just slipped my mind. I'm a scatterbrain this week. I walk into a room and not only forget why I went in there but also where I am. It's crazy. I'm sure he's a little offended at being forgotten, but I can't be worrying about him when we have bigger problems."

Madison smiles sadly. "Hopefully tonight's vigil will be splashed all over the news networks and someone will get in touch."

Wendy Dranfield

Carla doesn't look convinced. "I can't believe you haven't heard from her family yet. I mean, who doesn't keep tabs on their daughters and sisters?"

Madison's thoughts exactly. "I don't know anything about her family other than the fact her mom is deceased. Has she mentioned them to you?"

They keep getting interrupted by people asking for candles, but eventually Carla says, "No. I've never heard her mention her mom or dad, or any siblings; I didn't even know she'd lost her mom. She clams up if you try to delve too deep, so there's obviously a story there."

Madison agrees. "Perhaps she became homeless when she got pregnant." By her calculations, based on Ashlee's real date of birth, she would have been nearly sixteen when she conceived Ellie. That would have come as a shock to her and whatever extended family she has. It couldn't have been easy for her, being pregnant at such a young age.

"It's really sad," says Carla. "Especially now we know she's only seventeen."

"Is she religious, do you know?"

"Only as much as the rest of us. I'm not a regular churchgoer, but I've seen Kacie here at least once." Carla realizes she's used the wrong name and looks tearful again. "I'm sorry. I've got to get used to calling her Ashlee, but it's hard. Who took her, Madison? Where is she?"

"I don't know, but I will find out. I won't let this case go cold, I promise. I want to see Ellie back with her mom." Madison is hopeful that a family member will get in touch when they see Ashlee's face on the news. But families are complicated and she knows she can't rely on them contacting her. There could be old resentments holding them back. Or maybe they were involved in her disappearance.

Carla walks away to greet a couple just as Madison's phone rings. It's Detective Douglas.

"Hi, Don. Any luck with the search?"

"No, we've found nothing of interest yet. We'll start again tomorrow, but it's looking like we won't find anything in the White Woods. What about you, have you discovered anything?"

She notices his voice is a little slurred, possibly a result of the pain medication he's on. "I've got a few possible leads but I'll fill you in tomorrow. I'm at the vigil for Ashlee."

"I thought you would be. Do I need to come?"

Mindful that he's probably exhausted from searching all day, she decides to let him get some rest. "No, it's fine. I'll cover it. See you tomorrow."

"Thanks."

She sighs as she pockets her phone. Maybe he'll mellow toward her over time. She spots Ashlee's neighbor, and former boyfriend, huddled in the church doorway, trying to keep out of the bitter chill. When he sees her staring, he quickly looks away. It makes her head straight for him.

"Justin. I take it you haven't seen or heard your neighbor moving around in her apartment since we spoke?"

His eyes are restless; he wants to get away. He pushes his hands into his coat pockets and tries to act casual. "Nope. It's just silent. Kind of creepy, actually. I've been playing my music to fill the silence where Ellie's cries would normally be." He nods to Kate in the distance. "Is what she said on the news true? Kacie's real name is Ashlee?"

"That's right." Madison eyes him suspiciously. "How come you never told me you dated her for a while? And did you know she was only seventeen? Because what are you, about eight years older than her?"

A look of panic crosses his face. "Hey, come on! I'd just woken up when you banged on my door, and you didn't actually ask whether we dated. Of course I didn't know she was that young. I don't go looking for minors, Detective. You can check the ages of my previous girlfriends if you don't believe me. Anyway, we didn't date for long. She was pretty uptight about me smoking pot. I don't know why; it's not like it's illegal anymore."

"Uptight? Huh. I'm surprised that's your opinion of her, because when we first met, you told me you thought she was cool." He looks like he's about to flee, so, knowing she's got no power to stop him, she says, "How about you show me around your apartment so I can eliminate you from my list of potential suspects?"

He takes a step back and opens his mouth. "What? Why would *I* be a suspect?"

"Come on, Justin. You're more intelligent than you're pretending to be. You live next door to the girl who's vanished, you dated her, and I heard she constantly asked you to turn your music down and to stop smoking pot outside her window." She pauses. "What happened? Did she interrupt your high that night and you suddenly lost control? You lashed out when you weren't in your right mind? Because that could be used in your defense, you know."

He's angry now. "You cops are all the same." He starts walking away, but shouts over his shoulder, "You can search my place when you get a warrant."

She can only get a warrant if she finds some evidence that Ashlee has been harmed and that Justin was involved, but by then he'll have disposed of any potential evidence in his apartment, if he hasn't already. She's not sure what to think of him, but she'll have some uniforms keep an eye on his movements over the next few days.

A bright light suddenly blinds her and most of the attendees. She hears Kate shout, "Sorry, everyone. It's just while I do my piece to camera!"

Madison blinks to help her eyes adjust. She can see the banners people have made: *Bring Ashlee Home!* and *Think of her daughter!* They're praying together too. This vigil is thoughtful, but she knows it won't have any effect on the perp. She firmly believes there *is* a perpetrator now. Ashlee hasn't vanished of her own accord. She was taken. And if whoever took her watches this on the news, he or she won't be moved by anyone's emotions. She thinks of Shane Kennedy. If she can find evidence he was involved in Ashlee's disappearance, his fame will help word spread quickly. It will be difficult for him to stay hidden.

She stands out of view as Kate gives a moving overview of the vigil to camera. Owen suddenly appears to her left, and he's panting. "Sorry I'm late."

Madison hugs him. "I wasn't expecting you, but thanks for coming." She looks in surprise at the two coffees he's holding. "Is one of those for me?"

"Sure. Here."

Half of it appears to have spilled out through the hole in the lid, but she can't believe he actually thought to bring her something.

"No sign of her yet?" he asks as he unzips his jacket. He must have run some distance if he's warm on a night like this.

She shakes her head, then sips the coffee. It's lukewarm, but still better than nothing.

"Is the baby here?" He looks around.

"No, child services probably wouldn't agree to that." Ellie will be tucked up asleep by now in her new temporary home. She looks at him. "Do you remember Maya Smith from child services?"

He averts his gaze to his feet. "Of course. I didn't like her."

"Really?" She had no idea. She tenses as she wonders whether Maya was mean to him back then. "Why not?"

"Because it was obvious she hated kids. I mean, she didn't hurt anyone, but she was so uncaring. When I visited you in jail the day after your arrest, I got upset when I was made to leave. In the car afterwards, she told me I was a crybaby and the sooner I forget about you the better off I'd be."

Madison's blood boils. She did the right thing telling Maya's boss about her. She would've done it sooner, but as an ex-con, she wouldn't have been taken seriously. She puts her arm around Owen and laughs when he glances about nervously.

"My friends might be here."

"I don't care. I just need you to know that I'm sorry for what you went through: with her, with the McCoys, with your girlfriend."

He looks her in the eye for the first time. "None of it was your fault, Mom. I know that. But I don't know why we're finding it so hard to get along. I thought that by having you back, things would feel like you'd never left."

She swallows hard. "You were ten years old when they took you away. We've both been through so much since then; we're different people now. You can't imagine what it was like seeing you again for the first time. You were—you are—this tall, handsome seventeen-year-old who doesn't need me anymore. Every single time I look at you I'm reminded of how much I missed out on." She blinks back tears.

Owen looks like he finally gets it. "I still need you in some ways. I mean, you're going to help me pay for college, right?" He's grinning now.

She laughs with relief. Owen wants to study law at college when he graduates from high school next summer. He says he wants to be one of the good guys, but that just means he'll end up working in the public defender's office for peanuts. She doesn't say that, though, as she doesn't want to dampen his enthusiasm. If successful, he'll be the first Harper to get a degree, something she wishes she had done before joining the police academy. Something her mom wanted her to do. But she couldn't afford it back then, plus there was the fact that she unexpectedly became pregnant with Owen at twenty.

Staring intently at every person present, he says, "Do you think the perp could turn up and pretend to be a grieving member of the community? Is it true that kind of thing happens?"

"I can't tell if you're watching too many crime shows or if you're thinking like a cop." But her thoughts turn back to Justin, who did turn up. "Have you had any more calls from Nate?"

"No. I hope Brody's okay."

"As long as he has Nate, he'll be fine. That dog's obsessed with him."

Owen smiles. "I was teaching him some new tricks. I wonder if he'll remember them when they eventually come home."

Madison smiles at the word "home". Something she lost for so long. She and Nate are good friends and nothing else, but he fits into their family well. Sure, he can infuriate her with his impulsive—but thankfully few and far between—coke binges, but she's never met anyone like him before. He's been through so much, yet he still puts other people first. It must be why he felt a calling to become a priest in the first place; it comes naturally to him.

She hopes he can find a way to prove he wasn't responsible for Rex's murder, but she can't see how he can do that without knowing what the evidence is and without someone giving him a fair chance to explain himself. She doesn't know whether the detectives in charge of the homicide investigation are the kind of cops who will do a proper investigation, or whether they'll arrest Nate because he's the easy choice. Unfortunately, she and Nate both know from experience that some cops are all about closing cases, no matter who they pin the crime on.

Her phone buzzes with a text from Douglas.

San Diego detectives have confirmed they'll be here in the morning. They're getting ready to release Monroe's name to the media if he doesn't hand himself in.

She feels dread creeping up through her stomach. Nate is running out of time.

CHAPTER THIRTY-NINE

Listening to the birds singing their morning chorus as the sun rises on a new day, Nate rubs his tired eyes and walks to the edge of the lake. The sun's reflection is bouncing off the gently rippling water, giving the illusion that all is well in the world. He runs a hand through his newly cut hair and checks his cell phone, but there's still no response from Father Connor to his suggestion that they settle things once and for all.

There is, however, a message from a number he doesn't recognize. He soon realizes it's from Marcus Alexander, presumably via a burner phone.

> *Turns out your guy was discharged from the navy after an investigation into the death of a female petty officer by the name of Julia Martinez. There were no criminal charges brought and I can't get any more details about her death or the investigation, which suggests an internal cover-up to me. You might want to try speaking to the victim's family, because they could be open to exposing whatever Vince Rader did. Will forward her next of kin's phone number as soon as I get it.*

So Vince has a shady past. Nate doesn't know whether contacting the victim's family is a good idea. Some wounds run deep, and if they get wind that Vince might be involved in the disappearance and possible murder of someone else, they could go to the press. It has to be handled delicately. In the meantime, he needs to let Madison know. Checking his watch, he realizes Owen will be in class already, so he has no choice but to call her. He can destroy this phone afterwards and use one of the many others he has ready.

"Madison Harper." It sounds like she's driving.

"Hey, it's Nate. Are you free to talk?"

"Nate! Thank God. Yes, I'm on hands-free and alone. Are you okay? Where are you?"

"I'm around. Just not too close. I've got some information about Vince Rader."

"Good or bad?"

"Possibly bad. Turns out he was discharged from the navy after an investigation into a female officer's death."

"Jeez, I wasn't expecting that. Think he killed her?"

"I don't know yet; the details are sketchy. My contact is getting a number for the victim's family, so I can see if they're open to talking about what happened. Or would you rather call them?"

"I'll do it. Chief Mendes wouldn't be happy if she found out I asked you to get involved in police business. Besides, the family might open up more to a detective than a PI."

Nate disagrees, based on his own experience with the cops, but he lets it go. "I'll forward you the number as soon as I get it."

"Thanks." She pauses. "I have to go. I'm still looking for Ellie's mom. When are you coming home?"

He smiles. Part of him thought she would be relieved to be rid of him and his problems. "That depends. Are the San Diego cops in town yet?"

"They're due this morning. I'll be speaking to them as soon as I can. I'll make them see they should be looking at Father Connor for Rex's murder."

He wishes he could believe they'll take her word for it. "I'll be lying low until I know I'm cleared. I have to, Madison. You know that, right?"

She doesn't answer. Changing the subject, she says, "Just keep in touch."

"Sure."

Brody wanders over and sits close to his feet as he ends the call. He doesn't know how long he can hide out here like a criminal. It's not good for him or the dog. After receiving the email from Rex's attorney, he wrestled over whether to take the risk that would come with calling him—giving away his location to a hostile agency—or whether to pack up and drive out of Colorado for good. He can certainly afford to disappear if he wants to; to forget his friend was murdered and who by, and to end all communication with Madison and Owen, giving them an opportunity to move on with their lives.

But he found there was some fight left in him and eventually chose to call the lawyer. He doesn't want to live his life on the run like Father Connor. He doesn't deserve it.

Now he takes a seat at a picnic table and waits for Rex's lawyer to pick up.

"Hank Collins."

Nate hesitates. There's still a chance this could be a scam. "Hello?"

He bites the bullet. "Mr. Collins, it's Nate Monroe. Rex's friend."

"Nate! I'm glad you got in touch. That can't have been easy given your current predicament."

Nate hears a door closing and he assumes the lawyer has gone somewhere private. "No. It wasn't. I'm taking a leap of faith here, Mr. Collins, and believe me, since my incarceration, that's not something I do very often."

"I understand. And please, call me Hank. I'd like to offer my condolences. Rex was one of a kind and I'm sure we're both going to miss him more than we can appreciate right now. If I ever needed a boost, I'd pick up the phone to him and he'd reassure me that not everyone in this world is bad. You know what I mean?"

Nate smiles. He knows exactly what Hank means. "I do. But I don't know anything about what happened at his place. His neighbor called me and said she saw cops there but didn't know what had happened to him."

"Arlene called you? That was smart of her. I wondered how you found out before the police managed to get to you." Hank takes a deep breath. "I'm sorry to be the one to tell you, but it's looking like Rex was poisoned. The autopsy is scheduled for this morning, but the initial signs are pretty clear."

Nate shakes his head and has to swallow back his sadness as he thinks about how painful and terrifying Rex's final moments must have been. "He didn't deserve that."

"I know, I'm sorry." Hank sighs. "It doesn't even help to know he would've been gone soon anyway. When he found out he was dying, he gave me some packages for you."

Nate has jumped out of his seat. "Wait, what?" His whole body freezes over with goosebumps, and Brody immediately leaps up and sits close to him, staring up intently, ready for action. "What do you mean, he found out he was dying?"

"Shit. I'm sorry, I thought he would have told you. He had cancer. It was terminal. Said the doc gave him no more than six, maybe seven months."

Nate whispers, "When was that?"

"About four months ago. He could have tried some cutting-edge new treatments, but he didn't want to be a guinea pig. He hated hospitals." Hank lets the information hang in the air while Nate processes it.

"I had no idea. I just spent almost two months with him." He thinks of Rex's weight loss. "He told me he was on a diet."

"He probably didn't want any sympathy. Don't blame yourself for not noticing. His energy levels were still good, from what I could tell. I think he would have lasted well into next year." Hank pauses. "His study was smashed up, you know? It suggests to me that he put up a good fight against his attacker, and maybe even harmed the asshole."

That might explain why Father Connor hasn't responded to Nate yet. He's probably hiding away, licking his wounds. Trying hard to stay in control of his emotions, Nate wishes more than anything that Rex had told him about his cancer diagnosis during his recent visit. He would have stayed by his side until the bitter end, which could have denied Father Connor the opportunity to kill him. But he also knows Rex wouldn't have agreed to Nate becoming his carer. He wouldn't have wanted to burden him.

Hank continues. "He's made provisions for the animals and left his ranch to the local animal welfare group. But he left me a pack of documents for you. He was working on finding someone for you, I understand."

"That's right. Did he tell you who?"

"Mr. Monroe, he told me everything. I may have been his lawyer, but I was also his friend. We'd have long drinking sessions a couple of times a year at his place, and I can tell you, his only regret on leaving this earth would be that he didn't track down Jack Connor for you. I won't call him Father Connor, because I'm a God-fearing man and that guy has nothing to do with God. He's a demon."

Nate's finding it hard to take everything in. "Had Rex made any headway?"

"Well, I need to send you these envelopes. They're sealed, so I don't know what's inside. I haven't had a chance to enter the property; the cops aren't letting anyone inside." He hesitates for a minute. "I should tell you, I've heard your name mentioned at the precinct. The lead detective is getting pretty excited about pinning this on you. Apparently she's hoping that if she can find you, it will be a big deal in the media. I can see the headlines now—*Killer priest strikes again after wrongful exoneration*. She probably thinks the case might even expedite her move up the career ladder."

Nate can't worry about her intentions. He feels ever so slightly better that Rex's death wasn't as premature as he originally believed, but the method is absolutely unforgivable. "Can you open the envelopes and scan every page, then send them to me by email?"

Hank is silent as he considers the request. Finally he says, "What if there's something in here I shouldn't see? I'm thinking ahead to any possible trial you get dragged into, Nate. I wouldn't want to have to testify against you. I could give it to a paralegal, but I think the fewer witnesses to the contents, the better."

Nate leans against a tree as he tries to think. Hank's right: if the San Diego police find him, he's sure to be arrested, and there's no way there won't be a trial. But whatever is in those documents could help him find Father Connor. If the information is so important, why didn't Rex just tell him while they were at the ranch together? He considers the possibility that Rex didn't want him to find Stacey's killer, because he knew what Nate would do to the priest, and he wouldn't have wanted him to go back to death row for that man.

"You still there?" asks Hank.

He stands up straight. "Yeah. Go ahead with scanning the documents. If you have to testify against me, I'll understand. But I need to know what Rex found out."

Hank sighs down the phone. "Sure. I understand. I guess I'll try not to read anything so I don't perjure myself in court."

"Thanks. I appreciate your help. And maybe once all this is over, we can throw Rex one hell of a memorial service."

Hank laughs. "He'd love that. You should have the documents by the end of the day."

Nate slips his phone into his pocket and tries to ignore the overwhelming urge to go back to Lost Creek so he can read the documents with Madison. For some reason he feels as if he'll need someone with him when they start coming through.

CHAPTER FORTY

Madison arrives at Ashlee's apartment. Alex should already be there doing a forensic sweep of the place, and she wants to take a closer look for herself. As she pulls into a spare parking space, she thinks about Vince's discharge from the navy. Without knowing what happened to cause it, she can't make any assumptions about him, and if the investigation has been covered up by the navy, she knows there's no point going to them for information. They won't talk to her if it means trouble for them. His discharge doesn't prove Vince is a danger to women, but she wants to speak to the victim's family as soon as Nate's contact comes through with a phone number.

She sighs as she gets out of her car, acutely aware of the clock ticking. Having checked in with Stella first thing, she knows that no credible tips or sightings of Ashlee came in overnight, which is frustrating, but if anything, it's making her more determined to follow every possible lead. Stella did mention that a lot of locals had called to volunteer in the search efforts, which is positive. It means Ashlee was well liked by the diners she served. There has been no suggestion so far that she was in trouble with anyone. She was just living her life when she vanished. Like so many other victims before her.

Madison nods to the uniformed officer stationed outside Ashlee's front door, but she doesn't go in straight away; instead she heads to the last apartment in the row, the one next to Justin's place. She bangs on the door, but there's no answer, and it still smells damp from the burst pipe. Her gut tells her she should get the landlady down here to check if anyone's hiding out in there.

When she walks into Ashlee's apartment, she finds Alex on all fours in full protective equipment, scraping samples of residue from Ashlee's bathroom floor. It's not a job she envies.

"Found any blood?" she asks.

He bumps his head on the sink as he looks up. "Bugger."

She smiles. "Sorry, I didn't mean to startle you."

"Morning, Detective." He pulls his mask down and rubs the back of his head. "No, I haven't found anything to suggest anyone was hurt in this apartment or that there's been a clean-up to hide it. This is the last room to investigate, but it's looking like nothing happened in here either."

"Good. Hopefully that means Ashlee's still alive." She checked the local papers and online news sites earlier to make sure everyone has included the girl's disappearance as headline news. "Have you seen the papers this morning?"

He nods. "Her disappearance has knocked Cody Stevens off the front pages at last. I expect the press are secretly glad to have something new to report on."

"I'm relieved she made the front covers; I need as many people as possible looking for her."

Alex stands up to stretch his legs. "By the way, I went through Ashlee's friends and posts on Instagram as you asked. There was nothing to link her to Shane Kennedy, I'm afraid. They don't follow each other on there, although he does have an Instagram account and a Twitter account. But it looks like they're both managed by a publicist, as they just appear to contain standard promo posts for his books."

Pity. She needs something concrete to link them. "Is Ashlee on Facebook or Twitter, or any other social media sites?"

"Not using her real name, her fake name or her Instagram profile name. But that doesn't mean she's not on them under a different identity. We really need her phone in order to find relationships and messages."

She nods, disappointed. "Would Instagram give us access to her messages?"

"Not normally without a search warrant, which would be difficult to get considering we don't have any proof she hasn't disappeared voluntarily. But now we know she's under eighteen, we could submit an emergency request to Facebook, who own Instagram. I've not had to do that before, so I don't know how successful we'd be, but I can certainly try if you'd like."

She doesn't hesitate. "Do it. If I can gain access to them, I might be able to find out what she was planning to do the night she went missing. Because she was excited about something, and the star marked in her calendar backs that up." Madison knows Ashlee wasn't going anywhere with her friend Joely, or with her co-workers, so it's likely that whatever she had planned was arranged online and with someone her friends don't know about.

"No problem, let me just finish up here," says Alex. He pulls his mask back on and continues swabbing the floor.

She wanders into the small living room to have a closer look at Ashlee's belongings. Her bookcase is mostly full of framed photos of Ellie, half-burnt candles and cheap plastic Halloween decorations. But two shelves are dedicated to books. There are some fantasy novels as well as some non-fiction books about notorious criminals. As Madison snaps on a pair of latex gloves, she notices there's another row of books behind those at the front. Pulling out a couple of the true-crime books, she sees Shane Kennedy's name on the spine of three novels behind. His bestseller *Bitter Road* is amongst them.

She gets a horrible sinking feeling as she realizes the implications. Ashlee must be a fan of his. She takes the novel from the shelf and sees the spine is cracked in several places and the pages are well thumbed, suggesting it's been read more than once. It's not signed by the author.

Vince said that the only person he'd told about Shane Kennedy being his guest that night was Carla. But what if Ashlee overheard them talking? She notices a gap on the shelf that would fit two more books. Are those books missing? Ashlee could have gone to the diner to wait around for Shane to appear after his interview. Perhaps she wanted him to sign her copies.

Then another scenario crosses her mind. What if he took a liking to her? It wouldn't be the first time, if the previous allegations against him are to be believed. He could have tried to assault her, and maybe she fought back for the sake of her baby. Foreseeing more bad press and the end of his career, never mind potential prison time, Shane could have hurt her to shut her up. That would explain why he left the baby behind. Some people can hurt a child or an adult, but they can't bring themselves to harm a baby, especially if they hadn't planned on killing anyone.

Her thoughts go further then. What if Ashlee and Shane had met before, at a book event, and that's why she made a special effort to hang around after midnight to see him again? They could have hooked up previously. "Oh shit." He could be the father of her baby. Her adrenaline kicks in, making her hands sweat inside the gloves. It's looking increasingly clear that he's the person who abducted Ashlee Stuart. She tries to ignore the dread that's creeping through her. She was so determined to reunite Ellie with her mother that she hadn't once allowed herself to consider it might not happen. That Ellie might have to grow up with strangers the way Owen did.

She pulls her cell phone out and calls the station, asking Pamela—the day shift dispatcher—to put her through to Sergeant Tanner. "Steve? Any luck getting the cell phone records for Ashlee Stuart or Shane Kennedy yet?"

"Not yet," he says. "I'm still trying to pin down who their service providers are, but I've been distracted by other things this morning."

"I need you need to prioritize it immediately."

Without question or hesitation he says, "Understood."

"I also need you to get Ashlee's landlady to let an officer into the empty apartment two doors down. It would be a good place for someone to hide, so it needs checking."

"Got it."

"Then I need you to locate the detective who dealt with Kennedy's arrest in 2016. I need to know if they believed he was actually guilty of the assault, and how credible the accusations were."

"I'll give it a try. Do you want to speak to the victim?"

"Sure, if she'll agree to it." Madison can't imagine she would, but it's worth a try.

"I'll ask them for her contact details."

"Great." Depending on the detective's opinion of Kennedy, she might arrange for a paternity test to see if he's Ellie Stuart's father.

"Want me to issue an APB for the guy?" Steve asks.

She tries to think. Is she jumping to too many conclusions? She doesn't want to make another serious error after what happened at the real Kacie Larsons's house yesterday. She has to be methodical and certain of any action she takes before she takes it, especially as Shane Kennedy has a level of fame. Her only other suspects are Justin Carmichael—though there's no evidence to link him to Ashlee's disappearance—and Vince Rader. But again, she has no evidence against Vince right this minute, and the fact that Shane's books are on Ashlee's shelves and that he was at her place of work just hours after she finished her shift decides it for her. Because she has to be decisive if she's to beat the odds and find Ashlee alive. "Do it. Let everyone on the team know I want Kennedy brought in for questioning."

"I'm on it."

"Thanks, I appreciate the help." Before she hangs up, she asks, "Is Douglas in yet?"

"No. Search-and-rescue are reconvening at lunchtime. He'll be meeting them out at Lake Providence."

The lake sits between Fantasy World amusement park and Grave Mountain. It's a good place to dump a body, but Shane's rental car was found on the opposite side of the woods. Still, as that area has already been searched, it makes sense Douglas would try somewhere else.

"By the way," continues Steve, "the San Diego detectives are currently in with Chief Mendes."

Her heart rate speeds up. "What are they like?"

He takes a deep breath. "Unfriendly. Detective Russell thinks she's some kind of hotshot and her partner doesn't say much. They've been here for an hour and I've already heard your name mentioned three times. I don't suppose you've had any contact with your friend?"

She hesitates. "No. Nothing."

He sighs. "I know we've only known each other for three days, Detective, and I hope you don't mind me being frank, but in my opinion you should be advising him that if he's got nothing to hide, he should come in and face the music. Because once his name gets released, things will turn nasty."

Madison doesn't reply straight away. It's easy for Steve to say that because he's never been framed for something he didn't do. "I have no problem with your frankness. Thanks for the heads-up. Now if you could get me those cell phone records asap, I'd appreciate it."

"Sure. No problem."

She ends the call. When she turns around, she sees a woman standing in Ashlee's doorway. Her face is crumpled with despair. "Is it true?"

"Can I help you?"

"Is it true my niece has been taken?" says the woman.

Madison's eyes widen. "You're related to Ashlee Stuart?"

"Just tell me," she says. "Is she dead?"

Something about the look of inevitability on this woman's face makes Madison's heart sink.

CHAPTER FORTY-ONE

Nate is considering his next move while he waits for Hank Collins to send through the documents Rex wanted him to have. He won't be staying another night at the campsite. It's too cold overnight and Brody's getting just as restless as him. As he pulls the minivan's seats into an upright position, his phone buzzes in his pocket. It's a text from Owen.

Call me asap when it's safe to talk.

Concerned, he calls Madison's son immediately. "Everything okay?" he says when Owen answers.

"Someone's been in the house."

He clutches the phone a little tighter. "What do you mean? Are you and your mom okay?"

"Yeah, Mom's at work, so she doesn't know. I have a free period so I came home from school, but when I went to put my key in the front door, it was already unlocked." He stops like he's out of breath with either panic or excitement.

"Could your mom have forgotten to lock it when she left?"

"I left after her because she went to work really early. I know I locked it. And when I stepped inside just now, the house felt weird. I don't know how to explain it, but I could just tell someone had been here. I thought you were back, so I tried shouting your name. When I got no answer, I was going to phone Mom, but... well, instead I did what all those dumbasses do in the movies and I investigated for myself." He laughs nervously. "I can't believe I was that stupid. I mean, I literally shout at the TV when people do that."

Nate shakes his head. He can't believe it either. Owen could've been attacked. "So do you know for sure someone was inside?"

"Yes."

"How?"

"Because there's an envelope taped to our TV."

The phone nearly slips out of Nate's hand as dread creeps through his body. "Have you opened it?"

"No, I didn't want to contaminate any potential DNA. But Nate…" Owen pauses.

"What?" He thinks he already knows what the boy's going to say, and he doesn't want to hear it.

"The envelope is addressed to you."

He takes an involuntary step back. "Son of a bitch."

There's only one person who would dare enter Madison's house uninvited and leave something behind for him. Anxious that Owen could be in danger, he speaks clearly and forcefully. "Owen? Listen to me. You need to get away from your house right now. Do you understand?"

"But why? There's no one here now, I've searched the whole house."

"I don't care. Father Connor could be watching you from afar. Get out of the house and call your mom. Tell her what you found but don't open the envelope until I get there."

"You're coming back?" There's relief in his voice.

"I have to. He's left me no choice. He's dangerous, Owen, and he's a threat to you and your mom. By doing this, he's sending me a message. Why else would he break into your house?" Nate's trying hard not to panic as he thinks how easy it would have been for Father Connor to kill Owen. Or Madison. Or both of them. He should have left Brody behind to protect them.

He swings open the driver's door and slips into the car, looking around for the dog. "I'll be there as fast as I can. Do *not* tell anyone but your mom that I'm coming, and make sure she's alone when you speak to her. In the meantime, get out of the house."

"Okay, okay." Owen sounds scared now.

Nate shouts for Brody, and within seconds the dog is running toward the car from the woods. He pushes the passenger door open from the inside, and Brody jumps in and barks inquisitively at him.

"That's right, boy. We're going home."

CHAPTER FORTY-TWO

Madison has to coax Ashlee's aunt into the small apartment; it's clear she's reluctant to come in. "Just take a seat for two minutes while I ask you some questions. Please, you might be able to help me find her."

The woman follows her to the worn couch, and slowly sits down whilst looking around the room. She's dressed warmly in a thick winter coat and well-worn boots. Her face is lined and her hair is curly and badly dyed. She looks like a woman who's been through a lot and now wishes everyone would just leave her alone.

Alex appears in the hallway, so Madison gives a nod toward the bathroom door to suggest he leaves them alone while she quizzes this woman. He disappears.

"How did you hear about Ashlee's disappearance?" she asks.

"Saw it on the news last night. I battled with coming down here, but I was worried about the baby."

Madison's phone starts ringing; it's Owen. She has to reject the call and reluctantly set her phone to silent, because she can't interrupt this woman while she talks. She could provide crucial information.

"Can I take your name?"

"Barbara Fletcher." Madison writes it down, but the woman eyes her suspiciously. "I don't want to get involved in this mess."

"Why not? Aren't you concerned for your niece's well-being?"

"I used to be." Barbara looks away. "Ashlee came to live with me after her mother passed away. I couldn't afford to take her in, but there was no one else. Her dad has never been in her life—"

"Do you know his name?" Madison wouldn't normally inter-rupt, but she senses she has limited time before this woman bolts.

"No, I can't remember. He was just some guy my sister worked with, but he moved up north over a decade ago. They weren't in a proper relationship when they conceived Ashlee. Anyway, Derek, my husband, wasn't happy when I took her in, and it caused countless arguments." She's wringing her hands.

"About what?"

Barbara shakes her head. "He never wanted his own kids, so why would he want someone else's to come live with us? I'm surprised he didn't leave me, to be honest."

Madison has to hide her contempt for him. "Do you think Ashlee picked up on not being wanted?"

The woman shoots her a sharp look. "Don't say it like that. I know what you're thinking. I took care of her the best I could with what little we had. But that girl's not right."

Madison frowns. "What do you mean? Does she suffer with mental health problems?"

"She suffers with something alright. One minute she's nice as pie and then the next she's like a big ball of anger waiting to explode. We never knew which version we were getting from one day to the next. She's… troubled." Barbara's face shows the pain she's been through. The sleepless nights.

"Did you take her to a doctor? She might have needed therapy after losing her mom. Or medication."

Barbara scoffs. "We can't afford to take ourselves to the doctor, never mind her. You have to understand that we were doing her a favor by letting her live with us, and we tried hard to make her feel comfortable. I would make sure she went to school every day and even helped her get a part-time job. So when she didn't try to fit in, lost her job and started drinking her way through our liquor cabinet, we'd had about enough. Once she got pregnant at fifteen, it was the final straw for Derek. We couldn't afford to feed another mouth, so he told Ashlee she could stay until the baby was born, but then she'd have to move out and stand on her own two feet."

It's clearly painful for Barbara to recount all this, and Madison can tell the woman has some love for her niece, despite what she's saying. She was put in a difficult position and Ashlee didn't help herself. *Couldn't* help herself, probably. Which means she could have been suffering from an undiagnosed mental health issue. Or from the consequences of suffering grief and rejection at such a young age. She needed her aunt more than ever, yet instead she was asked to leave her home. And with a newborn baby. "Do you know who Ellie's father is?"

Barbara doesn't react. "No idea. I heard on the news that the baby is alright. Will she be okay with child services? They'll keep her safe?"

Madison takes a deep breath and nods. "Ellie will be well looked after no matter what happens, but the sooner she's reunited with her mother, the better."

Barbara clearly doesn't agree. "She's better off with a new family, whether or not you find Ashlee. Ours is cursed."

Madison looks away, trying hard to remain professional. She can't agree that Ellie is better off without her mother. Especially as there's no evidence to suggest Ashlee wasn't taking care of her. Some people clearly don't understand what it's like to lose a child to the social care system, and what it's like for that child to grow up with no biological family around them. "We don't have any real leads yet as to Ashlee's whereabouts. She was waitressing in the local diner and raising Ellie alone, with some help from friends and co-workers. They all think very highly of her and can't understand where she might have gone. But if you leave me your number, I'll keep you updated."

The woman hesitates. "I don't really see any point."

"What do you mean?"

"Well, if she turns up dead, we can't afford to bury her, and if she turns up alive, we don't want her living back with us. She's not the little girl I knew when my sister was alive, so it's like she's already dead to me. I watched my sister die from alcoholism and I can't watch my niece go down that road." She pulls a tissue from her pocket and wipes her watery eyes. "I know how I sound, but I can't take any more heartache. It's time for me to move on." She stands, stuffing the tissue in her coat pocket. "I don't want my name released to the press. I know what they're like."

Madison stands too, disappointed in Barbara's attitude. She's completely given up on Ashlee. Something Madison refuses to do. But it's clear she won't change this woman's mind. "If you hear from Ashlee or hear any rumors about where she's gone, please call my department." She still doesn't have any business cards to hand out. "Ask for Detective Madison Harper."

Barbara smiles sadly. "I hope she's alright, I really do. But I think it's unlikely. I think this was destined to happen."

Madison watches the woman leave the apartment. She can't help but feel sorry for Ashlee. Her mother was an alcoholic, she never knew her father, and the only family member she had left just washed her hands of her for the second time. No one in Lost Creek has mentioned Ashlee having an alcohol problem, so she doesn't know what to believe. She walks to the kitchen and checks the cupboards and refrigerator. There's nothing in there except sodas, puréed baby food and some sandwich meats and condiments. Maybe having Ellie helped her clean up her act.

Turning away, she glances at her phone. There are fourteen missed calls from Owen. "Shit."

CHAPTER FORTY-THREE

Madison's heart is pounding out of her chest as she tries not to drive too fast in her rush to get home. Owen told her what he found in the living room, and she's furious that Father Connor had the nerve to break into her home and put her son's life in danger.

She spots Owen walking down the street in the direction of their house, and skids to a stop next to him. "Get in."

He does what he's told, and when she glances at him before pulling away, he looks pale and afraid. "Are you okay?"

He nods. "Yeah. Nate freaked me out earlier. Made me realize I could have found that priest in our house and got myself killed." He laughs nervously. "I mean, Jesus, Mom, how embarrassing would that have been when my friends found out I got killed by a seventy-year-old priest?"

She finds herself laughing at his absurd train of thought, then skids away from the sidewalk. "In all seriousness, you need to learn to think on your feet. You shouldn't have entered the house, Owen. What were you thinking? He may be old, but he's deadly."

"I know that now. I don't need a lecture."

She glances at him, but he's turned away from her. "I'm sorry. I was worried about you. But I'm glad you're safe." She swings the car into their driveway and slips out, grabbing her gun out of its holster. She knows it's unlikely Father Connor has returned, but she refuses to be caught unawares. "Stay behind me."

They silently climb the porch steps as she tries to listen for movement from the inside. There is none. Owen locked up behind him, so she pulls her keys out and slowly opens the front door. A quick scan of the downstairs tells her no one is in the house, but she checks upstairs too. Before she can look at the envelope Father Connor left, they hear a dog barking from out back.

Owen heads to the kitchen and is out through the back door before she can stop him. When she hears him call Brody's name, though, she relaxes. Outside, she sees Nate cautiously emerging from the barn as Owen kneels down on the damp grass, petting the dog.

She rushes toward Nate, relief washing over her. He steps forward and they embrace. He lets her hug him longer than necessary, which is a huge step forward from when they first met. "I'm so sorry about Rex," she says into his neck. "He was one of the good guys." His cheek feels soft, and she realizes he's shaved his usual two-day stubble off and even got a haircut.

"Thanks," he whispers. As they pull apart, he fixes his serious blue eyes on her. "Are you okay?" He looks concerned. "Hey, why the tears?" He rubs them away with his fingers.

She hadn't realized she was crying and she has no idea why. Waving a dismissive hand, she says, "Something in my eye."

He laughs as they walk toward the house.

"Wait, watch this!" calls Owen.

They turn back to face him. Brody is standing to attention in front of him, waiting for a command. Owen makes a shooting gesture to the dog. "Bang, bang, Brody."

Madison raises her eyebrows as Brody drops to the ground as if hit. She glances at Nate, who's laughing. "This is what you taught him?" she says. "Owen, of all the tricks you could have practiced, what a waste of time!"

Nate gently nudges her shoulder. "It made us laugh, though."

"That's not the only trick I taught him," says her son defensively. "There's others."

She smiles. "I guess we can look forward to them another time."

They enter the kitchen, where Owen pours some kibble and water for Brody. Then, wiping his hands on his shirt, he looks at

Nate. "I wasn't going to tell you this, because I didn't want you to freak out, but I found a recent video of Father Connor online."

Nate frowns. "What do you mean?"

"I had time to kill until you both got here, so I was googling the priest to see if there had been anything in the news about him recently. I had to go through so much crap, but eventually I found this website that keeps track of wanted criminals." He pulls his cell phone out. "This video was taken in Shadow Falls, California. I recognized the name; it's where Mom told me you two first worked together to find that missing girl in the summer. Apparently he was caught on TV in early July giving a brief interview to a reporter who was asking about the case. The reporter must have thought he was from a local church, because it looks like he was put on the spot."

Nate steps forward and takes the phone off Owen. Madison watches from his side. She's surprised the guy would get caught on camera. When Nate hits play, the priest appears.

Father Connor is wearing a black suit, and a large crucifix necklace rests on his chest. He looks irritated. He's obviously been ambushed whilst eating his breakfast; Madison can make out the dining room of the guest house they were staying in during their investigation. She's a little unnerved that he was so hot on their trail.

The reporter who ambushed him speaks from behind the camera. "As you'll know, Father, twelve-year-old Jennifer Lucas went missing from Camp Fearless at the beginning of summer, and the case has recently been solved with the help of two private investigators. Do you have some comforting words at this time for the shocked community of Shadow Falls?"

Father Connor fixes a grim look on his face, but Madison notices a flash of annoyance before he does. "I'm not privy to the details of this young girl's tragic case, and I wasn't in town during the police investigation, but it's always devastating when a child suffers. God will help people through their pain, and we must trust that He knows what He was doing. It's time for the community to pull together, because together we are always stronger."

He's clearly trying to keep his sound bite as short and generic as possible, in the hope they won't use it.

The reporter leans in. "And what would you say to the girl's mother, if she's listening?"

Father Connor hesitates. "She should seek counsel from her own spiritual adviser in these difficult times. Now, if you don't mind…" He smiles at her, but there's no warmth there. "I'm trying to eat my breakfast."

Just before the camera cuts to the reporter, Father Connor bites into a sausage and lets the greasy pork fat run down his chin, landing on his gold crucifix.

"Eugh." She's seen Connor before, in old news reports showing Nate's trial. He was parading around in front of the cameras, clutching his Bible and demanding sympathy. But that was almost twenty years ago. He left Texas with his sister after Nate's conviction, and then disappeared when Nate was finally cleared of Stacey's murder. Mainly because he became the primary suspect for her death. He must have left Shadow Falls soon after this sound bite was recorded, knowing the FBI could see it and come for him.

Her first reaction of disgust is quickly followed by noticing how badly he's aged. Although he still has hair, it's white and wispy, not thick and brown like it was. His clerical collar looks too big for his wrinkled throat. He's not wasting away, but he's clearly not as fit and strong as he used to be. He's an old man now, and really, how much of a threat could he be to Nate like this?

She watches Nate's reaction to seeing him again. He's fiddling with the rosary beads sitting under his T-shirt. It's something she's seen him do a few times. Usually when he's thinking about the priest. His grip on the phone is tight and his eyes have a new fire behind them. It unnerves her.

CHAPTER FORTY-FOUR

"That was short and sweet," says Nate as he passes Owen's phone back to him and tries to control the tremor in his hands. It's been a long time since he's seen Father Connor. Anger burns in his chest from knowing Stacey's uncle is living a seemingly normal life while he himself is still trying to piece together his shattered existence.

"How does it feel to see him again after all this time?" asks Madison.

He looks away from her, because he hates seeing the fear in her eyes. She knows what he's thinking and she knows this whole fucked-up situation won't be over until either he or the priest is dead.

Realizing he's drumming his fingers loudly on the kitchen counter, he's overwhelmed with a craving to use, to forget everything for the next twenty-four hours and go under into the comforting numbness that helps him forget. Flashbacks to Stacey's crime scene begin. Closing his eyes doesn't help; they become more vivid. "I guess I need to see what he left me in the living room."

Madison tenses, and he can't blame her. She knows that whatever's in the envelope has the potential to destroy him. She steps in front of him. "Before that, I need to tell you the San Diego cops have arrived. They've been with Chief Mendes this morning and she's given Detective Douglas the task of liaising with them and helping them track you down."

He nods, but he's numb to it. He just wants to find Father Connor while they're both still free men. "At least you're not the one who has to arrest me, I guess."

Her eyes soften. "Hopefully no one will arrest you. You look tired, Nate. Where have you been the last two days? And where's your car?"

"I had to swap the Jeep for something they wouldn't be looking for. My new car's in the garage. I wasn't sure if you would arrive before the cops, so I waited in the barn just in case." He pauses. "I've been contacted by Rex's lawyer. He told me Rex was battling terminal cancer."

She closes her eyes. "Oh God. And he never told you. I'm so sorry."

Owen must sense they have a lot to talk about, because he leads Brody out of the kitchen. Nate hears them running upstairs.

He steps closer to Madison. "How long do you think I have before the detectives turn up here?"

She leans against the counter and crosses her arms. "I'd like to think they'll speak to me at the station instead of ambushing me here, but who knows? They could turn up any minute, considering Douglas knows you've stayed with me before. As soon as I get a chance, I'll make them aware of Father Connor. They have to know he's responsible for Rex's murder. It might buy you time to clear your name if they at least consider another suspect."

He's doubtful. "How can I even begin to clear my name? I can't get to Rex's home to search for evidence, I don't know anyone on the inside at the San Diego PD to ask for help, and I have no way of proving it was Father Connor." He sighs. "The way I see, it I can either turn myself in for questioning and risk being sent down for murder again, or I can disappear for good."

She struggles to reply. He wonders if that's because she wants him to stick around. He'd like to, but how can he? He touches her arm. "Let me see what's in the envelope. That might change everything."

She nods slowly. "Owen said it's stuck to the TV."

He walks into the living room and approaches the large white envelope. The handwriting is messy but unmistakable.

"Put these on." Madison hands him a pair of latex gloves. "Both the envelope and the contents can be dusted for prints if necessary."

He slips them on and stares at it. Should he give Father Connor power over him by reading the contents? Probably not. But it could contain some clue as to where he's been staying. It might contain answers about why he killed his niece. With shaking hands, Nate pulls the envelope from the screen. As he turns it over, he can see it's unsealed, so he pulls out what's inside.

"Oh God!" He throws it on the floor and moves his hands to his head. "Oh God, no!"

"What is it?" Madison crouches down and studies the photo. She looks up at him. "That's not Stacey."

He turns away. "It's Kristen Devereaux."

He wants to unsee it, but he can't. The photo shows her bruised and bloodied face, her eyes closed against the attack. If she's not dead, she's close to it. She was bludgeoned, just like Stacey. If Kristen hadn't taken Nate's case on for her students to dissect, this would never have happened. She wouldn't have been a target of the madman who won't let him move on with his life.

Madison stands up, clearly shocked. "She might still be alive. We can't assume she's dead. Her lips aren't blue and…" She stops, struggling for the right words.

Brody appears in the doorway and runs to the photo. As he sniffs it, he inadvertently turns it over. There's something written on the back. Nate has to lean in to read it.

Madison's next.

He picks it up before she sees.

"What did it say?" she asks.

"It doesn't matter." He won't let that happen. Adrenaline and hatred sear through his body. The pained expression on Kristen's face in the photo tells him all he needs to know about the attack. It was as brutal as Stacey's. It's time to find the son of a bitch responsible.

He has to make him pay. "You and Owen need to stay away from this house in case he comes back."

"He won't be stupid enough to return here after pulling this stunt." She doesn't look sure of herself, though.

Father Connor probably *is* long gone, knowing his freedom is more at risk now than ever before, but they don't know that for sure, and Nate won't take the risk. "Owen should go stay with a friend for a while, and you need to book into a hotel."

"I agree about Owen, but I'm not booking into a hotel. This is my home and I'm not giving in to that asshole. I'll be ready for him if he comes back."

He shakes his head in frustration. "You're being naïve. He managed to take Rex unawares, and—" He stops. He doesn't want to tell her what's written on the photo, but he can't risk her being blasé about this. "Look." He holds it out to her.

Instead of scaring her, the words light a fire in her eyes. "That won't happen, Nate. I'm experienced with guns and I have bolts on all the windows and doors."

"Those bolts didn't stop him getting in today, did they?" Experience tells him he won't change her mind. "If you're insisting on staying here, you should keep Brody with you. He can guard the house while you're at work, and when you're not, make sure he's always by your side. Don't make it easy for Connor. Stay armed and assume he'll turn up any minute."

She stares at him, unimpressed. "You sound like you're leaving again."

He doesn't reply.

"If you're that concerned about me, why won't you stay?" Her eyes are imploring him, but he doesn't think it's because she's fearful for her own life. She's worried about what he's going to do.

He looks away. "I can't live like this, with that demon taunting me."

Madison steps closer. "Don't do anything stupid, Nate. He's baiting you because he knows you'll react emotionally. You have to stay calm."

He shakes his head. "It's time to end this. He's never going to stop. He's killing everyone I love." He looks at her. Could he live with himself if Madison or Owen were killed because of this man's hatred of him? There's no way.

She touches his arm. "I need you here with me, Nate. Together we can try to clear your name and get this guy caught, then focus on finding out what happened to Kristen. She could still be alive. You know how well we work together. And once we find this sorry piece of shit, we can hand his ass over to the FBI."

He can't think straight. Images of Stacey's crime scene are taking over. She had the same look on her face as Kristen. The only other thing they have in common is him. "Where's your gun?" he asks. "Not your service weapon; the one you bought illegally when you got out of prison."

She swallows and takes a step back, shaking her head. "I'm not giving you that. If you kill him, you're guaranteed to go straight back to death row. Can't you see that's what he wants?"

Owen appears in the doorway. He's holding Madison's second-hand gun. "He needs to finish this, Mom. It's the only way."

Nate takes the weapon from him before Madison can react. He's never fired a weapon in his life, but he knows there's no other way. Looking at her he says, "Don't follow me. I need to do this alone."

She steps forward. "But—"

"No." He holds his hand up and raises his voice. "I mean it, Madison. This has to end and I don't want you getting in the way."

He leaves the house before she can stop him.

CHAPTER FORTY-FIVE

Madison is fuming with Owen for giving Nate her gun, but Chief Mendes has ordered her to the station, so he's off the hook for now. He's arranged to stay at his friend's house for the next two nights. But Madison has no intention of booking into a hotel. She's left Brody at home in case the priest is planning to break in and lie in wait until she returns from work.

She has to steel herself before entering the police station. What's happening with Nate can't affect her search for Ashlee. But when she walks into the chief's office, she sees two strangers sitting there. Chief Mendes stands up. "Madison, this is Detective Christine Russell and Detective John Purdue. I'm sure it'll come as no surprise to hear they want to talk to you about Nate Monroe."

She swallows. All the way here she was trying to figure out what she was going to tell them. Does she admit she was talking to Nate less than an hour ago? That he's gone to kill the guy who's made his life a misery for twenty years? She doesn't know what's going to come out of her mouth when they start asking questions.

There's no attempt by anyone to shake hands, and the two detectives remain seated. With no spare seat for Madison, she stands while Chief Mendes perches on the corner of her desk.

Detective Russell pulls out her cell phone. "Instead of taking notes, I prefer to record conversations. It's easier all round. Do you mind?"

Madison is tempted to say yes, but only to be difficult. She shakes her head.

"Good. Let's get right to it. When and where was the last time you saw Nathaniel Monroe?"

The most difficult question first. She hesitates. She's a cop; she should be honest with them. But she also wants to be loyal to Nate, even though he didn't ask her to lie for him. She considers whether being found by these guys would be better for him in the long run. It might stop him from killing Father Connor and securing a life sentence. But would he get one anyway, for Rex's murder?

"What's taking you so long, Detective?" asks Chief Mendes.

She swallows. "Sorry. I'm in a difficult position, as I'm sure you can all appreciate."

"Not really." Mendes crosses her arms. "You tell the truth or you lose your job. It's as simple as that."

Madison studies her face. She's serious. "Before I answer the question, I want to know why Nate is even a suspect in Rex Hartley's murder." She turns to the detectives. "What evidence are you basing that on?"

Detective Russell crosses her legs and smirks. "With all due respect, that's none of your business."

Madison bristles. "It is, actually. As a detective myself, I wouldn't be chasing someone across the country without hard evidence that I'm after the right guy. I would like to assume you wouldn't either, yet here you are. So do you have something that implicates Nate? Or is your whole investigation based on a Google search of a formerly exonerated guy who on paper looks easy to reconvict?"

Russell's face flushes with annoyance and Detective Purdue looks uncomfortable. Maybe he's not used to people challenging his partner.

"I have a witness who confirms Monroe was staying with the deceased at the time of his death," says Russell. "And I have security footage showing him leaving the property around the time our ME thinks the victim died."

Madison shakes her head. "That's it? Nate stayed with him for two months and left on the day of his murder, but Rex was still alive when he left."

"You know that for sure?"

Madison doesn't like the smirk on Russell's face. "I guarantee you Rex was killed after Nate left. So are you saying you don't have any real evidence that he was responsible; anything linking him to the body or the poison? Because if so, you don't have a case."

Russell is undeterred. "I won't disclose everything to you—after all, we don't know if you can be trusted—but I will say we're expecting the autopsy report to come in shortly, followed by the lab results of the DNA found under the victim's fingernails."

Incredulous, Madison says, "How can you come here to arrest someone when you don't have any of that yet?"

Chief Mendes steps in. "Just answer the original question, Madison. Time is of the essence."

She shakes her head, knowing she can't avoid it any longer. "Nate unexpectedly appeared at my house earlier today. But he's gone now, and I don't know where."

Detective Russell shares a look of contempt with her partner. "Why didn't you arrest him?"

"Because I was asked to stay away from this case. And I haven't seen any evidence to suggest he killed his friend. I know him, and he's not a killer."

Russell rolls her eyes. "In other words, you're screwing him and you don't want him to go to prison. Great."

Madison steps forward, making Russell's partner spring up from his seat. "Whoa! I suggest you calm down, Detective."

Russell slowly stands.

Chief Mendes is shaking her head in frustration at Madison. "Do you know where he was going? Or what he was planning on doing next?"

"No."

"Is he still driving the Jeep Grand Cherokee?" asks Russell.

"No idea."

"You didn't see it parked outside your house earlier?"

"I didn't see any car."

Clearly pissed, Russell persists with her questions. "What was he wearing?"

"A T-shirt and jeans with a rain jacket over."

"What color were his clothes?"

"Dark, but I don't remember specifically."

"Was his dog with him?"

She hesitates. "Yes." Maybe that will buy Nate some time if the police only stop men travelling with dogs. Brody is obviously at her house.

"How long ago did he leave?"

She glances at the clock. It's one thirty. Nate left at around twelve thirty. "Sometime this morning. I didn't note the time."

The two detectives make moves to leave, but first Russell turns to the chief. "I need your department to issue an APB and make all local units aware that we're looking for a guy with a dog." She glances at Madison. "What breed and color is the dog?"

"German shepherd Siberian husky mix. Brown, cream, and white."

"Is he dangerous?" asks Detective Purdue.

"Only if he doesn't like you." She doesn't tell him how Brody has a thing for cops, since he was raised by one. He can spot one a mile off and he won't leave them alone until they've assured him he's a good boy. A good *officer*.

"I'll make all units aware who we're looking for," says Chief Mendes. "But I think Detective Harper could be right that you're pinning your hopes on someone who has no motive to kill his friend."

"Oh yeah? Then who would *you* suggest we go after?" asks Detective Purdue, clearly more willing than Russell to consider alternatives.

Madison doesn't hesitate. "Father Jack Connor."

Russell scoffs at that. "Does Monroe blame that guy for all his problems?"

"I think you'll find it's the other way around. Look." She takes the envelope containing the photo of a bludgeoned Kristen out of her back pocket. It's bagged up to protect the prints, so she pulls on a pair of latex gloves and then extracts the photo from the envelope. They all lean in to look. "This is Kristen Devereaux, the college law professor who went missing after helping secure Nate's release from prison."

"How did you get this?" asks Russell.

"Father Connor broke into my house earlier today and left it. He killed Stacey Connor twenty years ago, then attacked Kristen for daring to help Nate." Madison looks up. "And now he's killed Rex Hartley, Nate's closest friend. The guy is a psychopath, and if you can't see that he's a better suspect than Nate for Rex's murder, then quite frankly, you shouldn't be cops."

She drops the disturbing photograph on Mendes's desk face down so they can see what's written on the back. Then, pulling off the gloves, she leaves the office without another word. She's done all she can to make them see reason.

Now she needs to find her missing girl.

CHAPTER FORTY-SIX

Madison is reading emails at her desk whilst silently fuming. Her cell phone vibrates loudly on the desk beside her, making her jump. It's a text from Nate with the contact details for the family of the deceased navy officer. She doesn't hesitate, and places the call, determined to find out once and for all whether Vince is a killer.

A man answers in Spanish. He doesn't understand Madison's English, or her terrible attempts at Spanish. She manages to speak enough to ask him to put someone else on the phone who understands English a little better. He calls his wife over, and once Madison has introduced herself and confirmed that this woman is Julia Martinez's mother, she tells her why she's calling.

"I'm after some information about a man named Vince Rader. Do you know him?"

She's met with silence.

"Please, I wouldn't ask if it wasn't important. I have a missing girl to find and I'm concerned Vince might have been involved in her disappearance. I understand he was discharged from the navy for something to do with the death of your daughter."

"No, no, no."

At least the woman hasn't hung up. "Ma'am? Are you saying he wasn't involved?"

"Vince is a friend of our family. He tried to save Julia."

Madison hears the husband raising his voice in the background. It sounds like he's insisting she doesn't say anything else. "So Vince wasn't responsible for her death?"

"Not at all, you've got it all wrong. The navy used him as a... a... scapegoat?"

Madison's shoulders relax.

"I'm sorry, but my husband's right. I'm not allowed to talk about this since the lawsuit. We signed an agreement that we wouldn't discuss it with anyone."

She frowns. Sounds like there's a cover-up going on in the navy. But she can't get involved in that. At least she has answers about Vince. "No problem, I understand."

"You won't arrest him?"

She can't promise that. "Not unless he gives me a reason to, no. Thanks for your time, and please accept my condolences."

She looks up as someone approaches her. It's Alex. "Afternoon, Detective. Have you had a chance to look at the photos I sent you of the contents from the luggage found in our crashed car?"

She takes a deep calming breath, trying to switch her mind from Nate to Ashlee. "Yeah. There's nothing useful there." It was just two pairs of pants, a sweater and underwear, along with toiletries. Shane Kennedy travelled light, indicating he wasn't expecting to be in town long. They've yet to locate his cell phone, so it must be with him.

"I agree. The results of the blood analysis have arrived from the state crime lab."

"That was quick. What do they tell us?"

"Well, the blood found in the Ford drew a match on the DNA database."

She leans forward. "Whose blood is it?"

"Shane Kennedy's."

He must have been injured when he lost control of the car. If the press gets wind that Shane's badly hurt and somehow involved in Ashlee's disappearance, it'll go nationwide within hours and all eyes will be on her investigation. "Are you able to tell from the amount of blood how badly hurt he might be?"

Alex shakes his head. "Afraid not, but it's highly likely he suffered a head wound. Obviously if it was fatal we'd have found his body."

"Is he a match for the blood on the sneaker?"

"No, we didn't find a match for that specimen. As you're working on the assumption that it's Ashlee's shoe, it's likely she also suffered an injury at some point."

Which means they both left the car as walking wounded. The sneaker is definitely Ashlee's, because Vince Rader identified it as being the same as the shoes the girl wore to work. Madison remembers she was going to order a paternity test on Ellie to see if Shane is her biological father.

Her cell phone buzzes with a text from Shelley.

Got hold of the CCTV footage from the gas station for the night Ashlee went missing. It clearly shows the red Ford driving by at 2.23 a.m. and there are two people in the front—a man and a woman, both Caucasian. Can't see a baby because the quality isn't great. Will bring it back to the station shortly.

She lets Alex read it as she watches the San Diego detectives leaving Chief Mendes's office. Without a glance in her direction, they exit the station, and Madison wonders where they're going next.

Mendes approaches them. "Alex, would you check the prints on this and see if they match those on record for a Father Jack Connor." She hands him the photo of Kristen Devereaux, along with the envelope. "I've noted down his DOB. He's wanted for the homicide of Stacey Connor in Austin, Texas, back in 2000."

"Of course." Alex turns it over and reads what's written on the back. He looks at Madison. "Are you in danger, Detective?"

Chief Mendes butts in. "Madison, you'll need to be extra careful in case he tries to make good on his threat. I can have Officer Williams stationed outside your home overnight until he's found."

Madison's surprised by the change in attitude. "Not necessary. I've made arrangements for better protection." She can't tell Mendes that Brody's at her house, because she told the San Diego cops that he was still with Nate. "Plus, my son has gone to stay with a friend for a few nights, so I think we'll be fine. Are Tweedledum and Tweedledee going to look for Father Connor now instead of Nate?"

Alex excuses himself as Mendes crosses her arms. "No, they won't be swayed. Detective Russell's convinced Nate is the most likely suspect. If it was Father Connor, he's likely to be long gone by now, but I'll get Steve to make all units aware we're looking for him, plus I've put a call in to the FBI to alert them he could have been here at some point."

"Could have? Don't you believe he put that photo in my house?"

The chief's expression doesn't give much away. "We have to consider the possibility that Nate planted it there for you to find, knowing you'd jump to conclusions because you want to protect him. You need to stop letting his problems distract you, Madison. Focus on finding Ashlee Stuart instead." She walks away.

Incredulous, Madison has to bite her tongue. Mendes didn't witness Nate's reaction to seeing Kristen Devereaux's battered face. If she had, she wouldn't accuse him of planting the photo.

Steve finishes a call and comes over. "Hey. So I managed to speak to the detective who interviewed Shane Kennedy back in 2016."

"And?"

"He says the guy was pretty shocked in his interview and insisted he was innocent. He said he did invite the girl up to his hotel room, but only so he could sign her book. Apparently he got her confused with a competition winner and thought she would be coming up with her family. According to Kennedy, it was *her* who made advances toward *him*, but he declined and asked her to leave, which is when things turned ugly. She wanted photos for social media, to prove she'd met him, but he wanted her out of there."

"Did the detective feel he was telling the truth?"

"He had mixed feelings, but he thought Kennedy probably had his attorney pay the girl off to make the allegations go away."

Madison doesn't doubt young fans can get over-zealous when meeting their idols, and some teenagers can be particularly manipulative when they don't get what they want, but that doesn't mean the girl isn't to be believed, and if he bought her silence, that's worrying. "Would she speak to me, do you think?"

Steve shakes his head. "When the case was dropped, she made it clear she wanted no further contact with the police and just wanted to forget anything had ever happened. He said she seemed embarrassed by it all and didn't want her parents getting mad at her again."

Madison frowns. If she was embarrassed, it suggests she might have made it all up. "Okay, thanks. Any luck with Ashlee and Shane's cell phone records and last known locations?"

"I've figured out who their cell providers are and I'm just waiting on management to approve releasing the information to me."

"Great. And everyone knows they're to be on the lookout for Shane Kennedy?"

"Right. If he's still in Colorado, we'll know about it soon enough."

"Good. Because Alex says it was his blood in the car, and footage from the gas station shows both a man and a woman inside before it crashed."

Steve nods. "It's just a case of bringing him in, then."

She hopes so. "If we can find him."

She leans back in her seat as he walks away. She wishes she could relax, knowing the crime writer will find it hard to hide now they're all looking for him, but until she knows where Ashlee is, she can't.

CHAPTER FORTY-SEVEN

"Madison?"

She blinks. She was concentrating on the security footage brought in by Shelley. It's too grainy to make out a baby on the woman's lap, or even to tell whether Ashlee was alive. And the angle at which the car passed the camera means the license plate is impossible to decipher. She looks up with raised eyebrows.

"Want me to answer that?" Stella says.

Madison looks at her cell phone. It's ringing. Detective Douglas's name is on the display. "Sorry, I was miles away." The phones are always ringing in the station; she's learnt to ignore them when she needs to concentrate. She answers it. "Hey, Don. How's the search going?"

"We've found something."

Her mouth goes dry. "What? A body?"

"Not yet. A set of car keys and a cell phone, but the phone is badly damaged and won't switch on."

Madison stands up, grabbing her own car keys. "At the lake?"

"Right. We're only searching the area around it at the moment. My gut's telling me we're getting close to finding a body." He sighs. "I could really do with a sniffer dog out here."

Madison hesitates to offer Brody's services, but he could help them find Ashlee, so she's prepared to take some heat for misleading the San Diego cops. "I can get hold of a dog. I'll be right there."

It takes less than half an hour to get home, collect an excited Brody and drive to Lake Providence. She pulls her big winter coat on as she gets out of the car, bracing herself for the cold wind, and Brody immediately speeds ahead of her. By the time she reaches Detective Douglas and the search leader, he's sitting to attention at their feet.

The search leader glances at her, amused. "This one's ready for action."

She smiles. "He always is. Brody's a former cadaver dog, so if there's someone out here, he'll find their scent."

"Perfect. I'm Mark Fuller, pleasure to meet you."

She steps forward to shake his hand. "Madison Harper." He has a firm grip, and his hands and face are weathered from all the time he spends outdoors. She'd guess he's nearing sixty, and there's not an ounce of fat on him.

"My team have covered a large area already, but we've only found the car keys and cell phone—well, other than discarded beer bottles and used condoms." He smiles. "But we're happy to continue around the rear of the lake, where it gets a little trickier to reach the edge. If you want the water searched, that'll require someone with diving experience, because it gets deep in the center."

She looks out over the lake. It's reflecting the afternoon's heavy rain clouds. Thankfully, they're holding for now. A whiff of alcohol passes in front of her nose. "Keep going. Let's give Brody a chance to search the area where the items were found before we call it off for today and reassess. It's already starting to get dark, so we don't have much time."

"No problem." Mark looks down at Brody. "Come on then, boy. Show me what you're made of."

Brody barks up at him and runs ahead. Mark follows.

Madison turns to Douglas. "I'm almost one hundred percent certain now that Shane Kennedy abducted Ashlee." She tells him about the 2016 allegations against Shane, and how the lead detective felt he probably paid the girl for her silence.

Douglas doesn't look surprised. "I'd ask why he would risk his successful writing career, but assholes like him think they can get away with whatever they want. Is Ashlee Stuart a fan of his?"

"Yeah, she owns some of his books. I'm working on the theory that she found out he was going to be on Vince's podcast and decided to try to get a selfie with him or a book signed. She's an attractive girl, so he could have seen her interest in him as an opportunity to make a pass at her."

"And maybe she fought back."

She nods. Fighting back should be a good thing, but there's always the risk of escalating what was meant to be an opportunistic grope into a deadly assault. Because some men don't take rejection well. "How are you doing now?" she asks. "I noticed you were rubbing your shoulder when I got here."

Douglas seems surprised by her concern. "The aching is driving me nuts. And not functioning at one hundred percent is frustrating as hell. I miss working out properly. I feel like—" He stops himself.

"Go on."

He seems wary. "I don't know. I just feel like I'm not a cop anymore. Working part-time and doing light duties isn't what I want. In all honesty, I'd rather be following the real leads in this case. But here I am babysitting the search-and-rescue team and waiting for something to happen." His dark eyes look angry. "I didn't become a detective to wait for things to happen."

She feels for him. She's noticed a deterioration in his body shape: formerly strong and muscly, he looks like he's dropping weight. Almost four months of not being able to hit the gym will have an effect on someone who used to go twice a day. "Listen, I can totally appreciate how you feel. Before I got my job back, I was working for Nate as a PI, but it was frustrating because I had no real power over anything and Nate called all the shots. I couldn't have done that long-term. I like having a badge to open doors, and a team around me."

He turns to her and sighs. She realizes then that the smell of alcohol is coming from him. She tries to hide her surprise.

"So what would you have done if Chief Mendes hadn't agreed to rehire you?" he asks.

She shrugs. "I have no idea. I'm not qualified for anything else. Although I did pick up some waitressing experience earlier this year." She smiles. "If this job doesn't work out because Mendes thinks I'm not good enough, then I'm screwed."

Douglas is watching her closely. "You know what? I've always dreaded retirement. But if my shoulder doesn't heal properly, I might have no choice." He shakes his head. "And I'm only forty-five."

So he's drinking because he's worried he'll have to retire early. She'll keep an eye on that. Hopefully he'll pull himself together before it becomes a problem, but if Mendes smells it on him, she might take away the option of retirement. She tries to lighten the mood. "Let's make a pact: if you have to retire and I get fired, we'll start up our own private investigation company. Harper and Douglas Investigate."

He laughs. "I prefer Douglas and Harper."

"Of course you do. But after what you did to me seven years ago, the least you can do is let my name go first." She winks, knowing she's pushing her luck, but he takes it on the chin.

Brody starts barking in the distance and Douglas's radio crackles to life. They hear Mark's voice through it. "Detective Douglas?"

"What is it?"

"Brody's found a body. I repeat: cadaver located."

Madison shares a look with Douglas and finds herself swallowing back a lump in her throat. Is it Ashlee?

He must know exactly what she's thinking because he places a hand on her back as he passes. "Let's take a look."

CHAPTER FORTY-EIGHT

Nate's attempt at finding Father Connor is fruitless. He's been asking around town, showing the priest's photo to anyone who will stop to look, but no one has seen him, which seems impossible as the guy clearly showed up long enough to break into Madison's place. He must have left straight after.

Nate has just managed to avoid the stare of a passing patrol car when he gets a text. He pulls over in the parking lot of a liquor store to read it, keeping an eye on the two guys out front who look like drug dealers. They're watching him too, probably wondering whether he's an undercover cop or a potential customer.

The text is from Hank Collins. *I'd like to speak to you before I send these documents through.*

His stomach dives with dread and his mouth goes dry. All of a sudden he doesn't want to know what's in the documents Rex asked Hank to keep safe. It can't be good news, because Rex would have told him while they were together. He realizes that he doesn't want any more updates on Father Connor. He wants to move on with his life. Accept what happened, be the bigger guy and start afresh. But that's not fair to Stacey and Kristen. Or to Rex, for that matter.

He calls Hank's personal number. "It's Nate. What's the problem?"

Hank is hesitant. "Hi. To avoid anything leaking to the press, I scanned the documents myself, and although I tried hard not to read them, I was pulled in by what Rex found out."

Nate feels tremors of fear running through his body.

"I could just email them to you," continues Hank, "but I felt Rex would probably haunt me until my dying days if I didn't at least prepare you first. Are you alone?"

Nate swallows. "Yes."

"Do you have anyone you trust who could read these with you? For moral support."

He gets a familiar sinking feeling. How much more bad news can he take? "Not right now, no. Just tell me what's in them so I don't have to go through it all myself. I assure you I can handle it."

Hank takes a deep breath and appears to consider it. "Okay, if you're sure. Well, Rex found out through an online obituary that Father Connor's sister—Deborah—has recently passed away."

Nate is surprised to feel sadness for Deborah. He always got along with her until she turned on him in court. She was a meek woman who never stood up to her brother, but in the end, she was complicit in Father Connor's lies. Still, it's not like she was young; maybe she succumbed to cancer or some other disease. "Is that it?"

"No." Hank sighs. "Nate, she hanged herself."

Stunned, Nate lets it sink in. "But she was deeply religious. I can't believe she would take her own life. And why now? Why not after she lost Stacey?" He puts two and two together. "You don't think her brother killed her, do you?"

Hank is fast to reply. "I know for a fact he didn't."

"How?"

"Because I've got a copy of her suicide note. She obviously wanted to cleanse her soul before leaving this world, because she explains *everything*."

Nate is suddenly overwhelmed with relief. Has Deborah admitted that she lied at his trial? Has she finally admitted that her brother killed Stacey? This is huge. This is something concrete he can show the world to prove Father Connor is a cold-blooded killer, not the man of God he pretends to be. He wipes his eyes and clears his throat. "Does she admit what her brother did to Stacey?"

"Oh, she does much more than that."

His whole body is tense. He's finding it hard to sit still. The two drug dealers outside the liquor store have stopped watching him and gone back to checking their phones. They may have a new customer in a few minutes if Nate can't keep his shit together. "What do you mean?"

"You're not going to like any of what I'm about to tell you, I'm afraid, which is why Rex withheld it."

His hands start shaking harder. He runs one of them through his hair. "Just tell me."

"Actually, I think it's best I email you Deborah's suicide note so you can read it in private. Just remember that Jack Connor is not worth going back to death row for. You have to take emotion out of this and react rationally, otherwise things are going to end badly. You understand?"

Easy for Hank to say. "I understand. Email it to me now."

"Will do."

Hank ends the call and Nate's phone immediately pings with a new email alert. He opens it and downloads the attachment. The letter is written in delicate handwriting on lined paper. He suddenly wishes Madison was here, because he doesn't trust his own reaction.

With trepidation, he reads the first paragraph.

I'm sorry for committing the ultimate sin by taking my own life, but I know God will forgive me. In order for him to forgive the other sins I've committed, I need to unburden myself. I need to confess to my part in my daughter's brutal murder.

The hairs on Nate's neck stand up and he shivers. He's been waiting years for this.

I didn't want to believe it at the time, but that's no excuse, because deep down I knew the truth and I let another person pay the terrible price.

My daughter was murdered by her father.

Nate stops reading and looks up. "What?" Stacey hadn't known who her father was; they never met. Deborah told her she split up with him before Stacey was born and that was why she moved in with her brother. He keeps reading.

Jack isn't my brother or Stacey's uncle. He's my partner—and he's Stacey's father.

Blood roars in his ears. His stomach feels like lead. "That sanctimonious son of a bitch!"

So that was what Stacey was going to tell him the night she died. She must have found out that her mother and her supposed uncle had been living a lie. Father Connor spent his days preaching to others the necessity of living their lives by the Bible, all the while breaking every commandment himself. Nate finally understands what Stacey was dealing with in the weeks before her murder; why she had been drinking so much to cope.

Suddenly the penny drops.

That's why Connor killed her. He must've realized she'd found out he was her father and panicked that she was about to expose him to Nate, which would have risked his parishioners finding out he was living in sin and had fathered a child. He would have been dismissed from the Church and shunned by his community. He would have lost everything. It probably would even have made the local news. But to kill his own daughter to stop that from happening? They must have argued over it. He must have lashed out in anger.

He carries on reading.

Jack and I had separate bedrooms so that Stacey didn't find out, but it was still sinful. We started a romantic relationship when I was a young parishioner at his church. He told me we had to pretend to be siblings in order for him to be able to continue his church work, which reached so many people, so I changed my last name to Connor. Stacey found my birth certificate, with my real name on, and got suspicious. It didn't take her long to figure things out. I didn't know that it was Jack who killed her until the murder trial. He never admitted it to me, but it became painfully obvious as the case against Nathaniel Monroe was so weak, and Jack was entertaining Detective Diaz regularly.

Detective Diaz was the cop who ensured Nate looked guilty of the murder by planting evidence. He was the detective who made Nate distrustful of all cops. He finally has confirmation that Diaz took a bribe from Father Connor.

I may not have struck the fatal blows, but I lived the lies that preceded and followed Stacey's death, and for that I am eternally sorry to my daughter.

Tears are running down Nate's face. He's been hunting for the answer to why Stacey was murdered without considering how painful that answer would be. Just when he thinks he can't read anything worse, he sees the next revelation.

There's something else. A woman called Kristen Devereaux was another victim in all this. I don't know if he killed her, but her house keys and driver's license are buried in the backyard of our last rental in New Mexico.

"Oh Christ, no." The photograph found in Madison's house confirmed Kristen's run-in with Connor, but Nate has been praying she managed to get away before he killed her. But if she did, wouldn't she have shown up by now? Wouldn't she have contacted Rex? The police? Maybe not if she was afraid Father Connor would find her again.

He realizes he might never know what happened to her.

Jack Connor is the devil. I can see that now.
God will forgive me because He is good.
Deborah Connor

He lets the phone drop from his hand as he slumps forward onto the steering wheel. The repercussions of Father Connor's actions are never-ending, and Nate doesn't know if he can continue to live the life this man has forced upon him.

CHAPTER FORTY-NINE

Madison's legs feel like lead as she walks toward the heap lying at Mark Fuller's feet. She tries to keep images of Ellie out of her head, but the thought of breaking her promise to find the little girl's mother alive threaten to consume her as she draws near. She nods at Mark before looking down. Then gasps.

The body is easily identifiable, as it's been dead no more than two days. The wildlife and weather haven't yet eroded the features on the face that is staring up at them with a look of horror etched in the open mouth and pained eyes.

She shakes her head before turning to Mark and Douglas. "That's Shane Kennedy." She's astonished to see him lying here and not Ashlee. This raises so many new questions.

All three of them crouch down in the wet leaves for a closer look, and Madison scans his face, neck and body for clues as to his cause of death. Dried blood from his nose and mouth is spilled down his face, and his right eye is completely bloodshot. He looks nothing like the photos she saw of him online, making her think he's avoided the camera for a long time. Perhaps since his brush with the law.

Douglas takes hold of Shane's blue jacket and carefully pulls him forward just enough to reveal the back of his head. Madison sees the injuries that show his head has been bashed in. Splinters of wood stick out of the wound, caught in his bloody matted hair, and it's clear this was done by a tree branch, which suggests it wasn't premeditated.

Mark stands up as his team appears behind them. "What's your next move?" he asks. "Do you want us to continue searching for Ashlee?"

Douglas joins him. "It's getting too dark to continue now," he says. "Thanks for your help today. Why don't you and your team head off and I'll update you tomorrow."

"Sure." Mark lets the other volunteers know they can go home, and Madison envies them. For her, the hard work is just beginning.

Brody is eagerly awaiting the reward he's due for finding the body. Luckily, Madison remembered to bring one of his many balls with her, just in case. Even though she's sickened by their discovery, she throws the ball as far as she can, making him wade into the water to retrieve it. He's so fast he's brought it back within seconds, and he happily munches on it between his two front paws as he lies in the damp undergrowth.

Douglas phones the coroner, followed by Alex at the station. They're going to need him to process the crime scene before the medical examiner removes Shane's body.

Madison tries calling Veronica Webb to get a number for Shane's next of kin, but there's no answer. She has another close look at him. There's no doubt it's the writer, which means the car keys and cell phone found here earlier must be his. She shakes her head, trying to understand why he would be dead. What the hell happened out here?

She thinks about Ashlee. Was she wrong to assume the girl was the victim in all this? They already know she was living a lie; with her false name and fake next-of-kin details. And her aunt didn't have many good things to say about her. Could she be hiding something else? Maybe she lured Shane here to kill him. They could have been in a secret relationship that went wrong. Maybe he was cheating on her and it tipped her over the edge. Or maybe he came to break it off and she took the news badly. Really badly.

No. Madison can force herself to believe Ashlee is capable of attacking Shane. But she's more inclined to believe she did it in self-defense, in order to get away from him. Neither theory explains why the red Ford Fusion was found a mile away from here, and why her baby was left in the car. If Ashlee was the one who killed Shane, wouldn't she have come straight back for Ellie after managing to get away from him?

The image of Ashlee as a killer doesn't reconcile with what her friends have said: that she's a loving mother to Ellie and a hard worker at the diner. There's no way she left Ellie behind by choice. Shane must have abducted her. She must have fought hard to get back to her baby, but for some reason she didn't make it. Even though her aunt made her out to be troubled and hard work, Madison considers whether Ashlee left her aunt's home for different reasons. Perhaps she ran away because she was being abused or neglected. But what's any of that got to do with Shane Kennedy? It doesn't make sense.

Douglas returns. "Alex is on his way, as is Dr. Scott. The officers who were helping with our search are about to cordon off this whole area and search for the murder weapon. Although," he looks around at the broken branches on the ground around them, brought down by the recent stormy weather, "I don't know how we'd find the specific branch used."

She agrees. "It's highly unlikely we'll find it, and it could have been thrown in the lake anyway, washing away any traces of DNA. But we might get lucky." She looks at him. "Do you have any theories on who killed him, and why?"

He crosses his arms. "Well, we've got to look at what he and Ashlee have in common." He waits for her to figure it out.

"He writes crime and she reads it?"

"No. Think about it: Ashlee works at the diner and was reported missing by her boss. Shane Kennedy was at the diner to give an interview for the *Crime and Dine* podcast."

She nods. "Vince Rader."

Douglas says, "He was the last person to see Shane alive, other than Ashlee. And what if he called Ashlee to come back to the diner for something after the other staff had left?"

"But what's his motive to kill either of them?"

Douglas's theory falters there. "Okay, maybe he intentionally killed Shane, and was taken by surprise when Ashlee unexpectedly witnessed the whole thing by coming back to meet the writer?"

She's not so sure that's a sound theory. But she thinks of the podcast interview Shane gave. She uploaded the copy Vince gave her to the cloud earlier so she could listen to it as soon as she had a chance. "Give me a minute." She pulls out her cell phone and wanders up the hill that overlooks the town. The sun has almost completely set, so the buildings are illuminated beneath her. It looks pretty, despite what's decomposing just a few feet away.

She finds the recording and speeds ahead of what she already listened to with Vince in his apartment. Letting it play she waits to hear about the case Shane was in town to research for his next book.

SHANE: So when you got in touch and told me about what had happened to your wife and grandson, I thought it would be a good case to look into. The more I delve, the more interesting the case appears to be. I'm hoping I can find some lead that was missed. Something that results in answers for you.

VINCE: Well, a fresh pair of eyes on the case certainly can't do any harm.

SHANE: What can you tell me about Ruby and Oliver's disappearance that I won't find online? Are there any leads the police failed to follow?

VINCE: Oh, plenty. Unfortunately, Lost Creek PD aren't the most competent police department. Detective Douglas has a stick so far up his ass I'm surprised he can still talk.

She presses stop. Goosebumps cover her arms as she realizes Shane was working on a book about the disappearance of Vince's wife and grandson. A feeling of both excitement and dread runs through her body.

Douglas looks alarmed as she fills him in. "And Vince was helping him with it?" he says.

"Apparently."

Douglas looks down at Shane's body. "No way. Something doesn't add up." He thinks about it for a minute. "I led the investigation into Ruby and Oliver's disappearance, and I've got to tell you, I always felt like Vince was involved somehow. But without the bodies, I had no evidence."

Wiping away the fine drizzle that's starting to fall, Madison says, "He told me you'd come to the conclusion that she'd run away with a lover, presumably taking her grandson with her."

"That was one theory Mike went with, but I always believed Ruby Rader and her grandson were killed in this town, and I just know that one day their bodies will be found by a dog walker or a jogger."

She's not surprised Vince was the main suspect in their disappearance, but with no evidence or new leads, how will they ever know what happened to them?

Douglas looks serious. "What if Vince was afraid that Shane Kennedy was getting too close to the truth and needed to be silenced?"

That's exactly what Madison is thinking.

CHAPTER FIFTY

Nate has no leads on Father Connor and has to assume the guy is long gone. The next time he hears from him will probably be via another delusional email. He's feeling drained, both emotionally and physically, with both his bones and his mind longing for some kind of rest. He knows he can't go on like this for much longer, chasing a madman. He needs peace.

He feels for Madison's gun. It's still in his jacket pocket. He's never fired a gun in his life, so it's not like he'd be a great shot even if the moment ever comes when he's face to face with Stacey's killer.

With nowhere else to go and the sun setting fast, he heads to the only Catholic church in town. He needs comfort right now, and even after everything he's been through, there's still no substitute for being surrounded by the calming environment of a church. Most people leave prison having found God, but Nate was the opposite. He went in believing and came out uncertain, which is why he keeps returning. He's seeking some kind of sign.

Sitting on a pew in the empty building, he stares ahead at the statue of Jesus Christ. The familiar musty smell helps him relax a little, and he finds himself wondering whether he can ever allow himself to truly believe again. He closes his eyes and tries to pray, but the words sound hopeless in his head. What does he ask for? That Father Connor dies soon? That he himself doesn't die? That he goes back in time and stops any of this from happening?

Quiet footsteps pass him and he opens his eyes just as one of the doors to the confessional box closes. Perhaps the parish priest could see the tension in Nate's shoulders, or perhaps he could sense his wavering faith. A good priest always knows the signs of a troubled person. That's his job.

Nate considers whether to go and talk to him, but something holds him back. Does he have anything to confess? Would it help him to speak his thoughts aloud? Does he really want to be reconciled with God?

He figures it can't do any harm. After all, he has nothing left to lose.

His legs are heavy as he walks over to the confessional. His hand hesitates at the door. Eventually he opens it and steps inside.

Once seated, he says, "Bless me, Father, for I have sinned. It has been…" he tries to think back, "a long time since my last confession."

The priest remains silent, giving him the time he needs to list his sins. The confessional box smells of polished mahogany. The confined space makes him think of his tiny prison cell on death row, and the lack of fresh air makes his chest tighten. He tries not to panic. He needs to remember that, unlike his cell, he can leave this box at any time.

He takes a deep breath. "I've had impure thoughts."

"Of what nature?" asks the priest.

Nate hesitates. A smell hits him that brings back long-forgotten memories. "I want to kill a man."

The priest remains silent. Is any priest shockable? Probably not. They speak to all kinds of desperate people and they hear all kinds of sins.

"And I want his death to be long and painful, in retaliation for the pain he caused the people I loved. For the murders of people I loved. For taking them away from me too soon, and for not letting them live the lives they were entitled to. I want him to live one day of my life, to experience what he's put me through." He pauses. "And I want his death to be violent."

As he unburdens himself, Nate realizes that the thoughts he's been having aren't sinful. They're understandable. Because they're human. He's supposed to feel this way. If he didn't feel his losses this deeply, if he didn't want revenge, what kind of person would that make him? It's a relief to finally come to this conclusion, because he has felt like a monster for wanting another person dead. It's been a heavy weight on his shoulders. Perhaps if he accepts he's only human, he can stop turning to drugs for comfort.

He feels his chest relax and he takes a deep, cleansing breath. Maybe he can finally stop punishing himself. He doesn't know if this insight has been bestowed upon him for confessing the thoughts aloud, but he'd like to believe that. He'd like to believe that if he hadn't set foot inside this confessional box today, inside this church, he wouldn't have been enlightened. He'd like to leave here believing in God again. Believing there is somewhere every person can go to for reassurance and comfort. To accept that doing their best, for themselves and others, is all anyone can do.

"Do you intend to act on your sinful thoughts?" asks the priest.

Nate slowly nods. He feels lighter than ever before. He turns to the voice behind the screen. "I'm afraid so, Father Connor."

He pulls Madison's gun out of his pocket, but before he can lift it, Father Connor has his own gun against the screen between them.

"Then you truly are going to hell." The priest fires the first shot.

Nate ducks in time, feeling the wooden splinters hitting his face, before leaping forward, out of the booth. It was the smell of Brylcreem that gave Father Connor away. He's the only guy Nate's ever met who uses the stuff, and he hasn't smelled it for a long time.

He rolls over and gets to his feet just as Father Connor pushes his own door open, aiming the gun at Nate's head. He hears the bullet whistle past him.

Even though Nate figured out it was him, it's a shock to see the man in person after all this time. He's fantasized about this moment for so long. But the man in front of him is old and withered; it's no longer a fair match. He does, however, still bear a strong resemblance to the woman Nate intended to marry. It's a shock to his senses, making the moment feel surreal.

He lifts Madison's gun, aims it at Connor's chest, and pulls the trigger. It clicks, but it doesn't discharge. Has he left the safety on? His inexperience with guns is going to get him killed. Panicked, he launches forward, knocking Father Connor over and headbutting a pew on his way.

Nate experiences an overwhelming dizziness as the priest manages to get up and run past the altar and out of sight. A cold knot of fear threatens to consume him. He feels like he's about to suffer an anxiety attack, now of all times. His chest is constricted, making him gasp for air, so he stumbles in the opposite direction, out of the church and into the safety of the darkness.

Outside, he feels compelled to call Madison, to hear her voice. It might calm him down. It might stop him from getting killed here tonight. He collapses behind a large headstone.

She answers quickly and all he can say is, "It's me."

"Nate? Where are you?"

"I'm with *him*." He looks at the gun in his hand. "Madison, your gun." He's struggling to steady his breathing. "I can't think straight and it's not working. How do I switch off the safety?"

"No. Nate, don't even think about it."

"Madison!" he yells, desperate for her to help him. "Listen to me: he's armed and he almost killed me. I tried shooting him, but nothing happened. Is your gun broken?"

"Holy shit, Nate. Where are you?"

"I'm at the Catholic church."

"I'll head there now, with backup."

"No! No backup. If you bring anyone else, I'll leave and you'll never see me again."

She goes silent.

"I can't trust the police, Madison. I want to finish this. I have every right to kill him."

"No, Nate!" She's pleading with him now. "You'll be no better than him if you do that! And when all this is over, I know you'll regret it. Leave him to me and my team and get out of there, because nothing good will come of you killing him."

He shakes his head. "You can say that because you didn't know Stacey or Kristen. You barely knew Rex." He peers around the headstone. He can't see anyone in the dark.

"I'm only five minutes away. I'm going to meet you there, and I promise I'll come alone. Just do not kill him, Nate."

Before he can protest, Madison hangs up. "Shit." He can't risk getting her killed. He has to go back inside and finish this.

CHAPTER FIFTY-ONE

As soon as Nate is through the door, Father Connor appears from the darkness and strikes out at his head. Nate drops to the floor near the pews, Madison's gun sliding away from him. His ears are ringing and he feels something warm running down his temple. His fingers find the wound and his sticky blood, making him wince.

Father Connor hovers over him with his gun outstretched. "You're the reason my daughter died. *You're* the reason my life was ruined."

Nate shakes his head. "You killed her, not me."

Connor ignores him. "Seeing as you're in the mood to confess, tell me how you ruined my daughter. Tell me how you turned her to a life of sex and alcohol. To a life of *sin*."

Nate's eyes feel like they're never going to focus properly again. A sudden pain pierces his brain when he tries to move. He looks up at the priest, who's just a misshapen blob, and feels anger building in his chest. "Stacey died a virgin." He's shouting now. "And she was drinking because she found out about *your* sins." His eyes clear a little and he can tell Father Connor looks unsure of himself. The sneer is fading from his haggard face, so Nate continues. "She discovered you lied to her her whole life; that you were her *father*, not her uncle. She knew you were pretending to be a godly man while you were the one living in sin and projecting your own imperfections onto her. You let her down in every single way imaginable, and then you killed her." His hatred is giving him strength. He intends to get up off the floor and lunge at Father Connor when he can catch him off guard.

The priest's face is contorted in rage. "My hand might have delivered the fatal blow, but your presence in her life caused her death. You brought ungodliness to her under the guise of love. *You* made her sin."

Nate can't control himself. "She didn't sin!" he shouts at the top of his voice. His vision finally focuses and he kicks out as hard as he can into Father Connor's looming face. As the priest falls backwards, dropping his gun, Nate pulls himself up using a pew. He grabs for the gun, knowing from the priest's earlier shots that this one works. Standing over Father Connor with his foot pressing down on his chest, he has to clutch the pew for support with his spare hand because of the pain in his head. "You killed Rex, didn't you?"

The look of satisfaction on the old man's face is sickening. "He was complicit in getting you out of prison. He tried to put up a fight, but then quickly gave up when he realized he'd already drunk the poison."

Nate shakes his head in disgust. "He was already dying before you murdered him."

Again, uncertainty flashes across the priest's face.

"He only had months to live, so you didn't win anything by killing him. You actually stopped him suffering months of worse pain."

Father Connor remains slouched against the holy water font. Any movement has it rocking back and forth, spilling water onto his forehead. His nose is leaking blood down his white dog collar. Nate takes immense satisfaction knowing he's broken his nose. Rubbing his own blood from his eyes, and feeling like his head is going to explode, he leans back against the pew. Instead of using his weight to keep the priest in place now, he points the gun at his chest. Killing this despicable man won't bring Stacey or Kristen back, but it will relieve all the emotions he's bottled up for nearly twenty years. It will put an end to it all.

Won't it?

He aims the gun at Father Connor's head now, his shaking hand giving away his need to get this over with.

"Nate, no!" Madison rushes through the door, bringing a blast of cold air with her. He risks a quick glance in her direction to see if she's come alone. Brody runs up to them and quickly realizes something's wrong. He stands over the priest, staring intently whilst emitting a menacing throaty growl. Nate watches as Madison draws her gun. He waits to see who she'll aim it at.

She hesitates, and he can tell she's trying to assess how likely it is that he'll shoot the priest. Eventually she points her gun at Father Connor. He's relieved. It's reassurance that he's not going to be completely alone now Rex is gone. Maybe she can fill the gap he's left.

He looks down at the coward at his feet. He wants to rip him apart with his bare hands. A bullet is too good for him. Too fast.

Madison steps into his line of vision, holding her free hand out for the gun he's holding. "Give it to me."

He wipes his eyes. "I can't do that, Madison."

Placing her hand on his outstretched arm, she lowers her voice. "Nate? You'll be no better than him if you kill him."

At their feet, Father Connor laughs. "Go ahead, Nathaniel. You'll end up back where you belong: on death row with the other sinners. Except this time you'll be executed, because neither Rex Hartley nor Kristen Devereaux is around to help you."

At the mention of Kristen's name, Nate kicks the priest hard in the ribs. "What did you do to Kristen?" Then, shouting, "Where is she?"

Wincing at the pain, Father Connor has to compose himself. "I'm not telling you that. I want you to wonder whether she's dead or alive for the rest of your life."

Nate sees red. His hand is sweating and he's losing his grip on the gun. It's now or never.

Madison looks down at the priest, her own gun still trained on his chest. "We're going to make sure everyone knows what you did and who you really are under that crucifix around your neck. And I'm going to make sure you're still alive to suffer the repercussions."

He sneers at her. "That's not going to happen."

Nate can't understand why he's so sure he won't pay for his crimes. Is it because he's intending to kill himself at the first opportunity? No, he doesn't think Father Connor would do that. In which case, there's only one explanation: he wants to be killed. He wants a way out that doesn't involve taking his own life. He wants Nate to do it for him. Not only will that end his misery, it will put Nate back in prison.

Madison turns back to him. "Give me the gun."

He looks into her sincere blue eyes. She cares about him, he can see that. But at this moment in time he doesn't care about himself. He realizes then that he *would* be willing to serve another long sentence if it means Stacey's killer is dead. He would sacrifice the rest of his life for her.

"Let him have his turn on death row." She gives him a reassuring nod. "Let him suffer like you did."

He gulps back his anguish. He wants to be the one to kill the priest. What kind of person does that make him? "What if your department lets him go? They'll arrest me instead."

"I'll notify the FBI. They'll take it seriously."

He doesn't know if the feds are trustworthy.

Madison slides her hand toward his. It feels warm and reassuring. Soft and feminine, like Kristen's when she was the first person to touch his shackled hands in prison after years without human contact. He looks up at the high ceiling, blinking back his torment.

"Nate." She's running out of patience.

Father Connor sniggers beneath them, getting ready to say something else designed to push Nate over the edge.

Nate swallows. Then, surprising himself, he relents, letting Madison take the gun from him.

"You're doing the right thing."

He looks at her. "So why doesn't it feel like it?"

"You're a coward," says the priest with a hate-filled expression. "My daughter was too good for you."

Nate takes his final look at Father Jack Connor. He's nothing but a pathetic old man now. Chasing Nate around the country has clearly taken its toll. Losing Deborah to suicide must have been humiliating. Killing his own daughter must surely weigh heavily on his conscience, no matter how much he tries to convince himself it wasn't his fault.

Nate wonders if he can take satisfaction in knowing that this man is already suffering for what he did. He may have killed two, maybe three people, and got away with fooling his parishioners, but ultimately, he's had no life himself because of his actions.

He turns to the statue of Jesus before closing his eyes and saying a brief prayer. Yes, he thinks he can find solace in that, rather than in Father Connor's death. He has to. He feels the fight go out of him. His shoulders lift. With no words good enough to do justice to how he's feeling, he turns away.

He walks out of the church and into the darkness.

CHAPTER FIFTY-TWO

Madison pulls into her driveway. It's pitch black out and she's exhausted. Nate drove away from the church, but she doesn't know where he went. She had to stay behind to deal with the FBI. They arrived within the hour, and she had the satisfaction of watching Father Connor being taken away in handcuffs. She wishes Nate had stuck around to see it. It might have helped him with closure, if such a thing exists.

As she switches the car's engine off, she watches the light from the TV dancing in the living room window. Owen's staying with his friend tonight and has no idea of what went down, so it's not him. Which means Nate's come home. That's something at least. She was worried she might never see him again. That maybe he'd either driven right on out of Colorado or decided to end his life. She retrieves her spare gun from the passenger seat. She's already checked it over for faults, but there were none. The safety was switched off, so she doesn't know why it didn't work for Nate. She's just thankful it didn't, because if it had, he *would* be on the road right now, fleeing the authorities.

Letting Brody out of the car ahead of her, she climbs the porch steps and enters the house. The dog immediately goes to find Nate, while she locks the front door behind her.

She finds him on the couch in the living room, in sweatpants and a T-shirt. His hair is wet, and he has a large Band-Aid over his right temple and bruising around his left eye socket. Brody immediately sprawls out next to him, upside down with his head in Nate's lap, demanding a belly rub. He looks more like a pet dog now, not the highly trained K9 he was out by the lake earlier.

Nate looks up at her, and she can see his eyes are red. He gives her a remorseful smile. "Sorry for ditching you. I just had to get out of there."

She nods.

"But I stopped for this on my way home." He picks up a bottle of bourbon.

Madison smiles. "Always the best way to apologize. Let me grab a glass."

She opens kitchen cupboards. Once she finds a suitable glass, she checks the back door is locked and then returns to the living room. She closes the drapes in case Detective Russell and her partner swing by looking for Nate, then flops down on the couch next to Brody, kicking her boots off. There are no lights on, just the TV, which is showing music videos from the nineties. She recognizes Kurt Cobain smashing up his guitar. Maybe this was Nate's best era. He would have been a teenager, with the promise of his whole life ahead of him. It was before he ever met the Connor family.

He pours her a double and she downs it immediately. It's been that kind of day. The heat warms her throat and instantly relaxes her. She holds her glass out for another shot.

Quietly Nate asks, "Is it done?"

She turns to him. He looks exhausted, but the frown lines that usually adorn his forehead are gone, and his blue eyes are different somehow, brighter. Maybe the result of a heavy burden being lifted. "Special Agent Lisa Baxter from the FBI will be in touch when she needs your statement."

He nods.

"She's nice, not how I expected the feds to be. They're going to look into Kristen's disappearance now they have him in custody. I'll be turning over the photo of her."

He sips his drink. "Thanks for handling all that. They're going to have a lot of questions and I just don't have it in me to relive the whole sorry saga right now."

"I know. I made her aware of what a long road this has been for you. She says she's got plenty to be getting on with, but there's no getting away from the fact that she'll need to interview you at some point soon."

He nods again.

"And I've spoken to Douglas about the San Diego police. He's been told that Rex's autopsy report confirms he was poisoned but not by what substance yet. The toxicology results should help with that. They're also waiting for the results of the DNA they found under his fingernails. They'll check to see who it matches." She doesn't remind him that his own DNA is on the database from his original arrest, and now they have Father Connor in custody, they can take a sample of his too. "You and I both know it will be Connor's DNA, but until they can confirm that, they still want to interview you. Douglas has managed to talk them into leaving it until the morning, but only because I gave my word you'd go and see them and not flee overnight."

He looks at her. "How did you know I'd still be in town?"

"Because you left this one behind." She strokes the dog. "You'd never bail on Brody."

He smiles, but it vanishes quickly. A cloud crosses his face. Looking down at his drink he says, "Did he say anything as he was taken away?"

Madison thought he might ask that. Should she lie and say Father Connor apologized at the end? Pretend he showed remorse for his actions? It might help Nate if she does. But he probably knows the man is incapable of remorse, and there's his eventual trial to get through yet. No doubt the priest will be just as scathing about Nate during that. Still, she won't tell him what he did say. What only she and the feds heard. She won't give Connor the satisfaction and she refuses to allow his words any power over Nate. "No. Nothing."

He looks at the TV and her heart aches for him. What happened this evening might lead to the fresh start he needs, or it might tip him over the edge. Only time will tell.

Her cell phone rings. It's Kate Flynn. "Hey. How are you?"

"Hey. I hear you've found a body at Lake Providence, but I can't get anywhere near the crime scene. Detective Douglas is keeping all media away. Is it true? And is it Ashlee Stuart?"

Madison runs a hand through her hair. "All I can tell you is that we did find a body with the help of a sniffer dog, but I can't confirm who it is yet."

"Oh God, that's terrible. Is there a reason you can't confirm the identity? What was the cause of death?"

"I can't say anything else. We only found it late this afternoon and we're still processing the scene. Sorry, Kate. You know how it is." She can't risk the press alerting Vince or any other potential suspects. They need to wait on Alex's forensic report to know who might be responsible for Shane's death. "I'll be visiting the morgue in the morning to see Dr. Scott. I should be able to release the victim's ID and cause of death once she's confirmed it."

Kate sighs. "Fine. Just keep me updated, will you? I don't want any of the other guys beating me to it."

"Sure."

Nate looks at Madison as she places her cell phone on the coffee table. "Did Brody find the body?"

She smiles. "He sure did."

He rubs Brody's belly as the dog yawns. "That's my boy." Turning back to her, he asks, "Is it Ashlee?"

"No. It's my prime suspect for Ashlee's disappearance." She sits back and uses the last of her energy to fill him in on what he's missed.

He's clearly surprised. "So do you think Ashlee attacked him in order to get away?"

"It's possible, but unless she was also fatally injured in her escape attempt, she would have come home by now. There's no way she would have left Ellie behind voluntarily. I've asked Douglas to check with the local hospitals again to see if they've had any recent patients with critical injuries. But to be honest, with Shane dead, that leaves Vince Rader as my prime suspect for both his death and Ashlee's disappearance. Although I can't say I'm one hundred percent convinced he's capable of hurting anyone."

"Did you manage to speak to the family of the navy officer who died?"

"Yeah. Vince wasn't involved in her death. They consider him a friend of the family, so that's a dead end."

He considers it. "He tried to get me on his podcast the other day."

"Me too. And I've heard he's trying to get Cody Stevens next."

"The child rapist?"

"Right. So he clearly doesn't care if his interviewees are guilty or innocent as long as he gets the scoop." She takes a sip of her bourbon and thinks about the whole *Crime and Dine* podcast and the fact that Vince is a true-crime fanatic. It leads to a crazy thought. "What if Vince is some kind of vigilante who goes after criminals? I mean, Shane Kennedy had a sexual assault charge that went away when the accuser dropped the charges. Cody Stevens is assumed guilty by everyone, no matter how much he protests his innocence. Maybe Vince thinks Cody got away with his crimes by accepting that plea deal, and now he wants to execute his own form of justice."

"What about Ashlee?" Nate asks. "Does she have a criminal past?"

She sighs. "No. She must have got in the way somehow."

"It sounds to me like you're at the point where you're thinking about this case so much your mind has stopped seeing the bigger picture. You need to get some rest, because that's when your brain will start linking everything together."

"You think?"

"Sure. The answer will come to you when you least expect it. I guarantee it. Besides," he places his empty glass on the side table, "I should probably go to bed. This has gone straight to my head. I didn't eat much today and I'm exhausted." He rubs his temple, near the Band-Aid. "Father Connor hit me so hard my head's throbbing."

"Do you need to go to the hospital?" She hadn't realized.

"No, I'll be fine after a good night's sleep. If not, I'll go tomorrow."

"But you must be hungry. I can order takeout?" She doesn't want him to leave. It's nice having company, and she can't tell whether he's going to spend the night getting high after everything that's happened today. To be honest, she wouldn't blame him.

He looks at her and hesitates. It's as if he wants company too but doesn't want to burden her. "No, that's okay. I'm going to hit the sack." He stands and Brody jumps up too. Looking at the dog he says, "I guess you're sleeping with me?"

Brody barks an affirmative.

"Not before you visit the little boys' room, my friend." Nate turns to Madison. "Thanks for what you did at the church. I'm actually glad you stopped me from killing him. But if the FBI let him escape, or if he somehow gets away with murder…"

He doesn't finish his thought, but she knows where it was going. She smiles sadly. "I don't believe you would have killed him if I hadn't showed up. You're a good person, Nate. No matter how much you believe otherwise."

He doesn't seem convinced. "See you in the morning."

She listens as he takes Brody out into the backyard, and hopes more than anything that he begins to heal now that his ordeal is finally over.

CHAPTER FIFTY-THREE

Early the next morning the sun makes an appearance as it slowly rises between the mountains, giving Madison hope that today might bring better weather at last. It was perfectly clear last night, so frost is glimmering on the ground and her breath materializes before her as she pulls her hat down over her ears and walks from her car to the entrance of the dull building ahead. Although she can see her breath, the sun feels warm on her face and she's tempted to stand basking in it for a few minutes to catch some vitamin D. She doesn't have time for that, though, as she and Nate have been summoned to Chief Mendes's office for nine a.m., so she needs to get her morgue visit over with as quickly as possible.

She yawns. After such an active day she found she couldn't drop off last night, so she listened to the full podcast interview between Vince and Shane Kennedy. Vince sounded genuinely helpful in it, providing Shane and the listeners with all the finer details of his wife and grandson's disappearance. It made it less likely in her eyes that he killed Shane to stop him finding their bodies and discovering he was their killer. She's actually warming to the guy. But without him she has no suspect, so she has to remain open-minded.

As she approaches the door, she remembers Detective Douglas was going to meet her here, but he's nowhere to be seen. She checks her phone and sees a text.

Running late so skipping the morgue, sorry. Also, just received confirmation there was no one found in the empty apartment near Ashlee's or anything to suggest someone had been hiding out there.

She rolls her eyes at his no-show. Inside the building she makes herself known to the receptionist, then waits for the medical examiner to appear. Within a few minutes, a door opens to her right and a tall woman with long brown hair holds her hand out for Madison to shake. "I'm Lena Scott. Pleased to meet you, Detective."

"You too. Call me Madison."

The woman is striking, with a beautiful smile, and has an air of confidence. Madison follows her through to the medicinal-smelling autopsy room, where two assistants are moving a couple of cadavers to the large freezer. Lena walks her to an examining table and pulls back a blue sheet.

Shane Kennedy is naked and the skin on his face is beginning to slide downwards as it disconnects from his skull. His eyes are closed and sunken. Lena moves his head to one side so Madison can see his injury. Now that it's been cleaned and the hair around it shaved, the damage is clear. "That must have been incredibly painful."

"Yes. It would've taken two or three hard blows to cause these fractures to his skull."

"So that's what killed him?"

"Absolutely. I can find no internal injuries or bruising elsewhere, so assuming no drugs show up on the toxicology results, I'm planning to list his cause of death as blunt-force trauma to the head. There are no pinpricks on his arms or nasal damage suggesting drug use, although he could have taken them in another form. Either way, the injuries speak for themselves and tell us this was definitely a homicide."

"Understood."

Lena refers to her notes. "I've cross-referenced his fingerprints and DNA from the database to confirm his ID. It's definitely Shane Kennedy. I hadn't realized he had a previous arrest until my co-worker told me about him. She's a fan of his work, apparently. I only knew him through the *Bitter Road* movie that was based on his book."

Madison nods. "Me too. I'll track down his family so I can deliver the death notification." She'll trying calling his assistant again. She got sidetracked by Nate and Father Connor's showdown after her failed attempt to speak to Veronica Webb yesterday afternoon, and she'd bet Douglas didn't think to call her. Once news gets out to the media, there's going to be intense interest in this case. Maybe that will be good for Ashlee, as it will raise awareness of her disappearance. The more eyes looking for her, the better.

"We'll keep him here until you confirm we can release his body to family." Lena pulls the sheet back up over his face. "Any luck with finding Ashlee Stuart yet? It's just that I know her as Kacie from the diner, so I'm hoping she'll be found alive and well. I'm kind of bracing myself for a Jane Doe to come in any minute that might turn out to be her."

Madison takes a deep breath. "We haven't found her yet, no. Her disappearance is a real riddle at this point, especially now he's turned up dead." She looks down at Shane's covered body.

Lena looks confused, but before Madison can explain how he might be linked to Ashlee's disappearance, the doctor is called away to the phone. She stops long enough to say, "Let me know when you have a next of kin for him."

"Will do." Madison checks her watch. It's time to meet Nate at the station.

Nate's waiting for her outside the front entrance to LCPD. He hasn't brought Brody, and he looks well rested for a change.

"Ready for this?" Madison asks. For all they know, Nate could find himself arrested within the next few minutes.

He shrugs. "Hey, it can't be worse than what I've already been through, right?"

She laughs. "Oh my God. Please don't tempt fate. I just want one week where neither of us is being arrested for something. Is that too much to ask?"

He smiles, but he appears tense as he moves to follow her into the station. He must be expecting the worst.

The detectives from San Diego are already in Chief Mendes's office as Madison and Nate walk in, and Madison notices that Detective Russell appears to have lost her former confidence. She won't make eye contact with anyone, with the exception of a curious glance at Nate every few seconds. She's never actually met the man she was chasing.

Chief Mendes *has* met Nate before. "Thanks for coming, Mr. Monroe," she says. "I understand you had an eventful day yesterday."

He nods. "You could say that. Is this about Rex Hartley or Father Connor?"

"Both, actually." She looks at Detective Russell, who stands up.

"You shouldn't have disappeared when you heard we wanted to question you, Mr. Monroe. That was a cowardly thing to do and any detective would assume it pointed to your guilt."

Madison is quickly overcome with anger. "How dare you call him a coward? You can't even begin to appreciate what—"

Nate touches her arm, cutting her off. "I'm not here to soothe your ego, Detective Russell. Am I still a suspect for Rex's murder or not?"

They all look at Russell, and it obviously pains her to say it. "No. The DNA found under his fingernails matches that taken from Jack Connor overnight. And Connor has been photographed by the feds. He has some scratch marks around his neck that appear to be defense wounds made by the victim."

Nate's shoulders lower with relief. "So I assume you've arrested him for Rex's murder?" he says. "And that he'll also be arrested for the murder of his own daughter?"

Detective Russell turns to her partner, unsure of herself. "His daughter?" she says. "I'm not aware he had a daughter. I mean, he's a priest, he should be celibate." She laughs sarcastically.

Unsmiling, Nate clarifies. "Turns out he didn't take his vows seriously. Stacey Connor was his daughter, not his niece. Deborah Connor was his secret partner." His voice falters and Madison resists the urge to place a reassuring hand on his back. He filled her in on these new revelations over breakfast earlier, and although she was surprised, nothing about Father Connor can shock her anymore.

Russell looks alarmed. "I wasn't aware of that. Do you have evidence?"

"I've seen Deborah's suicide note, where she confirms everything. I'll be giving a copy to the FBI."

Chief Mendes picks up on Nate's discomfort. "I'll make sure all the relevant agencies know what they should be doing. Leave it with me. You're free to go. And I'm sure the detectives will join me in offering you our deepest sympathies for the loss of Mr. Hartley."

Nate looks at everyone in turn, to check they're serious. "When can I bury him?"

Russell shrugs. "The San Diego coroner will probably release his body within the next week or two, once we have everything we need to secure a conviction."

He nods, and Madison leads him out of the office. All eyes are on them as they leave the station, and she takes him around to the side of the building, which is out of view of any windows. There she pulls him to her and hugs him tight. "It's over, Nate. It's finally all over."

His body is tense at first, but he eventually relaxes into her and squeezes her tight. Father Connor will be convicted of murder. He has to be. Which means Nate can start living again.

Her phone rings, but she ignores it, until it rings again immediately. Letting go of Nate, she checks the display. It's Chief Mendes. "I have to go back in. Are you going to be okay?"

He nods. "I'll be fine. I'm going to head to Ruby's Diner to order the biggest breakfast they do."

She laughs. "I don't blame you. Hey, if you get a chance, would you collect Owen from school this afternoon? I called him last night to fill him in on everything that's happened and said I'd give him a ride home, but I might get caught up here." Really, she's just giving him something to do. He needs to keep busy while he processes everything.

"Sure. I'll text him to arrange a time. Maybe we'll pick up some takeout and candy on the way home, seeing as today's Halloween."

She'd forgotten about that. "Thanks."

His smile fades as he looks over her shoulder. She turns and watches the San Diego cops drive out of the parking lot. "Good riddance to bad rubbish." Turning back to him, she says, "Any other plans for today?"

He nods to his new minivan. "I need to trade that bad boy in for something better." He smiles. "I mean, it's not exactly a babe magnet, is it?"

She laughs as he walks away. She has a feeling he's going to be okay. As long as he can find something to occupy himself with now that he's not hunting the priest.

Back inside the station, she heads straight to the briefing room, where Detective Douglas is updating everyone on the body found at Lake Providence. "So, given everything we now know, our primary suspect for Ashlee Stuart's disappearance and Shane Kennedy's murder is Vince Rader. I'm going to bring him in for questioning after this meeting, but we still don't know where Ashlee is, so we need to step up our efforts. It's highly unlikely at this stage that she'll be found alive, but we can't say that to the press or her friends and co-workers."

Madison is annoyed. She should be giving this briefing. She steps forward. "I really don't think Vince is our guy. I understand why he makes a good suspect, but with everything I now know about him, I just can't see it."

Douglas crosses his arms. "With all due respect, unless you have anyone else in mind, I'm bringing him in."

Chief Mendes says, "I agree with Detective Douglas. He was the last person to see Shane Kennedy alive, and Ashlee obviously worked for him. Plus, we know now that Kennedy was in town to research the disappearance of Vince's wife and grandson. Sergeant Tanner, do we have Ashlee's cell phone records yet?"

Steve steps forward. "I've been promised they're coming to me by lunchtime."

Alex speaks up. "I was unable to access Shane Kennedy's phone as it was too badly water-damaged, so we'll be relying on his cell provider to send us his call logs."

Steve adds, "They've been less forthcoming than Ashlee's provider, but I'll keep at it."

Chief Mendes turns to Madison. "I assume you've searched Ashlee's apartment already?"

She nods. "Alex has checked it thoroughly, but nothing was found to suggest she was hurt or abducted from there. I've been to the morgue this morning, and Dr. Scott confirmed what we already know: Shane Kennedy died from blunt-force trauma to the head. I'll be tracking down his family as soon as possible."

Chief Mendes nods. "Okay, people, let's locate Ashlee Stuart before the press find out a hotshot writer has been murdered in our town."

As Madison watches everyone disperse, Douglas approaches her.

"I'm going straight to the diner to bring Vince in for questioning. Do you want to be in on the interview?"

She shakes her head slowly. "I don't like this, Don. It doesn't feel right. He's been nothing but helpful when I've questioned him about both our victims, and he was more than cooperative with Shane when he was questioned about his wife and grandson's disappearance. I really don't want to bring him in unless we have some concrete evidence, as he's been through so much already. I just don't think he's our guy."

"Well, I guess we'll find out." Douglas ignores her concerns and walks away.

CHAPTER FIFTY-FOUR

Madison sends a request for a DNA test to be done on Ellie Stuart to see if Shane Kennedy was her father. If he was, it will finally explain the link between the pair of them and give her a possible motive for Ashlee's disappearance. Perhaps Ashlee was suing him for child support and he didn't want to pay it. In the meantime, she needs to break the news of his death to his assistant.

Veronica Webb answers straight away and sounds harassed. Madison cautiously tells her she has an update on Shane's whereabouts.

"Well, if he doesn't call me soon I'm going to quit, because I'm sick of the lack of respect. I have three other authors I work for, yet he's the one who takes all my time!" Veronica pauses. "Go on then, where's he been hiding?"

Madison takes her opportunity to get a word in. "It's not good news, I'm afraid. Shane was involved in some kind of attack and succumbed to his injuries. I'm afraid he was found dead here in Lost Creek late yesterday afternoon."

A sharp intake of breath. "What? You're kidding, right?"

"I'm afraid not. I'm sorry to be the one to break it to you. We're investigating his death as a homicide."

"Oh my God." Veronica is sniffing back tears.

"I know, I'm sorry. And I hate to ask you questions at a time like this, but you're my only link to information about Shane at the moment." Madison pauses, giving Veronica some time to compose herself, before saying, "There's a young mother who we believe was with him at the time of his death and who is now missing. We have reason to believe she's also at risk of harm, so I need to ask whether you know of any other allegations against Shane other than those from 2016?"

"I can't believe it." Veronica's voice is quieter now. "Who would do such a thing?"

"That's what I'm going to find out. Does he have a partner?"

"Not that I know of."

"What about kids?"

"No, none."

Madison wouldn't be surprised if he chose not to disclose anything about his private life to his assistant. "Do you know of anyone who might have a vendetta against him?"

"Not at all! And those allegations were false. Anyone who knows Shane knows he's not into teenage girls. The accuser was just a bored schoolkid who wanted some attention, either from her parents or from her favorite writer. I mean, I'm not victim-blaming or anything, because I know these things *do* happen with famous people abusing their power—all the time—but not with Shane. I think she was embarrassed when he asked her to leave as soon as he realized she'd come up to his room alone. And so in retaliation she accused him of coming on to her, not realizing the implications of her actions. Not one other person has made any allegations against him before or after that, and even if they did, it would be lies. Shane was devastated by it and almost quit writing altogether. I mean, it's because of those allegations that he turned to drink."

The guy paid her wages, so she's bound to be on his team, but Veronica is so passionate about his innocence that Madison is inclined to believe her. But then why were Ashlee and her baby in his car? She considers the weather that night. It was raining hard; maybe he was simply giving her a ride home. Could it be that innocent? But then how did they come off the road? And why is Shane dead? "Okay, thanks for clarifying things. I'm going to need the contact details of his next of kin; parents ideally."

"His parents have passed. He has one brother, but they have no relationship anymore."

Madison straightens up. "Why not? Is there animosity between them? Could his brother have wanted to harm him?"

"No, nothing like that. Last we heard he was living in Hawaii running a T-shirt store on the beach. He's an addict who probably couldn't even afford a flight over here. There's been no contact between them for years."

Disappointed, she relaxes. "So who would you recommend I call to sort arrangements for the release of Shane's body?"

Veronica breaks down at the mention of his body, and Madison has to wait for her to compose herself again. Finally she says, "Sorry. He has friends. Let me make some calls and get back to you. It might take a couple of days."

"No problem. I appreciate your help and I'm sorry for your loss." Madison ends the call and takes a deep breath, then looks up when she hears Douglas's voice from across the office. He's walking Vince Rader through to one of the interview rooms, and Vince looks pissed.

Stella has noticed them too. She removes her headset. "What's Vince accused of now?"

Madison gets up from her desk and approaches her. "Nothing yet. He was the last person to see our dead guy alive, and we need a clearer understanding of what happened that night."

Stella gives her a look to suggest they're wrong to bring him in and she's itching to give her two cents. But instead she says, "I'll keep my opinion to myself, as I wouldn't want to upset you."

"Spit it out, Stella. I can take it."

She turns in her seat to face Madison. "That poor man went to hell and back when Ruby and little Oliver disappeared. Since then, he's had to live with the constant speculation about whether or not he hurt them. But think about it: why would he stay in town if he was involved in their disappearance? It was six years ago;

he could be long gone by now. And it's not like he's been able to claim any life insurance for Ruby, because there's no body so she's not considered dead."

Madison crosses her arms. "Some killers think they're too intelligent to get caught, so he could be staying because he's confident he hid or destroyed their bodies well. Besides, it won't be much longer before he can have his wife declared legally dead. That's when the life insurance would pay out."

Stella waves a dismissive hand. "Oh peesh. He's no killer. And if I'm wrong about that, I'll quit my job."

Madison eyes her suspiciously. "Are you two dating or something?"

Stella flushes bright red from her neck to her temples, which is something Madison's never seen her do before. "Don't be stupid. Now leave me alone, I've got work to do."

Madison smiles. It's clear that Stella has the hots for Vince Rader. But that doesn't make her the best judge of character.

Back at her desk, she opens the CCTV footage from the gas station. As she's been working on other leads, she asked Douglas to watch the whole tape—not just the clip of the abandoned car driving by—in case there was anything of interest. He said he hadn't found anything, so she feels like watching it again could be a waste of her time, but she wants to make sure they're not missing anything. No tiny detail that could prompt a new lead.

She starts it at the moment the red Ford drives past the camera and watches for what must be the tenth time. The footage is dark and grainy, with no sharp outlines on any objects, making her eyes distort the more she focuses. She doesn't have time to watch the whole tape from the beginning, and she shouldn't need to now Douglas has watched it, but she rewinds to ten minutes before the car arrives on screen and hits play. No other cars drive by. She watches as the gas station employee takes a quick cigarette break under the camera before heading back inside. She had Shelley question him about that night, but he hadn't noticed anything out of the ordinary, which means that whatever happened started after Shane and Ashlee passed by.

Once the car has driven past, she's tempted to switch the video off, but she leaves it rolling. After two minutes, nothing has happened. Three, four, five long minutes of nothing but a spider making a web to the left of the camera. It looks huge this close to the lens, and the sight of it makes her shudder. Then it falls away. She rubs her eyes and considers grabbing a coffee from the kitchen. Until headlights appear on the left of the screen, beyond the camera's view.

She leans forward, waiting to see if it's a customer for the gas station. The car approaches slowly, appearing to speed up as it passes the station. "What the…?" It's heading in the same direction as Shane's car. "Dammit," she mutters. "Why didn't Douglas tell me about it?" The obvious answer is that he didn't watch the whole tape like he promised.

She calls Alex. "There's a second car on the security footage. I need the make, color, and license plate if possible. And I need to know who's driving it—male, female, any passengers."

"That could be difficult based on the quality of the footage, but I'll do what I can," he says. "What time stamp am I looking at?"

She checks her screen, which is paused on the second car. "It's two thirty-one a.m. when the second car appears."

"Leave it with me."

"Thanks." She thinks of Vince being the last person to see Shane alive. Did he follow the novelist after the podcast interview was over, with the intention of silencing him? Was Ashlee accidentally caught up in it? If Vince didn't know Ashlee was in the car, he could have been surprised. It would explain why the baby was left unharmed. Ashlee would have been a witness, and witnesses need to be silenced, but babies don't talk.

She heads straight over to the interview room, where Douglas and Vince are sitting opposite each other. "Hi," she says, trying to keep her demeanor light. "I hope you don't mind me joining you a little late. Thanks for agreeing to answer some more questions."

Vince sighs. "I've told you all along that I'm happy to help." He appears relaxed, maybe a little too relaxed. Is that because he knows he's innocent or because he managed to fool the police once before?

Douglas is leading the interview. "What time exactly did Shane Kennedy leave your apartment on the morning of October twenty-eighth?"

"I double-checked the recording and that ended at precisely one fifty-three a.m. It only took him a few minutes to pack up and leave, so he was out of my apartment by two."

"And when you opened the door to let him out, did you see anyone hanging around outside in the shadows?"

Vince gives him a wry smile. "It was pitch black outside of the reach of my security light, so there was no way of seeing anyone who didn't want to be spotted. But I certainly didn't hear anyone. Mr. Kennedy walked away in the direction of the White Woods after telling me he'd parked a distance away."

"Why do you think he did that?" asks Madison. "I mean, he could've parked in the diner's parking lot easily enough at that time of night."

Vince sips a coffee Douglas must've made him, taking his time. "I have no idea. I can only presume it's because he wasn't completely sure he wouldn't get spotted at such a public venue. Like I said, he's camera-shy these days."

"Did you drive after him for any reason?" She's thinking of the second car in the CCTV footage. "Maybe he left something behind and you decided to catch up with him?"

Vince eyes her suspiciously. "Absolutely not."

Until Alex confirms the make of car and who was driving it, she doesn't want to give anything away.

"About Kennedy being camera-shy," says Douglas. "During your interview did he make any mention of the allegation against him?"

"Not directly, no. He just made some jokes about his notoriety in general and about how he struggled with it."

Douglas shifts in his seat. "I understand he was here to research the disappearance of your wife and grandson. It seems odd to me that you'd want to help him do that."

Vince leans forward and rests his elbows on the table, hands clasped. "So here it is." He shakes his head. "I know exactly where you're going with this line of questioning, Detective, and it doesn't surprise me. It does, however, disgust me that you're willing to pin this man's murder on me in the hope of closing a cold case."

Sitting back and remaining calm, Douglas says, "What do you mean?"

Madison feels the tension rising and she actually feels sorry for Vince. It must be difficult living under the shadow of doubt for so long, whilst grieving for your loved ones. But is he fooling her? She's normally a good judge of character, and even now she can't believe he's a killer. On paper it looks bad for him, but taking into account his personality and circumstances, she thinks Mendes and Douglas are wrong to suspect him, even if that leaves her with no one in the frame for Shane Kennedy's murder.

"So let me get this right," says Vince. "You think I killed my wife and grandson, and when I heard this hotshot crime writer was going to investigate—was going to do what *you* failed to do properly—in order to write a book about it, I got worried he would find their bodies and expose me as the killer." He laughs sarcastically. "Have you ever thought of writing soap operas, Detective Douglas? You could make a fortune with outlandish storylines like that."

Madison glances at Douglas, who's clearly finding it difficult to remain composed. He also looks tired and disheveled. His tie is pulled loose and he undoes his top button. She thinks she can smell liquor on his breath again, only faintly. Is he unraveling? She'll need to take him to one side and warn him. He won't take it well, but it's better than Mendes firing him.

Her phone rings and she's grateful for an excuse to get out of here. "Sorry, I need to take this." She hears Douglas continue the interview as she gets up and leaves the room, closing the door behind her.

"Madison? It's Shelley."

"Hey, what's up?"

"I've just been called to Ashlee's apartment because her neighbor noticed the door was open. It's been ransacked. The whole place is turned upside down."

Alarmed, Madison heads for the exit. "I'll be right there."

CHAPTER FIFTY-FIVE

Ashlee's apartment is a mess. Every book, ornament and Halloween decoration is on the floor. Framed photos are upside down, and all the drawers are pulled open, their contents haphazardly spilled.

Alex whistles as he slips past Madison and Shelley. "Wow. I guess someone was looking for something." He turns to them. "Put on some protective gear, please, so you don't drop DNA."

Madison steps into a disposable coverall and covers her shoes, then looks around. It took either desperation or anger to make this kind of mess. Everyone in town knows this apartment is empty while Ashlee's missing, so could it have been a burglary? Snapping on a pair of latex gloves, she checks the front door. The yellow police tape is flapping in the wind. "The lock appears to be busted, but it's so flimsy it wouldn't have taken much to get in."

"Do you think Ashlee came back?" asks Shelley beside her.

"God, I hope so." She thinks of Ellie. It would be amazing if Ashlee were still alive. "Maybe she needed to collect some spare clothes and toiletries in order to skip town. If she did injure Shane in a bid to escape, then she could be panicking that she'll be locked up for murder if she comes forward." But that's assuming she was the one who killed Shane, and Madison doesn't think that's what happened.

Alex pulls open his hard case. "I'll dust everything again to see if there are any fresh prints."

Madison thinks of Ashlee's Instagram account. "Alex, did Facebook ever reply to your request for access to her DMs?"

He shakes his head. "Not yet, but they're notoriously slow in replying to anything."

She rolls her eyes. The social media giants have a lot to answer for when they won't allow law enforcement agencies access to information that could save the lives of thousands of young people every year. She turns to Shelley. "I assume it was Justin who called this in?"

Shelley nods. "Said he didn't hear anything and doesn't know how long ago it might have happened."

Alex gets to work as Shelley searches the other rooms. Madison carefully steps over the mess, approaching the copies of Shane's books, which are now lying on the floor. Opening each one at the front, she looks for signed dedications, but there's nothing. The other books are all true crime written by a variety of authors.

She picks up Ashlee's copy of *Bitter Road* and wonders what all the fuss was about with this book and its subsequent movie. She's never read or seen it. Having only glanced at the back last time she was here, she reads the whole blurb this time.

On a quiet summer morning in sleepy Paradise Falls, two twelve-year-old girls, best friends Ella and Kate, set out for school like any ordinary day.

It's only when they arrive home hours later that it becomes clear something terrible has happened. Why was there no tick by their names on the roll call? Why are their classroom seats cold and their lockers unopened? Why has the sparkle in both their smiles disappeared, never to return?

When they later jump to their deaths from Paradise Bridge—holding hands, friends to the bitter end—only two people alive know the truth, and it's up to Detective Brian Blackwood to find them…

Madison frowns. This sounds familiar, but how if she's never read the book? She pulls out her cell phone and googles it. There are hundreds of forums dedicated to talking about the real-life inspiration behind *Bitter Road*. One name jumps out at her: Cody Stevens.

Her stomach leaps in dread. She reads on to confirm what she already knows. Cody Stevens sexually assaulted two young girls who went on to kill themselves, but after serving seven years of his life sentence, he was released from prison last month after taking an Alford plea. Shane Kennedy fictionalized that case in *Bitter Road* and made a ton of money out of it. She tries to think: what's the link between Cody Stevens and Ashlee? Just because one of her favorite books is based on his crimes doesn't mean she's ever met the guy. He was in prison for the last seven years anyway, so she couldn't have.

Fearing the worst, she rifles through Ashlee's true-crime books. Her heart sinks when she finds one about Cody Stevens.

She opens it. The inside page has a personalized dedication in biro: *To Bunny, always yours, love Ace.*

CHAPTER FIFTY-SIX

Madison googles Cody Stevens and quickly learns that Ace was his nickname in prison. "Oh shit." Ashlee was writing to him inside. She must have been obsessed with both the writer of the book and the criminal it was about. And now the criminal's been released.

Madison remembers Nate telling her how many women would write to him when he was on death row. The guards called it fan mail, and that's pretty much what it was: women, and less often men, who were looking for attention from famous killers and convicts. Sure, some of them actually believed that they could help these prisoners, by changing them from their evil ways or helping them to find God, but Nate said it was pretty clear from their letters that most of them were looking for help themselves. For someone to love them.

She stands up. Was Ashlee stupid enough to use her real address in her letters to him and he decided to pay her a visit once he was released? She feels sick when she thinks of the implications: a thirty-four-year-old convicted sex offender building up a relationship with a vulnerable seventeen-year-old fan of true crime. *The mother of a baby girl.* It doesn't bear thinking about.

It could have been Cody in the car that followed Shane and Ashlee toward the White Woods in the early hours of that morning. Maybe Cody was the one who killed Shane, in order to leave no witnesses to his abduction of Ashlee. Or, thinking about the alternative scenario, maybe Shane was the intended victim, for making money out of Cody's crimes. For keeping his name and conviction in the spotlight, reducing his chances of ever being able to get away with assaulting someone else so easily.

Regardless of who Cody's intended victim was, he needs to be located immediately. She keeps hold of the two books and rushes from the apartment without stopping to tell Alex or Shelley where she's going.

Madison bursts into the station. On the way to her desk, she almost knocks out Chief Mendes, who appears unexpectedly from a doorway. All she can do is watch as the coffee Mendes is holding spills down the front of her clean white shirt, even soaking her bra in the process.

She winces at the growing stain. "I'm so sorry, Chief! I didn't see you." Before Mendes can unleash her obvious anger, Madison blurts out, "I've just figured out who might've taken Ashlee Stuart." She tries to catch her breath.

Stain immediately forgotten, Mendes buttons up her navy suit jacket and asks, "Who?"

Steve joins them, and Stella is watching over her computer screen as she talks to a caller. Detective Douglas is nowhere to be seen.

"Cody Stevens."

Mendes opens her mouth but doesn't find any words. She stops shaking the spilt coffee from her hand.

Madison elaborates. "He's the guy who—"

"I know who he is."

She explains what she found at Ashlee's apartment; about the inspiration behind *Bitter Road* and the implications of Ashlee having a signed copy of a book about Cody and his crimes. "As you can imagine, I have a ton of work to do in order to prove my theory. I need Douglas to speak to the prison to find out Cody's last known location." She takes a deep breath. "This should never have happened; they should've been watching him closely, knowing he was at a high risk of reoffending."

"I saw on the news that he's been spotted in Vietnam," says Steve with skepticism. "You sure it could be him?"

She doesn't have proof yet, just a hunch based on the books and the strange circumstances that link both Shane and Ashlee to Cody Stevens. But her gut is telling her he's their best suspect yet. She needs to find out for sure whether Ashlee was writing to him in prison before his release. "I'll know shortly."

Chief Mendes says, "Douglas is off this investigation." She looks like she's doesn't want to tell them why, but eventually she explains. "He's been suspended. He's not fit for work at this time."

Madison's heart sinks and she glances at Steve, who's shaking his head. "Is he okay?"

"No, actually. He has a drinking problem and I caught him about to drive whilst under the influence of alcohol. This information is not to leave the station. I'll be investigating what's going on, but for now we're a detective down."

Madison closes her eyes and sighs. "Poor Don." She already feels like she's been working alone for most of this investigation, so she's confident she can see it through, but she'll need help with some things. "I was hoping he'd lead the search-and-rescue team in checking the lake. We only searched around it before, and with Shane's body being dumped there, maybe we'll find something in the water. Some clue as to where Ashlee is, or maybe her cell phone."

Steve says, "You know who used to be the water search-and-rescue leader, right?"

Both Mendes and Madison stare at him.

"Vince Rader," he says. "He was good at it too, on account of his navy background. But Douglas pissed him off after the investigation into Ruby's disappearance, so Vince quit. Since then, Mark Fuller does the land searches but we have no one qualified to handle a search of a lake that big."

Madison knows what she has to do. "Has Vince been released without charge?"

Mendes nods. "For now." She turns to Steve. "I need you to liaise with the prison and find out where Cody Stevens is living now. I'll make all units aware they should be on the lookout for him and that he could be dangerous."

"Can you authorize the search of the lake?" asks Madison. "I'm going to try to get Vince onboard to lead it."

The chief hesitates as she considers the implications of asking a suspect to get involved in the investigation. "How sure are you about your Cody Stevens theory? Enough to take the heat should you be wrong and it turns out Vince Rader was responsible?"

Madison takes a deep breath. "Even if Cody is the wrong guy, I'm pretty sure Vince is too."

Mendes must decide it's time to trust her. "Okay. Then go ahead. Keep me updated."

Madison rushes to her desk and looks up the number for the prison Cody was incarcerated in. It takes four transfers through the switchboard to be put through to the team who handle inmate post. Once they verify she's a detective, she can finally ask them what she called for. "I understand you keep scanned copies of all incoming and outgoing mail to prisoners, am I right?"

"Sure. Which prisoner are you interested in?"

"Cody Stevens. I know he's been released, but I'm looking specifically for letters from someone who called themselves Bunny and to whom he signed his letters Ace."

The clerk seems amused. "Bunny?" He laughs. "It might take a while. Some of these guys get a lot of fan mail. How about I send you copies of everything he ever received or sent, and you and your team can sift through it all?"

She tries to hide her annoyance. "Sir, there's a seventeen-year-old girl currently missing and this convicted rapist is probably the person who has her. Time is of the essence, so I need you to drop whatever you're doing, locate his mail and only send me letters between him and this Bunny person. There could be something in them that tells me where he's taken her. Until then, her life is in your hands. Do you understand?"

She hears him swallow. "Sure, I understand."

"Good. You can send the scanned copies to me at this email address." She gives him the details.

"I'll start looking through them right away."

"I appreciate it."

As she hangs up, she realizes everyone in the station was listening in.

Stella looks as pale as a ghost. "I really hope that son of a bitch doesn't have her."

Madison nods. "Me too, Stella. Me too."

Steve slams his desk phone down. "I just spoke to a Dave Burrows at the prison, who said he last checked in on Cody a week ago and he was at home. Apparently he's been living in an apartment just outside Denver, but he hasn't secured a job yet—go figure. Dave tried calling him while I waited on the line, but there was no answer to his landline or cell phone. He's going to send officers to his address. They'll break in and search it if they have to, in case he's hiding Ashlee there."

"He wouldn't be that stupid. Sex offenders are careful." Madison shakes her head. "He's involved in this somehow, I just know it. Let me know if they find him."

"Sure thing."

She pulls out her cell phone and heads to an empty interview room, dialing as she goes. Nate answers after two rings. "Nate, I need a favor."

"Sure," he says. "What's up?"

"I think that guy in the news, Cody Stevens, is the one who killed Shane Kennedy and abducted our missing girl. I have a hunch she was writing to him while he was still inside and she probably unwittingly gave him her real address, assuming he'd never get out of his life sentence."

"Holy crap, that's not good."

"How would he have got away with writing to a seventeen-year-old? Did you ever get letters from kids that young?"

He hesitates, and she suddenly realizes she's asking him to go back there, to his time inside. To his credit, he responds. "She probably lied about her age. In theory, prisons check all incoming and outgoing mail, but things are bound to slip through the net. Especially for guys like him. He would have been one of their most popular inmates for mail because of all the news coverage of his trial and the documentaries that've been made about him."

The thought of it makes her feel sick. "I just learned that Shane Kennedy's bestseller, *Bitter Road*, was a fictional account of Cody's crimes. He unwittingly helped build the guy's notoriety with that book and the movie adaptation." She sighs. "I bet he regretted that right before he was killed."

"So you think Cody came for Shane, and Ashlee got caught up in it somehow?"

"He could have come for either one of them. But yeah, that book probably got Shane killed. We're trying to locate Cody, but the prison has lost contact with him. Patrol are being asked to look out for him, but I could really do with getting the search-and-rescue team to search Lake Providence. We might find something that confirms Cody's our guy. Normally Douglas would be in charge of overseeing that, but he's… unavailable. I've been told Vince used to be the volunteer leader for water searches, but we just questioned him about Ashlee's disappearance, so he's not going to want to talk to me right now, never mind help me." She pauses. "Think you can work your magic?"

She can practically hear the smile in his voice. "I'll give it my best shot."

She exhales, relieved to have some backup. "Thanks. Remember, no one knows yet that it's Shane Kennedy's body we found, so try to keep it between the two of you. I suspect Vince will be good at managing the search, but I need you as my go-between. I'll check in when I can."

"No problem."

She slips her phone into her pocket and says a silent prayer that between them they can bring Ashlee home alive.

CHAPTER FIFTY-SEVEN

Nate is at the diner within minutes of Madison's phone call. He runs through the rain to the entrance, leaving Brody waiting in the car. Inside, he runs his hands through his wet hair and looks around for Vince, not sure what kind of welcome he'll get after what Madison told him.

"Hi," says Sue, one of the full-time waitresses. "Can I get you something?"

"Just Vince if he's around."

"Sure." She pours him a coffee. "Take a seat, I'll go find him."

Nate chooses a stool at the counter and looks around. It's quieter than usual. He glances up at the TV, which is switched to some reality show. He suspects the waitresses have grown tired of watching the speculation around their friend's disappearance play out all day on the news.

Vince appears behind Sue; he doesn't look happy. "What do you want?"

Nate spots Carla out of the corner of his eye. She's pretending to be busy, but clearly she's listening in. "I need your help," he says. "You see, I've accepted a job that has me feeling way out of my depth, and I have it on good authority that you're much better placed to help with it than me."

"What are you talking about?" Vince looks like he's about to walk away.

Nate lowers his voice. "This is strictly confidential, but Madison's arranging for the search-and-rescue volunteers to go into the lake and see if they can turn up any clues to Ashlee's disappearance, or maybe some of her belongings."

Vince crosses his arms. "I can read between the lines, Mr. Monroe. You're telling me the police think Ashlee's body could be down there."

Carla gasps and walks away, not wanting to hear any more. Sue leaves to take an order, but not before shaking her head.

"Madison hasn't given up hope of finding her alive, but I'm sure you'd agree it needs checking." Nate looks over his shoulder to see if anyone else is listening in. No one is even looking at them. He turns back to Vince and leans in. "Especially as Shane Kennedy was found dead there yesterday evening."

Vince's arms unfold and fall to his sides. He takes a step forward. "Say what now?"

"That's just between you and me. We need to find Ashlee before the media get wind and risk alerting whoever has her."

"How was he killed?"

"All I know is that he's dead. But there's something else." He gets off the stool and leads Vince to a quiet corner. "I don't know all the details because my call with Madison was brief, but Cody Stevens is now her primary suspect."

"Cody Stevens?" Vince whispers in disbelief. "Christ almighty. If he's got her, she'll be wishing she was dead by now."

Nate hasn't let his mind go there yet; to what Ashlee might be going through with the suspected rapist. But he understands Vince's response. Cody might have been released from prison, like him, but he didn't get a clean slate. He wasn't exonerated. He chose to accept the Alford plea, which means the public will never know for sure whether or not he was guilty of attacking those two little girls. "If you and I can find evidence Cody Stevens has been in town and was involved in Shane's murder, we'd be helping the investigation."

Vince looks torn, and Nate gets it. Why help the department that treated him so poorly after his wife and grandson's disappearance? Eventually he asks, "So I'm not a suspect anymore?"

"I guess not."

"Then why aren't the detectives here asking me?"

Nate shrugs. "All I know is Detective Douglas isn't available and Madison's got a ton of other leads to follow. Besides, she said you'd be the best person to lead the water search because you have experience in that. I'm just the go-between." A customer walks past them and Nate lowers his voice. "Plus, my dog has certain talents."

Vince raises his eyebrows, instantly catching his drift. "You know, the police chief who was in charge before Mendes took over this summer wouldn't search Lake Providence for Ruby and Oliver. The son of a bitch had the audacity to claim the department couldn't afford it, as if they weren't important enough to spend money on. I found out later that he thought I'd killed them and assumed I was focusing on the lake as a way of diverting attention from their real burial place." He shakes his head in disgust.

"That's tough, I'm sorry. And I get your reluctance to help, trust me I do, but we have to think about Ashlee. There's still a chance she could be found alive."

Vince takes a deep breath and nods. "You're right. If I can help find her, then I'm in. But you do realize that you and Detective Harper will owe me a favor?"

Nate raises his eyebrows. "Oh yeah?"

"Sure. I think being guests on my podcast would just about cover it."

Nate laughs. "You're nothing if not persistent."

"Is that a yes?"

He sighs. "I can't speak for Madison, but I'll think about it. Now let's go."

While Vince loads his diving equipment into Nate's new car—he replaced the minivan for a Chevy Traverse earlier today—Nate sends Madison a text to say his mission was successful. She confirms the rest of the search volunteers are already at the lake.

Vince gets in the passenger side and meets Brody for the first time. "Hey, boy. You're a fine-looking beast. I've heard you have a good nose for trouble." Brody leans in from the back seat to sniff every square inch of Vince's face and torso, his tail bashing the window in excitement. Vince chuckles to himself as he strokes the dog. "You're friendly, aren't you? I hope you're not this nice to felons."

Nate has never seen this less serious side of Vince before. It makes him wonder whether his grumpiness is all an act to keep people at arm's length. He knows that feeling. When the worst happens, you feel less able to let people in. He's learning himself that the only way to move on from grief is to take a risk with people, because not trusting anyone is no way to live.

"I used to have a Rottweiler," says Vince. "Most loyal creature I've ever owned. Only problem is, he damn near ate everything in sight." He laughs. "When I'm scraping diner leftovers into the bins at night, I wish he was still alive. He would have eaten the lot and still expected his regular food afterwards."

Nate smiles. Dogs certainly have a special way of getting under your skin.

As he approaches the lake, he notices Kate Flynn's news van. She's standing behind a line of crime-scene tape talking to a police officer.

"Looks like word has already got out about Mr. Kennedy's death," says Vince. "Gloria will keep them out of the way. No one will dare cross her."

Nate parks alongside a cruiser and they all get out of the car. Vince heads straight over to the officer. "How are you, Gloria? I see the vultures are circling."

Gloria laughs and waves a dismissive hand. "They're no match for me. It's good to see you, Vince. I hear you're going to be in charge of the search."

"Well, I'll see what I can do." He moves on to the group of volunteers, who are ready and awaiting instructions. Nate watches as he shakes their hands and confidently issues orders. Within minutes, three of them are entering the water and Vince is pulling on a wetsuit.

Someone calls Nate's name from behind him. Kate beckons him over. "Hey, Nate. Can you tell me anything?"

He shakes his head. "This isn't my investigation. I'm purely here because Brody's assistance was required."

She looks over at the dog, who's waiting by the embankment, eagerly sniffing the scents coming from the water. "So you're looking for another body?"

He gives her a look to suggest he can't say a word.

She rolls her eyes good-naturedly. "Can you at least confirm whether the body found yesterday afternoon was Shane Kennedy? I mean, speculation's rife since his assistant released a press statement to say he had passed away during a trip to Lost Creek."

"I'm sorry, Kate. Like I said, it's not my place to confirm or deny anything. You know what Madison's like: as soon as she's able to tell you something, she will."

Kate's shoulders slump. "Fine." She lowers her mic. "Did something go down at the Catholic church yesterday too?"

He bristles but remains silent.

"It's just that I had someone call in to say they saw Madison and some FBI agents in the area. And apparently the feds took some old guy away in cuffs, but by the time I got over there, the place was empty."

Nate's stomach flips with dread. He's been trying not to think about all that, and of what Father Connor is probably telling the feds about him. And he could do without becoming the latest hot topic again. "If something happened, she didn't tell me about it, sorry. I better go check on Brody."

He walks away before she can ask anything else.

CHAPTER FIFTY-EIGHT

With the daylight slowly fading, Madison sits at her desk staring out of the window while she tries to piece everything together. It's Halloween night, so the street outside is busier than usual, with several families and groups of teens walking by in a variety of costumes. She smiles. Owen used to love trick-or-treating. It makes her wonder whether he's outgrown it now he's seventeen. He must have, surely? Still, maybe she should have dressed up the front of the house a little ready for visitors later.

Looking back at her computer, she sighs. She's been trying to figure out where Cody Stevens could have taken Ashlee. He must've taken off in his own car after running Shane's off the road that morning, but Alex has been unable to identify the license plate from the gas station's security footage, or the make of car. Hazarding a guess, he said he thought it could be a dark-colored Honda Civic.

She takes a sip of water, then searches for Cody's criminal record. In his mugshot he looks cocky, with a smile playing at his lips. He's gazing into the camera like he's on a goddam date with it. There's no fear in his eyes at being arrested. He must've thought he was smart enough to get away with his crimes. The fact that he was right and is now a free man makes her skin crawl. What a creep.

She reads how he coaxed two twelve-year-old girls into his car—a silver Volvo—with a promise of a ride to school. Instead, he drove them to a secluded wood. What he did next is unsubstantiated, because the girls never felt able to give details to the police about their ordeal; it was their families who raised the alarm. The subsequent investigation into their suicides found security footage from various homes and businesses in the area that showed them in the back of Cody's car on the way to the woods. She leans into the screen as she reads. What led to his arrest and subsequent conviction was a mixture of the security footage, witness testimony from people near the area at the time, DNA found at the wooded crime scene, and information gained from a family member who one of the girls confided in shortly after her ordeal.

She skims the extra notes section, which has details of his sentencing. The reason he was sentenced to life without parole, which is perhaps harsher than most rapists get, was because of the victims' ages and their subsequent suicides. Seven years later, he was offered the plea deal that led to his release. All because of the witness who'd lied in court during the trial.

Madison's computer pings with a new email notification and she spots the sender's name flash up in the corner of her screen. It's the guy she spoke to on the phone at the prison earlier. She opens it.

Detective Harper,

I've attached scanned copies of all letters to and from "Ace" and "Bunny" during the period of their correspondence, from 2017 to just before his release from prison last month.

  Ace is definitely Cody Stevens and Bunny is a nickname Cody gave to a woman named Kacie Larson after she first started sending him letters.

Her heart sinks. She wanted to be wrong.

She initiated the contact and used a PO box for the return letters, which is what we advise everyone to do regardless of the fact that inmates don't see correspondence addresses. However, in her final letter she let slip that she resided in Lost Creek. Unfortunately, it wasn't picked up by any of my staff. If it had been, we would have redacted it.

There was nothing in her letters to suggest she was a teenager, but in hindsight, some of the content could have given her away. She included a couple of photos of herself, which inmates are allowed to receive if they're not nudes or sexually provocative. Both were edited with filters making her appear to be an adult, but the matter of the information about her home town getting through to the inmate undetected is an internal issue I intend to investigate. Unfortunately, it wouldn't be the first time something like this has slipped through the net. You have to understand the volume of correspondence we're dealing with on a day-to-day basis, given the number of inmates at this prison.

If you need anything else clarifying, let me know.

Madison shakes her head at Ashlee's naïvety. By telling Cody she lived in Lost Creek, she made herself easy prey. The town is small enough for someone to be found easily, especially because of where she worked. Madison is a little surprised that someone with an interest in true crime wouldn't realize the danger they'd put themselves in. But then child abusers can be clever and manipulative, and perhaps Cody sweet-talked her into it. She'll have to see for herself.

She spends the next thirty minutes reading their correspondence. Several phrases from Cody's letters ring alarm bells:

You look great, much younger than your age.

Do you have a boyfriend?

I'm single right now.

It's best you keep our correspondence secret. I wouldn't want people to get the wrong idea.

I'm including a present for you.

I think it's time we met each other in real life.

I consider you my girlfriend now.

Each letter read in isolation would cause concern to someone in Madison's position, but all of them together like this make her shudder at Cody's obvious attempt to groom Ashlee over the two years they were corresponding. When she's finished reading, she feels sick. She wonders whether Ashlee might not have got into this predicament if her aunt and uncle had supported her better when she most needed it. She was too young to be parentless, living alone and raising a baby.

As she leans back in her seat, she hears Stella on the phone behind her. "Calm down, ma'am. Just take a deep breath and tell me your location."

Madison's interest is piqued.

"And what exactly happened?" probes Stella.

She watches as Stella turns around to give her *that* look. The one that suggests something awful has happened and a detective is needed.

"How long ago was that?" Silence while she types the details onto her screen. Followed by "And how old is the baby?"

A creeping sensation of dread spreads through Madison.

"Are you the baby's mother?" Stella listens, then swings around to look at Madison again as she speaks into the headset. "You're saying that the baby who was snatched from you whilst trick-or-treating is Ellie Stuart?"

Madison's mouth drops open and the hairs on her neck stand up. "Shit." She jumps to her feet and grabs her car keys.

Stella scribbles a location on a piece of paper and hands it to her whilst saying to the caller, "There's a detective on their way right now. Please stay where you are and remain calm."

CHAPTER FIFTY-NINE

Madison tries hard not to think of the possible danger Ellie is in as she takes charge of the situation. She's alerted all units that a baby has been snatched, making it clear that Cody Stevens could be responsible, and that if they spot him, they shouldn't approach in case he harms her. Not unless the situation demands it. They should keep him under surveillance from afar until she can get there. She wants to be able to keep the situation calm and controlled so that he doesn't do anything stupid in his bid for freedom.

Shelley's cruiser skids into the parking lot in front of the stores on Delta Lane, the ones under Ashlee's apartment, just moments after Madison arrives. Its flashing lights are reflected in the glass storefronts. A crowd is building. Madison spots a man, woman and young child sitting inside the drugstore. She already knows the foster carers' names are John and Sarah Bryant. As she enters, she sees the pharmacist trying hard to reassure them. There's an empty stroller next to the mother, Sarah, and she's sobbing. She looks up at Madison and Shelley with hope as they approach. "Have you found her?"

"Not yet," says Madison as she retrieves her notebook. "But I will. I'm going to need full details of what happened."

Sarah tries to catch her breath. Her son is around six years old and he's wearing a Spider Man costume. He's clutching a bag of candy, but his eyes are big and wide like saucers and it's clear he's on the verge of crying too. His frightened expression reminds Madison of Owen's reaction the night she was arrested.

Shelley leads the little boy away by the hand to distract him from their conversation. John Bryant speaks up. "We were out trick-or-treating and just stopped to speak to our neighbors as they passed. When we turned back to the stroller, the baby was gone."

"We'd only looked away for a minute!" says Sarah.

"Did you see who took her?" asks Madison.

"No," says John. "There are so many people out tonight and at least six different families passed us while we were chatting. When I realized she'd gone, I had no idea which direction to go in." He looks distraught.

"Please try not to blame yourselves. I'm sure we'll find her." Madison uses her cell phone to google a photo of Cody. "Do you remember seeing this man anywhere tonight?"

Sarah gasps. "That's Cody Stevens."

"Right. Have you seen him here?"

The woman shakes her head. "No. I would recognize him from the news and keep well away if I ever saw him near me or the kids." Putting two and two together she says, "Is that who took Ellie's mom?"

Madison doesn't want rumors to spread about Cody being in town, so she tries to play it down. "It's highly unlikely to be him, but I just had to check." He must have been in a Halloween costume. It would have been easy for him to blend in tonight. "What was Ellie wearing?"

Sarah tries to think. "I'd dressed her like a pumpkin. She was in an orange sweater with a black smiley mouth and eyes hand-stitched on the front, and she had stripy pants on. Red and green, I think." She looks up at her husband for confirmation.

"And she was covered in a cream-colored knitted blanket. That's gone too." He pulls his cell phone out. "Here, I snapped a photo of her before we came out."

Madison can't help but smile. Ellie looks adorable with her gummy grin and chubby pink cheeks. She feels a deep pang of guilt, along with a determination to get her back unharmed. "Can you send me that photo? I'll get it distributed right away."

She gives John her cell number, and while he sends the photo, she leans in to look at the empty stroller. Is there a more depressing sight after a baby has been snatched? It just highlights how tiny and vulnerable Ellie is. "Did you hear her crying while you were talking to your friends?"

They both shake their heads, but Sarah looks uncertain. "There were just so many people about, and all the kids are loud and excitable tonight. I really don't know if I heard her or not. Oh my God, I'm a terrible foster mother."

Madison tries to keep her focused. "Where are your neighbors? I'd like to interview them."

"They've gone home," says John. "Their children got upset when we started shouting at people, trying to find out if anyone had seen the baby. I think it scared a lot of kids."

"That's actually a good thing," she says. "It will make it easier for people to remember the moment you discovered she was missing. Try not to worry, we'll interview as many of them as we can, including your neighbors. And I'll be in touch as soon as I know anything."

John Bryant steps forward. "I can promise you nothing like this has ever happened to us before. We're good parents."

She realizes he's worried about losing their status as foster parents, and potentially having their remaining child taken from them. The little boy looks like John, so she assumes he's their biological child. "I don't doubt it," she says. "Trust me when I say this could have happened to anyone. Don't worry, I'll find her."

Relief swamps his face.

She nods for Shelley to join her outside. At the cruiser, she says, "It's probable that Cody Stevens has taken Ellie. If I'm right, time is of the essence."

Shelley nods, acutely aware of what Madison is worried about.

"Get the whole street cordoned off and don't let anyone come or go. Put a call in for all on- and off-duty officers who aren't currently searching for her to come here as backup immediately, including Detective Douglas if he's up to it and Chief Mendes agrees." She just hopes he hasn't been drinking tonight.

Her phone rings. It's Nate. She considers ignoring it, but he could have news. "Hi, Nate, I have a situation here so I can't talk for long."

"Vince's team have found something in the lake. They're getting ready to bring it up and I think you need to be here."

Her mouth goes dry. "I'll be right there." She turns to Shelley. "Call Chief Mendes and tell her I can't be in two places at once. She needs to take over here."

Shelley raises her eyebrows, looking nervous. "Think she'll listen to me?"

Madison's heart is beating out of her chest. "If she doesn't, Ashlee's baby could die tonight."

CHAPTER SIXTY

When Madison reaches Lake Providence, the whole area is lit up, not just by floodlights but by all the news stations who have set up their own lights and cameras on the grass. It won't be long before they'll hear about Ellie being snatched. Perhaps that will see most of them heading into town to chase that story instead.

There's a flurry of activity as they realize the lead detective has arrived, and Kate tries to catch her as she walks from her car to the yellow tape, zipping her jacket against the evening chill. "What can you tell me, Madison?"

"Nothing yet," she shouts over her shoulder. "I'm just about to get an update myself."

Kate pulls back, clearly frustrated, but Madison can't show anyone favors. The press should all find out what's happened at the same time. And that should be *after* she finds out herself.

Nate nods as she approaches. She turns her back to the cameras so their conversation isn't picked up. "An hour ago Cody Stevens snatched Ashlee's baby from the foster carers."

He looks horrified. "You're kidding?"

"I wish I was."

Brody is barking loudly at the edge of the lake. He wades in as far as he can without being submerged. Nate flashes Madison a look of dread. "He can smell someone."

The barking is relentless and the buzz of the reporters dies down. They've noticed. All focus is on the dog.

Madison feels like her heart could burst right now. The pressure of trying to find Ellie whilst potentially pulling her mother's dead body out of this lake any minute is threatening to overwhelm her. She can feel the tears building behind her eyes and panics that she might not be able to hold them back. The press would love that. She clears her throat and blinks. She has to remain in charge. "Gloria?" She walks over to Officer Williams. "Move the boundary further back. If we find Ashlee's body down there, I don't want her remains caught on camera to be played on repeat for weeks to come. Get them as far back as possible."

Gloria nods. "Yes, ma'am." She walks toward the crowd and waves her arms in a forward motion. "Everybody move back. We're extending the boundary."

She's met with groans and a variety of frustrated cuss words, but she's persistent. "Wash your potty mouths out. Get back or spend a night in the cells. The choice is yours."

Madison watches them reluctantly move further away as another officer helps Gloria move the crime-scene tape.

Nate's trying to get Brody to retreat from the lake, but the dog won't stop barking. Madison joins them just as Vince appears from underwater and pulls himself onto one of the inflatable dinghies. He removes his goggles and yells, "We've got a body!"

Madison's shoulders slump; she doesn't want to believe it. "Oh God. Please don't let it be her."

Wordlessly, Nate places a comforting hand on her back.

Over the next twenty minutes, all they can do is watch as the volunteers free the body from the clutches of whatever's holding it. Madison can hear the reporters over her shoulder, doing solemn pieces to camera. Kate's broadcast is live, and she's desperately trying to fill airtime with a summary of what's happened so far: the red Ford Fusion being found abandoned with Ellie inside, followed by rumors of a famous crime writer's body being found, and now this. Madison bets they all heard Vince shout the news she'd been dreading.

Vince is the first one out of the lake, and he joins them as he removes his diving gear. She wonders why he's left the other volunteers to do this critical part of the rescue. The bright lights illuminating the scene already make everyone look pale, but Vince is looking ghostly. There's no blood in his face. He struggles to undo a clasp and she realizes his hands are trembling badly. "Are you okay?"

He looks at her and gives up on the clasp. There's fear in his eyes. "I know it's likely to be Ashlee. Logic and reason tell me that. But what if it's Ruby?" He swallows hard. "Or Oliver." He turns away.

Madison's heart goes out to him. She hadn't even considered it could be his wife or grandson. She should never have suggested he lead this search. She closes her eyes, mentally kicking herself for being so insensitive. Even if it's Ashlee down there, she's still someone Vince cared about. She puts her hand on his arm. "I'm sorry, I should never have—"

He waves away the thought before she finishes. "I knew the risks." He stands up straight and wipes his face with his hands. "At least I could bury them at last. My son could come back to say his final goodbyes."

Nate manages to coax Brody from the water as Mark Fuller and two other volunteers pull something onto the dinghy and start moving toward the embankment. They've wrapped the object in tarpaulin to make it easier to transport, and probably to prevent the cameras filming it. As they lift it ashore, Brody's barking finally stops and Madison and Vince both step forward.

The lump under the sheet is bigger than that of a baby or toddler, so it's not Vince's grandson, and for that, she's thankful. She doesn't want any nasty surprises.

Mark Fuller looks up at them. "It had been weighed down with rocks in the pockets."

Vince is silent, but he's holding his stomach with one hand and Nate's shoulder with the other.

With a creeping feeling of dread, Madison steps forward and lifts the tarpaulin.

CHAPTER SIXTY-ONE

The face staring up at Madison is not the face she was expecting to see. One of the eyes has had tiny bites taken from it, by fish or some other underwater creature. The nose looks broken, but whether it's a fresh injury, she can't tell. The mouth is slack and questioning, with bloated purple lips that look like slugs.

"Holy crap, that's Cody Stevens," says Vince, his voice a little shaky.

She kneels down and immediately spots the painful-looking gash across Cody's neck. The skin around it is wrinkled from being submerged in the water, and she can see his windpipe behind the slit. He must have bled to death, but it's difficult to tell how long he's been down there.

Nate kneels next to her. "What's going on?"

She's dizzy with relief. "I have no idea. I was fully expecting this to be Ashlee." She can hear Kate calling her name behind them, but she'll have to wait.

Brody's barking again, so Nate stands up. He pulls the dog's ball out of his pocket and throws it as far as he can. Brody is back with it in seconds, looking pleased with himself. But he quickly drops it and turns back toward the water.

"You sure he wasn't barking because he can smell someone else down there?" asks Vince.

"It's possible," says Nate, nodding slowly. "We should keep looking; Ashlee could still be down there."

Madison shakes her head as she stands. "No. She's not down there. She must be responsible for this, and for Shane Kennedy's death." Though even as she says it, she has her doubts.

"You sure about that?" asks Vince.

"As much as I don't want to be, it's the only logical explanation." She looks at Nate. "She must have been the one to snatch Ellie and to ransack her own apartment. She probably made it look like a burglary on purpose so we wouldn't figure out it was her coming back for supplies: clothes, diapers, food."

Nate looks down at Cody's body and Madison can tell he isn't convinced that a seventeen-year-old girl could have done this, but he gives her the benefit of the doubt. "Are you thinking she was fanatical about both Shane and Cody? Perhaps writing to both of them?"

Madison turns to Vince. "You know her better than anyone else in this town. Did she ever ask you about them?"

He considers it. "I've never heard her mention Shane Kennedy, but she was the one who suggested I try to get Cody Stevens on the podcast. I'd heard of him, of course, from the news, but I hadn't followed his case, so I've only just started researching what happened."

"She owned a non-fiction book that detailed his crimes," says Madison. "It was signed by him and dedicated to her."

He raises his eyebrows. "So, what, she met up with him after his release?"

"She was writing to him while he was in prison. They sent a lot of letters back and forth via a PO box, and he signed her book for her."

Nate rubs his jaw. "Cody must have thought she'd be an easy target, what with her being young and naïve. He probably came here specifically to assault her, but he obviously wasn't banking on her fighting back. I bet she thinks she'll be arrested for killing him, even though it must've been in self-defense. She's probably terrified and in hiding."

Madison isn't convinced. "What about Shane Kennedy? No. Something weird is going on. This whole situation is screwed up.

The fact that Shane wrote a book based on Cody's crimes must have something to do with all this."

Nate offers another theory. "Maybe Cody came after Shane, annoyed that he had made money out of his incarceration, and Ashlee just got in the way."

"It's a big coincidence that Ashlee of all people was in the wrong place at the wrong time, given that she was a fan of them both."

"Coincidences do happen, Detective," says Vince.

She knows that. She can think of countless crimes that occurred due to people being in the wrong place at the wrong time. But something about it doesn't sit right with her.

"Do you want us to go back in?" Vince nods to the water.

Nate's right about one thing: there is a small chance Ashlee could also be down there, and that they've completely overlooked another suspect who might have killed all three of them. "Yes. We should keep looking."

Vince walks over to the volunteers to update them. Although it's cold, dark and starting to rain, to their credit they all agree to go back in with him. Madison is impressed.

Nate looks at her. Keeping his voice low, he says, "Vince is doing a great job and all, but I'm wondering for real now whether he's our best suspect at this point."

She raises her eyebrows. "But he obviously wasn't the person who grabbed Ellie, and he seemed genuinely shaken just now before we knew this was Cody."

He glances at Vince to make sure he's still out of earshot. "Maybe because he already knew Cody was down there. I mean, it can't be nice to have to retrieve a dead body you've hidden yourself. He could be starting to worry that now we've got a body, we'll find some evidence to pin this on him. As for Ellie, maybe he had someone else take her."

Madison rubs her face. "We need to be careful what we tell him. Stick with him, would you? Just in case you're right."

"Sure."

She tries calling Chief Mendes to update her, but there's no answer, so she fires off a quick text about the body they've found. Putting her phone away, she nods toward the reporters. "Time to update those guys."

As she approaches them, she tries to think what she can and can't say at this stage. It's a fine line between confirming the facts and giving the killer a chance to stay one step ahead of them.

The questions come hard and fast, and she has to raise her hands to shut them up. "I'm about to update you, so just give me a second to speak before you bombard me with questions." She takes a deep breath and tries not to cover her eyes against the glare of the lights. Everyone pushes their mics close to her face, making her take a step back. "I can confirm a body has been found in the lake here tonight. It has obviously not been formerly identified yet, so I won't be giving you a name."

"Is it an adult or a child, and can you tell us the cause of death?" asks Kate.

"I can't answer those questions yet."

"What about the body found here yesterday? Can you confirm who that is?"

Madison weighs up the pros and cons of confirming it and decides to go ahead. "Shane Kennedy was found at this same location, although not in the lake, with serious injuries to his head. I'm investigating his death as a homicide and I have reason to believe both the deaths are linked."

Everyone launches into follow-up questions, but she hears Ellie's name being mentioned. "Is it true Ellie Stuart was abducted from her foster carers on Delta Lane earlier tonight?" asks Gary Pelosi.

Madison nods. "Yes, while the family were trick-or-treating. We have officers interviewing everyone who was in the area, but we're looking for a twelve-month-old baby girl wearing an orange sweater that resembles a pumpkin, as well as red and green striped pants.

She was wrapped in a cream woolen blanket, so if anyone finds that discarded somewhere, get in touch with LCPD immediately. And bear in mind the baby might have been changed into other clothes by now." She pulls her cell phone out and sends the photo of Ellie to Kate. "I'd be grateful if you would all distribute this photo that I've just forwarded to Kate Flynn. If anyone watching this hears or sees a baby where there wouldn't usually be one, get in touch with us immediately. We currently have no leads on Ashlee Stuart's location, so she's still considered a missing person. That's all I have time for right now."

Most of them wander away to record their updates or send off their articles. Kate stays back. "Is Ashlee now considered a suspect?"

Madison studies her face. Kate has been quick to jump to the same conclusion as her. "For what?"

"Your two murder victims and grabbing the baby."

She hesitates. "To be honest with you, Kate, and this is off the record... I have no idea."

CHAPTER SIXTY-TWO

Madison drives back to the drugstore to brief Chief Mendes, who looks to be in her element ordering officers around and helping to take statements from witnesses who were in the area when Ellie was snatched. When she spots Madison, she casts a critical eye over her. "You look like a drowned rat."

"I've been at the lake and got caught in a heavy downpour." She really doesn't care how she looks right now. "Any luck with finding Ellie?"

"Not yet, no. If it wasn't Halloween, we'd be in a better position, but everyone out tonight was in some kind of costume. It was perfect conditions for her to be snatched without anyone noticing."

"Did you see my text?" Madison asks.

"No, I've been busy."

"We have another body. Pulled from the lake."

Mendes looks alarmed and leads her out of earshot of anyone else. "Do we know who it is?"

"Cody Stevens."

"What? You're sure?"

Madison nods. "His throat was cut. There's still no sign of Ashlee, but I'm starting to think she was the one who took Ellie."

Mendes realizes the implications. "You think she killed Cody?"

"I don't know if she'd be capable of that." She thinks about what Nate said. "Vince Rader is the only other suspect we have. But apart from his links to Shane and Ashlee, I have no evidence to suggest he was behind any of this. He's currently leading the search of the lake, so he could be contaminating evidence for all we know."

Mendes considers it. "But he clearly didn't snatch the baby, because he was with the search party at the time."

"Right. He would've needed an accomplice, and I don't know anyone who would have reason to help him." She thinks about something that's been bothering her that she could really do with following up, but she can't be in more than one place at a time.

Mendes picks up on her conflict. "Talk to me, Detective."

Madison decides to go for it. "I want to follow a hunch I have. I feel like the girl who accused Shane Kennedy of assault could help me with it." She looks around. "Is Don here?"

"No. He's a liability right now and it's more important he focuses on his health, so I haven't requested his help." Mendes pauses. "I don't think we'll be seeing him at work for a couple of months, and that's only if he can overcome his problems."

Madison nods slowly. "If I go and chase my hunch, do you have this covered?" She glances at the witnesses talking to various officers.

"Sure. Go ahead. Just keep me updated."

"Will do." Madison gets in her car and places a call to the person who worked the case against Shane Kennedy: Detective Lutz.

The dispatcher tells her he's on his way home from work. Madison insists it's urgent she speaks to him, and to his credit, he accepts the call. She fires questions at him about Shane Kennedy, and he answers readily, although some of his memories are hazy. "Did anything stand out about the case?" she asks. "Anything unusual?"

"Not really. Like I said, it was a typical he-said-she-said case," says Lutz. "And unfortunately the accuser backed down before it went to trial."

"Do you think you would've got a conviction if it had gone ahead?"

He sighs down the phone. "Probably not. Jurors want hard evidence. If I remember rightly, there wasn't even a photo to suggest the pair were in the room together."

She nods, disappointed that he's told her nothing about the accusations that helps her. "Just out of interest, what was the victim's name?"

"Er…" he stumbles. "Let me check. It was a few years ago, and you know how many of these accusations we get. I'll call the station now and text you the name when I have it."

"Great. Thanks for your help, I appreciate it."

"No problem."

She drops her phone in her lap and leans her head against the rest, closing her eyes. "Where are you, Ashlee?" she mutters. Could a petite young mother really be capable of killing two men? She considers the practicalities of it and thinks of cases she's read about where victims have found seemingly superhuman strength to get away from their attackers. Shane was slim in stature, but Cody was stocky. He would be hard to overpower for someone of Ashlee's size. But if she was desperate, she might have managed it.

Her cell phone buzzes with a text. It's Lutz. When she sees the name of the person who made the allegations against Shane, her mouth drops open in shock. Without hesitation, she starts the engine and drives out of Lost Creek.

CHAPTER SIXTY-THREE

It's just after eight o'clock when Madison pulls up outside the Larsons's home. It's raining hard, and the house is lit up throughout, suggesting someone's in. She quickly walks up the driveway and rings the doorbell.

Mr. Larson opens the door with a mug of coffee in his spare hand. He looks at her incredulously. "What do you want at this hour?"

"Can I come in? I wouldn't ask if it wasn't important, and I won't be long." He looks like he's going to say no, so she adds, "Please, a baby's life is at risk."

He rolls his eyes and steps to one side. As she enters the living room, Mrs. Larson is clearly shocked to see her. She drops the book she was reading and gets up off the couch. "Is everything okay?"

Madison is reluctant to upset this couple again, but she says, "I need to speak to your daughter, and it's urgent. I'll explain as soon as Kacie joins us. Is she home?"

Mrs. Larson nods. "She's upstairs doing her homework."

"I knew you'd come back." They all turn to see Kacie standing at the bottom of the stairs. "I'm in trouble, aren't I?" she says.

Madison feels a jolt of adrenaline. Finally she's going to get some answers.

Tears start streaming down Kacie's face as she moves toward the couch. "I knew this would all backfire."

Mr. Larson looks confused. "Will someone tell me what the hell is going on? Kacie? What have you done now?"

Madison takes a seat next to the teenager. "It's okay. You're not in any trouble. I just need the truth and I need it fast."

Kacie wipes her eyes and Madison can see fear there. Just how much does she know? She looks up at the girl's parents. "You remember I told you there was a missing nineteen-year-old mother down in Lost Creek who'd been using your daughter's name and given your address as her next of kin on a job application?"

Mr. Larson swallows. "Of course, but she's nothing to do with us."

"Well, after my visit, I found out that her real name is Ashlee Stuart and she's actually only seventeen."

"Ashlee Stuart," says Mrs. Larson, trying the name out for size. "I think I saw something about her on the news. Was she the waitress?"

"That's right." Madison turns to Kacie. "You told me you didn't recognize her from the photo I showed you, but she's your friend, isn't she?"

Kacie's eyes fill with tears again and she glances at both her parents. Quickly looking away again, she nods.

Madison's heart is beating hard against her chest. She was right to come here.

"She can't be," says Mrs. Larson. "I've never met her."

Kacie clears her throat. "She was the kind of friend you don't bring home because you know your parents won't approve."

Madison tries not to shake her head disapprovingly. "Why wouldn't they approve?"

"She was…" Kacie hesitates, "poor. She enrolled in my school after her mom died, when she was thirteen. Her aunt and uncle sounded mean and didn't really want her living with them, and I felt sorry for her because she had no one else to hang out with. My other friends didn't like her, so I kept them separate from her. She was funny and we had a good time, mostly. But she went through a period of drinking a lot and she had awful low times where she was almost, like, suicidal or something."

Madison's reminded of the semi-colon tattoo Ashlee has on her wrist. "Can you tell me why Ashlee was writing to Cody Stevens in prison?"

"Cody Stevens?" says Mr. Larson incredulously. "The rapist?"

Kacie wipes her eyes and avoids her dad's stare, but she doesn't appear shocked that Madison knows. "She was obsessed with him. She said she wanted to meet him one day, even though he was serving a life sentence. I thought she was crazy for writing to him, but plenty of people write to prisoners apparently. She said it would be funny. I had no idea she was using my name until I saw an acknowledgement slip from the prison to say her letter had been received. We fell out over it, but she insisted it didn't matter because he'd given her a nickname to go by."

"But why Cody?" Madison presses. "Is it because he was the person *Bitter Road* was based on? Was that her favorite book?"

Mrs. Larson gasps. "*Bitter Road*? That's the book by Shane Kennedy."

Madison nods. She knows Kacie's parents won't be happy with what's about to come out.

Kacie shrugs. "I mean, I guess. That would make sense. I know she tried contacting Shane Kennedy through social media to get her books signed or whatever, but he never responded, no matter which platform she tried." She fiddles with her bracelet.

"You both attended a book signing of his in 2016, didn't you?"

Mr. Larson takes over. "That man put my daughter through hell by trying to sexually assault her. We don't discuss him in this house. I don't see where all this is going, Detective."

Madison takes a deep breath and looks at Kacie. "It was Ashlee's idea, wasn't it? To make the false allegation about him sexually assaulting you?" When Detective Lutz had confirmed Kacie Larson as the girl who'd accused Shane of sexual assault, she knew it couldn't have been Ashlee using her false identity, because he'd talked about the girl's parents and how they'd wanted to sue Shane for what he'd done. Ashlee doesn't have parents. That was when she'd realized there was a link between Ashlee and this girl who had previously claimed not to know her.

"That's it, Detective, you're way out of line!" says Kacie's father, clearly angered by the implication that his daughter caused them all that trouble for no reason. "I'm calling your superior right now."

Mrs. Larson tells him to shut up. Then she looks at her daughter. "Kacie? Did you make it all up?"

Kacie can't even meet her mom's eyes. Staring intently at her lap, with tears running down her face, she nods.

CHAPTER SIXTY-FOUR

Nate watches the last reporter drive away from Lake Providence. He doesn't blame them for leaving. The search team haven't found anything else in the lake apart from Cody's body, and they're packing up now too.

Vince claps him on the back. "How about I treat us to some food at the diner while we fix the arrangements for your interview on my podcast?"

Nate smiles. "It'll have to be a damn good meal." Keeping in mind that Vince might have played a role in Ashlee's disappearance, he's determined to stick with him.

He opens the back door of his car for Brody to jump in, then joins Vince in the front. A quick check of his phone shows he has no updates from Madison. It's past eight o'clock now, and he wonders what's going on with the baby. He calls Owen. "Hey, it's me. Has your mom been in touch?"

"Yeah," says Owen. "Apparently she's had to go to Prospect Springs, so I've had takeout for dinner, yet again. I ordered you two a pizza to share, but if you don't get here soon, I can't guarantee it'll still be around."

Nate smiles. "I'm eating at the diner while I take care of something there, but I'm sure your mom would appreciate it if you kept some back for her. She's had a long and difficult day."

"Sure, I'll try. Has she found the baby yet? It's all over the news."

"Not that I know of. I'll shoot you a text when I'm on my way home."

"Okay, bye."

He slips the phone back into his pocket. Owen's obviously not his son and Madison's not his partner, but it feels good to have someone else to care about.

When they step inside the diner, out of the rain, the place falls deathly silent and all eyes turn to them for answers. He glances at the TV and sees Kate Flynn on the screen.

Carla rushes up to Vince. "Was it Ashlee?"

It's like everyone is collectively holding their breath. Vince glances at Nate, clearly unsure how to answer, so Nate says, "We can't reveal that information, I'm sorry. I'm sure Detective Harper will update the press as soon as she's able to."

One by one their eyes turn back to the TV above the counter. Kate appears just to be repeating the few facts they already know, and it looks like she's standing outside the police station now, probably hoping to catch Madison coming or going.

"Find a seat," says Vince. "I'll order us some food and grab my laptop from upstairs." He turns to Brody. "You follow me, young man. I can't have the health inspector catching you down here."

Nate's grateful that he's letting Brody wait in his apartment rather than making him stay outside in the car. As he watches them walk behind the counter, he spots Brody carefully but swiftly stealing the remains of a beef patty from a dirty dish he passes. It makes him smile.

He chooses an empty booth and gratefully accepts the hot coffee Carla pours for him. She's hovering, so he decides to put her out of her misery. Keeping his voice low, he says, "It wasn't Ashlee."

Tears spring to her eyes and her spare hand goes to her chest. "Oh, thank goodness."

"It wasn't anyone local, so try not to worry. And I'm sure Madison won't rest until she finds the baby."

Carla squeezes his shoulder before heading back behind the counter.

Vince quickly joins him with his laptop and immediately starts searching for information about Cody Stevens's past. He turns the screen so Nate can read what he finds. They scour all kinds of websites to learn what Cody's been up to since his release last month.

"He managed to keep a low profile," says Vince.

"So did I after my release. Every news station and documentary producer wanted the first interview with me. I was lucky enough to have a friend collect me from prison and take me to his place to hide out while I acclimatized to the outside world. It was all so overwhelming." Rex was there for him when Nate had no one else in the world to turn to. He taught him how to use modern cell phones and computers. He even taught him how to drive again. Thinking about his friend brings a lump to his throat.

Vince leans forward. "I don't like to pry, but I heard the feds caught Father Connor. I have a friend who lives near the church where it happened. He got straight on the phone to me as soon as he saw a priest being led out in cuffs. I'm assuming the fact that he was captured here in Lost Creek has something to do with you, so tell me: did you get any time alone with the asshole before the feds turned up?"

Nate hesitates, but he feels more comfortable talking to Vince now. He looks him in the eye. "I wanted to tear him apart limb from limb. I wanted to kill him. Maybe I should've done."

The look on Vince's face tells him he sympathizes. Since prison, Nate's been a good judge of character, and the look on Vince's face is enough to satisfy him that this man had nothing to do with his wife and grandchild's disappearance. Which means he probably wasn't involved in Ashlee's either.

"You didn't, though," says Vince. "That must've been difficult. It tells me you're a good man, Nate, and you'd make a fine priest. Why don't you start afresh and build your own church here in Lost Creek? Sure, we have a few weirdos and sociopaths living

amongst us, but no more than any other small town in America."
He smiles.

Returning to the Church has obviously crossed Nate's mind
many times since his release, but a man who almost shot someone
out of revenge and still has a mild coke habit can't represent God.
He suddenly realizes he hasn't used since before his trip to visit
Rex two months ago. Not even after his showdown with Father
Connor. That's no guarantee it won't happen again in the future,
but it's progress at least. "I don't know. How can I guide others
when I still have so much to fix in my own life?"

Vince looks thoughtful. "You'll never be perfect. No one is.
But I'd sure as hell rather listen to someone who's lived your life
preaching to me every Sunday than some asshole whose character
has never been tested. You know what it's like to be human. Some
of those other guys are just paying lip service. I mean, just look at
Father Connor."

It's a good point.

Carla places a huge plate of food in front of Nate. Some kind
of stew. It's exactly what he needs after spending so long outside.
Rain lashes the large window next to them as they eat.

After a while, Vince sits back in his seat and studies Nate, like
he's trying to decide whether to trust him with something. "Think
you'll carry on as a PI, even though you've dealt with Father Connor
and can afford to never work again?"

Nate swallows his mouthful of stew. "Probably. I mean, it's not
like I have anything else to do now." He thinks of Kristen. The
photo wasn't proof she was dead; just that she was badly beaten.
Could she have got away? Maybe. And maybe one day he'll have
the strength to go look for her. But not yet. Father Connor's murder
trial might reveal some useful information about what happened
to her, and that could stop him unnecessarily chasing ghosts.

Glancing behind him and keeping his voice low, Vince says,
"How would you feel about looking for Ruby and Oliver?"

Nate is stunned. He sets his knife and fork on the plate, humbled that Vince would trust him with two of the people he loves most.

"I'd pay you, of course. I don't expect any favors." Vince appears embarrassed at having to ask for help, which shows how helpless he must be feeling. Nate can tell he isn't pretending to be a grieving husband and grandfather. He *is* grieving. He needs answers.

"Are you sure? I sometimes have… depressive episodes that render me useless."

Vince scoffs. "Oh please, who doesn't? You managed to find the missing girl in Shadow Falls, and you helped Detective Harper find out who framed her for murder. My gut tells me you're the right man for the job."

Nate feels the excitement that comes with a new case. Normally he gets his jobs from Rex, but that's never going to happen again. He decides to go for it. "I'd love to try. But you need to be prepared for what I find. I know from experience that clients don't always get the answers they're hoping for, and sometimes those answers are worse than not knowing."

Vince doesn't even have to consider it. "To be honest with you, Nate, it's been so long since they vanished that anything is better than nothing."

Nate nods, thinking of Kristen. He can understand that sentiment. "Then count me in."

CHAPTER SIXTY-FIVE

Madison leaves Kacie's parents in a state of shock. They're under-standably angry at learning that their daughter and her friend put them through months of hell with an unnecessary police investiga-tion. She knows it's not the first time friends that age have lied for each other, but she does feel sympathy for Shane Kennedy and the ordeal he went through because of a scheme to make him look bad. And for what reason? Kacie wasn't even sure why Ashlee wanted to ruin his reputation. She just knew her friend was obsessed with him. Was it just a normal teenage obsession gone bad? Or is there a deeper meaning to all of this?

Madison didn't disclose to the Larsons how both Shane Kennedy and Cody Stevens have been found dead, and that their deaths are somehow linked to Kacie's friend. She didn't have time, and they'll see it for themselves on the news soon enough. Instead she took Ashlee's aunt's address from Kacie before leaving, because she can't think of anyone else who might know why Ashlee was obsessed with the two men. It has something to do with that damn book, she just knows it. It's the only thing that links them.

The drive to Barbara Fletcher's home, just north of Prospect Springs, takes ten minutes, and once there, she can immediately tell the woman wasn't lying about not having enough money to feed Ashlee and a newborn. She lives in an apartment block in community housing. The walls are covered in graffiti, with adults hanging around on the street corners and kids running riot, despite it now being after nine o'clock. It reminds her of the halfway house she lived in after her release from prison. It might be rough around the edges, but she'd bet these residents look out for each other more than those living in affluent areas.

Avoiding the curious stares, she presses the intercom for Fletcher. When she announces herself, she's buzzed right in and Barbara greets her at the top of a long, narrow stairway. She doesn't smile; she just turns and walks inside her apartment. Madison follows and closes the door behind them.

"You've found her, haven't you?" Barbara perches on the edge of an upright chair and pulls out a cigarette. Her husband doesn't appear to be home, and the place is cramped but tidy. It would be a tight squeeze with three people living here, and Madison can see how adding a baby to that mix would have raised tensions. She takes a seat on the small couch, which offers little comfort.

"No, actually, I haven't."

Barbara raises her eyebrows. "Then why are you here?"

"Because I have two dead males in Lost Creek and they both appear to have links to your niece."

Barbara inhales deeply on her cigarette. "So she had two boy-friends at the same time, is that what you're saying?"

Madison can't tell if the woman is acting or not. Kacie told her that Ashlee had been obsessed with Cody Stevens ever since she'd first met her at the age of thirteen. Ashlee was living here then. "Who's the father of Ashlee's baby?"

Barbara's eyes narrow over the smoke and her hostility is obvious. "How would I know that?"

"Because she was in your care when she got pregnant. By my calculations, she was one month shy of her sixteenth birthday. Kind of young to be getting pregnant, wouldn't you say? Was she in a relationship at the time?"

The sound of a key in the front door makes Barbara glance over with fear in her eyes. Madison turns to see who it is. A tall white male around the same age as Barbara takes one look at her and stops where he is. "Who are you?"

Madison stands. "Detective Harper from Lost Creek PD. I'm here to talk to your wife about Ashlee."

Barbara walks over to him. "Give us some time, would you? Maybe fetch something for dinner?"

Madison doesn't want him to leave, as he might be more talkative than his wife, but he looks at her with mistrust. "Sure. I'll leave you to it."

She has a horrible feeling gnawing away at her because of the tension in here.

When he's gone, Barbara turns toward the kitchen counter and rests her hands on it. Madison can't see her face as the woman talks. "Like I told you before, I tried looking after her. When she first came to live with us, she was a sweet, scared little girl just about to hit puberty. But she started having anger problems. She didn't know how to channel the grief from losing her mom, and I couldn't afford to send her to therapy. The school tried counseling, but she was already drinking by then. We'd have to hide our liquor from her by the time she turned fifteen. It wasn't until she got pregnant that she stopped drinking and seemed to be turning her life around. Said she wanted to be healthy for her baby."

"Ellie's been abducted."

Barbara spins around. "What?"

"She was taken from her foster carers earlier this evening. I have no idea where she is."

The woman collapses into an armchair. "I should never have made them leave."

"No," says Madison. "You shouldn't have. They needed you. I take it you were Ashlee's only family after her mother passed?"

Barbara nods.

"Remind me how her mother died."

"Liver failure. She slowly drank herself to death on account of what happened. So to watch Ashlee turn to alcohol scared me, because I knew she'd probably be dead by twenty."

Madison is confused. "What do you mean, on account of what happened? Why was your sister drinking heavily?"

Barbara searches her face. "You don't know?"

"No. I don't know anything about Ashlee's parents."

Barbara pulls out another cigarette with yellowed fingers and lights it. The smoke doesn't bother Madison. It's actually kind of comforting, and she knows it wouldn't take much for her to take up the habit again. Barbara inhales deeply before saying, "Ashlee had an older sister she adored, called Kelly." She rubs her forehead. "That's why she named her baby Ellie. I don't know why she didn't go one step further and call her Kelly, maybe it was too much of a reminder."

"A reminder of what?"

"A reminder that Kelly was just twelve years old when she and her best friend killed themselves."

Blood roars in Madison's ears and her mouth drops open as she realizes where this is heading. Everything suddenly makes sense, but she doesn't want to be right. Her mouth is dry as she says, "Her sister was one of the girls raped by Cody Stevens, wasn't she?"

Barbara nods. "They jumped off a bridge together. Ashlee was only ten years old at the time, and she witnessed the whole thing." She takes another long drag on her cigarette.

Madison shakes her head as she tries to process everything Ashlee's been through. She tries to picture what it was like living here knowing she wasn't wanted. Standing up, she asks, "Mind if I have a look in the bedrooms?" She needs to check it wasn't Barbara or her husband who took Ashlee and her daughter.

Barbara looks like she wants to say no, but thinks better of it. She points to the doors beyond the kitchen.

In the dark hallway, Madison pushes open the first door. There's a double bed, a small desk in the corner with a computer on, and a double closet. She looks inside. Nothing but shoes and clothes. The other bedroom is tiny, with just a single bed. There are few signs that a teenager lived here: just some posters on the wall and a noticeboard with various photos. Madison steps up to it and studies them. Ashlee's a young child in these. She's with a woman who bears a strong resemblance to her, obviously her mom. It's clear from the tint of the woman's skin that she was drinking heavily. Another photo shows Ashlee squeezing an older girl tight, with their mom standing behind them laughing. The two girls look happy with their wide grins. It must have been a huge ordeal for Ashlee to lose her older sister.

She pulls open some drawers, not really sure what she's checking for. There's nothing obvious that suggests anyone was trapped or harmed in here. She opens the small closet and finds a box of paperwork buried under blankets. Sitting on the bed, she starts rifling through it and realizes it's full of court documents related to Cody's sexual assault trial. One in particular stands out: a transcript of a session between Ashlee and a child psychologist in which they discussed Kelly's suicide.

She glances at the door and can hear Barbara making a hot drink. Looking back at the document in her hand, she decides she needs to know what Ashlee witnessed on the day her sister died.

CHAPTER SIXTY-SIX

The transcript states that Ashlee was eleven years old during this session, and the number at the top of the page shows that it was used as evidence in Cody's trial, held the year after he raped the two girls.

DR. PHILLIPS: Ashlee, would you tell me what happened that day at the bridge last July?

ASHLEE STUART: I remember it was sunny and I thought we were going to play at the park, even though it was really early. It was before breakfast and I was already hungry. We were collecting large stones on our way, stuffing the best into our pockets and backpacks. Only two cars passed us on the bridge and Kelly and Janie were quiet the whole time. There was no laughing or chatting. When we got to the middle of the bridge, Kelly pulled something out from her pocket. She said, "In a minute you need to go to the phone booth I showed you and call Mom. Tell her what happened."

DR. PHILLIPS: What did you think she meant by that?

ASHLEE STUART: I wasn't sure. I looked down at the coin and the slip of paper she'd given me. There was a phone number on the paper. It was our home number. Mom had made me memorize it years ago, so I didn't know why Kelly had written it down. I looked up at her to ask, but the sun blinded me, and before I could say anything, she and Janie had crossed the road without me. I wasn't supposed to cross roads unsupervised, so I stood still and waited for them to come back for me.

DR. PHILLIPS: And did they?

ASHLEE STUART: No. They walked to the metal thing next to the sidewalk.

DR. PHILLIPS: The bridge railings?

ASHLEE STUART: Yeah. Janie looked back over her shoulder and gave me a weird smile. I wasn't sure if I was supposed to be copying them. They'd already taken my stones off me and put them in their backpacks and pockets.

DR. PHILLIPS: And what happened next?

ASHLEE STUART: Do I have to? [Unintelligible mumbling]

DR. PHILLIPS: It's really important that we know, Ashlee, because then you don't have to talk about it again if you don't want to.

ASHLEE STUART: Okay. Kelly started climbing the railing. Then Janie did too. But she got her foot caught in her skirt and some stones fell out of her pockets and I laughed. She climbed back down to pick them up. Then they were both sitting on top of the railing. I was so scared for them because the bridge was high over the water. I thought they were just trying to scare me, because I don't think Janie ever really liked me.

DR. PHILLIPS: Why do you think that was?

ASHLEE STUART: Because I always wanted to come along wherever Kelly went. I liked being with her.

DR. PHILLIPS: Now, Ashlee, I need you to think really carefully. Can you remember what happened next?

ASHLEE STUART: They held hands and disappeared off the side of the bridge. I couldn't see them anymore. I forgot to breathe for what seemed like forever. I waited for them to climb back over and laugh at how scared I was. Except they didn't. I heard two big splashes underneath me but it took a while before I realized it was them hitting the water.

DR. PHILLIPS: Was there anyone else around at the time? Any other pedestrians or cars?

ASHLEE STUART: Yeah. A car drove by and the driver looked at me before looking away. He didn't see what happened. My legs were shaking bad, like real bad, so I carefully crossed the road and took hold of the railing. I couldn't see over the top as I was too small, so I climbed up a little. It made me go dizzy to see how high up the bridge was. When I felt safe, I looked over the top and down at the river below. It took a few minutes to spot Kelly's white cardigan. She was floating face up but the weight of the backpack pulled her under the water really fast. She had blood on her head so I think she hit a rock. She wasn't holding Janie's hand anymore because Janie was ahead of her. She was all the way under by the time I remembered to blink.

DR. PHILLIPS: What did you do next?

ASHLEE STUART: I jumped down off the railing and pulled out the piece of paper. I'm glad Kelly wrote our phone number down because my mind had gone totally blank so I forgot it. I had to find that phone booth and… tell Mommy that Kelly was dead. [Unintelligible mumbling]

DR. PHILLIPS: It's okay, Ashlee. You don't need to talk about it anymore, it's over now. Let me go get your mom.

Madison rubs her temples. This might just be the most devastating thing she's ever read.

CHAPTER SIXTY-SEVEN

Madison needs to get back to Lost Creek as fast as possible. But she's not done with Barbara yet. She carries the box of court documents into the living room.

"Do I have your permission to take these back to the station with me?" It's evidence. If Barbara won't let her take it, she'll have to get a warrant.

Barbara glances at the box and silently nods.

"Did you know Ashlee was writing to Cody Stevens in prison while she was living here with you?"

Barbara's eyes widen. "What? Of course not. Why would she do that?" Her shock is obvious, and Madison believes she didn't know.

"You tell me. I mean, why would she write to him knowing what he'd caused her sister to do?"

Barbara looks away. "Ashlee's always made bad decisions. Probably because she's traumatized. Kelly wouldn't tell any adults what that son of a bitch did to her and her friend Janie, not the police or her mom. But she told Ashlee. They were close; they shared a bedroom and Ashlee followed her sister everywhere. It's a miracle she wasn't with Kelly and Janie when they were…" She shakes her head. "Kelly told her that Cody Stevens got them into his car by pretending to give them a ride to school. He told them he was the new janitor there, so they trusted him. Instead he drove them to the woods. First he attacked Janie while Kelly watched from his locked car, then he swapped them. Kelly told Ashlee it hurt more to watch what he did to Janie than to have it happen to her.

"You have to understand that Janie was a shy, sensitive girl who didn't have any other friends. She was obsessed with mermaids, sweet thing, but she was mercilessly bullied for it. If you ever saw the girl, you'd know she was the kind of child you just feel compelled to protect from the world. I believe that's why they both took their lives after. Janie couldn't cope with what had happened to her and Kelly couldn't cope with seeing her friend in pain." She shakes her head and wipes away tears. "Ashlee was too young for that kind of information to be dumped on her. She didn't say a word to anyone. Then, just days later, before she could tell anyone, the girls took her with them to the bridge so that afterwards she could tell their parents what they'd done, and why."

Madison is trying hard to hold back her own tears. In all her time as a cop, and during her six years in prison listening to cellmates share their horrific stories of abuse and neglect, this is the saddest story she's ever heard.

"That animal should never have been released from prison." There's hatred in Barbara's eyes, and rightly so. She has dealt with the loss of one niece to suicide and her sister to alcoholism, and now her remaining niece is missing. And all of it happened because of Cody Stevens.

Clearing the lump in her throat, Madison says, "We found his body earlier today. He's been murdered."

Barbara leans forward in shock and rests her head in her trembling hands. "Oh my God, Ashlee. What have you done?"

So she thinks it was Ashlee too. The girl must have wanted revenge. The letters to him in prison were a ruse to gain his trust, and that was why she used Kacie Larson's name instead of her own, so he wouldn't know she was Kelly's sister. But she couldn't have known he'd ever get released from his life sentence, so what was the point? Maybe coming to that realization herself—that he was untouchable inside—would account for the break in her letters to him. She must have realized the futility of corresponding with her sister's rapist. The break was also around the time Ashlee gave birth. Perhaps she wanted a fresh start for herself and her baby. But of course then came the news of Cody's mistrial, along with his imminent release. She would have been devastated that he was going to be a free man after everything he'd done to her family. She saw her chance and she took it by rekindling their correspondence.

It dawns on Madison then that Ashlee didn't include her location in that last letter to him through naïvety. She wanted him to find her. She wanted to kill him in retaliation for what he'd done to her sister. But he must have taken her unawares. That's the problem with felons. They're experienced in violence. Ashlee wasn't.

"Did she ever talk to you about him? Tell you she wanted him dead for what he did to her sister?"

Barbara shakes her head.

"Do you have any idea where she might be hiding? Maybe the house she was raised in? Or does she have a friend who would look after her?"

"Her mom's house was demolished a couple of years ago for a new office complex. I don't know any of her friends, but she hasn't been here in six months, so if anyone was hiding her, it must be someone she met in Lost Creek."

That would make sense. Madison thinks about Shane Kennedy's role in all this, and then it dawns on her. "Shit," she says out loud.

"What?"

Of course. "*Bitter Road* was based on what happened to her sister."

Barbara looks confused. "Yeah, it was. She hated that book. She said the author was making money out of Kelly's death. He even approached us on social media to give our version of events for his research. Even though he was writing a fictional account, and he didn't use Kelly and Janie's real names, he wanted to interview Ashlee to hear in depth what Kelly had told her."

Madison's adrenaline is kicking in now. She stands up. "Did he ever meet her?"

"No. I wouldn't allow it. And she was still too traumatized to talk about it back then."

Madison runs a hand through her hair and tries to think. "Shane Kennedy is dead too. He was murdered and dumped in the same location as Cody Stevens."

Barbara starts sobbing, and all Madison can do is put an arm around her shoulders while she releases her grief. She still doesn't know how Ellie Stuart ended up in Shane's car, but she's certain it's Ashlee who snatched her tonight. In a way, that's better than anyone else taking the baby, but they still need to be found, because she doesn't know what state of mind Ashlee is in. After killing two men, is she capable of killing her own daughter too? Maybe, if one of them was Ellie's father. Because Ellie would be just one more link, one more reminder of what happened to Kelly. But Madison can't believe Ashlee would do that to her baby. Ellie's all she's got now.

Barbara looks on the verge of breaking down. Her eyes are bloodshot and she's still shaking. "She's going to get life without parole for this. And what will happen to Ellie then?"

Madison withdraws her arm. "That depends on who her father is. Something tells me you know the answer to that."

After wiping her tears away with a tissue, Barbara stands up and goes into the small bedroom. Madison hears a floorboard being pulled up. Barbara comes back with a small notebook in her hand. "This is Ashlee's journal. She left it here when she moved away and I only discovered it because the floorboard was creaking when I stepped on it. But I left it down there and I've never read it. I never wanted to confirm my suspicions, because I wouldn't have been able to stop myself from shooting my husband."

Madison's heart sinks. The journal is pink and childish and she wonders how long Ashlee was writing in it. She doesn't want to read it either, but she needs answers. "If you suspected your husband was abusing her, why didn't you take Ashlee and get the hell out of here? I mean, at the very minimum." She can feel anger rising in her chest.

"He wasn't abusing her. I mean, he couldn't have been in an apartment this small. I would've known! It must have been a one-off. It *must* have been." But she's not doing a very good job of convincing herself. She breaks down again.

Madison stands. She doesn't tell Barbara she'll be making sure the local police pay her husband a visit tonight. Instead, she lets herself out.

CHAPTER SIXTY-EIGHT

Nate leaves the diner with Brody after closing. It's nearing eleven and the clouds have long dispersed, revealing a clear night. He takes a second to admire the stars that are shining brightly overhead before turning his collar up against the crisp breeze. The minute he and Brody are inside the car, his cell phone rings. It's Madison. "Hey. Where are you?" he asks.

"I've just got back from Prospect Springs. Where are you?"

"Leaving Ruby's Diner."

"Can you meet me outside the drugstore where Ellie was snatched?" she says.

"Sure."

It's only a five-minute drive, and he spots Madison standing next to her car, staring at a small pink notebook. She snaps it closed and slips it into her pocket as he approaches. He can't help noticing she looks exhausted. "Have you eaten anything lately?" he asks.

"Not for a long time. I just called Owen and he's about to order pizzas for us all." She sighs. "I cannot wait to get home, but at the same time I don't feel like I should stop working."

It sounds like Owen went ahead and ate the pizza he was saving for her, then. Nate listens while she fills him in on what she learned from Ashlee's aunt about the tragic link between Ashlee, Cody and Shane. It takes him a minute to get his head around everything. "I don't know what to say other than it's like a horror story." He leans against the black car parked next to hers. "You really believe Ashlee killed them both on purpose?"

She shrugs. "I don't want to, but what other explanation is there? I certainly don't believe Vince was involved anymore."

"I agree. Tonight he asked me if I would look into his wife and grandson's disappearance."

She raises an eyebrow. "That's interesting. I'd actually quite like to investigate that myself. Not that Chief Mendes would let me reopen a cold case when we've got all this going on. I've just updated her on why Ashlee's now my primary suspect. She told me they've had no sightings of Ellie, so she's going to notify all the relevant agencies in Colorado to be on the lookout for Ashlee in case she's already left town, plus she'll hold another press conference first thing tomorrow."

He nods. The street is empty and the stores are in darkness, with all officers now gone. The pumpkins sitting in the windows of the drugstore and hair salon stare back at them with empty eyes and devilish grimaces.

"I just wish I could find them both tonight," says Madison. "Or at least leave the case in another detective's hands while I get some sleep."

Nate realizes he hasn't seen Detective Douglas for a while. "Where's your partner?"

She hesitates, but she knows she can trust him. "He's suspended. Unfortunately he's been drinking whilst on duty. I can't tell if it's his gunshot wound affecting him, or PTSD from losing his daughter and his detective partner, but I get the impression Mendes will fire him if he doesn't find another coping mechanism fast. In the meantime, I'm the only detective working this case, and the thought of leaving Ashlee alone with the baby in her current state of mind doesn't sit right with me. God, I hope she hasn't already hurt her."

He raises his eyebrows. "Why would she hurt her?"

"Because I found out tonight that the baby's father is Ashlee's uncle." She pulls out the pink notebook she was reading when he arrived. "This is her diary. And it confirms that the year before they kicked her out, he started visiting her bedroom uninvited at night. It happened four times as far as I can tell. She wanted to leave but she had nowhere to go. She was only fifteen. I've notified the police up in Prospect Springs and they're sending a couple of officers to arrest him. The abuse is another trauma on top of everything else Ashlee has been through, so she might not have Ellie's best interests at heart."

It looks to Nate as if Madison's not totally on board with that view. "That would explain why she left her baby alone in Shane Kennedy's rental car. That doesn't sound like something a loving mother would do."

"True. But then why bother abducting her if she didn't still care about her? There must be another reason."

He doesn't have an answer for her.

They watch Brody as he takes a leak against a dumpster. Nate looks up at Ashlee's apartment, which is also in darkness. He can hear music coming from the neighbor's place, but it's not too loud.

"Where would a mother need to be close to for supplies for their baby?" he asks. "She would need diapers and formula, surely?"

Madison nods. "That's why I came here. I thought she might break into the drugstore at some point tonight. I was considering parking up the street and watching the place for a couple of hours." She yawns, and Nate doesn't think she'll last an hour, never mind two.

"I could drop Brody at home, then come back and keep you company?" he suggests. "Maybe pick up some coffee and donuts on the way back."

She looks him in the eye with a smile playing at her lips. "Donuts?"

"Sure." He smiles. "I've seen stakeouts in the movies. They always have donuts. Otherwise, why would I even bother?"

She laughs loudly. Brody picks up on it and bounds over to them, wagging his tail. "Oh my God, Nate. You have such a clichéd view of cops!"

"So… you're saying you *don't* want donuts?"

She pulls her coat tighter against the chill. "Hey, if it contains sugar and fat and comes served with hot coffee, I'm in."

He heads to his car and calls Brody over, shutting him in the back seat. Before he can get in himself, he hears Madison whispering his name. He spins around.

"Did you hear that?" she asks.

He stands still. He can't hear anything. "No."

Madison quickly but silently climbs the steps to Ashlee's apartment, pulling her weapon as she goes. He follows her. At the top of the stairs, she turns to look at him. "I swear I just heard a baby cry."

CHAPTER SIXTY-NINE

Madison doesn't have the key to the apartment on her. She pushes her shoulder against the front door, but it's definitely locked. She pulls away the fresh crime tape and stands silent, trying to hear whether there's anyone inside. Turning to look at Nate, she says, "We need to get in there."

On the count of three, they both force their weight against the door. It gives way easily and Madison enters first. "Police! Make yourself known!"

Brody barks from the car, annoyed to be missing out on the action. Nate switches the light on, and it's clear there's no one in the living room. Madison moves forward toward the bathroom and kitchen, gun ready to fire, but both rooms are clear. They creep toward the bedroom, and after a second's hesitation, she swings inside, gun first. It's pitch black in here, so she reaches for the light switch. With the light on, she can see the small room is empty.

An engine revs loudly outside, followed by the slam of a car door. It takes a second for Madison to realize that whoever has the baby must be escaping. "Shit."

Nate's ahead of her, running down the steps, but they don't get there in time. The black car that was parked next to Madison's speeds off toward the White Woods. "Get in!" he shouts.

They jump in his car and race out of the parking lot, tires skidding with the speed.

"There she is!" Madison points ahead, but there's really only one direction they can go in this part of town. They're heading toward the woods, which will bring them out at Lake Providence and Fantasy World, and eventually on to Gold Rock, the small gold-mining town a half-hour drive away.

The car in front is speeding up and Nate's headlights illuminate the driver from behind. It's definitely Ashlee. Her dark hair flies every time she spins around to check if she's still being chased.

Madison can't bear to watch. "She's going to kill herself if she keeps driving that fast!" The road through the woods is winding, and she knows from experience that these bends have taken many drivers unaware. "Ellie must be on her lap. Drive carefully, Nate. I don't want her to crash the car."

When Ashlee almost hits the only vehicle they pass coming in the opposite direction, Madison hears the driver yell "Asshole!" out his window. Her heart is in her mouth.

"She's slowing down," says Nate.

He's right. Maybe the near-miss scared her. Madison feels their car slowing down too.

Eventually Ashlee pulls over to the side of the road. Madison thinks she's going to make a run for it, into the woods, so she's out of Nate's car before he even stops. This time she doesn't draw her gun. She pulls out her cell phone to use the flashlight, then slowly and cautiously walks up to the passenger window, which is open just a crack, and shines the light inside the car.

Ashlee is leaning over the baby on her lap, her forehead resting on the steering wheel. She's sobbing uncontrollably. Ellie looks unharmed, but she's becoming distressed at seeing her mother that way. Madison allows herself a deep, calming breath as relief washes over her. She spots a clown mask on the back seat. Ashlee must have worn it out tonight when snatching Ellie from the foster parents.

"Ashlee? My name's Madison. I'm not going to hurt you. Do you understand?"

The girl doesn't respond. She's too distraught. Nate slowly approaches the driver's side, careful not to get too close. After a quick look inside, he walks round to where Madison is standing and whispers, "She has a gun in her left hand."

Madison peers closer. He's right. "Shit." The hairs on her arms stand up. She doesn't want to draw her weapon and scare the girl into doing something stupid. A closer look of Ashlee reveals greasy hair and mud-stained clothes but she doesn't appear to be harmed at all. The driver's seat looks to be stained with something underneath her.

"Should I call for backup?" whispers Nate.

Madison shakes her head. "No. Not yet. Keep your distance. I don't want to spook her." She leans in slightly and tries again. "Ashlee? Can you look at me?"

Ashlee starts wiping the tears from her face using the sleeves of her sweater. She must be freezing without a jacket on a night like this. Slowly she looks up at Madison. Her eyes are red and bloodshot; she's clearly exhausted. Her left hand falls to the other side of her daughter, gun now hidden from view.

"If I open the door, will you pass me the baby?"

Ashlee squeezes Ellie tight with her other hand and starts crying again. For the first time, Madison hears her speak. She sounds young and afraid. "She's all I have."

"I know. I just need to make sure she's okay, that's all. We can take you both to the hospital to get checked out before we discuss anything else."

Ashlee doesn't trust her. There's fear in her weary, red-rimmed eyes. "You're going to take her away from me."

Madison understands her fear better than most. Having Owen taken from her was worse than spending six years in prison. But Ashlee might've killed two people. No matter what her reasoning, she isn't in a fit state to care for her child right now. Madison slowly opens the passenger door, keeping her eyes on the girl. Then she crouches down and rests a hand on the seat. "Ashlee? I was supposed to be saving you, not arresting you, but you've put me in a difficult position." She pauses. "I've found the bodies of Shane Kennedy and Cody Stevens."

Ashlee looks up at the car's ceiling as tears stream down her face. "Oh God." She's rocking Ellie harder now and the baby is whimpering, reaching out for her mother.

"I understand that Cody caused your sister's death and that Shane profited from it. I understand why you would want them dead. But the law exists for a reason and you can't take matters into your own hands." Madison thinks of Nate and the way he almost shot Father Connor dead. She thinks of the people who framed her for murder. Ashlee will never appreciate how much she understands the temptations of revenge. Softening her voice, she says, "Do you want to give me your side of the story before the rest of my police department turn up?"

A car passes them, its headlights illuminating Ashlee's pale face. This girl is still a child, and she's been failed in every way imaginable. The thought of her serving a life sentence for murder feels unjust somehow, but inevitable nevertheless. Madison doesn't know if a judge and jury will take her past into consideration and show her leniency.

Ashlee wipes her eyes with her forearm, then looks at Madison. "My sister's rapist was freed on a *technicality*." She shakes her head in disbelief. "I watched her kill herself because of him."

Madison can see the pain in her face and her heart goes out to her. "Is that why you killed Cody?"

She swallows, then nods.

"You can't fight evil with more evil, Ashlee. It doesn't work."

"I know that now," she says quietly. "When it comes to my daughter, I can always do the right thing, but with him… I become a different person."

"And Shane? Did you kill him too?"

"No. Cody did."

Madison can't tell if she's lying. "It's cold out here; can I get in? Then you can tell me the whole story."

Ashlee slowly nods. Madison glances back at Nate, who looks alarmed. He clearly doesn't want her to get in the car while Ashlee has a gun in her hand. She climbs into the passenger seat and closes the door.

It smells bad in here. Of stale blood. It's too dark to see much, but she can't make out any obvious injuries on Ashlee. She gently takes Ellie from her and holds her close, trying to keep her warm. She's so relieved to have the baby in her arms again. "Tell me what happened that night."

CHAPTER SEVENTY

Ashlee painfully relives what happened three nights ago. She's waiting outside the diner, out of reach of Vince's security lights, as she checks the time on her cell phone. It's just shy of 2 a.m.; she's been here twenty-five minutes already. She's hoping Vince's interview will be over soon, because she knows it was booked to start at midnight, and they rarely last more than two hours. She takes a peek at Ellie. She is asleep in the pink baby carrier harnessed to her chest and is zipped up under her big winter coat, protected from the wind. A mist is building at ground level, but at least it's not raining.

She feels for the paperback in her coat pocket. She overheard Vince telling Carla who he was secretly interviewing tonight, and she knew she couldn't miss the opportunity to meet the man who used her sister's tragedy to make money. To write a book about Kelly and Janie's suffering and label it fiction was despicable. She remembers how Shane was all over the media discussing his fictional version of Kelly. The press hounded her and her mom all over again, wanting their opinion on what he'd written and digging up and showing over and over the CCTV footage of the girls in the back of Cody Stevens's car on the way to the woods. And the focus returned to Stevens again too. It was unbearable. Ashlee had to watch as her mom drank herself to death, while Shane Kennedy never once stopped to consider how his stupid book and movie deal would affect them.

She hears movement ahead of her so she steps further back into the shadows.

"Drive safe," says Vince before closing the door to his apartment.

Shane is illuminated by the bright yellow glare of the security light fixed above the door, and she watches as he lights a cigarette. Not wanting him to think she's some kind of crazy stalker, she holds back and watches him walk away. She wonders where his car is and why he didn't park outside the diner.

She hesitates to follow him, but decides it's now or never if she wants the opportunity to tell him what his book has done to her. She needs to convince him to get *Bitter Road* pulled from bookshops so she can move on with her life.

With that in mind, she sets off after him, trying to build up the courage to speak. He must hear her soft footsteps closing in on him from behind, because he suddenly spins around, looking afraid. She smiles to reassure him she's not some kind of murderer.

"What do you want?" he asks.

She's practiced this. "Mr. Kennedy, I'm sorry to bother you, but I'm a massive fan of your books and I work in the diner so I thought—"

He doesn't let her finish. He's already walking away.

She follows him again, needing to engage him in order to explain. "I just want my book signed. Please, I'm a huge fan of yours."

Over his shoulder he says, "I'm sorry, I don't do signings anymore, and I can't be seen with you."

She knows what he's referring to, of course: Kacie's allegation against him. It's clear he's paranoid that someone else will make similar accusations, and she feels a little bad for that, but didn't he deserve it after what he put her through? She told Kacie to accuse him of trying to kiss her so that his reputation as a crime writer would be overshadowed by the allegation, and maybe he'd be dropped by his publisher and his books would be pulled from stores. She wanted people to stop selling *Bitter Road* and to stop featuring him on their talk shows. But Kacie accused him of attempted rape instead, getting carried away with all the attention.

She eventually backed down when her parents made her life hell, trying to send her to therapy and insisting she take the allegations as far as possible to see him put away.

His book actually went up in the bestseller lists as a result of their stunt and all the press attention. That was a bitter pill for Ashlee to swallow: knowing the public would still support a man who might be guilty of attacking a teenager. She realized then that the only way to stop him pursuing the follow-up book was to appeal to his better nature. And the only way to find out whether he had one was to explain to him the damage *Bitter Road* had done.

He stops at a red car parked under a street light near the water tower, and within seconds thunder claps above them and a heavy downpour comes out of nowhere. Ellie jolts awake under Ashlee's coat and immediately bursts into angry tears. After he unlocks his car door, Shane looks back at her. "You brought a baby with you?"

"It wasn't raining when I left home." She's getting soaked fast.

Shane slides into his car and closes the door, denying her the opportunity to tell him what she came for. Disappointed, she walks ahead of his car, in the direction of home. Ellie cries as the downpour starts hitting her head, so Ashlee zips her coat up higher, mindful of leaving enough room for air. It's only a ten-minute walk, so she increases her pace and tries not to cry at her missed opportunity. She played it all wrong.

Shane's car pulls up alongside her. "Get in, or your baby's going to catch a cold."

Surprised, she slips into the passenger seat.

"I'm just giving you a ride home, okay? I really don't want to sign anything or take a selfie. I'm sorry."

"Sure. I understand." She strokes Ellie's hair. The baby has stopped crying now and is resting her head against Ashlee's chest. She must be able to feel how fast Ashlee's heart is thumping.

"Which direction?"

She doesn't want him to take her home. She needs more time than that. "Straight ahead. Through the woods."

He pulls away and then glances at her. "So you're a fan, huh?"

She almost nods, but instead she surprises herself by saying, "Actually, *Bitter Road* ruined my life." Her hands are shaking badly, but she focuses on her sister and how her death was exploited by this man.

Shane seems surprised by her response, and before he looks away, she can see fear in his eyes. He's wondering if he's picked up a crazy woman. The road ahead becomes winding as they drive through the White Woods. "I'm sorry you feel that way, but I don't really see how a book could ruin someone's life."

Anger surges through her. "I'm Kelly Stuart's sister."

He looks like he's about to slam on the brakes, but it would be dangerous to stop right here. "What the fuck? What is this, some kind of ambush?" He shifts in his seat.

Before she can reply, they're blinded from behind. A car's headlights are bouncing off their mirrors. The vehicle's lights, full beam, cut through the fog with ease and light up the road ahead of them.

"What the hell's going on?" yells Shane. "Have you brought someone with you?" He tries to see behind him, but it's too bright and the rain is still heavy.

Ashlee hugs Ellie close, not sure what's happening. "It's probably just a drunk driver. Let him pass."

But when the vehicle doesn't use the opportunity to overtake, Shane speeds up. Ashlee's suddenly afraid. This isn't a good place to speed. When the car behind lurches threateningly toward them, Shane makes a mistake and their car goes off the road. Ashlee screams as Shane instinctively puts his arm out in front of her and Ellie. The passenger airbag doesn't deploy fully, but Shane's does. It hits him in the face, dazing him.

It's not a big drop into the woods below, but the impact shocks her, and Ellie is instantly crying. The airbags slowly deflate as they sit there stunned. The engine cuts out.

"You both okay?" he asks.

She nods, but her neck hurts. Almost immediately, someone dressed head to toe in black, including gloves, pulls open Shane's door, grabs him by his jacket and punches him hard twice. His nose takes the full force and she winces at the cracking noise. She feels blood spatter on her face, making her lean away in disgust.

"Get out of the car, asshole! I'm gonna teach you a lesson for screwing my girlfriend!"

Ashlee's blood runs cold. She can't see the man's face, but she recognizes his voice from TV interviews. She scrambles back against the car door, trying to get away from them both.

"I don't know what you're talking about," protests Shane, holding his leaking nose with one hand and trying to reach the glove box with the other. "I'm just giving her a ride home!"

But Cody Stevens doesn't believe him, and to prove it, he strikes him again in the face. Ellie's screams grow louder, and Ashlee can't believe what's happening. Cody drags Shane out of the car, and she hears more thumping, louder this time, followed by something dropping to the ground. Then, abruptly, there's silence.

"Oh my God." With a surge of adrenaline, she tries to open her door. It's stuck. She closes her eyes and squeezes Ellie, who refuses to be appeased.

Footsteps approach the car. She desperately wants it to be Shane Kennedy who survived. But when she opens her eyes, she sees her sister's rapist staring at her with a malicious grin on his face.

"Hey, Bunny. How about you hand me the baby?"

It takes every ounce of self-control not to scream.

CHAPTER SEVENTY-ONE

Madison can barely breathe. She can tell Ashlee was traumatized by what happened, because reliving it is causing her to visibly tremble.

"I'm not a bad person, honest. By getting in his car I didn't plan for Shane to die. I just wanted to tell him what he'd done to my mom. It was his fault she drank herself to death. Not just Cody's." Ashlee turns to look at her. "Imagine if your biggest loss was repeated over and over on the news, in a movie and in a book. Everyone's read it or seen it and everyone's got an opinion on what happened to your family. You never get the chance to forget it. To move on. I just needed to tell him, for my own sanity, because it seemed unlikely he would ever come back to this town again. I thought maybe he might pull the book from sale or not write the sequel that everyone was waiting for." She pauses. "The planned sequel was going to be about me and my mom. About how we tried to cope with the aftermath of what happened." She shakes her head. "People love their true-crime documentaries, but what they don't realize is that there are real people behind the sensational crimes. People like me and my mom, trying to live broken lives." Her voice catches.

"I can understand how difficult that would be."

Ashlee looks at her with anger behind her eyes. "No you can't."

Madison takes a deep breath. "I can, Ashlee. I served time in prison for a murder I didn't commit. I was a detective when I was arrested, but I lost my job, my freedom, and my son. My life was discussed in the media for years. I know all about trying to move on in a world that never forgets."

Surprise crosses Ashlee's face. "You're that cop. The one the old guys talk about in the diner. I thought I recognized you."

Madison smiles sadly. "I'll never convince people like them I'm innocent, so I've had to learn to live with it."

Ashlee raises her hand and strokes Ellie's soft cheek.

Madison shivers. Now that she knows some of what happened that night, she realizes Cody Stevens arrived in Lost Creek at exactly the wrong time. If he'd turned up even a day later, Shane would have been long gone. He'd still be alive. Turns out Vince was right: coincidences do happen.

"So Cody killed Shane."

Ashlee nods. "He's strong. He worked out a lot in prison. He hit Shane too hard."

"But that's not what killed him," says Madison. "He died from a blow to the back of the head."

Ashlee looks down at her hands. "All I know is that eventually Cody threw him in the trunk of this car, dead."

"This is Cody's car?"

"Right."

Madison thinks about all the evidence they can pull from the vehicle. But not before she knows everything. "So what did Cody do next? Had you ever met him before?"

"No. I'd written to him in prison using a friend's name."

"Kacie Larson. I've been to see her. I know she faked the allegations for you. But why would you write to Cody in prison?"

Ashlee looks surprised. "I bet Kacie hates me. I started writing to Cody when I was too young to know better, thinking I could try to understand the kind of man who would rape two little girls. We were linked, he and I, whether I liked it or not. But as I got older and was trying to move on from it all, I stopped writing to him, and eventually I had Ellie and moved here for a fresh start."

"Why live under a false name?"

She looks away. "I didn't want my aunt or uncle finding me."

Madison closes her eyes. Of course. She would have been afraid her uncle would come for his baby one day, or that her aunt would find out Ellie was his. It dawns on her that this girl has never known a day's peace since her sister told her what happened in the woods. "Did you start writing to him again when you heard about his upcoming release?"

She nods through her tears. "It was all over the news about how he'd been offered a plea deal. The guys in the diner wanted to watch it every second of every day, and they all had their opinions about my sister. They didn't know she was my sister, of course, but they said she was stupid to get in the car with him in the first place, like it was her and Janie's fault for trusting an adult!"

Madison gives her time to cry. She rubs Ellie's soft hair and holds back her own emotions. "It wasn't your sister's fault, Ashlee. The only person responsible for what happened that day was the rapist." She exhales. "Trust me, I've been there."

A different wood and a different rapist, but she's been there.

Ashlee looks up at her. "So do you want to kill the man who raped you?"

Madison has to swallow the lump in her throat. "I did kill him."

CHAPTER SEVENTY-TWO

Nate is worried about Madison's safety. Brody is sitting alert in the passenger seat next to him, but he's not barking. He appears to sense they're in a delicate situation and Nate's been stroking him to keep him calm. They've both kept their eyes on the car in front. Ashlee is desperate, so there's no guessing what she'll do right now. He makes the decision to call the station. Within fifteen minutes, Chief Mendes and two police cruisers pull up a short distance behind his car. They cut their lights as he instructed.

He gets out, leaving Brody inside with the window down, and closes his door gently so as not to alert Ashlee to what's happening.

Chief Mendes is the first to approach him. "What's the latest?"

"They're just talking. Ashlee hasn't appeared to make any threats with the gun yet. The baby hasn't cried for a while, but I think I saw Madison take her from Ashlee."

Mendes nods. "So Madison is in the passenger side, correct?"

"Right." He studies her face. "Why? You're not going to go in heavy-handed, are you?"

She gives him a look. "I'll do whatever I think is best, Mr. Monroe."

They both turn to see another car pulling up behind the cruisers before the uniformed officers manage to cordon off the road. Nate watches as Vince approaches them. "A friend of mine called to say he was nearly run off the road close to where Ashlee's baby was found. I wanted to check it out for myself in case it was Ellie's abductor."

"This is a potentially volatile situation, Mr. Rader," says Chief Mendes sternly. "I'm going to have to ask you to leave."

Vince ignores her and turns to Nate. "It's Ashlee, isn't it? Is she okay?"

Nate nods. "She's got Ellie with her, but she's armed."

Vince looks shocked. "Ashlee wouldn't hurt that baby."

"I think it's more likely she might hurt herself," he says.

"Or my detective," says Mendes.

They all turn to stare at the car in the darkness ahead of them. Nate feels completely useless.

CHAPTER SEVENTY-THREE

Madison's getting cold. The car's engine has been switched off for almost forty minutes while they've been talking. She can see Ashlee's teeth chattering and knows it will be a mixture of the falling temperatures and the stress of reliving what happened. In her wing mirror she's spotted a couple of cars pull up behind Nate's. He must have called the station. She's grateful that for now they're all keeping their distance. She has to find out what happened to Cody before she can get them out of here; she knows that teenagers usually clam up once they reach the station and are put in an interview situation.

"Did it feel good to kill your rapist?" asks Ashlee.

Madison looks her in the eye. "No. It didn't make me feel any better at all. You should know it wasn't something I set out to do. He died after trying to kill me, but, well… it's complicated."

Ashlee nods, and Madison thinks that if anyone knows how complicated life can be, it's her. "You must know how I was feeling and why I wanted to kill Cody."

Madison has to be careful, because she shouldn't—and doesn't—condone what Ashlee's done. "I understand why you would want him dead, of course I do. But tell me what actually happened once Shane was in the trunk. Then I'll treat you to a hot meal and some food for Ellie."

Ashlee nods. She puts the gun in her lap and rubs her hands together to keep warm. "Cody was livid. He told me he'd been following me all day, since he arrived in town and found out where I worked from one of the locals. He followed me to the diner that night and was watching me as I waited outside. When he saw me get into the car with Shane in the early hours, he thought the two of us were lovers and that Ellie was Shane's baby. You see, I'd never mentioned being a mother in my last letter to him. I told him I lived in Lost Creek because I wanted him to show up. I was carrying a knife on me at all times, a hunting knife in a leather pouch strapped to my ankle that I'd bought especially. I knew he would turn up eventually but I didn't know when."

Madison tries not to react to her naïvety in thinking she could defend herself against someone like that. By giving her location to Cody, she not only put herself at risk, but her daughter too.

"He thought I'd cheated on him with Shane. To stay alive, all I could do was pretend I desperately wanted to be his girlfriend. I told him I didn't care about Shane or the baby, I only wanted him. He said I had to prove it." She swallows. "Ellie was crying hysterically and it was winding him up. I was worried he'd kill her. He said I had to leave her behind in Shane's car and drive away with him before the police showed up."

What a terrible choice to make: abandon your baby or both of you die.

"I had my knife on me but I needed the upper hand in order to overpower him, and he was so worked up that I could tell I wasn't going to get that then. So I agreed to leave Ellie behind, knowing I'd come straight back for her as soon as I could. I thought I'd be an hour max, and it was almost three a.m., so I didn't think there was much chance of anyone finding her." She swallows. "I genuinely thought she'd be safer alone in Shane's car than with me and *him*." She wipes away a tear. "When I got out of the car I stumbled on some branches and lost a sneaker. I didn't dare pick it up. I placed Ellie on the back seat and when I kissed her goodbye I didn't know if I'd ever see her again. Cody didn't know the town, so I told him to drive to Lake Providence, where we could hide and I could show him how much I wanted to be his girlfriend. I was trying to stop him from driving us straight out of town and probably out of the state."

Madison can guess what happened next, but she has to know for sure. There could be some detail that means Ashlee can claim self-defense at her inevitable trial. Or perhaps a detail that ultimately proves premeditated murder.

"What happened once you left Ellie behind and got Cody to the lake?"

Ashlee squeezes her eyes closed against the memory.

CHAPTER SEVENTY-FOUR

It's hard to go back there. To put herself in the car with that monster. Once they're parked in the dark, by the lakeside, Cody slaps her hard across the face, taking her completely by surprise. "Who the fuck was that guy? You been cheating on me, Bunny? I mean, Jesus, you've got a baby. Looks like I'm going to have to keep you on a tight leash from now on."

Stars appear in front of her eyes and her cheek stings from the slap. Fear threatens to consume her as she realizes there's no way on earth she'll ever be able to overpower him. She's going to have to find another way to get out of this alive. She faces him in her seat and is struck by how his good looks—blond hair and blue eyes, tanned skin and muscly arms—can mask such evil. "I've never cheated on you, I promise. Do you even know who that guy was?" She tries not to put her hand to her hot cheek.

"Why do I give a shit who he was?"

His arrogance is astounding. She leans in to him. "Because that was *Shane Kennedy*. The guy who made a hell of a lot of money from writing about the allegations that put you in prison."

His mouth drops open before turning into a grin. "You're shitting me? What were you doing with him?"

She has to lie on the spot. "He was in town to give an interview, so I tricked my way into his car so I could accuse him of sexual assault and see how he liked being locked up like you were. I was going to do it for you."

He raises his eyebrows, clearly impressed. "I fucking hate that guy. Do you know how many copies of his goddam book were sent to me in prison by people wanting me to sign them? Hundreds! Some of them were already signed by him. And the son of a bitch never once offered to split his royalties with me."

She's stunned. She can't believe Cody would expect Shane to share the book's royalties with him, the guy who committed the crimes. She can't help herself when she says, "Maybe he should have split them with the victims' families."

Cody frowns. "Why should they get anything? Those girls didn't have to kill themselves. It was only sex. They should've just forgotten about it. I mean, it's nothing they probably weren't already doing with their boyfriends, right?" He laughs, and it's clear to her that he feels no remorse for what he did to Kelly and Janie. He doesn't even deny doing it. Neither does he care that he killed a man less than an hour ago. He's the epitome of evil.

She once read that pedophiles can't be rehabilitated, and she remembers hoping it wasn't true. But listening to Cody Stevens talk, she realizes it *is* true. He doesn't see his actions as crimes, so how can he be rehabilitated? Anger threatens to overwhelm her. She wants nothing more than to scream at him. To make him see they were innocent little girls who stood no chance against him, just as she probably doesn't.

He lunges forward and his hands are suddenly all over her, pinching her skin and tearing at her clothes, grabbing her hair tight. He forces his lips against hers, probing her mouth with his tongue while he gropes her everywhere. Is this what her sister experienced? And what about poor little Janie? She would have been confused and horrified by the touch of this monster; how was she ever supposed to forget it? She winces with pain, no longer having to imagine how they thought killing themselves was the only way to forget what he did to them.

That's when she makes the decision to see this through to the end. Otherwise he'll do this to other children. Maybe he already has. She can feel bile rising in her throat as she desperately thinks of a way to gain some control over the situation. "Wait! Please, Cody, wait a second."

He pulls back, but his eyes are menacing. "I prefer Ace, remember? Why are you blowing hot and cold all of a sudden?"

She tries to smile at him, but it probably looks more like a grimace. "I just want our first time to be special, that's all."

He laughs, then considers it. "You've got me all hot. It's already going to be special, Bunny. How old are you anyway? Fifteen?"

She ignores him. "Let me slip into the back seat and get undressed for you. I'll tell you when I'm ready."

He can't resist. "Be quick. We've got to get out of here before someone finds that car."

She gets out and opens the back door, sliding into the seat behind Cody. He's watching her in the rear-view mirror, so she unbuttons her jeans, letting one hand slide down to her ankle. To her knife. "Put the radio on."

He humors her and his eyes divert to the car's stereo.

She uses the opportunity to pull out the knife and lean forward. Taking him by surprise, she grabs his hair with one hand and pulls his head back against the rest. She imagines her sister guiding her shaking hand to his throat. Before he realizes what she's doing, she stabs deep into his neck and pulls the blade from left to right. His hand is immediately on hers, pulling at the knife. He makes gargling noises as his eyes widen, staring at her in the mirror. He still doesn't understand what she's done.

As she locks her gaze with his, she whispers into his ear, "Kelly Stuart was my big sister, and Janie was her best friend. You're going to hell for what you did to them."

Tears are streaming down her face as she watches the information sink into his confused brain.

CHAPTER SEVENTY-FIVE

Madison swallows back her anguish at hearing what happened. She doesn't trust herself to speak, so she remains silent.

Ashlee is wiping her tears away. Eventually she says, "He genuinely thought I was going to have sex with him. Can you believe that? I have so many bruises on my chest and thighs. He did so much damage so quickly."

Madison will get her bruises photographed as soon as possible. It's looking more likely that Ashlee can use self-defense at her trial.

"I swear to God someone else took control of my hand as I leaned forward and slit his throat." She bursts into tears again. "I want to believe it was Kelly. That my sister got the revenge she deserved."

Madison squeezes baby Ellie gently for comfort and places a hand on Ashlee's knee, near the gun. In her wing mirror she spots Nate by the front of his car, watching carefully.

A few minutes pass while Ashlee collects herself. "I'll never forget that feeling. I watched him die. It wasn't as fast as I expected and it didn't bring me any peace. I just feel like a terrible person now." She wipes her nose. "I went to sit under a tree while I tried to calm down. I ended up blacking out. I think my mind just shut down with shock or something. When I woke up, I thought it had all been a nightmare until I saw Cody's car. I knew what I had to do. I had to get him and Shane out of the car so I could go back for Ellie and leave town before I was caught. It took forever. Cody was so heavy and he was covered in blood, making him slippery. I moved him first. I weighed him down with rocks so he'd know what my sister went through and then dragged him out into the lake. I had no energy left by the time it came to Shane, and I knew I wouldn't get him far enough into the water. My whole body was shaking and I kept going faint. So I drove the car behind the lake, out of sight, and used all my remaining strength to pull him out of the trunk, and just left him where he landed. I honestly didn't intend for him to get killed. I just wanted to tell him what his book had done to my family." Her shaky voice hitches.

"By the time I'd driven back to the woods to get Ellie, there was a car parked on the road above where Shane's car landed."

Madison doesn't explain that it was her who discovered the car.

"I couldn't see the driver, but it was obvious they'd gone down to look inside. I couldn't risk them seeing me, because they would've noticed the blood all over me and known I'd done something bad. They would never have let me take Ellie away. So I drove on by, distraught at having to leave her behind."

As Ashlee's sobs get louder, Ellie wakes and begins crying. She's probably hungry. Madison makes a decision that she hopes she won't regret. She opens the car door just a little, and within seconds Nate is there. He silently takes Ellie from her and gives her a look to suggest she should follow. She reluctantly closes the door and watches him walk away with the baby.

"It's all over now, Ashlee." She places a hand on the girl's back before pulling her in for a hug. She feels so fragile. "You did what you thought was right."

Eventually Ashlee draws away and composes herself. A blank look comes over her face as she realizes Ellie is gone. She picks up the gun from her lap and Madison wishes she'd got out of the car while she had the chance. Although it quickly becomes clear she's not the one in danger.

"I found this in Cody's glove box," says Ashlee. "I thought a lot about killing myself while I was hiding out in the empty apartment next to Justin's."

So that's where she was hiding: the apartment with a leak. She must have concealed herself from the officer who searched it and covered her tracks. Madison wonders where the car was parked, but it doesn't really matter, because none of them knew for sure what car Cody was driving, and they didn't have his license plate.

"I won't ever be allowed to see her again, will I?"

Madison swallows. "Of course you will. A baby that young needs her mother. You'll have to be supervised, but believe me when I say you'll be allowed contact with her." She feels bad for lying. She certainly hopes Ashlee is allowed supervised contact with her daughter if she's locked up, but she herself wasn't allowed to see Owen once she was convicted. Although she suspects that's because the people who framed her fixed it that way.

She looks closely at the girl, who appears to be giving up the fight. That's not good. Madison reaches out. "Give me the gun. Let's go to the diner and get something to eat with Ellie."

Ashlee shakes her head. "That's not where you'll take me. I'm a killer now, aren't I? No better than Cody Stevens."

Before Madison can respond, someone appears at her window and she tenses. Vince waves through the glass before slowly opening the door. He spots the gun immediately, but he acts unfazed. Crouching down, he says to Ashlee, "You're late for your shift, young lady."

Ashlee unexpectedly laughs through her tears. Her face lights up. These two clearly have a bond, and Madison feels guilty for suspecting that Vince could've been involved in her disappearance.

"Vince, I've done something terrible."

His eyes are watery, but he manages to keep it together. "Oh, I don't know about that, Ashlee. I mean, word on the street is you killed a child rapist. If you ask me, you deserve a pay rise."

Madison resists the impulse to scold him, because Ashlee is smiling through her tears, clearly relieved that Vince doesn't hate her at least.

"Come on, sweetheart," he says. "Let's go and see your friends at the diner. Carla's been worried sick about you."

As Ashlee slowly nods, Madison takes the gun from her.

CHAPTER SEVENTY-SIX

Surprisingly, Chief Mendes does let Ashlee have a quick stop at Ruby's Diner before she's taken to the station to be arrested. But not for something to eat. It's almost midnight, but Carla, Sue and a couple of younger waitresses have been allowed to come and say goodbye to her.

It gives Madison an opportunity to quickly assess Ellie for any injuries, but she's unharmed, and when she hands the baby back to her mother, Ellie happily stares up at Ashlee from underneath her beautiful long eyelashes. Unfortunately, Ashlee hasn't got off as lightly. As well as the bruising inflicted by Cody, she has a long road to recovery ahead for the emotional trauma he's caused her. She keeps apologizing to her friends, telling them she's a terrible person and she's sorry she lied to them about her name. Madison hopes she'll get the support she needs if she ends up in prison.

As they watch Carla hug the girl, Madison turns to Chief Mendes. "How come you let them see her one last time before we take her away?"

Mendes looks thoughtful. "I know you all think that because I'm the boss I'm some kind of ice queen who doesn't have feelings, but this girl is still so young. I want her to be rehabilitated inside, to get the therapy she should have had after the deaths of her sister and mother. Having close relationships within the community and knowing there are people who will be waiting for her when she eventually gets out of prison—*if* she gets out—will help her. She's not a lost cause by any means. Plus, it will help the baby to have these links to the community too."

Madison is overwhelmed with gratitude toward the chief; she knows her predecessor wouldn't have acted the same way. She feels like working under Mendes will be different. That for her it's not all about having a one hundred percent conviction rate, or worrying about what the media thinks of the department.

Vince approaches them and holds out his hand for Mendes to shake. "Thanks for letting us see her before she's taken away. I know my staff appreciate it."

Mendes is clearly taken aback by Vince's softer side. "Not a problem."

He turns to Madison. "I knew you'd make a good detective from the way you took down the McCoys over the summer. I wish you'd been in charge when Ruby and Oliver went missing."

She has to swallow the lump in her throat at his compliment. "Thank you. I wish I could reopen their case, but…"

He waves a dismissive hand. "I know, I know. No one likes working a cold case." He winks at Nate. "Except my new buddy here."

Nate laughs. "I must be crazy."

Vince claps a hand on his back and laughs before Chief Mendes ruins the moment. "If Detective Douglas didn't find them, it's unlikely a private investigator with no law-enforcement history will."

To his credit, Nate lets the dig slide as Vince says, "If Douglas is such a good detective, why isn't he here tonight?"

Mendes raises a perfectly plucked eyebrow. "With all due respect, that's none of your business." She nods to Officer Williams. "It's time to go."

Gloria looks regretful as she takes Ashlee's arm to lead her outside. Ashlee stops in front of Madison, handing her the baby. "Make sure Ellie is looked after for me, would you?"

Madison can't stop the tear that runs down her face, knowing exactly how Ashlee is feeling right now. She bounces the baby and nods. "I'll do my best."

Ashlee leans in and kisses her daughter for a final time. "I'm going to do everything I can to make amends and get back to you as soon as possible." She strokes the baby's cheek. "Don't you forget about me, Ellie."

Madison feels Nate slip his arm around her shoulders as they watch Ashlee being led away to the police cruiser. Brody is waiting outside and happily sniffs them both as Gloria cuffs the girl.

Mendes gently takes Ellie from Madison. "I'll return her to the foster carers. They've been beside themselves with worry."

Vince goes to comfort Carla and his waitresses, who are all in tears.

Turning to Nate, Madison says, "Ashlee told me that Cody killed the crime writer but she killed Cody. He was going to rape her, but I think she would have killed him no matter what happened. She wanted retribution for her sister's death."

He chews on it for a minute. "I'm not condoning it," he says at last. "But I can see why she felt compelled to do it. I have faith that any good judge will show her leniency based on what Cody would have done to her had she not retaliated. It sounds like it was just a matter of time before she became one of his victims."

Madison has never heard him talk positively about the justice system before. She's surprised. Does this first sign of optimism mean he's going to be able to move on from his own ordeal and restore his faith? She hopes so. She hopes it's possible for both him and Ashlee to overcome their pasts. Wiping her tired eyes, she looks up at him. Something's bothering her. "Ashlee killed a man, Nate. As a cop, I should be itching to see her charged and locked up, shouldn't I? Or am I in the wrong job?"

He hugs her to him as she tries hard not to break down. "No, Madison," he says into her hair. "That's not who you are. And that's why you're going to make a great detective." He squeezes her shoulders. "Come on. We should head home. I really don't know how long Owen can resist our pizzas."

She snorts with unexpected laughter.

A LETTER FROM WENDY

Thank you for reading *Little Girl Taken*, Book 3 in this series. As always, I hope you enjoyed spending time with Madison and Nate (and Brody!). You can keep in touch with me and get updates about the series by signing up to my newsletter here, and by following me on social media.

www.bookouture.com/wendy-dranfield

I love seeing your posts about this series on social media and I've had so many of you get in touch with me with wonderful feedback about the characters. I have a lot of fun writing about Madison and Nate, and it's satisfying to see Father Connor finally get his comeuppance. Vince Rader has become a new favorite character for me. From the minute he popped into my head, he wouldn't stop telling me his story and giving me his strong opinions about how the investigation into Ashlee's disappearance should be run! Something tells me he and Nate will become good friends in the future, and perhaps he can fill the void left by Rex.

If you enjoyed this book, please do leave a rating or review (no matter how brief) on Amazon, as this helps it to stand out amongst the thousands of books that are published each day, thereby allowing it to reach more readers. The more readers it reaches, the more likely you'll get more books in this series!

Thanks again.
Wendy x

wendydranfield.co.uk

WendyDranfield

WendyDranfield1

ACKNOWLEDGMENTS

For those readers who have stuck with me from Book 1 in this series: thank you! I love reading your reviews and social media posts. I get to see the characters through your eyes and that helps me with the next book, because I always write with you in mind.

To the bloggers who come on my book tours or who write reviews for my books just for the love of it: thank you. I love your enthusiasm and you make social media a fun place to be.

Thank you, as always, to Jessie Botterill, my editor on this series, and to the whole team at Bookouture.

Finally, my husband said he wanted to be acknowledged not just as my beta reader but as the researcher for certain things in this book. So if you spot any errors, it's a hundred percent his fault! (But my thanks go to him for trying.)